Gems from World Literature

Gems from World Literature

The Greatest French Classics

Alfred Capus and the Younger Generation

Edited by

J.A. Hammerton

CREST PUBLISHING HOUSE
G-2, 16 Ansari Road,
Darya Ganj, New Delhi-110 002

Published by Crest Publishing House
G-2, 16 Ansari Road
Darya Ganj, New Delhi - 110 002

The Greatest French Classics
Alfred Capus and the Younger Generation
ISBN 81-242-0475-6

First Crest Impression : 2004

Printed by Saurabh Printers Pvt Ltd
A-16, Sector IV, NOIDA 201 301

Editorial Board

Editorial Note

A SHORT story may be a mere anecdote of three hundred words or a work of ten or fifteen thousand. In content it may be anything from a glimpse of character, an incident, to a highly finished picture of life. But it should be a complete work of imagination, its effect achieved with a minimum of personages and events.

To select the best thousand examples was a task that could be achieved only on arbitrary lines. As to length, three thousand words was the ideal average, but this excluded some of the finest stories, so exceptions had to be allowed. National characteristics also had consideration. Another test was the value of a story as illustrating the development of the art.

PROBLEMS of arrangement were not entirely solved by classification according to the country of each writer's origin. This puts Richard Steele into the Irish volume and separates those ideal literary partners Agnes and Egerton Castle. But it is the best possible arrangement for the work, and the index makes reference easy. The inclusion of a series of stories of the War became possible when the War itself ruled out all modern German work.

A WORD as to the method of selection. The general editor prepared a trial list of titles, which was submitted to all the members of the Editorial Board, who rejected and added according to their individual tastes and knowledge, These individual lists were then collated and the final list evolved. The thousand stories selected are therefore representative of the combined opinion of the whole group of editors. A very few modifications of the final list were made necessary by difficulties of copyright and considerations of Anglo-Saxon taste in certain translations from foreign literatures.

MOST of the foreign stories have been specially translated, and all copyrights, in both stories and translations, the use of which authors and publishers have courteously permitted, are duly credited at the end of each volume.

J.A. HAMMERTON

Contents

CONTENTS

The French Story-Tellers

Alfred Capus and the Younger Generation

THE younger generation in France, in the eighteen-nineties, had much in common with their contemporaries in England. They were weary of the works of their elders, touched with despondency, and yet anxious to find new fields in art and letters. The end of the century was near, and for some inadequate reason this artificial division of time told upon the spirit of many of the new writers.

As a matter of fact, France, like Great Britain, was full of energy, and her younger men were acquiring a passion for sport unknown since the Middle Ages, while her inventors were developing new means of power and making an engine that could scale the skies. France should have produced somebody like Mr. H. G. Wells as interpreter of her new age. But the literary men of the younger generation rather affected a decadent mood, and left to Anatole France, Maeterlinck, and foreign writers read in translations, the task they pretended to be too weary to accomplish.

Alfred Capus

ALFRED CAPUS (*b.* 1858) was the representative of this strange young France. He became famous by his gospel of luck, by which it appeared that effort and sustained work were scarcely worth considering in comparison with the art of being born fortunate. His story of "Presence of Mind" is typical of his nonchalant, pleasant, easy-going way of looking at things. Smiling irony and witty depravity are the notes of his style and principal characters. The exquisite dubiousness he maintains in his study of crime in "The Marion Affair" remained characteristic of his art, until he became the political writer of the *Figaro* during the Great War.

Ginisty

Paul Ginisty (*b.* 1858), represented by a tale with an uncommon plot, "A Capitulation, also has an ironic touch, though he is on the side of honest men, instead of being the apologist for amusing adventurers. In Remy de Gourmont (*b.* 1858) we come to the young master of French literature at the close of the nineteenth century. Gourmont began as an understudy to Anatole France, after dabbling in mediaeval mysticism. He adopted the Prussian philosophy of Nietzsche, and developed it at times in a coldly outrageous manner. In his principal works his race indeed seems to be utterly decadent, yet the man himself is one of the ripest fruits of French culture. His keenness of intelligence is extraordinary, and his art, of which "The White Gown" and "The Magnolia" are examples, is perfect. His was the sweetest poison poured, just before the final struggle for life and death, into the brain of France.

Remy de Gourmont

Ferdinand Beissier (*b.* 1858), in his comedy of love, "The Helmet," recovers the old gaiety of the Gaul, showing that the current of life still ran fresh and bright among the people. But Anatole Le Braz came to Paris from Brittany with a gift of poetic sadness derived from the new Celtic movement in the British Isles. Le Braz (*b.* 1859) was the disciple of Luzel, the Breton folk-lore gatherer, and he desired to found a French-Celtic movement on lines similar to those along which the Irish and Scottish schools were working. In his study in superstition, "The Blood of the Siren," he attains in a French way an effect like that which William Sharp produced by more archaic means.

Beissier and Le Braz

WITH "Georges Courteline" (*b.* 1860) laughter is again heard. Courteline is one of the best of modern French humorists, but there is usually something serious beneath his fun. His farce of "A Gentleman Finds a Watch" is really a bitter thing. The class of officials that ran the French Republic before the war was generally bad. They owed their positions of authority to professional politicians, who shared the spoils of government among their immediate supporters in the manner of the old Tammany organisation of the United States. Courteline continually attacked the French bureaucracy in short stories and one-act plays, and his special weapon of ridicule told in the end with considerable effect.

"Georges Courteline"

Henri Lavedan (*b.* 1860) is a vivacious cynic engaged in painting fashionable life, until he was moved by fear of the abyss which his country seemed approaching. He wrote one of the greatest of sermons in his play, "The Marquis of Priola," which is pure literature and distilled worldly wisdom, yet ends in a tremendous moral effect. In his short tales Lavedan has a special love for the simple kindliness of French home life, as he shows in his exquisite picture of old age, "Years After." Quite as fine, original, and touching is his study of married life in "When He was a Little Boy." In the surprise story of "The Pocket-Book" he is still keen in seeing life's little ironies, and watching men and women sway under temptation.

Lavedan

Paul Margueritte (*b.* 1860) is another remarkable writer of the modern French renaissance. Being the son of one of the ablest generals in the war of 1870, he set himself to combat the early influence of Zola, and restore the spirit of heroism in literature. His curious tale of "The Dead Hand" is not only interesting itself, but symbolical of the author's constant view of life.

Paul Margueritte

For the dead hand that was an object of terror becomes an inspiration to healthy action.

IN his tale of French peasant life, "The Treasure," Georges Beaume (*b.* 1861) analyses the intense love of money prevailing, for both good and evil, in his country. It is a source of French power that enables the peasant to increase his hold upon the land and gradually break up the large estates into small holdings, and that gives the country its wonderful financial influence. It has made the French farmer monstrous in the eyes of Zola and Maupassant: yet without this national passion for saving, with all the laborious work it implies, France would never have maintained her greatness. During the war it was not until the hard, frugal peasants took the field that the fierce underlying tenacity of their race was fully revealed to the world.

Georges Beaume

Though Lucien Descaves (*b.* 1861), one of the finest men of the realistic school, has never won the popularity of Mirbeau, his work has been appreciated by the best minds. In his apparently slight sketch, "An Interior," he lights up the main problem in modern French home life. The men are often sceptics of the anti-clerical sort, yet, despite all their efforts, their children continue to be brought up in the faith of their fathers. For the Frenchwoman cannot bring herself to follow the Frenchman, and wives, aunts, and grandmothers, even in the best political families, defeat the intentions of the Government.

Descaves

Charles Foley (*b.* 1861) is not concerned with any important political or religious problem in his picture of the Avignon waiter "Pirotou." His tale is of an ironic character, yet expressive of sympathy with the unfortunate man who is so completely eclipsed by his wealthy, brilliant brother.

Foley

FOR long the fashionable novelist of his period, Marcel Prévost (*b.* 1862) deserves his position by reason of his subtle, ranging power of insight. In work after work he has illumined dim corners in modern French society. For example, the foreign reader will find nowhere else so concise and well balanced an analysis of the French *mariage de convenance* as in his "A Young Girl's Diary." The marriageable maiden is far from being a pawn in the affair. Her parents do the best they can to obtain a good match for her, and she is keenly alive to all the facts of the situation, and, with the special talent of her sex and race, plays the game for her future life with zest and skill.

Prévost

In "Wolf-Solange" Prévost turns to the French peasantry for an example of the virile yet graceful type of womanhood he often celebrated in his longer works. For Prévost with all his faults is one of those energisers of modern France who were consciously or unconsciously preparing the people for the great ordeal. The strange ghostly tale of "Psyche" is not a mere essay in the uncanny. It is based on ordinary facts of life, the supernatural element being only a symbol of certain natural truths. The extraordinary plot of the next tale by the same author, "Mademoiselle Heudier's Husband," is again only an artistic vehicle for conveying one of Prévost's fine discoveries in psychology.

Although Prévost first appeared as a disciple of Paul Bourget, he is a more discerning student of human nature than his master. How slight is his material in his last tale, "The Beggar Child": yet what a train of thought he suggests in it! Doctor Johnson would have been pleased with this story, for he was given over to that curious kind of impulse that Prévost was the first to turn into the subject-matter of literary art.

D'Esparbès

"THE BUTTERFLY" of Georges d'Esparbès (*b.* 1863) is a winged and iridescent idyll of studio life, that hovers daintily between the poetry and prose of the rather drab world of provincial competitive examinations. Perhaps it is the classic atmosphere of the most famous legend in Greek art, which the writer skilfully suggests, that makes his tale so charmingly distinctive. It is clear that "The Butterfly" is a remote descendant of the bird that came and picked at the grapes in the ancient Greek picture.

Leon Frapié

Léon Eugénie Frapié (*b.* 1863) has classic qualities of a deeper character. Realistic in style, he is yet full of Virgilian tenderness. How vulgar is his title "The Missus," yet how beautiful is the idea and how fine the execution! As for Frapié's second tale, "A Simple Soul," which is written in a vocabulary befitting a music-hall sketch for a low comedian, the pathos and loving-kindness of it are incomparable. It is right to judge artistic works of art purely from an artistic point of view, but there is something larger than art in Frapié's tale.

Pierre Mille

Pierre Mille (*b.* 1864) scarcely believes in loving-kindness, as he shows in his dramatic story of "Mrs. Murray's Revenge." M. Mille began as a disciple of Mr. Rudyard Kipling, and developed into one of the ablest of the young professors of energy, with a fine, original vein of his own, until he put his literary work aside in order to labour at cementing Franco-British-American comradeship in feelings, ideas, and action during the war.

De Régnier

HENRI DE RÉGNIER (*b.* 1864) is an extreme contrast to Pierre Mille. Régnier represents the old, idle, finely cultivated French aristocracy, and while composing volumes of poetry in a freshened classic mould, he returned in his stories to the traditions of the eighteenth century. By the pure grace of form of his works he won a position in the French Academy, and had the happiness of pleasing the men of the old school as well as the symbolists and other innovators. In his tale of "The Sign of the Key and Cross" Régnier executes a masterly variation upon a theme used by Poe and Villiers d'Isle Adams.

Régnier is usually derivative, yet his perfect art makes him seem less of an imitator than an eclectic master. In his gift for form he is practically equal to Anatole France, but his mind and spirit are those of an aristocratic dilettante. No fire from hell or heaven has touched him. There is far more feeling in the tale of the Franco-German war, by Georges Renard (*b.* 1864), "Jacques Brulefert's Death," the ending of which is one of the most magnificent things in the literature of the short story.

Georges Renard

DURING the period immediately before the Great War, the French story-tellers of the younger generation appeared to lack the energy of imagination of the older men. They seemed rather to be training themselves for some national movement than bent on exploring new fields of individual art. Much of their work, however, was marked by qualities of high value. The curious study by "Fernand Vandérem" (*b.* 1864), entitled "Himself," has a fine originality of a subtle sort. "The Foolish Virgin," by the brilliant Philippe Monnier (*b.* 1864), owes its distinction to the way in which it is written. The idea of it is old, yet Monnier makes it new by means of his sympathetic and winning style.

Philippe Monnier

"The Nona," by André Godard (*b.* 1865), is a surprise story, like Maupassant's "Necklace," depending entirely on skill and execution. The trick is often attempted, but the little masterpieces in the art of surprise remain small in number. Marcel Schwob (1867-1905), who follows Godard, was a master of all the effects of the short story, and as is seen in the strange, mystic tale of "The Wooden Star," he had a good deal in common with R. L. Stevenson. Schwob had a rich imagination, but lacked driving power of will, and the body of work he left behind him is as small as it is fine.

Godard and Schwob

André Lichtenberger (*b.* 1870), on the other hand, is a profuse and varied writer. All his work is marked by distinguished qualities that would make the task of selection somewhat difficult, if it were not for the adorable "Trott." Trott is now the classic type of the French child living in pleasant circumstances, and the series of comedies in which he figures is a chain of delights. There is comedy also in "The Captain's Little Secret" by Rudolph Bringer (*b.* 1871). The idea of this story seems purely farcical, but it contains a telling satire upon a certain whim of pretension in oldish men, which, though especially noticeable in Frenchmen of the retired class, is not uncommon in other races.

Lichtenberger and Bringer

"ASHES," by Paul Renaudin (*b.* 1873), is a more serious work. Indeed, it is one of the most serious in the literature of its period. It marks the profound change that at the beginning of the century was taking place in the French conscience, owing to struggles of the new Labour parties in France. In the early work of Frederic Boutet (*b.* 1874), little of this new spirit of seriousness was to be seen, until the writer went into the fighting line. But his tale of "The Experiment" shows that Boutet was always a master of his art. He took little interest in the social study of human nature, and obtained nearly all his effects by means of situations in which some curious scientific idea was developed.

Later Writers

Paul Clesio, in his sketch "The Musgravius Monopoly," plays in an amusing fashion with those brilliant dynasties in the French world of science, resembling the Darwin dynasty, which is one of the glories of England. Jacques Constant goes far afield to Finland in his dramatic monologue "The Betrayal," while Georges Japy turns to Japan in his allegory of "The Mirror." With Marc Le Goupils, the neo-realistic movement greatly increased in strength, and, as is seen in the bitter tragedy of "The Cross-Roads," became one of the master currents in French literature of the twentieth century. During the war, this movement, with its union of French, Russian, and English elements, prevailed over all others; but in the years of troubled peace before the storm, there were many Frenchmen who, like A. le Hêtre in his poetic fantasy, "Tramp and Poet," continued to seek for delight and charm rather than for truth of facts.

PICTURESQUE romance also attracted young writers, with a talent for pictorial effect, such as Georges Maurevert. His "Gold Chain" is a superb exercise in the art of painting with words, and carries on the traditions of Merimée and Barrés. His "Suicide," which by its alarming title promises to deepen the gloomy impression of his first story, really serves to show the suppleness of his mind, being only a brilliant farce, set in the scenery of Monte Carlo.

"A Silver Coin," by H. Roguenant, is an idyll of the Latin Quarter, original in idea and pleasantly maintaining the tradition established by Murger in his "Vie de Bohème." All oldish artists and literary men seem to think that Bohemia vanished when they became middle-aged; but immortal youth meanwhile sweeps into the old streets of adventure, bringing with it perennial romance.

Maurice Saint-Aguet looks for romance in the age of Napoleon, in "The Croissey Yew." This is certainly the easier way, as in the moonlight of history everything seen in the past has a certain given picturesqueness. But M. Saint-Aguet's plot is so original and is told with such happy strokes that the little work deserves its position as an admirable example of the lighter historical tale.

"Nicette," by Saint-Juirs, is a bustling comedy of errors, compact with amusing situations. As Falstaff is as dramatic a figure as Hamlet, the art of the short story must also be allowed to range over the farcical side of life as well as the serious side. As Charles Lamb remarked, a laugh is worth a hundred groans in any market, and though the market price is not the only estimate of value, it represents often certain general human qualities overlooked by narrow-minded aesthetes. In striking contrast with the tale by Saint-Juirs is the study of Spanish court life, "The Princess 'Just Because'" by Raymond Schwab, with which the volume concludes. This is a remarkable study of the blithe soul of a child, suffocated by the pomp and circumstance of royalty, and, as the Infanta Eulalie proves in her memoirs, Schwab penetrated closely to the truth in his portrait of his imaginary child princess in Spain of the old régime. E. W.

ALFRED CAPUS
B. 1858

PRESENCE OF MIND

LITTLE SERQUY and Jules Debot, whom his friends usually called Bobo, were completely stone broke from time immemorial. Such was their position that no one remembered having seen them with money in hand, except perhaps the oldest men of the Boulevard. They had arrived at this state of things by paths that were different but equally sure. Bobo had in a few years wasted a fairly small inheritance, and as for Little Serquy he had never possessed anything of the slightest value. The necessities of life had always prevented them from exercising any kind of profession. No one knew their families; but they lived very well, and always dressed in the best style. They also moved in the best society. They were about the same age, forty, and their reputation, without being the kind required in judges in affairs of honour, was still enviable.

A charming good humour and unalterable gaiety brought them frequent invitations, social successes and profitable friendships. Thanks to their pleasant personal qualities, everybody forgave them the incessant "touches" that constituted their only resource. For, in plain truth, they lived entirely on that delicate and Parisian variety of loan which has had to be distinguished by a special name. "Touching" a man is not the same thing as borrowing from him, and though it is a financial operation of the same family, it is distinguished by some essential features.

If, for example, you ask anybody for a sum of money, promising to repay it at a stated period, you contract a loan; if, on the other hand, you merely say to a friend or acquaintance, or to a stranger, "Lend me fifty pounds," without in any way undertaking to return it, that is a "touch." Men lend one another money in all countries and under all conditions, but "touching" only goes on in Paris among people of a certain class. A loan is often painful: it places you for the moment in an inferior and slightly humiliating position. It is not so with the art of "touching," which must be practised with a large easy air, as if the act of touching were a kind of homage to a chosen friend.

Bobo and Serquy excelled in this formidable art. They each had a fixed method, whose power they had proved by long use. The ability of Little Serquy consisted in a surprising tact that enabled him to divine the exact minute when anybody could be tapped. He knew when his victim had had a good day at the races or the card-table. He watched the play of his features, he never overworked him, and he used but little speech. He was like a discreet dentist who pulls out one of your teeth with a strong wrist at the critical moment without showing his instrument. His triumphs were beyond reckoning.

Bobo was a dentist with a gift of the gab who seemed to think it was a matter of no importance if you had one tooth more or less. At his genial good fellowship, his smooth and amusing flow of words, pockets opened naturally. Thus both of them led an easy and joyful life, exempt from gloom, putting up with passing checks and trusting in the innumerable combinations of luck. They had even had brilliant times and periods of luxury. The months preceding the great panic were one of their bright memories, and also the period of the Rio Tinto boom. They were always hoping that such times would come again, for their destinies were based on the vagaries of the Public Funds. And after any great hit on the Stock Exchange you saw them hastening like gleaners in the track of their acquaintances.

But for several months Bobo and Serquy had been having a very critical time of it. Business was not moving, and they were the victims of a deplorable state of doldrums. They had just got through a week with small pieces of money, taking their meals in low-class restaurants, meeting at times at cook-shop tables on evenings when they had no invitation to dinner. They chatted to one another about the difficulties of life in Paris and the increased cost of living. Yet they maintained towards each other a perfect manner and affected merely to be living frugally until the money market improved.

By a sorry coincidence, most of their usual clients were down on their luck. Blache, who was always good for ten pounds, kept his pockets closed at the club. Dick lost an enormous sum at the races. Similar accidents struck their best chums. Never had they found themselves in such unfavourable circumstances.

At last one night, Bobo, coming into the card-room of the club, as was his daily custom, to gather news, learnt that Boisgenet, a very decent fellow, quite young, almost a beginner, had just made a splendid scoop in a flutter. After this great exploit, Boisgenet had immediately given up playing. Bobo hastened back to his rooms and left one of his cards on the hall porter's table, after scribbling on it that he wanted to be awakened at ten in the morning.

At half-past ten he entered Boisgenet's outer room.

" Master has gone out," said the servant.

Bobo murmured an "Ah ! " of disappointment.

" But he is sure to be back before twelve. He has some friends coming to breakfast."

" That is all right," said Bobo, " I will wait for him in the smoking-room."

He began to read the newspaper in a tranquil frame of mind, but he had scarcely glanced at the headlines, when the servant opened the door again and introduced another visitor, brilliantly dressed, with light gloves, patent shoes and a smiling face. It was Serquy. Bobo and Serquy shook hands with an almost imperceptible frown.

" How are things going ? "

" Not at all badly ; and how are you getting on ? "

" I say! How is it I did not see you at the club yesterday evening ? " asked Bobo.

" I came rather late," said Serquy, " and I was told you had just gone."

" Ah ! " An embarrassed silence followed. Bobo and Serquy knew too much about life to have the least doubt about the object of each other. On the other hand, they were too well mannered to indulge in untimely jests. Firmly resolved not to give way to each other, they stared coldly, gravely, attentively at one another. Then they began to chat about indifferent matters, avoiding the mention of Boisgenet, as though they were not in his house. Half an hour thus passed by.

Suddenly the features of Bobo relaxed. He called to the servant:

" Are you quite certain that Monsieur Boisgenet will return for breakfast ? "

" Absolutely certain."

" Very well."

The servant retired. Bobo turned to Serquy.

" Just fancy, my dear friend . . . Yes, there is no harm in telling you. . . . You know Boisgenet well, don't you ? What a charming fellow ! And obliging. . . . You see, then, Boisgenet last month lent me a hundred pounds. . . . And with such a good heart !

Ah ! People who will lend you a hundred pounds when you are hard up are becoming rare ! And I will admit to you that when I at last received my money this morning, I was vastly pleased to think I could go at once and return Boisgenet his hundred pounds. By Jove, he is making us wait a little, but I will stay here all the same. I should only gamble the money away this evening. . . . What a charming fellow Boisgenet is, eh ? "

" Charming," said the other; and as he was somewhat cast down by having to wait so long, Serquy for a minute lost the keen edge of his intelligence. He thought innocently, " This is turning out very well. I will look in after lunch." And, getting up : " Faith ! I merely came to get some information from him about the race to-morrow. I can see him this evening. That will be time enough. Good-day, old chap."

So it was Bobo who, on that occasion, touched Boisgenet.

THE MARION AFFAIR

ALFRED CAPUS

THE need for a quiet simple holiday led me one day to a little country town fifty leagues from Paris. At the inn where I left my luggage I asked if there was not some cottage I could take for the season. The innkeeper advised me to go and see Monsieur Marion, the owner of a pretty furnished villa.

" I don't think it has been taken this year," he added.

Monsieur Marion lived quite near to the town in a one-storeyed peasant hut. I found him smoking a pipe outside his door. He seemed from sixty to seventy years old. But his tall, upright figure, his big shoulders and lissom movements were those of a man full of vigour. He received me with the greatest civility.

" There is the villa," he said, showing me with his finger a square white building with green shutters. " If you like you can look over it at once. It is well furnished."

It suited me. Monsieur Marion put a very moderate rent on it, and I took it.

" You will be very comfortable here. The river flows two hundred feet away, and it is full of fish. Do you handle a rod ? "

I admitted I had a passion for fishing. I settled in the house that day, helped by a servant whom my landlord was kind enough to get for me. And the next morning I began to fish with fervour. Angling did not seem to be the favourite sport in that part of the country. The banks of the river were deserted, in spite of their cool shadows, in spite of the slow deep water, in which big fish could at times be seen leaping. However, towards the evening, as I was returning for a second attempt, I heard the noise of branches moving behind me. Looking back I saw, box in hand, rod under the arm, an old little thin gentleman looking somewhat serious and slightly frowning. By these signs I recognised that not only was he a fisherman like myself, but that, in all probability, I had taken his usual place. I rose up, excusing myself. At this mark of good-will, his face brightened.

" Don't disturb yourself," he said, " I will go farther up the river."

I replied I could not permit it, and that it was only because I was unaware . . . He insisted with a fine courtesy and bowed and went away.

I met him the next day, and little by little we began to chat together. He gave me special information about the best fishing places on the river, we lent each other tackle, and there was soon established between us the intimacy that comes of liking the same sport.

" It is you, isn't it, who has taken old Marion's villa for the season ? "

" Yes. Is Marion one of your friends ? "

" Not exactly," he said, with a smile ; " but I have known him for a long time. . . . Yes, for thirty-eight years."

" He seems to be a decent man," I said.

" Yes, very decent."

" Have you lived for thirty-eight years in the country ? " I asked.

" Much more than that. I have never left it. I was a notary, and I retired some years ago. My name is Lebrun."

" Possibly Marion was one of your clients ? "

" Well. . . . Somewhat."

These evasive answers in regard to my landlord began to puzzle me in a vague way, but I could not obtain any more precise information. A few days afterwards, as we were fishing side by side, I again mentioned the name of old Marion. Monsieur Lebrun had just caught a perch that leaped and twisted at the end of his line. He placed it carefully in his box, then said abruptly :

" How is it that you never heard of the Marion affair ? It is true you were young at the time. But it excited so much . . ."

I leant over to listen, and he continued in a low voice so as not to disturb the fish :

" It was in 1855 a terrible crime was committed in the parish : a woman and a child had their throats cut—Widow Berez and her little boy. Don't you remember it ? "

" Not at all."

" Suspicion fell on Marion, who was then a man of about thirty-two. I ought to tell you that there was a good deal of evidence against him, but I will spare you the details. He was only condemned to penal servitude, benefiting by certain points that could not be cleared up. He was taken to New Caledonia. Then, five years afterwards, in 1860, a rumour was started that Marion had been wrongly condemned. The real criminal, it was said, had confessed on his death-bed. That created an enormous scandal. It was observed that up to the moment of the crime Marion had always behaved well. Public opinion was very strongly moved. The Emperor took part in it, and after all the proceedings had been revised, Marion came back here. Since then, I must add, his life has been very honourable. He inherited the property of some relation and became a man of leisure. All this story is now forgotten. Most of the witnesses are dead. No one in the place thinks of making the slightest allusion to it."

I asked for details.

"Ah! It has all got mixed up in my mind. . . . Besides, to my way of thinking—and I was present at the trial—the case was extremely perplexing."

"But he is innocent . . . the confession of the criminal . . ."

"Clearly, he is innocent. There is nothing to say about that. The confession of the guilty person was made in legal form. I stand on settled things," added Monsieur Lebrun with a smile. "When Marion was condemned, I believed in his guilt. When the authorities decided that he was the victim of a mistake, I immediately believed in his innocence."

"But what is your own sincere opinion in the matter?"

"My opinion is that it is forty years since all that happened." And without another word, the old notary cast his line again into the river.

You always end by getting somewhat bored on a quiet holiday in the country. In one of those hours when idleness weighs as much on the mind as heavy work, I determined to find some occupation by getting old Marion, if possible, to tell me his story. I often met him, either at his door, or on the path by the river. He wished me a good catch, and I asked him about his health, and there our talk came to an end. After the revelation of the old notary, I tried to get on a more intimate footing with my landlord, whose case had excited my curiosity. One day I offered him some fish. He accepted it on the condition that I drank some plum brandy that he made himself with fruit from his garden. Then I invited him to dinner. It was only then a question of finding an opening. "You have struck up a friendship with the notary?" said old Marion. "I noticed it. He is just as mad about fishing as you are. I know him of old."

"Yes," I answered, "we are good friends. He is a delightful man." And I added rapidly, "We have talked . . . about you. I already knew about . . . your terrible affair . . . before I came." I shook him by the hand, saying, " My poor Monsieur Marion ! " And I thought to myself, " I have got him."

But far from being astonished or putting on a serious air as I expected, old Marion began to laugh.

" Ha ! Ha ! I don't doubt it. It made some noise at the time, that affair. It is well known in Paris, eh ? "

" Very well known," I affirmed.

The ice was broken. Old Marion filled his glass with plum brandy, then, still smiling with winning good nature :

" Eh ! Yes, that was an amusing story. . . . At first, when I returned they carried me shoulder high in triumph. Next they tried to get me into politics on the side of the opposition. I refused. I was always afraid of politics. Then I had scarcely been back six months when they began to say that my judicial error was a government invention, and that I had got off by intrigues and backstairs influence. Men shunned me in the street, although I didn't care a button. Some of our local newspapers attacked me, others took my part. It was comical ! For six months I was innocent, then crack ! I again became a great criminal, after I had spent half a year in being a martyr whom everybody honoured. Travellers had begun to ask to be introduced to me. But one fine morning all that changed, without rhyme or reason. I was nothing more than a monster of hypocrisy who had cheated the guillotine. Isn't it funny ? At last, everything was forgotten ; is it not so ? Just imagine, on the fourth of last September . . ."

Old Marion expanded with jollity, as though he were recalling a merry past.

" On the fourth of last September, as my name was very well known—they did not remember why—they came and asked me to stand as mayor. . . . Ha ! Ha ! You will guess I declined the honour. . . . Now it is all finished, finished. . . . It is a legend. . . ."

Such nonchalance and gaiety strangely surprised me. What especially astonished me was that old Marion did not display the slightest animosity against his persecutors, that he never spoke of his sufferings at Noumea, that he never appeared to retain the least grudge against his country for the horrible adventure of which he had been the victim.

As for myself, I inclined from one extreme to the other. Sometimes, looking at his white beard, his fine figure of robust old age, I took him for a philosopher, superior to common men by his simplicity, his pride of soul, his gentleness and resignation. At other times, seeing his clear cold eyes and thin lips, I conceived the most abominable suspicions.

Naturally I never dared ask him the question that was on my lips: "You are innocent, aren't you?" It was extremely curious, for during the three months that we chatted together he never said to me in a downright positive way, "I am innocent." On the eve of my departure for Paris we dined together. Then I went back with him to his cottage. We shook hands. Then looking me in the face, with a smile that seemed to me at the moment diabolical but may have been only a delicate and ironic allusion to the unjust suspicions he had divined in me, he said:

"Would you like me to tell you something quite extraordinary? To-day I am exactly sixty-eight years old. It doesn't matter now who committed or did not commit a crime in 1855. Well, they have told me so often that I was guilty and that I was innocent that, on my word of honour, I don't know myself what I am." And he disappeared into his cottage, giving me, behind the door, a friendly good-night.

PAUL GINISTY
B. 1858

A CAPITULATION

"OH dear, oh dear!" exclaimed M. Amalfi, after reading the letter which he had received.

As he always did when a matter seemed very important, he took off his glasses, blew on them, wiped the lenses with his handkerchief, and put them on again. This operation gave him time to think.

He was sitting at his study table, which was covered with documents, papers, cases full of written sheets, all of them heaped in a disorder which only he could regulate. An old bachelor, he never allowed a woman's hand to put his papers straight, and his servants were ordered not even to disturb the dust which gathered on his desk.

"Oh dear, oh dear!" he said again. "This is a trifle strong, all the same!"

M. Amalfi was a man about fifty years of age, who had been gifted by Nature with a ferocious-looking moustache, though he was really of a very pacific temper, thinking of nothing but his work as a historian, which had gained him a reputation for scrupulous accuracy, the result of his inflexible conscientiousness. When he had pronounced his decision, it was as certain as Holy Writ; for every one knew how careful he was, how scrupulously he verified every single source of information, and how anxious he was that there should not be a single error, however slight, in his facts. Ten large volumes, consecrated to the Wars of the Royalist Insurgents, bore witness to the admirable precision of his method, by which not a single word was written without absolute proof of its truth.

Yet this hard-working historian, whose eyes were worn by the constant examination of the manuscripts which he had laboriously got together, was not altogether devoid of feeling. He was impartial, but could at the same time feel sympathy for one side or another. A stranger to the present day, hardly knowing what was going on in the world around him, or at least not troubling about it more than he could help, M. Amalfi lived in the past. For the dead he felt pity, admiration, affection, just as he often felt for them anger and disapproval; he seemed to live in the lives of those whose deeds he described, and belonged only to the past which he evoked.

Being naturally kind-hearted, he was often sorry to have to fix irrevocably in print matters which he had so laboriously discovered. Thus, he had been known to visit a cemetery in the suburbs of Paris, where one of the heroines of the Vendéan War lay buried. She had died in the odour of sanctity, but he sought her tomb to ask pardon of her memory for the revelations which truth compelled him to make concerning her private life, for these revelations ill consorted with her virtuous reputation. On that occasion the good M. Amalfi was profoundly regretful. Nevertheless, the profession of historian has its own unalterable obligations, which may by no means be evaded.

The letter which he held in his hand referred to an important recent research, which he had lately had published in a magazine. He had been led by degrees, though not at first without surprise, to a conviction of the double part played, during the Royalist Insurgent War, by the Marquis de Villeroc. This warrior had been regarded by the Royalist party as one of the most faithful comrades of Larochejaquelein, and had received great honours and rewards under the Restoration, not for his own merit alone, but also for that of his former companions-in-arms, whom Fate had not spared to reap the final success of their cause. As a last recompense for his devotion to his King, he became a peer of France in 1827. Villeroc, one of the most celebrated leaders of the Catholic Royalist Army, one of the most active agitators of the Vendée, convicted of disloyalty! At first, M. Amalfi felt ashamed of harbouring the least suspicion of the man's probity, and accused himself of a lack of charity; for in his absolute regard for truth he never believed harm of any one, except when it was quite impossible to doubt it. But this mystery, upon which he had come, occupied his thoughts for a time, and ended by absorbing all his attention. In his usual scientific method, yet not without anxiety, he devoted himself to the study of the problem. If Villeroc had been a traitor—the ugly word must be faced—a careful examination of all the facts must some day show the truth.

When once he had set out on the trail, M. Amalfi never turned aside; and in the present case he was more than usually tenacious. He never allowed the doings of Villeroc to escape him for a single moment, and conviction soon followed what had begun as no more than suspicion. He grudged neither the journeys he had made nor the most patient inquiries, nor the most elaborate researches ; and at last, in the face of the world's opinion, he was absolutely convinced that what he stated was the astounding and lamentable truth. The hand of Villeroc, the "glorious Villeroc," was clearly to be traced in many of the disasters of the Royalist Army. He had played a double game. While leading the peasants of the West, and swearing all the time by God and King, he had kept the enemy informed of the movements of the Army to which he belonged, and had indicated at the same time the weakness of its positions. The "heroic Villeroc" had been the miserable agent of the destruction of his brothers-in-arms, whom he had basely sold. A dastardly hypocrisy had won his reputation for valour and loyalty.

Once sure of his facts, M. Amalfi had no fear of their refutation, for he had only too many proofs of the truth of his discovery. He therefore set to work at once, and wrote an article for a magazine, embodying the substance of the book which he was preparing, and unmasking with avenging indignation the Villeroc who had been so unjustly honoured.

The letter which he had this morning received was from the present Marquis of Villeroc, who bore the title with the tenacious pride of a man who has done little himself, and is therefore all the more indebted to his ancestors. By universal consent, his manner was perfect, and he was a notable ornament of the French nobility. His hereditary title gave him the distinction of being one of the Councillors of the Royalist party, though it must be said that his counsel was rarely asked. In a word, he represented traditional loyalty, unshakable faith in the monarchy, and chivalrous devotion to the Royalist cause, though he had never had occasion to prove his fidelity.

His letter contained a lofty protest. In a few dry lines, in which there were two mistakes in spelling, the Marquis spoke out his mind to the crazy historian who dared to upset history, and demanded a withdrawal of the facts which had been advanced. It was this that had caused M. Amalfi's exclamations. The tone of the letter was haughty. "As the guardian of an inheritance of glory," wrote the Marquis, "as the descendant of a hero, it is impossible for me to permit such an absurd attack on his memory."

"Very well," said M. Amalfi, "I will just go and show you what your hero was really like !"

An idea came to him. He took a case of papers out of the drawer of his desk, folded it in a rather worn leather cover, which had seen much service on the tables of public libraries and record offices, and though he was not as a rule very careful of his appearance, he put on his best overcoat. As he went downstairs he smiled and whistled, with the air of a man who knows what he is about. A cab was passing, and hailing it, he told the driver to go to the Rue de Varenne.

The Villeroc town-house was a magnificent building. Impressed by the noble lines of its architecture, M. Amalfi looked at it for a moment before entering. He was still smiling. He gave his card to the servant and was admitted into an immense drawing-room, looking out on a fine garden, and seeming as if it could not have changed much since the Restoration. The first thing which attracted his attention was a huge portrait, by Gérard, of the great Villeroc, in his robes of a peer of France. In another and smaller portrait, he appeared in his uniform of General of the Army of the Vendée, sword in hand, dealing out death to the enemy. Everything in this great room recalled him; everything was eloquent of his glory. Two autograph letters of Louis XVIII., in which he called Villeroc his " dear and faithful friend," were mounted in gold on either side of a sword of honour, which he had received from the former soldiers of the Royalist side, when he was created a peer. A glass case contained his plumed hat, with the white cockade. All spoke of the heroic past, and of the honours paid to the illustrious ancestor.

The Marquis at length appeared, after keeping his visitor waiting for a long time, no doubt to put him in his proper place. He was tall and thin, and singularly like Gérard's portrait.

" Sir," he said, without any other salutation : " I have seen your article."

" It is only an abstract of a large volume I am bringing out," interrupted M. Amalfi, whom the sight of all these souvenirs, impressive to others but not to him, inclined to obstinacy.

The Marquis shrugged his shoulders. " You ventured, sir," he continued severely, " to make most unwarrantable attacks. We despise them, sir, we despise them. Understand that clearly. They do not touch us at all. Still, we have the right to exact—— "

M. Amalfi had been carefully studying the Marquis. He was very solemn, but was evidently sincere.

" My Lord Marquis," said he, " I never write anything of which

I am not certain. Will you please look over some papers which I have brought with me ? "

" We despise them, sir, we despise them," repeated the Marquis.

" Very good," replied M. Amalfi, with annoyance ; " despise them if you like ; but do look at them all the same."

Very carefully he took from his case about twenty different papers, which he spread out one by one in due succession before the Marquis. The first was a letter from the Prior of the Marne to the Adjutant-General Savary, dated the 22nd of Frimaire (November-December) of the year II. In this letter the position of the Royalist camp was given, and certain information which came from " an unexpected source " in that very camp. The papers were full of details as to the occupation of Le Mans by the Catholic Royalist Army, and as to its defeat in 1793. A note from Villeroc, in a scarcely disguised handwriting, gave all particulars of the celebrated Council of War, held in the Hôtel de la Biche, between the two parties of Talmont and Larochejaquelein, under the presidency of the Bishop of Agra ; and mentioned the indecision of the Vendéan leaders. Then there were a few lines from Maignan, Commissioner of the Revolutionary Police, plainly stating the name of Villeroc as a man overwhelmed with need of money, and capable of doing anything to obtain it. Nothing was lacking to complete these successive revelations, graduated so as to admit of no doubt whatever. The travelling case of Garnier de Saintes, a member of the Convention, lost by him at Pont-Lieu, forgotten for a hundred years in the garret of a farmhouse, but the contents of which had at last been carefully collated and examined by M. Amalfi, left no room for the slightest shadow of doubt. For the sum of 500,000 francs, Villeroc had betrayed the Army which he served, pointing out the points at which it could most easily be attacked and routed. There was even an order from Turreau for the payment of the sum in question, confirming the shocking fact of the betrayal. And before that, there was a long correspondence with General Rossignol ; and a letter from him, describing in his coarse way and in cynical terms, the intrigues in which Villeroc had engaged with him.

It was all quite undeniable. The gorgeous legend faded pitiably. Villeroc had made use of the favour which he enjoyed with the Royalists only to betray them. And mark—it was not a moment of madness, a sudden impulse, but a long premeditated and steady course of treason, for the basest motives ; an appalling duplicity. It was infamy of this kind, which Villeroc had believed to be for ever concealed, that had been so splendidly rewarded by the foolish and ignorant gratitude of Louis XVIII. ; it was this tissue of crime and felony which had gained for the Vendéan leader the admiration of a deluded posterity.

The Marquis was stupefied. He could not speak. His face was flushed ; he wrung his hands in distress which could find no other expression. M. Amalfi, in absolute certainty of his facts, had proved the authenticity of these terrible documents, brought to light to show the truth which had been so long hidden.

"You see," said the historian, "Kléber and Marceau won the Battle of Le Mans ; their forces gave them the victory ; but knowing, as they did, what was going on in the town, they could easily have won it three days sooner."

Tears rolled down the thin face of the poor Marquis. M. Amalfi, who had been speaking quite absorbed by his subject, suddenly stopped and looked at him. He now felt very sorry for him. The blow had been a severe one.

"Permit me, sir," said the Marquis de Villeroc at last, wiping his forehead, "to go and consult my wife."

He went out. M. Amalfi, who was also very much upset by this too sharp revenge for doubt thrown on his good faith as a historian, began to arrange the papers in his case. A quarter of an hour went by. The Marquis returned, accompanied by the Marquise, a woman who had been very beautiful and was now very dignified. There had been a hasty but serious conversation between the husband and the wife.

She did not beat about the bush, but went straight to the point.

"Sir," she said, "you are bringing dishonour on our house."

"Madame," replied M. Amalfi, who began to feel very uneasy, "I am only an historian. It is a painful task sometimes."

"Sir," she said, "you are in possession of secrets which until now were unknown to us. I assure you on my honour that we knew nothing of them. If you make them known it will kill us ; I implore you not to publish your book."

"But it has been announced and is expected ! I also have my duty to do."

The Marquise was really tragic and imposing in her grief. M. Amalfi felt for the agony which he had inflicted on this family. In spite of his uncompromising reply, he felt softened. Moreover, the

Marquis had lost all his former haughtiness, and was now only a poor man who saw all his great position taken away. M. Amalfi was overwhelmed; he was sorry he had come.

"Sir," said the Marquise, "perhaps you will listen to a mother. We have a daughter who is about to be married to the heir to one of the greatest titles in France. Who knows what terrible consequences may result from the dreadful scandal which you will cause in our circle?"

She stretched out her hands toward him in appeal—she who was so proud, and had lived all her life in the prejudices of caste; and the downfall of her pride made her distress all the more pitiable.

Troubled by his innate kindness of heart, M. Amalfi murmured words of consolation, expressing his sympathy and sincere grief at having ever undertaken these researches, the result of which had been only too certain from the beginning. He excused himself humbly, and endeavoured to restore the courage of those on whom he had inflicted so deep an injury.

The Marquise saw that he was shaken in his resolution, and that he was truly grieved; and believed that only one last effort was necessary in order to obtain the victory.

"Be generous," she urged. "Our gratitude will be everlasting."

A struggle evidently took place in the mind of the honest historian, who had never in his life dreamed of tampering in the least with the truth, but had weighed so carefully every one of his words, and had given chapter and verse for every statement. And yet, he was miserable at the thought of the deep humiliation which he had inflicted on the Marquis, in spite of his arrogance at the beginning of their interview, and on his wife, who was plainly suffering acutely.

"Well?" asked the Marquise, anxiously.

"Well!" replied M. Amalfi, convinced in all good faith that he was about to make the greatest possible concession, and feeling rather uncomfortable in his conscience, which he was forced to bend before the pity which overpowered him: "I am so touched by your grief that I will give way. I will make a great sacrifice."

"And——?"

"Instead of saying in my book that Villeroc betrayed his party for five hundred thousand francs, I will say that in fact he only received half that sum."

REMY DE GOURMONT

B. 1858

THE WHITE GOWN

AH! How sorry I was to leave the corner of the railway carriage, where I had sat dreaming of views more interesting than the silent mills, the solitary spires, the gnarled apple-trees, and the melancholy hovels we passed, seeming, under the evening mist, to sleep the weary sleep of Nature freed at last from light and gaiety, from labour and from tears.

I had been invited to be present at the wedding of my friend, Albert de Courcy, whose best man I had agreed to be. I gave this promise with polite indifference, for I make it a principle never to seem to take too great an interest in other people's joys or sorrows. I maintain an air of dignity combined with friendliness, and the calm and somewhat melancholy smile which I bestow on my friends wins forgiveness for the flash of resentment which I sometimes cannot repress when it gleams for a moment in my eyes.

No one came to meet me, for I was not expected until the following day. I set out on foot, and walked through the woods for three-quarters of an hour, avoiding the open spaces and the moonlight, which bored me.

I did not feel anxious about the late hour of my arrival, for I had been here before and knew the ways of the house. The gate was unlocked; no dog made a sound; I entered as silently as a thief.

I crossed the smooth lawn so as to cut short the way by the winding avenue, and as I passed a group of syringas, whose poignant odour was spread around, I saw two windows lighted up in the dim white façade of the house.

These two bright windows were beside one another on the ground floor. Before tapping at the glass, I made bold to stop and look in.

In the midst of a small room littered with many garments, three women were gazing at a white gown which lay on an arm-chair, a gown white as the souls of the Holy Innocents. They were Rosa, a trusted maid of the family, Madame de Laneuil, and a girl whose face recalled my playmates of long ago, the little maidens with whom Alberic and I had sported ; I remembered how they had pretended to be our brides, giving us flowers from their bouquets to wear as favours, and gravely posing in that marriage ceremony which is so dear to the heart of feminine childhood. How many years ago was that ? A good many ; perhaps ten. How many days had passed since those childish games ! How many times since then the thrushes had sung in the tall chestnut trees round the house !

The place had been shut up ever since the death of M. de Laneuil, and had only been reopened now that Alberic was to take away a bride from here. My part was to lend to the marriage the indispensable stamp of social approval. Edith and Elphège had been our playmates, and now he was to marry Edith. The girl whom I saw before me, fair and pale, paler indeed than if she herself had been the bride, must surely be Elphège, my little sweetheart of other days. Elphège had always been fair and pale, and at the sight of her my boyish affection revived and my heart went out to her. Of course, she would be bridesmaid to her elder sister.

I yielded to the fascination of her charm and dreamed of the happiness of a double wedding, if that could be ; two couples kneeling at the feet of the priest, two wedding rings instead of one. Of course it was Elphège who stood there, and I felt that I had loved her all through these years unconsciously, and had come here now just to fulfil my destiny.

Yes, I had loved her, though far away ! My love had grown, even as I grew from boyhood to manhood, as the laughter of childhood softened into the serious smiles of youth, as the first gaiety of life melted into the dreams and strivings of manhood. And I seemed now to live those lost hours over again, and to listen once more to the songs of the thrushes every morning in the chestnut tops as they greeted the rising of the sun.

The perfume of the syringas was wafted on the night air, and went to my head like wine. I tapped at the window. The three women started, and after a pause and a word from the elder lady, Rosa pulled aside the curtain, and shading her eyes with her hands, asked who was there.

I spoke my name ; Madame de Laneuil disappeared ; the young girl smiled to me with the smile I knew of old, Elphège's smile ; and all hastened to unbar the door and welcome the midnight visitor.

My old friend greeted me warmly, and raising the lamp examined me closely, exclaiming, " How pale you are ! "

I hastened to assure her that I was very well, and that the moonlight made every one look pale ; it seemed to have had a special effect on me that evening.

" You find us in a great difficulty, my dear," she said ; " we hardly know what to do. Every one went to bed early. Elphège seems unwell ; she has that mysterious depression which attacks girls whose sisters are being parted from them by marriage. I wished Edith, before going to rest alone for the last time, to come with me and join me in prayer. We were just going upstairs when the wedding gown arrived from Paris—that white gown. We thought of making some alteration in the trimming of the bodice, and Rosa pinned it on. Imagine our horror when we found that it will not fit at all ! It is much too wide. Far too wide. We do not know what to do. We have been arguing and thinking ; each of us in turn took up the scissors, but we dare not touch it for fear of spoiling it. Still, we must do something, even if we have to stay up all night."

My voice was as lifeless as the white gown itself, as I said, vainly attempting a tone of indifference : " When I tapped at the window, I happened to see one of your daughters, and I supposed it was Elphège. I took for granted that it was Elphège."

" They are very much alike ; you might easily mistake one for the other, especially as it is so long since you have seen them. But come in ; perhaps you will be able to help us. Men often have good ideas as to these things."

I stood still, and she repeated, " Come with me."

As I followed her into the little sitting-room, Edith looked at me with some surprise ; but Madame de Laneuil explained who I was, and how I came to be there at such a late hour.

I vaguely heard her talking and laughing through the tumult of my thoughts. It was indeed Edith ; Edith, pale and fair, the bride of to-morrow. And it was Edith whom I loved, whom I had always loved. The force of passion so overwhelmed me that if I had been alone with her I could not have restrained myself ; I must have told her my mad desire to have her for my own, and to carry her off even at that hour, though against her will.

Madame de Laneuil continued to talk and laugh, explaining an idea which had come into her head.

And now I grew calmer ; I mastered my emotion and looked at Edith, for I felt that she was looking at me and never once took her gaze from my face. I looked at her, I say, and in that look I saw that my passion was returned. Our eyes met for a second, which might have been eternity, so much was felt, so much conveyed in that glance of mutual understanding and consent.

Then I heard Madame de Laneuil saying, " Well, what do you think ? Give us your advice."

I pulled myself together, trembling all over, and radiant with the happiness of the discovery I had made. Even my hostess noticed the change in my manner.

" Come," she said, " you look brighter already. A wedding is always a happy time, isn't it ? "

Edith smiled sadly.

" First of all," I said, trying to appear business-like ; " first of all, Edith must put on the dress."

" That is true ; of course she must."

I shaded my eyes with my hands like Rosa, and looked out of the window, while the change was being made. The moon was high, throwing the shadow of the great manor-house across the courtyard. I saw nothing outside ; another vision filled my brain, called up by the rustling of the silken fabric as they fastened the gown—the vision of the white throat and dainty form of my dear one, as she raised her arms, and from all her being a perfume was exhaled, sweet and poignant as the syringas in the night air outside. But now the white gown fell like an avalanche over all and blotted out my vision.

Edith still smiled sadly.

We talked like dressmakers. I gave my advice, which was taken. Rosa undertook to make the necessary alterations in the gown, and I saw by the way she looked at me that I had risen greatly in her estimation.

Madame de Laneuil took me to my room. Before leaving I said good-night to my love, just found and lost again, the bride of another. As we parted a sad sympathy welled up between us, the consciousness of a fatal secret shared by both. Her eyes followed me as I went out—her clear blue eyes now dimmed with tears.

The thrushes had long been singing to the dawn from the tops of the mighty chestnut trees. Alberic came into my room to talk of the morrow. He spoke of his bride, of his wish to make her happy, of his fear that he was not good enough for such a perfect creature. He rambled on like a good fellow who wants others to reassure him of what he tries to believe. I let him talk. It did me good to listen to him, for when one is unhappy there is consolation to be found, as Scripture tells us, in the anxieties of our friends. But all the time I thought, and thought incessantly, of the felicity which was not for me.

"The bride is coming!" A murmur went round the great drawing-room as Edith entered, fair and pale, beneath the pictured gaze of generations of her ancestors. She had not wept, neither had she slept; there were heavy shadows beneath the sapphire of her eyes. Her slender form was outlined by the white gown whose defects I had been called on to correct, and the virginal white veil fell over all.

Turning aside from the others, she approached her grandfather, who leaned against the mantelpiece, evidently deeply touched by the scene. As she passed close to me, barely moving her lips, her breath coming as in a sigh, her eyes cast down, these words reached me, so faint as to be no more than uttered—"Too late!"

I, too, lowered my eyes, thrilled once more by the forbidden joy of a secret understanding.

She offered her fair cheek to the old grandfather's kiss, and resting her two hands on his shoulders, she smiled up at him. But the smile was sad. The old man's kiss seemed to bring a blessing from all her ancestors on the nuptials of this daughter of their race.

I stood so near that the ample veil floated round my head, wafted by the breeze from an open window, and it seemed as if a breath of love came in to bear us, my Edith and myself, to the Paradise of parted lovers.

When she had again reached her mother's side, she looked at me for an instant fixedly, and then the white veil fell between her eyes and mine and hid them from my gaze—for ever! The perfume of the syringas, cruelly poignant, floated in through the open window. She was a wife!

During the ceremony, I repeated in my heart the bridegroom's replies to the questions of the priest, and when the nuptial blessing was pronounced, I bowed my head at the solemn words which bind together man and woman with an indissoluble bond.

I remembered my college days and the theological studies in which

I had delighted, and I knew that in every sacrament there are two parts, the essence and the outer form, the true spirit and the manner in which the hidden blessing is imparted to those who await it. That spiritual essence of marriage—what is it ? Not the blessing of the priest, nor the outer rites and ceremonies : but the union of hearts, the mutual consent of the lovers, and—that alone.

" My Edith," I thought, " bride of another, in this world you can never seem to be mine. But in reality you belong to me as you can never belong to him who outwardly possesses you, for his is only an apparent possession. You are mine in very truth. God knows of our mutual consent. *That* is His sacrament, and that alone."

I felt a bitter joy, as the priest spoke the solemn admonition to the wife—" Forsaking all others, she shall cleave to him and be faithful to him until death. And those whom God has joined together, let no man put asunder."

Silently I slipped away, and left the house as I had entered it—silently as a thief.

The thrushes had ceased their song in the tops of the high chestnuts, and the poignant syringas hung their perfumed heads, already faded, faded as the memory of a childish love.

THE MAGNOLIA

Remy de Gourmont

THE two orphan sisters came forth from the house where they lived—the young and beautiful Arabella and the old and ugly Bibiane. Arabella was like a daughter and Bibiane like her mother.

They came out of their sad dwelling and stopped under the magnolia, the magic tree which no one had ever planted and which grew so gorgeously in the garden of the melancholy house. It bloomed twice in the year: in the spring, before the green spikes had opened into leaves, and in the early autumn, before the great green leaves began to fade. In autumn, as in spring, the noble form of the magic tree was laden with chalice-shaped, lotus-like flowers, their waxen petals white as death, with a tiny crimson spot symbolical of life.

Leaning on the arm of her sister Bibiane, who was always kind to her fancies, Arabella stood under the magnolia, thinking, " He will die with the second blooming of the magnolia—he, whose blood should make me live, flower that I also am! Now I shall be pale for ever and must also die! "

" There is still one blossom left," said Bibiane.

It was only a bud, whose white unopened beauty showed bright amid the setting of deep green leaves.

" The last! " said Arabella. " It will be my sole bridal adornment. The last? No, there is still another, but it is faded and almost dead. Symbols of both of us! Oh, I fear and tremble at the sign, for what could more clearly show what we are than these two flowers? I pluck the one which is myself, Bibiane. Look, here I am. If I should have to die too? "

Silently Bibiane caressed her trembling sister, and, in fear herself also, led her from the sorrowful garden, and from the magnolia stripped of its last beauty.

They entered the house which was the abode of lost happiness and of early grief.

" How is he? " asked Bibiane, taking from Arabella's shoulders the white scarf of the bride.

Arabella sat down to contemplate the unopened blossom which she held in her fingers, and the mother of the dying man continued, " We must make haste, for he is dying and his last wish must be accomplished before he goes. Come, my Arabella, my daughter, bride of a dying man, whose beauty will lighten the last sad prayers, softening Death with Love. It is Death which awaits you, alas, my child ; the nuptial kiss pressed on your forehead will come from one who is already claimed by the cold tomb, who will pass from your arms into a darkness which will fall for ever between you both, a darkness which the light of your eyes will never pierce, my Arabella. My son will die ; he is already numbered among the dead, and you, so fair, so bright, so fitted for the joy of life and love, must be united to the endless gloom and corruption of the grave. Alas ! Alas for both of you, my child ! "

They wept together as the witnesses came in, to attest the union of Death with Life. The priest followed, prepared for two sacraments, that which should bless the ring of marriage and that wherein holy oil should ease the passage of the parting soul.

All went up in silence, their steps sounding dull and solemn as those of the bearers of a bier, to where he lay prepared for the sacrament of Life and the sacrament of Death. The nuptial couch and the coffin, how could they differ now ?

They ascended in silence, unbroken except by the words of the mother, repeating, " We must make haste, for he is going to die, and his last wish must be accomplished."

In the chamber of the dying man all knelt, except Arabella, who stood by the nuptial couch, her white robe falling round her like a shroud ; and when her turn came to kneel too, her face pressed on the pillow, all the company trembled, as if she too were claimed by Death. Her soft white hand was laid on the thin wasted hand of the dying man, lying outside the coverlet, and in her other hand was the unopened magnolia bud, symbol of virginity, which she pressed to the dying lips.

The solemn words of the service alone broke the stillness. All watched the son supported by his mother, fascinated by the expression of his face. No resignation, no peace of love fulfilled was there ; but the rage of despair, of passion unaccomplished, of struggle to retain the life which was fleeting away, of hatred and envy of the life which remained. The flame of his hollow eyes gleamed on Arabella as though in withering jealousy of her fresh young beauty, and all present thought, " How dreadfully he must suffer ! "

He raised himself with a supreme effort. He murmured with livid lips, over which the tint of death was stealing, amid the strained silence of the men and the low sobs of the women :

" Farewell, Arabella ; you are mine for ever now. I must go, but you must follow me. I shall be there. Every evening I shall await you under the magnolia, and you shall know no other love but mine. No other, Arabella. You shall have proof of my love ; yes, proof indeed, for yours is the soul which I must have ! "

And with a smile which gleamed like that of a satyr or a devil across the gathering shadows of his wasted face, he hoarsely repeated these words, which sounded like wanderings, but had the deep significance of a warning from beyond the tomb :

" Under the magnolia, Arabella, under the magnolia ! "

All day, and almost all night, Arabella sat and watched the magnolia, its blossoms all gone, its discoloured leaves ready to fall ; and at night, when the wind rustled through the stiff dry foliage and the magic tree stood tall and noble in the moonlight, which gleamed fitfully from among October clouds, Arabella trembled and cried, clasping Bibiane, " He is there ! "

He was there, under the magnolia, in the masses of the fallen leaves, like a shadow waved by the wind.

One evening she said to Bibiane, " We loved one another. Why should he do me harm ? He is there, and I will go to him ! "

" The wishes of the dead must be obeyed," replied Bibiane. " Go, and fear not. I will leave the door open and will come if you call. Go ; he is there."

He was there indeed, among the dead leaves rustling in the wind, and when Arabella reached the magnolia, the shadow stretched out its arms, twining them about her like cold and slimy serpents, writhing and hissing on her fair shoulders like snakes of hell.

Bibiane heard a stifled cry. She ran to where her sister lay dead, and carried her back to the house. On her neck were two livid marks like the pressure of thin and bony fingers.

Her eyes still kept an expression of anguished horror, and her hands were clasped on something dry and brown. It was the withered flower which they had seen on the tree on her wedding day, the last pitiful dead bloom which they had left there in compassion, the flower which had symbolised the other, the one who had passed beyond the grave.

FERDINAND BEISSIER
B. 1858

THE HELMET

"BUT, uncle—I love my cousin!"

"Get out!"

"Give her to me."

"Don't bother me!"

"It will kill me!"

"Nonsense! you'll console yourself with some other girl."

"Please——"

My uncle, whose back had been towards me, whirled round, his face red to bursting, and brought his closed fist down upon the counter with a heavy thump.

"Never!" he cried; "never! Do you hear what I say?"

And as I looked at him beseechingly and with clasped hands, he went on:

"A pretty husband you look like!—without a sou, and dreaming of going into housekeeping! A nice mess I should make of it, by giving you my daughter! It's no use your insisting. You know that when I have said 'No,' nothing under the sun can make me say 'Yes'!"

I ceased to make any further appeal. I knew my uncle—about as headstrong an old fellow as could be found in a day's search. I contented myself with giving vent to a deep sigh, and then went on with the furbishing of a big, double-handed sword, rusty from point to hilt.

This memorable conversation took place in the shop of my maternal uncle, a well-known dealer in antiquities and *objets d'art*, No. 53, Rue des Claquettes, at the sign of the "Maltese Cross"—a perfect museum of curiosities.

The walls were hung with Marseilles and old Rouen china, facing ancient cuirasses, sabres, and muskets, and picture-frames; below these were ranged old cabinets, coffers of all sorts, and statues of saints, one-armed or one-legged for the most part and dilapidated as to their gilding; then, here and there, in glass cases, hermetically closed and locked, there were knick-knacks in infinite variety—lachrymatories, tiny urns, rings, precious stones, fragments of marble, bracelets, crosses, necklaces, medals, and miniature ivory statuettes, the yellow tints of which, in the sun, took momentarily a flesh-like transparency.

Time out of mind the shop had belonged to the Cornuberts. It passed regularly from father to son, and my uncle—his neighbours said—could not but be the possessor of a nice little fortune. Held in esteem by all, a Municipal Councillor, impressed by the importance and gravity of his office, short, fat, highly choleric and headstrong, but at bottom not in the least degree an unkind sort of man—such was my uncle Cornubert, my only living male relative, who, as soon as I left school, had elevated me to the dignity of chief and only clerk and shopman of the "Maltese Cross."

But my uncle was not only a dealer in antiquities and a Municipal Councillor, he was yet more, and above all, the father of my cousin Rose, with whom I was naturally in love.

To come back to the point at which I digressed.

Without paying any attention to the sighs which exhaled from my bosom while scouring the rust from my long, two-handed sword, my uncle, magnifying glass in hand, was engaged in the examination of a lot of medals which he had purchased that morning. Suddenly he raised his head; five o'clock was striking.

"The Council!" he cried.

When my uncle pronounced that august word, it made a mouthful; for two pins, he would have saluted it bareheaded. But, this time, after a moment's consideration, he tapped his forehead and added, in a tone of supreme relief:

"No, the sitting does not take place before to-morrow—and I am forgetting that I have to go to the railway station to get the consignment of which I was advised this morning."

Rising from his seat, and laying down his glass, he called out:

"Rose, give me my cane and hat!"

Then, turning towards me, he added, in a lowered tone and speaking very quickly:

"As for you—don't forget our conversation. If you think you can make me say 'Yes,' try!—but I don't think you'll succeed. Meanwhile, not a word to Rose, or, by Saint Barthélemy, my patron of happy memory, I'll instantly kick you out of doors!"

At that moment Rose appeared with my uncle's cane and hat,

which she handed to him. He kissed her on the forehead; then, giving me a last but eloquent look, hurried from the shop.

I went on scouring my double-handed sword. Rose came quietly towards me.

"What is the matter with my father?" she asked; "he seems to be angry with you."

I looked at her—her eyes were so black, her look so kind, her mouth so rosy, and her teeth so white that I told her all—my love, my appeal to her father, and his rough refusal. I could not help it—after all, it was *his* fault! He was not there: I determined to brave his anger. Besides, there is nobody like timid persons for displaying courage in certain circumstances.

My cousin said nothing; she only held down her eyes—while her cheeks were as red as those of cherries in May.

I checked myself.

"Are you angry with me?" I asked tremblingly. "Are you angry with me, Rose?"

She held out her hand to me. On that, my heart seething with audacity, my head on fire, I cried:

"Rose—I swear it! I will be your husband!" And as she shook her head and looked at me sadly, I added: "Oh! I know that my uncle is self-willed, but I will be more self-willed still; and, since he must be forced to say 'Yes,' I will force him to say it!"

"But how?" asked Rose.

Ah! how? That was exactly the difficulty. But, no matter; I would find a way to surmount it!

At that moment a heavy step resounded in the street. Instinctively we moved away from each other; I returned to my double-handed sword, and Rose, to keep herself in countenance, set to dusting, with a corner of her apron, a little statuette in its faded red velvet case.

My uncle entered. Surprised at finding us together, he stopped short and looked sharply at us, from one to the other.

We each of us went on rubbing without raising our heads.

"Here, take this," said my uncle, handing me a bulky parcel from under his arm. "A splendid purchase, you'll see."

The subject did not interest me in the least.

I opened the parcel, and from the enveloping paper emerged a steel helmet—but not an ordinary helmet, oh, no!—a superb, a monumental morion, with gorget and pointed visor of strange form. The visor was raised, and I tried to discover what prevented it from being lowered.

" It will not go down—the hinges have got out of order," said my uncle ; " but it's a superb piece, and, when it has been thoroughly cleaned and touched up, will look well—that shall be your to-morrow's job."

" Very good, uncle," I murmured, not daring to raise my eyes to his.

That night, on reaching my room, I went at once to bed. I was eager to be alone and able to think at my ease. Night brings counsel, it is said ; and I had great need that the proverb should prove true. But, after lying awake for an hour without receiving any assistance, I fell off to sleep, and, till next morning, did nothing but dream the oddest dreams. I saw Rose on her way to church in a strange bridal costume, a fourteenth-century cap, three feet high, on her head, but looking prettier than ever ; then suddenly the scene changed to moonlight, in which innumerable helmets and pieces of old china were dancing a wild farandola, while my uncle, clad in complete armour and with a formidable halberd in his hand, conducted the bewildering whirl.

The next day—ah, the next day !—I was no nearer. In vain, with clenched teeth, I scoured the immense helmet brought by my uncle the previous evening—scoured it with such fury as almost to break the iron ; not an idea came to me. The helmet shone like a sun : my uncle sat smoking his pipe and watching me ; but I could think of nothing, of no way of forcing him to give me his daughter.

At three o'clock Rose went into the country, whence she was not to return until dinner-time, in the evening. On the threshold she could only make a sign to me with her hand ; my uncle had not left us alone for a single instant. He was not easy in his mind ; I could see that by his face. No doubt he had not forgotten our conversation of the previous evening.

I went on rubbing at my helmet.

" You have made it quite bright enough—put it down," said my uncle.

I put it down. The storm was gathering : I could not do better than allow it to blow over.

But suddenly, as if seized by some strange fancy, my uncle took up the enormous morion and turned and examined it on all sides.

" A handsome piece of armour, there is no doubt about it ; but it must have weighed pretty heavily on its wearer's shoulders," he muttered ; and, urged by I know not what demon, he clapped it on his head and latched the gorget-piece about his neck.

Struck almost speechless, I watched what he was doing—thinking only how ugly he looked.

Suddenly there was a sharp sound—as if a spring had snapped—and—crack !—down fell the visor ; and there was my uncle, with his head in an iron cage, gesticulating and swearing like a pagan !

I could contain myself no longer, and burst into a roar of laughter ; for my uncle, stumpy, fat, and rubicund, presented an irresistibly comic appearance.

Threateningly, he came towards me.

" The hinges !—the hinges, fool ! " he yelled.

I could not see his face, but I felt that it was red to bursting.

" When you have done laughing, idiot ! " he cried.

But the helmet swayed so oddly on his shoulders, his voice came from out it in such strange tones, that the more he gesticulated, the more he yelled and threatened me, the louder I laughed.

At that moment the clock of the Hôtel-de-Ville, striking five, was heard.

" The Municipal Council ! " murmured my uncle in a stifled voice. " Quick ! help me off with this beast of a machine ! We'll settle our business afterwards ! "

But, suddenly likewise, an idea—a wild, extraordinary idea—came into my head ; but then, who ever is madder than a lover ? Besides, I had no choice of means.

" No ! " I replied.

My uncle fell back two paces in terror—and again the enormous helmet wobbled on his shoulders.

" No," I repeated firmly, " I'll not help you out, unless you give me the hand of my cousin Rose ! "

From the depths of the strangely elongated visor came, not an angry exclamation, but a veritable roar. I had " done it " !—I had burned my boats !

" If you do not consent to do what I ask of you," I added, " not only will I not help you off with your helmet, but I will call in all your neighbours, and then go and find the Municipal Council ! "

" You'll end your days on the scaffold ! " cried my uncle.

" The hand of Rose ! " I repeated. " You told me that it would only be by force that you would be made to say 'Yes'—say it, or I will call in the neighbours!"

The clock was still striking; my uncle raised his arms as if to curse me.

"Decide at once," I cried, "somebody is coming!"

"Well, then—Yes!" murmured my uncle. "But make haste!"

"On your word of honour?"

"On my word of honour!"

The visor gave way, the gorget-piece also, and my uncle's head issued from durance, red as a poppy.

Just in time. The chemist at the corner, a colleague in the Municipal Council, entered the shop.

"Are you coming?" he asked; "they will be beginning the business without us."

"I'm coming," replied my uncle.

And without looking at me, he took up his hat and cane and hurried out.

The next moment all my hopes had vanished. My uncle would surely not forgive me.

At dinner-time I took my place at table on his right hand in low spirits, ate little, and said nothing.

"It will come with the dessert," I thought.

Rose looked at me, and I avoided meeting her eyes. As I had expected, dessert over, my uncle lighted his pipe, raised his head, and then——

"Rose—come here!"

Rose went to him.

"Do you know what that fellow there asked me to do, yesterday?"

I trembled like a leaf, and Rose did the same.

"To give him your hand," he added. "Do you love him?"

Rose cast down her eyes.

"Very well," continued my uncle; "on this side, the case is complete. Come here, you."

I approached him.

"Here I am, uncle," and, in a whisper, I added quickly: "Forgive me!"

He burst into a hearty laugh.

"Marry her, then, donkey—since you love her, and I give her to you!"

" Ah !—uncle ! "

" Ah !—dear papa ! "

And Rose and I threw ourselves into his arms.

" All right ! all right ! " he cried, wiping his eyes. " Be happy, that's all I ask."

And, in turn, he whispered in my ear :

" I should have given her to you all the same, you big goose ; but —keep the story of the helmet between us two ! "

I give you my word that I have never told it, except to Rose, my dear little wife. And, if ever you pass along the Rue des Claquettes, at No. 53, at the place of honour in the old shop, I'll show you my uncle's helmet, which we would never sell.

ANATOLE LE BRAZ
B. 1859

THE BLOOD OF THE SIREN

SHE was a very young woman, Marie-Ange, and as fresh and as gracious as her name ; she was like a water nymph risen from the waves as she seized the ladder of the *Louise* and slowly climbed on board.

" How is Jean ? " was the captain's question. " How many lobsters did he catch this season ? "

It seemed as if the question had disappeared far back in the depths of her sea-green eyes as she answered :

" There has been a wonderful catch this season. We had one hundred and fifty for our share alone ; and that is why Jean could not come with me to the christening. He had to sell them in the Isle of Saints. They pay more there."

I had listened enchanted. Her voice was pure music. She did not speak ; she sang. She was sitting on the bench beside me, her hands joined in a gesture of adoration. She crossed herself in silent prayer.

" It is because we enter Fromaveur," she said.

Suddenly the waves became choppy and rough and threw themselves against the sides of the ship and I remembered the old story I had heard in my youth. Here, they had told me, the sirens have their palaces, tormented by endless desires which they endeavour to quench in vain ; for the lips of the sons of men from which they wish to drink love are frozen by death under their kisses. Disappointed one day, they begin the next.

" Do you believe in sirens, Marie-Ange ? " I asked idly.

She grew pale, her lips compressed, and a shadow crept into her eyes at the question.

" Why do you ask that ? " she said fiercely.

" Only that the country people have told me such stories of this Fromaveur," I answered.

" From what part of Brittany do you come ? " she said, smiling once more.

Then we entered one of the two harbours of Ouessant. She flew up the rocky path like a bird and laughed as she watched my slow and awkward ascent. Each note of her laugh was like a pearl.

" You must have a charming voice, Marie-Ange. I should like to hear you sing," I said.

She became serious at once. " In our island the women never sing after marriage, except in church."

A delicious perfume spread about us, subtle and penetrating, made up of a thousand little secret odours.

" Do not look for it," she said. " That is the aroma of Ouessant. It fills everything here, even the stones of the old houses."

Then came the parting of the ways and she went to Cadoran, the oldest house of this island, the cradle of the clan Morvarch. She went down the hill and away from me.

Suddenly, as I walked along toward my destination, a sharp voice called behind me :

" Won't you ride, sir ? "

She who called was a little old woman with a fresh face framed by a small black hood from which escaped some locks of white hair like bits of uncarded wool. She crouched in the little waggon, drawn by a tiny horse.

" Nola Glaquin, sir—at your service."

I asked her abruptly: " Tell me, who is this Marie-Ange ? "

" Aha ! " she said. " Another one bewitched by the beauty of Marie-Ange ! There is a spell over that woman. She is married to Jean Morvarch, a fine fellow, a pilot and also a lobster fisher." Nola Glaquin made the sign of a cross and I heard her say under her breath: " God keep the dear fellow ! " Then she said : " They have a child, a perfect cherub."

" But what is it that is strange about her ? " I asked. " She seems unlike all the rest of us."

" Will you believe me if I tell you ? " said the old woman.

" Yes, because you believe," I answered.

" A long time ago, sir," she said, " twelve virgins, as lovely as angels in body, but demons in soul, had their summer home down there in that basin where the water of the sea comes in among the rocks. In winter they followed the storms, no one knew whither ; but as soon as the sunshine reappeared, they came back. They never came out of the water, for they could not walk on land ; and at night they sang.

The young men of the island grew wild. Many lost their souls because of these sirens and many ruined their parents, too, for these wicked ones. Then God took pity on the island and sent good St. Veltez, who was the bishop. He gave them his ring to kiss and they burned their lips fearfully and fled away, crying."

The little old woman shivered under her thin cape.

" They appeared here no more, but across there on the other coast you can hear their cries on clear nights. There are only eleven now."

" Where is the other one ? " I asked.

Then she looked at me. " Will you believe me if I tell you ? "

" Because you believe," I said.

" The old men who are older than I am," she said, " tell how the head of Cadoran was fishing one morning, and one of the sirens was resolved to have him, for he was the proudest and most handsome man in the island. When he had drawn her out of the water, she said to him :

" ' Let me be your wife after the manner of men, and I will make you king of the sea.'

" She spoke very sweetly, and he wanted to be king of the sea.

" ' But you are only half a woman,' he said.

" And she replied, ' Carry me in your arms to the door of your house.'

" She was as cold as ice when he took her up, but as they travelled the road to Cadoran she became warmer and warmer and the scales fell from her limbs. And when he reached the door and opened it, she walked in by herself."

The little old woman watched me to see whether I believed. Then she went on :

" She could only belong to him at night, and a little before dawn she always crept back to the sea. He became king of the sea, as she had said. The winds and the waves obeyed him. He was happy and rich, and a beautiful child came to them. One morning he said to her as she rose to leave :

" ' I need you by the light of day.'

" And she was sad. ' Do not ask such a thing. It would ruin us both and all our posterity.'

" ' If you refuse,' he said, ' it is because you do not love me ! '

" And the words hurt her so that she fainted, and when she opened her eyes again it was day.

"Since then"—the old woman spoke very softly—"trouble follows the race of the siren. In each generation her blood runs in a woman irresistibly charming, whose voice and face show the unquiet of the siren's soul, and an implacable destiny watches over her from the depths of the sea. In the midst of her joy, soon after her marriage, the blow falls. One fine day the husband goes out as usual to fish; evening comes and he does not return. Once more those eleven sisters have punished the offence of the twelfth, and while the widow cries from the rocks to him who never will return, you can hear afar off the light voices laughing. Marie-Ange is one of these."

I heard Marie-Ange sing the next day in church, and I could see her. And her face showed that she was the inconstant, divine being born of the dreams of primitive humanity in the illumined depths of the sea. The music of the waves trembled under her lightest note and her eyes shone with the mysterious fire of the sea. Her heart exhaled its perfume, her flesh reflected the morning and the evening glow, and the breath of the ocean breeze swept about her.

I asked where Jean was, her husband. He had stayed overnight, she thought, at Saint Isle. "He will probably return to-night; the winds are fair."

That night, when the breath of the sea came hot from the furnace of the tropics, we sat in the window of the Hôtel Stephan. The bells in the little church tower had rung for curfew, and there was one among us with his pipe to his lips who was telling the story of a shipwreck. "Do you recall the speech Nola Glaquin made that night before we got the news?"

"Who is Nola Glaquin?" I asked.

"An old fool. She pretends that she knows the misfortunes that are coming a couple of days before the rest of us. They nicknamed her the Death Gull. The people here swear that the gulls talk to her and she understands them. It is true," he went on, "that the hearth of her house is covered with the feathers of these birds, and when they are wounded they come to her and are cured; and in return for this attention they are said to bring her tidings from the sea."

"Yes," said another of the group to me; "one day she passed our house. My mother asked her if she would not come in and light her pipe."

"'Alas,' she replied, shaking her head; 'do not jest, Renée-Ann!

You will have me in your house sooner than you can possibly expect!'

" And that same evening I went for her, for my father was drowned; and she is a watcher with the dead in this village."

At this moment the hotel-keeper's youngest daughter came in in great excitement, followed by a man of enormous stature. His jacket was too short for him, the sailor's clothes hung in rags about him. The schoolmaster recognised him first.

" It is Mauet-Euss, the mate of Jean Morvarch."

The man looked like a frightened animal.

" What has happened ? " we asked.

He bowed his hairy face over his herculean breast and sobbed like a child. The air in the hotel office suddenly thickened with the sea-fog; and the lamp burned with a green light over the face of our companion. The schoolmaster gave him a drink of brandy, and he told us, brokenly, his sweat and tears flowing together, of what had happened to his master.

He had started the night before for home, very gay, for his pockets were full of money and the sea was as still as a pond. And Jean Morvarch had sent his mate to sleep and had sung an old song as he stayed by the helm. And then the mate heard a voice and awakened suddenly. He jumped up and ran to the helm—there was no one there! The sky was clear, and the sea even clearer, and it seemed as if there were lights under the water, and he called, " Morvarch! Jean Morvarch!" And the call had echoed as in a church, and then from the distance came a long, sad call, ending in laughter. And the laughter was all about the boat; and although they sought for hours, until the sun was high, they could find no sign of him.

The next day I saw Nola Glaquin as she stood before a table. In front of her rose the catafalque, upon which rested the waxen cross that represented the body of the one who could not be there. Marie-Ange was sitting by the oaken cradle where lay the baby.

"GEORGES COURTELINE"
B. 1860

A GENTLEMAN FINDS A WATCH

FROM the top seats of L'Étoile tram-car I perceived my friend Bréloc, who was just crossing the Place Blanche in such a state of excitement that I got down from the car on purpose to question him.

"Hey! *mon Dieu*! what is the matter, Bréloc? What is the meaning of this face of yours, more mournful than a shop closed on account of a death in the family?"

"Please don't mention it," he replied; "I've just had a narrow escape from being put in gaol."

Which led me to think that he had committed some dishonest action, and I began to ejaculate rather loudly, when he, guessing the turn of my thoughts, exclaimed: "You don't seem to understand! I was very nearly being put in gaol through an unlucky watch that I picked up last night on the Boulevard Saint-Michel, and which I honestly deposited in the hands of the commissaire (police inspector) of our district. Pretty rough, hey? I feel almost ill from astonishment and fright. But you can judge for yourself. Have you five minutes to spare?"

"Certainly. Why not?"

"Then listen, and I hope you may profit by my experience.

"About 9 A.M. I presented myself at the police station in the Rue Duperré carrying said watch—a beautiful timepiece, by the way, with gold case and platina monogram—and I asked to be shown to the commissaire. That gentleman had just finished drinking his cup of chocolate, when he gave orders that I should be admitted to his presence, and without deigning to say good-day or offer me a seat, he began:

"'What do you want?'

"I had composed my features for the occasion, with the smile of a man who accomplishes a meritorious act for which he expects to be almost crowned with glory. So I answered, 'Monsieur le Commissaire of Police, I have the honour of depositing in your hands a watch that I found last night, and——'

"Without letting me finish the sentence, the commissaire sprang up, repeating the words:

"'A watch! A watch!'

"The gendarmes were playing cards in the next room.

"He hallooed to them:

"'Hey! you there! Close the street door! There is more draught here than in a windmill!' And he remained grumbling until his order had been executed.

"Then, resuming his seat, he proceeded:

"'Please give me that article.'

"I handed him the watch, which he began to turn about, examining and turning the winder, opening the case and the chain swivel.

"'Yes,' he said gravely, 'it is indeed a watch, there is no denying.'

"Saying which, he deposited the watch in the depths of a very large safe, closing its three locks.

"I looked on with astonishment, and he resumed:

"'And where did you find this valuable article?'

"'Boulevard Saint-Michel, at the corner of Rue Monsieur-le-Prince.'

"'On the ground?' asked the commissaire; 'on the pavement?'

"I answered in the affirmative.

"'It is very extraordinary,' he said with a suspicious look at me; 'the pavement is not the usual place to leave a watch.'

"I remarked smilingly:

"'If I may call your attention——'

"Drily the commissaire said:

"'That will do! You may omit all remarks. I know my business.'

"I stopped talking and smiling.

"He resumed, 'In the first place, who are you?'

"I gave my name.

"'Where do you live?'

"'I have already said that I live at the Place Blanche, 26, second floor.'

"'What are your means of living?'

"I explained that I had an income of twelve thousand francs.

"'At what time, as near as you can tell, did you find the watch?

"'Three o'clock A.M.'

"'Was it not later?' he remarked ironically.

"'I don't think it was,' I said candidly.

"'Well, I congratulate you,' he said ironically. 'It seems to me that you are leading a somewhat singular existence.'

"As I was rather warmly protesting my right to live according to my fancy——

"'Admitted!' said the commissaire. 'But I have a right to know what the deuce you could be doing at that hour on the Boulevard Saint-Michel, corner of Rue Monsieur-le-Prince, you who *say* that you are living at the Place Blanche?'

"'What do you mean by that, I *say*?'

"'Well, you do say so.'

"'If I say so, it is a fact.'

"'That is what we must have proved. Meanwhile, please do not wander from the conversation, and answer courteously to all the questions that I feel it my duty to put to you. I am asking what were you doing at that unearthly hour in a neighbourhood that was not your own?'

"I explained (as was true) that I was coming from the house of a lady friend.

"'What does she do, your lady friend?'

"'She is a married woman.'

"'Married. To whom?'

"'To a druggist.'

"'What is his name?'

"'That is none of your business,' I answered impatiently.

"'Do you dare to talk like that to me?" bawled the commissaire.

"'Of course.'

"The commissaire's face became purple.

"'Well, my man! you will have to alter your tune; that strain of yours does not suit me. And—I fancy that I recollect your features.'

"'Oh, nonsense!'

"'Yes—I do have a recollection——'

"There was a moment of silence. Then:

"'Have you ever been committed for trial, Bréloc?'

"This exhausted my patience.

"'Have you?' said I.

"The commissaire sprang to his feet.

" 'You are a blackguard!' he cried.

" 'And you are an idiot!' I retorted.

" At that moment I thought my last hour had come. The commissaire bounded toward me, flushed and foaming with rage. Under his bushy eyebrows I could see the glistening of his wild eyes.

" 'What did you say?' he stammered. 'What did you say?'

" I attempted to utter a word, but he did not give me a chance.

" 'And I say that I am going to send you to gaol; and it will not take very long! It is just the hour for the patrol waggon! Ah! you are going to put on airs! Ah! you want to jeer at me, and at the law that I represent! Very well! you came to the wrong place!'

" He brought down his fist violently on the papers lying on his table with each of his sentences, adding:

" 'Do I know you? Do I know who you are? You say that your name is Bréloc; I don't know anything about it! You say that you live at the Place Blanche. Where are the proofs of it? You say that you have twelve thousand francs income. Am I bound to believe you? Show me your twelve thousand francs! Hein! you would have a hard job to show them to me.'

" I was stunned.

" 'All this is not very clear,' he concluded violently. 'I say—do you hear?—that it is not very clear, and I don't know that you did not steal that watch!'

" 'Steal it!'

" 'Yes, steal it! Anyhow, I am going to find out.'

" The gendarmes, hearing the noise, had come into the room. He called out to them:

" 'Search this man!'

" In a second they undressed me completely, even down to my socks.

" 'Ah! you think you are smart!' the commissaire repeated mockingly. 'Ah! you mean to trick us! Look well under his arms,' he said to the gendarmes. 'Search him thoroughly!'"

At the recital of these indignities Bréloc's voice became overexcited. But I was laughing, nodding my head approvingly, because I could recognise in his story the two implacable enemies of honest folk—the administration and the law.

" Catch me finding another watch!" roared my unfortunate friend, with a closed fist as if threatening the future.

HENRI LAVEDAN
B. 1860

YEARS AFTER

BETWEEN 1850 and 1855, in a little provincial town, in a deserted quarter, in an old room that was full of memories of the past, two old people, a man and a woman, sat before the fire on a Christmas night at a late hour.

Their hair was as white as the winter's snow that was falling without in slow flakes like little pieces of moonlight. Their faces were spiritual, tender, fine, full of charm and goodness. Sometimes a smile, like a pale ray of the late season's sun, lit up their faces, which one could see had in former days been very kindly. Even now they retained traces of their former beauty. One had only to see them seated there side by side in their well-worn arm-chairs, their knees almost touching, to be sure that they had loved each other very much.

They did not speak. They watched the fire flare up and die down again. The flames, short or high, rose and fell, dancing a little ballet in their red, blue and green skirts. The old couple followed them with their eyes, and one could well imagine that they were looking through the dancing flames in the old cast-iron fireplace at the long scroll of their youth. It was just because, if they had opened their mouths at all, they would have had thousands of things to say that would have taken them days and weeks, that they were silent on this Christmas night. But it is possible to understand one another without the aid of speech. Silence is the language of golden hearts, and this old married couple did not need to use words and phrases to question one another and reply. They knew beforehand, once for all, what they thought of themselves and of this world —and of the other, in which they both believed. They knew each other so well! Never had a cloud, however faint, dimmed the azure of their happiness; never had they had a secret from one another for forty years. They had had a secret all their lives, to tell the truth, but it was a mutual secret that they bore lightly, that of their quiet and delightful happiness, which they had guarded and concealed as best they could, because they knew that too great earthly happiness is lost as soon as one boasts of it or even tells of it in confidence. Tell your best friend under the seal of secrecy that you possess a treasure, and it is already stolen.

But it had been easier for them than for ordinary people of the regular world to conceal, and it may be forgiven them, for at that time they were both members of that free-mannered, slightly suspect, amiable, dangerous, madcap, unreflecting, rich and poor craft, whose vices honest people copy and in which virtue is so often to be found, that is called the guild of actors.

Yes, this couple of worthy and delightful old people, married hard and fast years ago by mayor and priest, before God and before man, as seriously as a grocer or a marquis could be—they were a couple of old player-folk, former treaders of the boards, beings created in the image of God—born on this very night—who had rouged their cheeks and blacked their eyes, who had recited verse and prose of which they were not the authors, on the stage, and all for money to make a living! And they were there, in the venerable white hair that was their own, dreaming before the hearthfire—their last footlights—on their return from the midnight mass to which they had gone, arm-in-arm, to wonder at the scenes of that adorable play, so simple and so popular that the number of its performances can no longer be reckoned, that has made the world weep and laugh, in which the principal actors are Joseph, Jesus, the Virgin, and the Ass, and, in the secondary rank, the Kings, who, with their poor offerings of gold and precious stones, play only secondary rôles. The husband was called Valère and his wife Lise. These were their stage names, the names they had had the modesty to assume to avoid dishonouring the excellent families to which they belonged and which included among their forebears a Roman prince, two barons, three generals, a king's favourite, a bishop, many bankrupts, a roué and one man who had been hanged.

Their sentimental history was as simple and naïve as the intrigue in a curtain-raiser, as the dialogue in a piece for school children. One evening, as they told each other their love on the stage, they had had a revelation of their own mutual love and had married soon after, like the end of one of Scribe's plays. They had had no children, but in spite of that they had been very happy. For five and twenty years they had played together in more than a thousand comedies, tragedies, farces and dramas. They had great talent. They had laughed, wept and portrayed adorably emotions that were at once sincere and simulated. They had died in a hundred different ways ; from joy and from sorrow, by cold steel and by poison, by fire and by shipwreck ; they had gathered bravos and laurels, celebrated their silver wedding and then retired to a little country town, as prettily planted and swept as a stage-scene, of which they had preserved a specially tender recollection ever since they had passed through it in the mail-coach while on tour, and where they had sworn by the prompter's box to come back and end their lives playing over their old parts. They were playing them over now in the mild calm and happiness of an eternal vacation, remembering the repertoire of their happiness that had been so pure, so complete, so rare.

As the hour sounded from a clock that was still older than they and had been saying the same thing over and over again since the days of Louis XIV., Valère, smothering a slight cough in his silk handkerchief, said to Lise :

" We are very silent, my Chloe."

She gave a slight nod of the head—if it was not the little perpetual trembling, the sad yes-and-no of old age—and sighed : " That is true, but I was thinking."

" Of what ? "

" Of something that it will cost me dear to tell you of, and yet I must tell you. I have a confession to make."

" A confession to make to me ? "

" Yes, and a very serious one."

" Does it concern love ? " and his eyes shone with a Don Juan flame.

" Yes."

" Bah ! Another ? "

" Alas ! "

" Why alas ? "

" You shall see," and she began : " You suppose I have always been faithful to you, do you not ? "

" Assuredly, and I suppose it still. By the devil who made woman ! " That was an oath from a romantic play in which he was inimitable.

" You are mistaken."

" You have deceived me ? "

" Yes."

" You ? " He sat up in his chair. " You, Lise, in whom I have placed the blindest confidence! What! You have—wicked and sacrilegious—you have thanked me in this way for the marked favour I have shown you by choosing you from among so many other princesses to elevate you to my rank and seat you on the throne of Spain!"

In spite of himself he was wandering and repeating to her passages that had formerly won him applause, and this last phrase that he had just uttered, tongs in hand, had come back to him from *The Caverns of Grenada*, in which he had electrified the house.

"Yes, sire," she answered, in a low tone. Then, returning to a more natural language, she went on: "I have deceived you without deceiving you, my friend, but it is almost worse and uglier than if I had deceived you by actually deceiving you."

"Explain yourself clearly, gypsy, or be on your guard!" Another sounding phrase, in spite of himself.

"Here it is. You know when you confessed your love to me——"

"Yes, and you to me——"

"Yes. You know that I was sought after?"

"Oh, Lord, do not remind me of it! I suffered enough through it. I was jealous—jealousy, infernal gnawing that——" He was going on with one of Othello's tirades, but she stopped him.

"You were wrong."

"Undoubtedly. But can a man control his impulses to mistrust and anger when he is in love? And I loved you! I love you still. Ah, you were so beautiful then, you are beautiful now!"

"Hm!" she observed. "The play has grown stale."

"How could I not have been jealous?" he continued. "You see, instead of being wrong, I was right, for this evening, forty-five years afterwards, you inform me that——"

"Do not be so quick to accuse me. Let me go on to the very end."

"Go on, my Celimène."

"Do you remember, one of the things that used to put you beside yourself in the height of our passion was the letters, the declarations, I received every day after the performance?"

"Ah, yes. They rained down on you from all directions, from all sides at once! They were from young fops."

"From old ones, too, and middle-aged."

"From poets and military men——"

"I had only to choose."

"And did you make a choice?"

"Do not interrupt me. Do you remember, too, that these burning love-letters, whose number was considerable, even when it was well known that we were madly in love with each other, fell off and became much more infrequent as soon as we were married?"

"We loved each other even more, however, if that was possible."

"Yes, but, as a lawful wife, I did not move the public to such extremes, I did not seem to promise so much, and, while I was resolved never to deceive you, while I loved you more than the richest and most fashionable man on earth, must I tell you?—well, I suffered from this falling off of homage and pursuit. All those false and high-flown declarations that I received, of course, I did not believe in in the least. I laughed at them——"

"As for me, I wept over them."

"Wait. We read them together. Really, I quite enjoyed it; it became a delightful habit that I could not do without, a divine tobacco whose smoke-wreaths I missed."

"Is it possible?"

"Yes, indeed. And didn't you ever notice it, Scapin?"

"Never."

"You have forgotten. You used often to ask me, 'What is the matter with you, Marinette? Why are you so sad? You never say anything. Your mind is wandering. What are you thinking of?'"

"Perhaps—yes—vaguely. So that was it—the rarity of those strange declarations?"

"Yes, that was it. But do not say the rarity, say the cessation, the total disappearance, for at the end of six months of married life I was not getting a single one. What a humiliation it was for me! The door-man at the theatre, the dressers, the stage-hands, who only a year before had been accustomed to deliver whole shovelfuls to me at all hours from my generous admirers, were never charged with the least clandestine message for me, and I could feel their pitying contempt in their looks. I grew thin. I contemplated the river, like Ophelia."

"And all this time I never noticed anything!"

"Men never notice those things, my lord, especially husbands."

"You should have told me."

"What could you have done? Nothing."

"That is true."

"I had arrived at that point of anger, humiliation and concentrated distress, when one morning, one fine morning—ah, Valère! Ah, Fantasio!"

"A letter?"

"Yes."

"Oh, Lise, that is what I feared. A love-letter?"

"Yes, and such a letter! I was happy again. And the next day another!—and the day after, and every day for a month. At last, I was beloved once more, I was courted, I was not looked upon as a strait-laced wife, married, settled down, finished, so to speak, having renounced the pomps and vanities of this wicked world——"

"Well, and afterwards? Go on."

"Afterwards the letters became less frequent."

"Ah, good!"

"But they continued to come with faithful persistency, sometimes every five or six days, sometimes every fortnight."

"For a long time?"

"For two years."

"The deuce! And who was it wrote them?"

"An unknown."

"A nameless admirer?"

"Yes, he never told his name."

He poked the fire, humming to himself, "And he never was seen any more."

"I have always thought," she observed, "that it was some great personage who wanted to preserve his incognito, for the writing was always disguised, as if he had written with his left hand."

"The sly dog! And so you have never spoken to him?"

"Never!"

"If that is the case, then you have never deceived me?"

"Oh, yes, I did!"

"How was that?"

"At first his letters were so ardent, so beautiful, so delicate, so tender, so subtle, so delicious—oh, you could not imagine them!"

"Have you kept them?"

"Yes, for a long time—and hidden them."

"Where?"

"I will tell you that—later."

"When?"

"When you are a hundred. Then, as my lover—my lover on paper, but he was my lover all the same, wasn't he?——"

"Well, I must certainly make up my mind about that. He was a lover after a fashion, there's no getting around that."

"As my lover had given me a mysterious address, where I could write to him——"

"Ah, the scoundrel! You replied to him? You have replied to him?"

"Yes, often and so ardently!"

"Oh, Jacqueline! Oh, Rosamonde!"

"Do not scold. If you could only imagine how imperious and charming his letters were! It was impossible to leave them unanswered. A heart of stone would have taken up the pen! What do you think of that metaphor?"

"It is like yourself, bold. And did the other man speak ill of me in his letters?"

"No, never. On the contrary, he besought me to respect your honour."

"Come, come. That is stranger still. And what did you reply to him?"

"Follies, the greatest follies!"

"Oh!"

"What would you have? It was better than to commit them."

"I do not deny that. All the same——"

"I repeat, if you had been able to read his letters, you would understand, you would forgive me."

"That is not so sure. But, more than the letters, what I would have liked to see—ah! how I would have liked to see them—was your replies. They ought to be still more interesting!"

"Enough, Horatio. Yes, unfortunately, or rather fortunately, he has carried them off or destroyed them. They belong to the things that will never be known this side of the other world!"

"So be it. We shall wait. But while we are on these confidences of long ago, you wicked little old woman, tell all to your knave of hearts. Did you never seek to learn who was writing to you?"

"Never."

"Did you never feel a temptation, a curiosity, to see him, to speak to him, to know him?"

"No."

"Strange! You never longed for the reality?"

"The unreal was too beautiful. I thought of it sometimes, but I was afraid, if I found myself face to face with my unknown, I would fall from my pinnacle. That was all. The lamp—don't you remember? I played Pysche when I was fifteen."

"Perhaps you were right. Even in their folly women are wise."

"Well, it is finished—there is my confession—and I am over sixty. I have deceived you, poor Organ, by correspondence. Do you forgive me?"

He took her hands in his: "Yes, madame," he said, in a gently tragic voice, "if you will give me the letters."

"Very good, sir; if you are going to use force, you shall have them."

She released herself with a smile, rose, and opened her large armoire, with its piles of linen bedecked with ribbons from old bouquets, and, away at the back, on the middle shelf, thrusting her little hand under a mass of fine chemises and gewgaws, she drew out a packet of faded letters, tied with an old gilt string from a bonbon box. She inhaled their perfume, looked at them, raised them to her lips, shrugged her shoulders, smiled with a little pout, and murmured:

"How silly we are when we are young!"

"And when we are old, too," he replied.

She handed them to him with the air of a duchess, saying, "Here, sir!"

"Very good, madame."

They were amusing themselves, they were playing comedy, they were doing "the big scene in the fourth act."

"You will allow me to read them?"

"Yes, sir. But not before me—I should be too embarrassed. No, not until I have withdrawn to my apartment."

"Her apartment," which she indicated with a wave of her hand, was her own little twin bed, which stood side by side with his.

"Turn around, sir."

He pivoted in his chair. "I have done so. I am not looking. But do not forget to put your slipper in front of the fireplace—it is Christmas Eve."

"Just as you please. But what shall I find in it?"

He made an evasive gesture. She brought over one of her little velvet slippers, on which the light of an old jewel sparkled in the buckle, and laid it on the hearthstone.

Then with three sighs and a faint rustling, she was in bed, with the linen sheet under her chin. In a voice that was already drowsy, she said, " Good-night, dear old friend."

He leaned over her and tucked her in. " Good-night, my life, my soul," he said.

The clock struck the half-hour. Two kisses passed between them, one from her on his cheek, one from him on her ivory forehead, and then she fell asleep, breathing regularly, one, two, one, two, like a child.

He listened to her, laughed to himself, and with tender mischievousness went softly on tiptoe over to the Louis XIV. marquetry secretary, pulled out a deep bottom drawer, thrust his arm into it, mysteriously drew forth a packet of faded letters tied together with an old silk cord, and, stooping down at first and then on his knees, deposited it in the rose-coloured slipper, murmuring to himself in a low tone :

" The answers. What a surprise it will be for her to-morrow ! "

WHEN HE WAS A LITTLE BOY

Henri Lavedan

MADAME DE PRÉCY said to her husband: "You wish to know what is the matter? Oh! I will tell you, if for a few moments you will condescend to lend me your attention."

In an icy tone he answered, "I will not lend, I will give it to you."

"Well, then, the matter is"—and a trembling voice betrayed her excitement—"that life with you has become unbearable and that I have resolved no longer to try to endure it. You are, I admit, an honourable man, and have, I believe, been a faithful husband. I, on my side, have never forgotten my marriage vows. Here we stand on the same ground. The trouble is that we are uncongenial. Everything I do annoys you, and to me all your ways are insufferable. What I say always vexes you, and your laugh drives me crazy. Even when silent, we provoke each other. About the merest trifles we have frightful scenes—about a hat, a dress, whether it will be best to carry a cane or an umbrella, or whether the meat is overdone or not—in short, everything—and everything makes us quarrel! Then, at home, either you talk so much that I cannot put in a word or else you do not open your lips, and you look about as cheerful as a mortuary chapel. I must be happy when you are happy, sad when you are sad. Your temper is changeable, odd, quick; you do not allow the slightest contradiction; if I begin to speak of something which does not interest you, I am not allowed to finish my sentence. For me to express an opinion suffices to make you take an opposite view. You insist that you understand music, and that I know nothing about politics, while, in point of fact, the contrary is the truth. You scold my maid until she cries, and your disgusting valet drinks all the wine in my cellar. You forbid me to smoke, and insist that my dresses shall not be cut too low. And when we quarrel, even about some very ordinary matter, instead of its being over in five minutes, it lasts for hours, and we try to outdo each other in saying bitter things which neither of us forgets. In short, everything about me is disagreeable to you. I feel it, and I know it: you hate the tone of my voice, the sound of my step, my gestures, even my clothes ; do not deny it, at this very moment I can read in your face that you would like to pitch me out of the window."

" Therefore ? " said Monsieur de Précy.

" Therefore I conclude that it is wiser for us not to prolong our experience of married life. Its having proved a failure is neither your fault nor mine, or rather it is the fault of both ; at any rate it is a fact. We were not made to live together ; until we cease to do so, neither of us will be happy. After all, there is nothing to prevent us from amicably parting. Fortunately there is no child to quarrel about, we have each an ample fortune, so I really cannot see why we should remain any longer on the same perch, pulling out each other's feathers. As for me, I have had enough of it, and you have had too much. I am quite sure you will be happy. Sometimes in the morning, while you are shaving, you will think of me ; and for my part I shall always remember you as a perfectly honourable, thoroughly disagreeable man. But for that I bear you no ill-will, because it is in your blood, all the Précys are so, and your own father and mother, as you have often told me, could never contrive to remain together for more than ten days at a time. However, I will waste no more breath in talking about the matter, but will now, Monsieur, retire to my own rooms, where until to-morrow I shall pass my time in thinking over the most practical way in which to arrange our separation."

Monsieur de Précy had received this avalanche of reproaches in silence, but his lips twitched, once or twice he sighed, sighed deeply, and toward the middle of the discourse he had begun to pace the floor. When his wife ceased speaking he stopped before her, and, looking at her with an expression which he strove to render as dignified as possible, said in a sad, somewhat victimised, tone of voice :

" Have you finished ? "

" I have finished, and it is finished."

" So be it, my dear ; the book is closed, and I, like you, think it best not again to open it. As you wish it, we will separate to-morrow and each try solitude."

" Oh, I permit you to enliven it ! "

" Thanks, and I forbid you to do so."

" Gracious ! I do not dream of such a thing. When I leave you, it is to become my own mistress, not to change masters. You can be quite easy ; to marry again would be a folly I shall never commit. Have you anything more to say ? "

"No, except that if we take this step without knowing to what it may lead . . ."

"Oh! I know. First to peace, then to old age, finally to Père Lachaise."

"Do not joke, but please allow me to finish. We will do as we wish, but it is not necessary that the world should be at once enlightened as to our disagreements. That is my opinion, and I think you will agree with me."

"I do not know, because, of course, people cannot long remain ignorant . . ."

"Yes, but for a time. Later the same objections will not exist. In short, this is what I ask: before taking any measures to obtain a divorce, let us separate by all means, but under special conditions which will save appearances, and excite no suspicions in the minds of our friends."

"What, then, is your idea?"

"As you wish to leave to-morrow, do so; but instead of taking refuge with some friend in the country or abroad, as is probably your intention, go to Meneaux, my château in Brittany, and as long as you can endure it—two months, if you have the courage—remain there. Madame Bénard, my parents' old housekeeper, who brought me up, is in charge. She will receive you, and in every way look after your comfort. You can tell her that I will soon join you."

"That, I imagine, will not be the truth."

"No, but you had better say so. The house is well furnished, pretty, and not more than four miles from Guérande. Under the pretext that Brittany is too far away from Paris, you have always avoided setting foot upon this family estate where my childhood was passed. This, before we each go our own way in life, is a good opportunity to look at it. If you let this chance escape, you will never have another. Now can I count upon you? Do you consent?"

"You have made your request with civility, and I consent. I will go to Meneaux, and will remain there for two months. You may send a telegram to Madame Bénard."

Then a few words more were exchanged with a coldness too intense to be quite genuine. "Thanks—good night—good-bye! yes, good-bye!" Their voices did not tremble, oh no; but their hearts, their poor hearts, ached! Each one privately thought, "What? Can it be true we are to part—and for ever? That is what we shall see, my wife! I'm not quite sure about that, my husband!"

But, nevertheless, the next day Madame de Précy departed.

. . . .

On a clear, fresh May morning the young woman arrived at Meneaux. It is at the seaside, a delightful place when spring, like a tiny child on its uncertain legs, hesitatingly treads there. The sparse, backward vegetation is more rugged than elsewhere, the blue of the sky has a deeper tint, and in the salt air there is something bracing and healthful which brings red to the cheek and peace to the soul.

For Madame de Précy's occupation, Madame Bénard had prepared, on the second floor, a large bedchamber, wainscoted in oak and hung with old sulphur-coloured damask; on one side it overlooked a wide expanse of flat country, broken only here and there by a rock or a thin cluster of reeds; and on the other a pine wood ceaselessly murmuring in the breeze.

After she had emptied her trunks and made herself at home in her room, Madame de Précy found plenty of time for reflection. Nature offers many consolations to those who at a moral crisis fly to her. By a sort of reflex action, she deadens pain, soothes and cheers. Her immutability, her apparent egotism, are good advisers. Before her who does not pass away one learns to see that everything else will do so, our little happinesses as well as our great sorrows; and the order which she observes in everything incites us to order also our hearts and minds. Madame de Précy began to think, and more seriously than for many and many a long day before. She reviewed her entire past life, beginning with the first white pages of cradle, dolls, first communion, long skirts and balls, next turning to the chapter of marriage. Her life had not been a romance, scarcely even a story, but very ordinary, without great joys, great catastrophes, or anything striking. Every night she had gone to bed with the secret hope that the next day something might happen. During the nine years of her married life, the sun had risen many times, but never had anything happened. Little by little she and her husband had become embittered, and perhaps he also, without being willing to admit it, had suffered from that monotony to some beings so irritating—monotony of things, hours, events, crimes, heroisms, vices, seasons, rain, sun, admirations, and anticipations. Her husband was not a man to be despised: cultivated, distinguished, honourable, sometimes (only sometimes) tender-hearted—in fact, admirable—yet impossible to live with. So, while deploring her fate, in the bloom of youth finding herself thus alone and in a false position, she did not, however, regret the impulse to which she had yielded. She would not know happiness, but she could have peace. One cannot expect everything at once. Without feeling that her dignity was compromised, she gladly accepted the society of Madame Bénard, the old housekeeper in charge of the château, and yet, as a rule, she was haughty. But Madame Bénard had brought up Monsieur de Précy, and moreover the country equalises; its solitude brings together human beings, raising a little those who are below, and lowering a little those who are above, so that Madame de Précy and the good old lady—for a lady she really was—soon became friends.

On the day Madame Bénard took Madame de Précy through the château, she went first to a large room on the third storey, and, as she pushed open the door, said:

"I want to begin by showing you everything connected with Monsieur's childhood. This is the room where Monsieur played and amused himself when he was a little boy."

Then she opened closets where lay balls, drums, trumpets, boxes of tin soldiers, games of patience, draughts, and dominoes, saying as she fingered them one after another:

"These were Monsieur's playthings when he was a little boy."

And suddenly she pulled from a heap a doll with a broken nose.

"See, Madame! he even had a doll, that boy; he called her Pochette, and when he kissed her he used to say, 'She shall be my wife!' Was it not ludicrous? Well, he would not say that now. He has something better."

Madame de Précy did not reply.

The housekeeper questioned: "It must move you to see all these things?"

"Yes, Madame Bénard."

Then the old lady took her to see the room where Monsieur used to sleep; sometimes forgetting herself, instead of Monsieur, she said Louis; and Madame de Précy was strangely moved at hearing pronounced by another that name she had so often said, but might never say again. The room where her husband used to study was next exhibited, with its shelves still filled by his old school-books and copy-books. One of the latter was seized by Madame Bénard, who, tendering it to Madame de Précy, cried, "See how well Monsieur wrote when he was a little boy." And traced in large, uncertain letters she read, " Let us love one another." Then she exclaimed, " I should like to go out into the air ; I do not feel quite well."

They went out of doors, and for some moments silently walked about. When a large pond, on which floated two beautiful white swans, was presently approached, Madame Bénard announced, " Here is the pond where Monsieur kept his boat when he was a little boy. One evening he came near drowning himself. I shall never forget that."

When, a few steps farther on, they reached an old straight-backed, moss-grown wooden bench, on either side of which stood a tall earthenware vase, she cried, " This is the bench where Monsieur used to sit and read when he was a little boy."

Next they entered the vegetable garden, and Madame Bénard, walking at once toward a little plot, enclosed by a hedge of box, said again, " This was Monsieur's garden when he was a little boy."

As they afterward crossed the servants' court, a glimpse of the farm horses in their stalls, afforded by widely opened stable doors, caused Madame Bénard to exclaim, " Oh, Boniface used to be kept there ! "

" What was Boniface ? " asked Madame de Précy.

" Boniface was Monsieur's pony when he was a little boy."

So clearly had Madame Bénard brought before Madame de Précy a little Louis who studied, read, wrote, laughed, and played, that she almost saw him now, in short trousers with sunburnt legs and bare head, running across the garden.

When later in the day they were both seated in the dining-room near a large window overlooking the sea, Madame Bénard began in a simple way to relate the story of Monsieur when he was a little boy. It was not very cheerful.

" I must tell you, Madame," said the old woman, " that Monsieur's parents were very peculiar. You never saw them, but I knew them well.

" Just imagine, they actually disliked each other, and without any good reason. That they were not ' congenial ' was the only excuse they could give for living almost always apart ; but think how wicked that was ! If the father was in Paris the mother travelled, and when she returned he went away. They both loved Monsieur Louis, but rather than share his society preferred entirely to deprive themselves of it. So he was sent here to me, and I had to be to him both father and mother. That is the way I happened to bring him up, and I did my best. His parents both died quite young, and he, poor child, wept as bitterly as if he had known them. I can forgive him, but I'm quite sure that when I die he will not grieve as much.

" I tell you all this, Madame, because perhaps he has never done so, and also that you may be able to make allowance for him if sometimes he appears nervous, quick-tempered, or moody. It is not his fault ; it is the fault of old times when he was a little boy. Had it not been for his deserted, lonely childhood, he would have grown up quite a different man."

All this Madame Bénard said and much besides, telling many anecdotes, and giving a mass of details, so that the conversation lasted until evening. Neither of the two women thought of ringing for a lamp, and darkness enveloped them. Therefore Madame Bénard did not observe that Madame de Précy was furtively drying her eyes. When she rose it was to say :

" All you have related about my husband has interested me very much, dear Madame Bénard," and she warmly pressed the good old woman's hands. This did not astonish Madame Bénard, nor was she surprised when the young woman handed her a telegram for Paris to be sent to the office at Guérande. What did the telegram contain ?

What is sure is that it was sent that night, and that the next day Monsieur de Précy arrived.

THE POCKET-BOOK

HENRI LAVEDAN

MONSIEUR CERVEAU crept cautiously, like a mouse, the whole length of the Rue d'Assas. As he was coming out of his office some of his friends had prevailed upon him to go to a café, and he had lost nearly three francs at dominoes. Now he was hurrying home, having learned by former sad experience that Madame Cerveau expected him punctually at her dinner-hour. He grew even more timid as he reached the door. What a scene there would be!

He climbed the stairs slowly, for he was covered with perspiration, and was breathing heavily. When he reached the second storey he heard a cough above him. Raising his head he saw his wife bending over the railing with a light in her hand, and he trembled still more. He continued climbing, however, trying to conceal his fear under the mask of a smile. She was standing on the landing, and the lighted lamp she held in her hand gave her the appearance of a vestal virgin. Monsieur Cerveau had already bent his humble head ready to submit to all her reproaches, to endure all her scoldings; but to his great astonishment she only said:

"Here you are at last! I have been watching so impatiently for you!" Then seizing him by the arm: "If you only knew! I have such a wonderful thing to tell you. Come!" They entered their room, and Madame Cerveau closed the door, repeating: "You will see, you will see!" Then she laughed, a forced, nervous laugh.

"You worry me, Léonie. What is the matter with you?" cried Cerveau.

"Why, nothing is the matter, but listen. Such an extraordinary thing happened to me an hour ago. You have read novels, haven't you?"

"Of course. What do you mean?"

"Can't you guess? Just try to guess."

"Tell me what it is, I beg. You are torturing me."

"Yes, that's true. No one could guess it. Well, as I was coming back from the Faubourg St. Honoré, this is what I found while crossing the Champs Elysées." With some difficulty she drew forth from the depth of her pocket a black stuffed thing which she held for a moment as though trying to decide how much it weighed. Then her face grew grave, as if she were about to do something important, and she held the object toward her husband with a gesture that said, " Look, and give your opinion."

Cerveau took it and said, after he had turned it over and over again: " It's a pocket-book."

" The inside—look inside ! " commanded his wife.

He opened it carefully. Several slips of paper dropped out. As he was not examining it quickly enough to suit her, she snatched it from his hands. " Give it to me. There ! " She opened the first piece of paper her hand grasped. " Do you understand ? These are foreign shares. I don't know how much money each one represents, but I'm ready to wager they mean quite a sum."

" Yes, yes, they do," stammered the amazed Cerveau. " It is very strange. They are certainly foreign shares. And you found this ? "

" Yes. In the Champs Elysées. I stepped on it. I almost fell over it."

" Somebody must have lost it."

" Of course."

" If you like, we will take it to police headquarters after dinner. It will give us some place to go for our evening walk. What do you say ? "

" Why, of course. I had no idea of keeping it," she answered impatiently.

They sat down at the table, both out of temper, like people who have a disagreeable task to perform. Suddenly she said to him:

" Morin, who is at the Bourse, is going to lunch with us to-morrow. I am rather curious to find out through him the value of those papers. Suppose we wait a while before we give them up. There is plenty of time."

He was overjoyed at finding her so willing and readily consented.

They told the story to Morin the next day, and after he had carefully examined the papers, he exclaimed: " Russian—Austrian railways. This is luck ! They are worth at least forty thousand francs ! "

Forty thousand francs ! They both jumped to their feet. Why, that was a fortune. " And you know," continued their friend, " in a few years they will double their value. I'm well acquainted with these things." Then he laughingly added: " Heavens! if I were only in your place!"

Cerveau was thoroughly shocked and interrupted him: "Oh, Morin!"

" Well, you may be right after all," answered the man from the Bourse. " Honesty is too complicated a thing for me to understand."

He seized his hat and left them somewhat coolly.

In the afternoon they went to headquarters, gave up the pocket-book, and returned relieved and pleased with themselves. Then life resumed its ordinary course, and eight monotonous months passed by. Toward the middle of the ninth month, Madame Cerveau gleefully said to her husband, " Would you believe it? The other day I went to find out who had called for the pocket-book. It has not been claimed! It is still there!"

" What difference do you suppose that makes to me?" he asked.

" Don't you know? The difference for you, the difference for us is, that if nobody appears within four months, as one year will have passed since we gave it up, the money will belong to us."

" Is that true?"

" Of course!" And she clapped her hands.

From that moment they lived in the most painful and continuous excitement. Cerveau would mutter each morning as he dressed, " If only the owner does not put in an appearance!" And each evening, on returning from his office, he would say, " Has he shown up?" They made so many visits that the chief grew weary of seeing them. They began to think that Providence was working for them as time went on, and they would startle each other by declaring together, " We shall have it!"

They could not sleep at night. They would seat themselves by the bed, and by the dim light of their candle they would build air-castles. They wavered between a farm in Beauce or a villa by the seashore. They had already decided to name the latter " Villa Léonie." In any case they would have a man-servant; they would buy a great deal of silverware. They would live to be very old, and would never be ill. Then, when they suddenly realised that this precious treasure did not yet belong to them—that they might lose it at the last moment, they would become furious, as if they were under the immediate danger of being betrayed, of being robbed. At times they would grow tender and would say with tears in their voices: " Our poor money!"

One evening, in a confiding moment, he said to his wife: "At any rate, we shall not have stolen it."

Only one week remained before the end of the time so ardently desired. Cerveau resigned his position. What was the use of working, now that he was rich? He saw on the fourth page of a newspaper, "Swiss chalet for sale at Petites-Dalles." He bought it for ten thousand francs, and promised to pay in fifteen days.

At last, on January 12, which was the happy, the blessed day, dressed in their best they both went to police headquarters and, after having signed their names, tremblingly received the pocket-book from the officer. The long waiting was over, and they went to the church and offered thanks by lighting a candle in that sacred place.

They had invited Morin to dinner, planning to surprise him, and if the truth must be told, in no wise sorry that they had an opportunity of crowing over him.

They gave him no hint of their good fortune until the dessert was brought on, and then they gave full vent to their joy, telling the good news with joyous, excited cries. Cerveau brought forth the pocket-book, which was hidden behind the handkerchiefs in a bureau drawer. Morin took it and cast his eyes over the papers.

"Russian and Austrian railway shares!" he exclaimed. "They've gone down during the last six months, my poor friends. Why, you will be lucky if you get three hundred francs for them now! Didn't I tell you that would happen?"

PAUL MARGUERITTE
B. 1860

THE DEAD HAND

I

RENÉ d'Yons came home at four o'clock in the morning. Since his mother's death he had lived alone in the great house, which now seemed so lonely. Its blank white face looked out over the dark garden, and there was no homeliness in its aspect. He pushed the key into the lock of the side door, and entered the gloomy house with a feeling of repugnance and dejection.

He had been to a party, which had not amused him. For one thing, there had been high play, and he had lost a good deal of money. He had also drunk too much champagne, which had depressed him, and he had been obliged to come home in a crawling night cab, which shook all his bones and set his teeth on edge. He pictured the uses of the cab when it was not taking fares. It served as a bed for the cabman, and as a granary for his horse. That was certain, for it reeked of tobacco and stale hay. And he also thought of its other possible uses—to take patients to the fever hospital, and all sorts of people to see them afterwards. He checked his thoughts with a shudder.

Since his mother had died and left him to his own devices, he had run after pleasure. And now, after all, what pleasure had he got ? An intolerable weariness and disgust, and the certainty that he could never pay the debt of honour which he had incurred under the promise that it would be paid by noon next day. He was the most unhappy and pitiable of creatures. That was what his pursuit of pleasure had done for him.

He went up the dark silent staircase. No one waited for him ; no one greeted him on his way. The two old servants who had remained with him after his mother's death had long since gone to bed, for he had told them never to sit up for him. He lit the gas in the passage and went into his bedroom, passing in haste the dark rooms which had never been opened since his mother's death. He shivered with cold, the cold of a sleepless night and the deadness of the time before the rising of the sun, that mysterious hour when all Nature seems to be at her lowest ebb, and to have resigned all part in the lives of men.

He had lighted the candle which was always left for him outside his bedroom door, but the draught blew it out as he entered his room, just as if it had been purposely extinguished by human means. He thought, "They always leave my window open, and of course the wind has grown stronger during the night."

Ten minutes passed while he hunted for matches. He did not like to wake the old servants, and he had to search through his cupboard, for his match-box was empty.

He succeeded at last in relighting his candle, and saw all the familiar objects of his bedroom. There were the bed, the sofa, the wardrobe with the long mirror in which he could see his form reflected. It was not a very nice reflection, for he was weary, dispirited, and untidy. His face was drawn and sallow after his night's exhaustion in search of pleasure.

Looking away from the mirror in disgust, his glance fell on the carpet in front of the wardrobe, and his complexion changed from sallow to green. He stood staring at the spot on which his eyes had rested. What did he see ?

There, on the thick red carpet just in front of him, lay a human hand. The fingers were spread out and slightly curved ; the wrist was cut short off, and still red as if from recent bleeding. It was unmistakably a hand cut from a person who had been alive only a short time before. What did it mean ? Why was it there on his carpet, in his bedroom, mute evidence of a crime of which he knew nothing ? No other trace was there. The ghastly hand lay before him, unconnected with any other object in his well-ordered chamber.

Certainly he was not dreaming. The horrid thing lay there so near him that he could just touch it by moving the toe of his patent leather boot. Who could have put it there ? Was this a practical joke played on him by one of his friends ? Was the hand made of wax, or was it some anatomical preparation ?

He reflected for a moment, and then, wishing to reassure himself, he gave it a little push with his toe, but without being able to repress a shudder of disgust. The object which he touched was soft and rather elastic, and he recoiled from the contact. The thing was flesh and blood. It had been alive a few hours before. When he became convinced of this, René trembled from head to foot, and the candlestick rattled in his hand like the little bell of a sacristan.

II

After some hesitation the young man ventured to look more closely at the object on the floor. Then he cast a glance round his room. He saw the bed, the wardrobe, the long heavy window curtains, and holding his breath he listened attentively. His open window admitted a breeze from the garden below, bearing with it the odour of moist earth. He went over and closed the window, shivering as he did so lest a dagger stroke between his shoulders should stretch him lifeless against the iron balcony. Taking a revolver from his pocket, he continued examining his bedroom so as not to leave a single nook or corner out of consideration.

Now a new fear assailed him, and he crept upstairs to the second storey as softly as possible to make sure that nothing had happened to the old servants who slept there. He listened at the door until their heavy breathing reassured him; and not seeing anything unusual in the appearance of the passages, he went down again, stopping at intervals on the stairs to listen. He descended to the lower floor, and opened the doors of the rooms which had formerly been used by his mother. All of these rooms had a damp and musty odour; and as nothing had been disturbed in them for a long time past, the carpets were covered with fine dust. The clocks on the mantelpieces had stopped, and everything spoke of the silence and immobility of death.

René returned to his own room. He felt terribly uneasy, but was a little reassured when he saw that the hand was still lying in the same place. He could not conquer his repugnance, but his anxiety to solve the mystery caused him to approach the object more closely, and he stooped to examine it by the light of his candle.

III

The hand was small, white, and delicate, and must have belonged to a woman or a youth. René began to picture to himself the actual commission of the crime. He seemed to see the blood flowing and the victim dying while the murderer prepared to cut the still warm body in pieces. The idea made him tremble, and he tried to banish it from his mind and to regain enough self-control to inspect the object calmly and with lucid judgment. That hand was too dainty not to be the hand of a woman; it had been very well cared for, but the points of the fingers were slightly darkened as if they had touched soot or ashes. René looked toward the fireplace, in which the fire had gone out some time ago. There could be no doubt whatever that the hand had fallen down the chimney, having been dropped from the roof by the crafty murderer, who was anxious to get rid of the proofs of his crime as easily as possible. It must have rebounded on striking the burnt-out coals, and fallen on the hearth-rug.

It was plump, fresh, and of youthful smoothness. It was the left hand. Where was the other, the right one? Perhaps he would find it in the garden during the coming day. Or was it also in his room? No, he dismissed that idea; he had searched too minutely. The third finger had a small white swelling at the base of the finger, evidently the mark of a ring which had been forcibly pulled off by the murderer. There was a scratch on the soft palm. The nails were prettily cut in almond shape.

That poor hand was still attractive-looking, dainty, and inviting, as it had been in the owner's lifetime. He looked at it closely and was able to see that it had belonged to a woman of the demi-monde, for it had been manicured with the aid of specially perfumed ointments such as were fashionable among some of those women whom he knew. He ventured to touch it gingerly, and found it soft as velvet, but cold as marble. He lifted it and was surprised to find it unusually heavy, with the heaviness of dead flesh. He tried to stretch it out flat, but the fingers contracted. He shuddered at what he was doing, which seemed indeed a sacrilege, but he could not help it; his curiosity was stronger than his self-control. Finally he stood up and faced his own reflection in the mirror, which gave him back a look of perplexity and alarm. What was he to do?

Well, first of all he had to wait for the daylight to come. He could not very well run off just then to rouse up the officers of the law, or wake the poor old servants to go hunting about in the dark garden or to help him to try to find the murderer in the deserted streets. The crime might have been committed somewhere very near his house, yet the criminal himself might now be very far off. It might even be that the murder had been committed at the other end of the town and the fragments of the corpse distributed broadcast. But in any case it could not be long since it had happened; and René, sitting by the window with his revolver within reach of his right hand, remained staring at the poor dead thing lying before him, admiring its fine delicate outlines, and trying not to see the ghastly stump in which it ended.

He tried to sleep, but found it impossible. First of all he thought he would hide the thing, and he picked it up in a towel and laid it on his dressing-table, carefully covered. Now he could not see it, but he knew it was there, and it was impossible for him to take his eyes away from its vague outlines. He put a screen before the table and looked at it. He felt a great pity for the poor creature who had met with a fate which is unfortunately not an uncommon one for women of the class to which she had belonged. His imagination pictured the details which the newspaper would publish with regard to this nameless and mysterious hand. He ran over in his mind all that was going to happen when day should come and he must go to the police station, where the tale which he had to tell and the interviews which would follow with the reporters of the daily papers would bring his name into every one's mouth for a short time at any rate. His pity for the victim of the crime was succeeded by a sort of vanity at his own share in the discovery, and at the attention which he was certainly about to attract.

A breath of air shaking the window frame caused him to start and grasp his revolver. He looked round with a shudder, and a cold perspiration stood out on his forehead. The question occurred to him : " Was it after all only by chance that his room had been selected as the spot into which the hand had been thrown ? Was there any idea of revenge in this apparent chance, any hint of the cruel reprisals of which we read in annals of bygone days ? "

The more he pondered on this, the more insistent the idea became, even when he felt its absurdity. He began to wonder if he had any special reason for being so much interested in that hand ; if it had even belonged to some one whom he knew. He was fascinated by the idea, and he thought : " I know now. I have seen that hand before. I know the girl it belonged it. I will think of her name presently, when my mind is less confused." He began to run over in his mind the personalities of the men and women with whom he had spent the evening at the supper party from which he had just returned. At last, by a violent effort of will, he drove away the terrible idea which was beginning to dominate his mind, and which, if he continued to entertain it, would end by driving him mad.

IV

He took up a book and tried to read one of the stories which used to interest him so much in former days. Impossible to keep his mind on it. Every sentence, every line, every idea, seemed to contain some one of the two words which hammered incessantly on his brain, " hand " and " death." At last he got rid of the thought of the first word, but the second became more insistent, and flooded his imagination with sinister thoughts. What was there real in this life except death ?

Visions of it flooded his mind: the death of his mother; the death of this unknown woman; perhaps his own death soon. When would that take place? Life is short, very short at best, and the end comes much sooner than any of us expect. How many things may lead to death! Illness, an apparently trifling accident, a chance cold, a whiff of foul air, a fall from a horse. All these things lie in wait for us at every moment of the day. And then there are other dangers which we bring on ourselves: the vengeance of a neglected woman or an angry husband, the murderous blow of one whom we have perversely made our enemy. René looked back into the years which had gone by, the years which he had wasted in the pursuit of his own idle pleasure. In his mother's lifetime, out of respect for her goodness, he had restrained his mad impulses. But since her death, what had been the case? He said with conviction:

"My present way of life is an insult, not merely to the memory of my mother, but also to the invisible presence of her spirit, which may be watching over me at this moment. This hand, a poor fragment of the mystery of another life, may have been sent into my presence to warn and advise me. Never could the thought of the unceasing menace of death have been brought so forcibly to my mind in any other way, or under any form so terrible and so insistent. I must make a better use of the days of my life which still remain to me, if I am not to be for ever lost to all possibility of good. I must try to control myself, to make some good use of what capacities I possess, to believe in something or in some one, to serve my fellow-creatures, to love those who deserve to be loved, to obtain the love of those whose love is worth having. Nothing else can make life endurable or the thought of death a matter to be borne with calmness. I see it all now. That poor hand which lies so cold, so lifeless, has served the purpose for which it was mysteriously sent to me; pulseless and still though it lies, it has pointed out to me the writing on the wall."

René sat absorbed in these reflections until the rays of the new day poured over roof and steeple, falling all about him, and lighting every corner of his room. He seemed to be suddenly delivered from the agony of gloomy thought which had weighed him down through the night, and without casting another glance at the screen beyond which he had placed the table with its ghastly burden, he rose from his chair and rang for his servants to give them the orders which would mean the end of this nightmare.

GEORGES BEAUME

B. 1861

THE TREASURE

I

FOR a long time Roch had lived alone with his son, in his house, built of reeds and stones, by the roadside, under the hill overlooking the far-off little town. He was the owner of rich lands, planted with vines, both on the hillside and in the plain. Only on rare occasions he quitted his own paths to climb into the mountain woods, to shoot the hare, or gather mushrooms and salads.

People sometimes came to see him, mostly on the eve of the vintage, to treat for the purchase of the fruit, which he sold on the vines for ready money, and on no other terms. At those times, after business, he would invite the dealers or his comrades to drink a bottle of wine, over which he would gaily talk about the doings of his youth, his health ; all the while laughing the laugh of the master, sitting at his door in the sun, his fowls picking and scratching in the straw and dust around him.

His son Michel resembled him closely—blonde, square-shouldered, with beard and hair tufted like the brambles in a ravine.

The old man was becoming grey, and bushy eyebrows protected his keen little eyes, which took a dreamy expression when, at the close of the day, he sat upon his stone bench and saw the trembling sea of darkness overspread the plain. He was a miser. He mended his own clothes, repaired his own ploughs, replastered the worn-out walls of his house and trimmed the hedges on his domain. He and his son, without any beast of burden to help them, did all the work. They dug deep, and opened out their cultures to the sun with energy and confidence. Their vines were the best in the country. They never quitted them—never ceased thinking of them day and night ; and so, lived by them.

Roch took pleasure in this kind of existence. He loved money—religiously, with all his strength. He hungered for gold, more and more gold, that he might handle it, imbibe its powers, hide it in corners, at the foot of trees, under heaps of rock.

On sunny Sundays he collected his fortune from its hiding-places, and heaped it on his table in front of his door, in the midst of his fowls, alone, and counted his silver and his gold pieces, making them glitter in the sunlight, and fall through his horny fingers in a clattering shower. Near him, within instant reach, he had his double-barrelled gun. And he laughed and fed his eyes with his large fortune. A glory sang within him, he swelled with the pride of being rich. He thought of Michel, of the happiness which this treasure, amassed with so much fervour and patience, would give him at some future time, when he would no longer be there. At ease in his solitude, he gave himself up to this enjoyment ; he enjoyed his lands, still full of riches, while his son, down yonder, behind the trees, dug bravely at the foot of a vine.

Then, suddenly, overtaken by terror, he hurriedly returned his gold to a canvas bag and bore it away ; made a fresh hole in the ground, no matter where, sometimes in the most open and noticeable spots, so as to ward off suspicion. And when he had thus buried his treasure, the old man stood powerless, oppressed with remorse, as if he had buried his happiness, his eyes lost in an ecstasy : he planted himself for a moment before his cottage, lifted his eyes towards the blue sky, scanned the high road along which were passing the dull and indifferent waggoners, and ever fearful of having been watched, he looked for his son, still working yonder behind the trees.

When he returned to labour and health, the joy of the soul came back to him abundantly. Yet he was pursued by an anxiety, a miser's care, a peasant's pride in his lands. After him what would become of the patrimony ? What would become of his gold ? He had confidence in his son—who resembled him ; but his son would not remain alone. He ought to be married already. And the young wife and the new relatives would, perhaps, destroy the order and prosperity of his possessions. He would himself choose a wife for his son.

Michel bowed humbly before his father, whom he regarded as a superior being, since, out of nothing, from the depths of poverty, Roch had raised himself to opulence. They went forth together, at dawn, one Sunday in spring. The clear sky hung over all like a robe of innocence. Fresh voices murmured in the solitude.

" We will not go into the town," said the old man. " We shall not find there what we want : the girls there are too fond of luxury and amusements. Let us try what we may see in the villages."

Michel followed him, his hands in his pockets, his head bent downwards, not daring to turn his eyes on the country, agitated by happiness and weakness, troubled in his virgin nature as a brooklet by the storm.

They went on for a long time without speaking : they were thinking of the old woman who, for five years, had slept at the foot of an oak, and for whom, at sunset, they said a prayer. She was wanted now. She would have given her advice, and Roch, supported by her, would have been enabled to maintain his authority ; as it was, he, for a moment, mistrusted his experience.

They visited the hamlets and villages, to the surprise of those who lived there, and were taken to the café, to the skittle and racket grounds, and to the spots where the crowd was promenading. They refused to drink, and walked about slowly, considering the girls.

Michel tired of these proceedings after a while : none of the girls pleased him. He thought them all too much dressed up and too forward in their bearing. The father grumbled at the young man's ill-humour and exaction. With quickening steps they made their way into the open country.

In the evening they returned home tired out. On the way the old man, angrily and with flashing eyes, attacked his son.

" What do you mean by all this ? " he demanded. " Don't you want to marry ? Are you hoping to find a princess, blockhead ? "

Michel shrugged his shoulders.

" I know nothing about it—only that I love the land—and that a girl who has sprung from it might please me."

The old man, dumfounded by this reply, bit his lips. He wished to get at the full meaning of what his son had said, suspecting that they implied the existence of a love as yet unknown to him. Something like a feeling of joy dawned upon him, but coupled with the agony of a fear, lest he might be deceiving himself.

But, blunt and rough as he was, he dared not ask any questions, conscious of his inability to touch the desire which, like a flower under water, was waking in the young man's simple soul.

II

On the farther side of the mountain, on the border of a torrent and shadowed by trees, stood a farmhouse, poor and isolated, the only house to which Michel sometimes paid a visit. Its inhabitants were a man named Bruno, taciturn, always at work, rusted by the sun; the wife, Olympe, a dried plant of the mountain, burned up like a cinder, like her husband, for ever at work, sewing, and tending the flowers and vegetables; then the daughter, a tall, brown-haired girl, sweet-smelling as the grass about a spring, the pure and caressing growth of the peace of the fields.

This was Justine, the sunshine of the hearth, the pride of her parents. For her sake Bruno put off his taciturnity after the day's work, and on Sundays went to the town and to the fêtes, exhibiting his heiress dressed in bright-coloured gowns, with gold chains about her neck—the jewellery of a long-forgotten grandmother. Justine was not yet twenty, and there had been no thought of marrying her.

Michel sometimes went to the farm, and he and Justine chatted, standing by the well, or, more often, under the mulberry trees, breathing the freshness of the leaves in the hours of rest and when the heat was too oppressive, looking through the hanging branches away to the far-off hills and the wide-stretching plain.

Then Michel returned home in company with Justine's father, examining by the way the vineyards, meadows, and olive gardens of their neighbours, comparing them with their own. But only Michel entered the enclosure. Occasionally Roch, putting down his spade, came forward, and he and Bruno, in their shirt sleeves, with their arms resting on the barred gate, chatted for a while, but in a tone of no great intimacy. Bruno never entered the gate, which Roch never opened, seeming to guard his domain on the threshold.

Sometimes Bruno received commissions from him which he executed in the town on Sundays; these were the only confidences between Roch and him. The old miser had never been across the mountain, and had only by chance seen Olympe and Justine as they passed along the hedges; when that occurred they only said "Good day" and smiled, without stopping to converse.

Michel and Justine had grown up together on the same soil. They regarded each other as if they had been old people, talking and laughing together without restraint, their conversation always turning on the same subjects, their labours and the seasons.

On the evening of the day following that on which he had been with his father on that strange excursion to the town and the adjacent villages, Michel met Justine; they looked at each other—then suddenly flushed, and their eyes grew moist with fondness.

They walked side by side.

At length Michel, with a thrill of contentment, clapped Justine on the shoulder.

" Are you going home ? " he asked.

" Yes, I am returning from the town—tired. Where are you going ?"

" I'm on my way home, too—but I'll go with you ; I have not seen your parents for a long time."

They walked on slowly up the hill.

As they went down the other side, the fresher evening breeze fanned their faces, and they were penetrated by a glory of health : a pleasure of calm and purity united them. Their eyes turned together to the same objects of interest. They had one and the same soul, and the same feeling of life.

When they were near the farm, already dim amid the shadows that were creeping to the brow of the hill, Justine asked :

" You and your father were away from home yesterday—why ? "

" Oh, yes !—Fancy ! "

And with laughter and abrupt gestures, fearing to offend Justine by ideas forbidden to her modesty, Michel related to her the story of the pilgrimage in search of a wife.

" It was all nonsense," he added ; " I don't know what my father has been thinking of lately. I have constantly seen him, spade in hand, removing his treasure from one place to another. And now he wants me to marry—a thing I never thought of," a look of dreamy helplessness in his eyes.

" Well, don't worry yourself about it, stupid ! " cried Justine. " One would think you were going to cry ! "

She bantered him noisily ; but he stopped and gazed at her in surprise, that she should mock instead of console him. They entered the farmyard. The young man's gravity had touched Justine ; she went to him with downcast eyes, vexed at having hurt his feelings. They went on to the house in painful silence. In the kitchen the mother was setting the supper table ; Bruno was sitting by it more than half asleep.

" Oh ! there you are ! " cried Olympe, putting down a glass and a yellow plate before her husband.

Bruno lifted his elbows, rubbed his heavy brow, admired his daughter ; the two young people seated themselves somewhat uneasily in front of the father.

" What is the matter with you ? " asked the mother, laughingly ; " have you two been fighting ? "

" No," murmured Michel.

" No," repeated Justine.

She sighed, and in turn recited in a breath, and forcing herself to smile, the quest of Michel and his father about the country in search of a wife for the young man.

The old people were taken aback, painfully disturbed, as if threatened with the deprivation of something. They looked at the young people. A heavy silence fell upon the hum of life which came from without. They were afraid to think, and the same idea, as by a miracle, entered and haunted their minds.

" I'm going," said Michel, abruptly. He rose from his seat. The silence still continued. Michel repeated : " I'm going."

" So soon ? " And Justine involuntarily held him, with a longing to ease her heart and win his forgiveness.

" Stay ! " commanded Bruno.

Michel resumed his seat beside Justine. They all looked at him. He blushed, dared not speak, bit his lips, and drummed on the table with his finger-nails.

" Do you want to get married, Michel ? " asked Bruno.

The young man blushed redder still, shrugged his shoulders uncomfortably, and replied :

" My father has ideas—stupid ideas that come into his head—and insisted on going about the villages——"

" But—what need was there to search so far away ? "

And Olympe, with her large hands widespread, boldly indicated her daughter. It was Justine's turn to blush.

" Why not ? " continued Bruno. " We are fond of you, Michel. But it was not for us to say anything : your father has money."

" Oh ! "

This question of money shamed the young man.

" My father would like it," he said, resolutely.

Justine raised her eyes to him, took his hands between hers, and extended them on the table. It seemed like an oath taken, and a bright vision passed before all of them in silence. Justine moved nearer to her lover, pressed closely against him, and encouraged him to trust and to will.

" Now I shall no longer dare to come to your house," she said.

" Nor I," added her father.

The anxious mother turned away, stirred the fire on the hearth, and made the soup ready.

" Already such big children," murmured Bruno.

This speech made them smile. Michel drew his hands from those of Justine, slowly, uneasily. She contemplated him as if she had found him again, after a long separation, grown, and handsomer, and better.

He went away, filled with regrets, tormented by a remorse. All accompanied him to the threshold, Bruno in advance. Then, with a movement of courage and will, Michel said to the master of the farm :

" My father esteems you : he will only do what I wish."

And he departed. Justine saw him, through the shadows, mounting the hill path. He walked quickly, agitated by his new emotion. For the first time in his life, he thought things no longer appeared to him as they had hitherto appeared. A voice spoke to him confusedly, awaking dreams in his soul, a joy in his flesh. He also felt a fear. He tried to drive away the memory of Justine ; but this memory clung to him, went before him, shining like a tender light. In his absorption he went by the gate of his father's enclosure.

On discovering what he had done he ran back, entered the cottage hurriedly, and, face to face with his father, felt as if he had suddenly been turned into a block of ice. Roch was grumbling.

" Where have you come from ?—from Bruno's ?—Oho ! " And bursting into a loud laugh, he added : " By your hang-dog look one would imagine that you have been up to some mischief. What ails you ? "

The old miser then tranquilly seated himself at table and helped the stew. While they were eating, Michel eyed his father furtively, watching for the moment to explain himself.

" Well—what's the matter with you ? " repeated the old man.

" I daren't——"

" I know : you need not tell me. It is this marriage business that worries you, and you have some notion of your own."

Michel nodded.

" Justine pleases you, then ? "

The young man looked at his father, and resolutely replied : " Yes."

" What about me ? "

Michel was silent ; his weakness and cowardice came back ; he was afraid of offending the miser.

"Don't be uneasy," said the old man. "Justine is to your taste, but what dowry will she have? Her parents are not rich, I believe, while you will have money and rich lands, you know."

"Yes."

"Oh! I know that they are honest people, and that with them my vines have nothing to fear."

Filled as he was with anxiety, Michel knew not what to say: his heart was overflowing with love and entreaty.

"You are an odd fellow; but well, after all, why should I not accept Justine? I prefer people who have surmounted privation and poverty." And with a decided tone and gesture he added: "Well, we'll see about it—that will remind me of past happiness and of your poor mother."

He scratched his forehead, dried his eyes: big tears were running down his cheeks.

"I'll have it so—but on one condition. It's a fancy of mine."

Michel turned pale and his lips quivered, and he leaned back a little in his chair, as if terrified by these strange exuberances.

"What is this condition?"

"You will marry—that is settled; but I'll not give you the money till you have given me a grandson—an heir to my name." And he laughed boisterously, Michel observing him dubiously.

"So be it, father—I accept!"

They struck hands on the bargain made.

Three months afterwards Michel and Justine were married and living at Bruno's farm by the torrent. Michel still worked at his father's vines, but Justine never went beyond the enclosure. All were happy. The miser's fortune slept tranquilly underground in some unknown nook.

But, near all this happiness and hopefulness, death was keeping watch.

One evening the miser, while doing something in the interior of his cottage, slipped, fell on his head, and expired. When he was found —the next morning—his body was cold and rigid. Naturally, the old man's treasure occurred to the minds of all: had he been murdered by some robber? Everybody on the farm, including Olympe, set to searching the whole of Roch's land; but nothing was discovered. The cottage, with its barred door, would speedily have fallen into ruins under the beating of the rain; but they kept it intact, as a sacred altar.

The spring arrived, and Justine became a happy mother. With the spring, too, came a long and heavy downfall of rain. Michel, Bruno, and the women, who sometimes tremblingly entered the dead man's domain, went to see what effect the deluge had had upon the empty cottage. They opened the door: a breath as from the tomb exhaled from the deserted dwelling. They sounded the walls: the rain had eaten into them on every side—the shattered building of stones and reeds was ready to fall at any moment. Michel sadly and vaguely gazed on the ruin.

But the clouds had passed to the far end of the plain; the sky cleared, and suddenly a flood of sunlight spread over the lands of the departed miser.

Then from the highest part of the roof of the desolate cottage broken tiles began to fall, and a shapeless something was laid bare to the sun—a coarse canvas bag, which moved and burst: the miser's treasure! The peasants sprang back, and pieces of money, white and yellow, poured down in a torrent.

Ah!—old Roch might well have laughed to himself! Vainly the domain might have been searched till Doomsday! Doubtless he met his death in the act of forming that final hiding-place for his beloved treasure. And still the shower of gold continued—slowly now—now at intervals—now drop by drop.

Michel collected the whole—thousands upon thousands of gold and silver pieces. Silently he and Bruno heaped the treasure upon a hand-barrow, covered it with a blouse, and wheeled it to the farm through the livid half-light of the evening.

Nothing was said of the dead miser, but the thoughts of all turned to him—a little more lovingly. Their wealth was great enough for them to have enjoyed ten years of luxurious life in the great cities far away; but Michel and Justine, in spite of their opulence, determined to live in the farm, to change nothing in their way of life—in the peace of their hearts and the joy of their love, and in the delight of dreaming of amassing a great fortune for their children. Who shall say what constitutes the *summum bonum* of human happiness?

LUCIEN DESCAVES
B. 1861

AN INTERIOR

MY old pal Rondeneux looked in to see me this evening, and we had a pipe together.

I have a great affection for him, going back to the days when we were in the army together, fifteen years ago. Even then I was able to appreciate the great qualities of his heart, which have never changed, although he has veneered them with a hateful covering of republican humbug. He has a rare native goodness, which always makes me think of some exquisite tropical plant dragging out its existence under glass at the door of a low public-house. He is a thoroughly good chap, absolutely straight and unselfish, and would certainly go gaily to death if he thought it would do me any good.

We disagree upon every subject under the sun, and on politics most of all. I cannot help pulling his leg when I see his name on the municipal posters asking for every one's votes. He takes the matter absolutely seriously, all the same. He revels in committee meetings and demonstrations, and in all occasions when the " representatives of the people " give an account of the " trust which has been reposed in them." I happen to know that he has given away much of his small savings to help toward the election expenses of the stupid old buffers who stand for our borough in the House and the County Council, and cannot help chaffing him. " Does not the collector of rates and taxes take enough off you already ? " I say. " My dear old boy, you must have lots of time and money to chuck away." But his answer is always ready. I do not " fulfil the duties of citizenship."

" Don't you understand," he says, " that it wouldn't matter a bit if you voted absurdly or on the wrong side ?· But the dreadful thing is that you don't vote at all. What would become of us if every one was as careless as you ? Nemesis will fall on you and your children, and you will only have yourself to thank for it."

But there is one matter above all others on which we fundamentally disagree. Rondeneux simply cannot stand the sight of a priest's cassock. I know quite well the origin of this, though he is always ready with other explanations. When he was a little lad he was indiscreet enough to imitate the cawing of a crow behind the back of a pompous priest, who turned and went for him. He has never forgotten that experience ; and from the day when that great formula appeared, " Clericalism is the enemy," he adopted it as his war-cry. He uses it in and out of season, and is always ready to hurl it at the head of an opponent. But I am not without my own stock answer, and I think that he gets as good as he gives. My point is this : " Look here, old chap, you are a back number ; that kind of sentiment is really out of date. The enemy is not Clericalism, but Capital, which is a long way more dangerous and subtle." Now, Rondeneux is an employer and has at least a dozen workmen. So my attack in flank is unwelcome and always puts an end to our discussion.

Of course he often has his revenge, and enjoys it thoroughly. When we are invited together to a wedding or funeral conducted under the auspices of the Church, he waits for me near the door to gibe at me : " Of course you will go in. When you have quite finished with all that play-acting, you will find me in the pub round the corner. So long ! " Good old Rondeneux !

He came in to-night when we were just leaving the table. My younger kiddie, a little white bundle in his high chair, was trying bravely all kinds of words, practising his lips and tongue upon them, and executing a design upon the tablecloth with a spoon. The elder, now six years old, was mad with excitement and jollity, as he always is after a meal, and was disciplining with hearty blows the beasts of his toy menagerie.

In a word, the noise was such that we could no longer hear one another. But a familiar voice came upon their games like a curfew bell. It was Granny, come to put them to bed. She brought them both up to be kissed, the eldest, still shaking from his interrupted activity, and the little one, whom she held out to us like a beaker of fresh water to the lips of a thirsty traveller.

Rondeneux really loves these babies, and is proud of having witnessed their entrance into the world. This means that he went with me to the registry office on the days of their birth to make the usual declaration. He is proud of having acted in this capacity. It would give him no pleasure, on the other hand, to have held them at the font. He gave expression to his inveterate dislike for these venerable rites when he said, as Granny carried the two away to their bedroom, " So that's the little kitten whom you had baptized last month ? "

"The very same," I replied.

"Do you know, there is something I cannot understand about you," he said. I saw the squall ruffling the waters in the distance, and took down a reef in my sail.

"What is it you don't understand, old man?" I said.

"Well, you know," he made answer, "you have nothing to do with religion, or its dogmas or practices!"

"That is true enough."

"I know very well," he continued, "that you regard baptism as worse than useless; it is even ridiculous. You cannot feel the need of washing away the stain of original sin when you don't believe in original sin. And then again, even if you were to take your stand by baptism as it was administered to the early Christians, full-grown men and women and full of faith, you cannot believe, any more than I do, in administering it in this way to these unconscious little wretches."

"I cannot deny it," I said.

"Let us be quite frank," he said. "You do not believe in the existence of Our Lord?"

"Very true."

"And yet—you baptize your children?"

"True, old man, I do."

"And then you will have them make their first communion?"

"Perhaps. I don't deny it. It all depends."

"And nuns will drill them in the Catechism! The Catechism—!" The smile of my friend—I should have told you he is a cabinetmaker —was notched as a plane is when it meets a nail in the plank. And then he added: "Do you know from what book my children learned to read?"

"I can guess," I said. "Out of one of those lovely illustrated alphabet books, with a long-necked giraffe beside the letter 'G,' and an elephant twining his trunk round the 'E,' and monkeys doing acrobatic tricks on the 'M.' It is a good enough beginning."

Rondeneux made a little gesture of annoyance, and said: "On the whole, I would rather talk seriously. My boys began with Paul Bert's *Manual of Moral and Civic Education*. I have used that wonderful little book in bringing them up, so that they shall be soundly formed in every way. Ask them any question you like on patriotism, taxation, property, justice, republican principles, military duties, universal suffrage, Léon Gambetta, and they will answer you straight off. If you have to carry a cargo of knowledge through life, that sort of stuff is infinitely better than the commandments of God and the Church. And now, if you do not mind my coming to the point, I have known you for a long time, you did not baptize your children because you were a hypocrite; you did it because you were weak. The fact is you have fallen under the influence of women; your will has been weaker than theirs."

"All that is perfectly true," I replied. "I plead guilty to weakness, an absurd tolerance, and even cowardice. The burden of your charge is that I was accessory to a solemn rite which I believe to be nothing more than an empty formality. Can you not understand that it is precisely because this rite has no meaning for me whatever, that I could not see my way to deny the pleasure of its performance to these women, tender-hearted and devoted people, for whom this trifle has such extraordinary value. I justify myself on the ground that I did not give way to them either for any personal advantage, as for money or a bequest, or anything of the kind. I took into account nothing but questions of love and esteem. You ask my reasons, Rondeneux. Listen!"

The muffled voice of the old grandmother came to us through the half-open door.

"In the name of the Father——" she whispered.

"In the name of the Father and of the Son and of the Holy Ghost. Amen," the two babies repeated, with folded hands.

"O Lord," suggested the old lady, "bless——"

The tiny lips babbled after her, "O God, bless Daddy, and Gran, and my brother, and the servants, and people who are unhappy and ill——"

"And grant, O Lord——"

"Grant, O Lord, that Daddy may be able to get us our daily bread; and that dear little Mummy, who has gone away from us, may rest in peace with You."

Was that profound silence which followed in the house and the world outside or in our hearts? Were those footsteps, which I think we both heard and knew so well—Whose were they?

Rondeneux rose and looked at me, as I at him, through a mist of tears. And inasmuch as there is no nonsense about him, he took my hand, and his grip said all that there is to say. And then he left.

Poor old chap! I can still hear him stumbling down the stairs, sounding as if he had a bad cold, caught in my house.

CHARLES FOLEY
B. 1861

PIROTOU

EVERY time I stopped at Avignon and spent the night at the little hotel, I found the same waiter there. Pirotou—for that was his name—seemed to do all the work of the place, and, I suppose, was the only man they kept. He used to meet the trains with the omnibus, carry the luggage upstairs as if it were as light as cork, sweep and dust the rooms, polish the shining floors, and twice every day, well-groomed, would act as waiter in the coffee-room.

The man always looked so genial and happy that he greatly attracted my interest. When he laughed, it was not with his lips alone, but with his dark bright eyes, his expansive nose, and even with his close-cropped hair and young moustache. He was the most obliging waiter I have ever seen, and was popular not only with the guests of the hotel but with every one in the vicinity. When he was perched high up on the bus, driving between the hotel and the station, he used to nod or wave his whip or smile to almost every one he passed. Indeed, he was pleased with all the world, and every one had a good word for him. Being so popular he had, of course, unusual privileges. He loved the sound of his own voice, and his manner was more intimate than one cares for in a waiter; but he was such a simple and natural fellow that no one could be offended.

When the dinner things had all been taken away and almost every one had left the room, Pirotou loved a chat with any one who had remained behind; but these conversations were brief, for the proprietor or one of the guests would always cut them short, when Pirotou was wanted to do this or that. Nevertheless, he managed to give me a good deal of information on my very first evening in the hotel.

"Just imagine!" he exclaimed. "My brother is an army officer. It is remarkable, is it not? One brother to be an officer and another a waiter! Yet it is true enough; my brother——"

"Pirotou, the lady in No. 10 wants her luggage." "Pirotou, take up coffee to No. 5." "Pirotou, get out the bus immediately."

And the astonishing fellow would whip out of the room and with swift good temper carry out all these orders.

After a time I discovered that his brother was his only subject. He did not know much about him, but was very proud of him, and might even be said to worship him. Just as a farmer is always talking about the weather and the sunshine, Pirotou was always talking of the brother whose image ruled all his life. But it was a little perplexing that, after dropping the conversation at one point, he would take it up again at the same point on the following day, just as if we had never been separated.

"I fancy you would like to know how it happened?" he suddenly remarked to me one day.

I was at a loss to know what he was talking of, and said as much.

"I mean, how my brother came to be an army officer."

"Yes, indeed; how did it happen?"

"Near our village there was an old lady, very rich, whose son had died. My brother and I were orphans, and she took an interest in my brother, for he was a handsome boy and about the same age as her son who had died. She supported him at school in Paris, near her house, and then sent him to the army school at Saint-Cyr. A few months ago she died, and very sorry I was to hear it, because my brother——"

"Pirotou, where are you? There's a bell ringing!"

Next day Pirotou's story was continued.

"The old lady——" he said.

"Whom do you mean?" I inquired forgetfully.

"The old lady who looked after my brother," he replied, a little annoyed that I had not remembered. "When she died she left him a large sum, so that he has now a good income. It was a great comfort to me that he should have an income suitable to his rank, for I had been somewhat anxious about him."

"And what did she leave to you?" I asked.

"To me?" he exclaimed with astonishment. "Nothing to me, sir. It was all to my brother, who was of the same age as her boy."

"Does he come here to see you?" I said.

"Oh, yes, he came five or six years ago, when he was on furlough. The governor gave me four days' holiday, and we went together to our old village. Four days seemed a very short time to have with him, but our holiday did not even last four days. I was here again for the third night. My brother could not give me more than two days, after all, for he had been invited to two or three big houses. And I think, though he did not say so, that our old village bored him. Of course, it was to be only expected that it should bore him—an army officer ! "

" Does he do anything to help you ? " I inquired.

The question gave Pirotou vast amusement. " Help me, sir? Why, no, sir. He is not used to the kind of work I do."

" Of course I don't mean that," I said. " As he is well off, does he not send you money ? "

" Oh, no," said Pirotou ; " and if he did, I would not accept it. I have good wages, and gentlemen are very kind in the way of tips, and I have no expenses such as he has ; if you think of it, sir, you will see that I am as well off as he."

" And has he not visited you again ? "

This question made Pirotou somewhat uncomfortable. He answered shyly : " He has promised to come soon at the time of my marriage. I am going to be married, you understand."

" Indeed ? I congratulate you."

" Thank you, sir. I am sure I thank you. Yes, sir, it is time that we should be married. I shall soon be twenty-four years old, and the young woman belongs to this neighbourhood, and we have kept company for three years. We have not been able to see much of one another, all the same, as she is maid in a family in Paris who come down here for three months every summer. I can only see her every Sunday after mass ; so we shall both be glad to get married."

" I suppose you will then take up some other occupation ? " I suggested.

" Not as yet, sir ; not for a time. We have not saved enough yet to set up in business. With luck we may do that in five or six years. But when we are married, I am to have a place in the house where Louisette is engaged. Louisette, sir, that is her name. My brother is coming to the wedding," he continued with enthusiasm. " Everything will be very well done, sir, as it would need to be, he being an officer of the army ! "

" Pirotou, where are you ? Fetch the key of No. 50."

. . . .

Several months elapsed before I visited Avignon again, and then I was painfully struck by the change for the worse which had taken place in poor Pirotou. His manner was dull and dispirited, and he could hardly call up a smile when he greeted me. It was evident that he wished to speak to me, but as usual he was wanted on every hand, and the proprietor was always shouting: " Quickly, Pirotou! Quickly! "

Pirotou sprang to the call, but not with the joyous alertness of old days. I remembered how he used to toss the trunks about as if they were empty, but now they seemed to be filled with lead. I remained at the dining-table when every one else had left; my anxiety to hear about Pirotou's marriage surprised me. He joined me as soon as he was at liberty, but did not stand beside me with his old intimate manner. He stood before me looking very depressed, and I guessed what had happened.

" Did not your brother come to the wedding, after all? " I inquired.

" Oh, yes, sir, he came. But let me tell you all that happened. On the first day, I was sure that he would take a room here, at our hotel, so that I might spend the time with him when I was free. I was very sorry, sir, to hear that he had gone to the Hôtel St. Yves, at the other end of the city. And even then, he did not come to see me, but sent a note telling me to meet him at a café, and that I was to remember to take off my apron and put on a coat and hat. It was perhaps well that he reminded me to make myself tidy, because I was so anxious to see him that very likely I should have run down the town just as I was. When I got there he looked so handsome, and his uniform was so fine, that I felt very proud of him, and would have embraced him; but he only held out his hand, and asked whether I would take wine or absinthe. He spoke very kindly and explained matters to me. He gave me to understand that he could not come to see me, but that I could meet him there. He was anxious that people should not know he was in the town; for the fact is, sir, I had stupidly talked about him a great deal too much, and he did not want to exhibit himself like a show. It was all quite right, of course; he is an officer, after all. I asked him if he would not come once and see the governor here; that seemed to me natural; but he pointed out that this would put him in an awkward position; and, of course, I saw that he was right. But you will understand, sir, that it has made it a little uncomfortable for me, because my employer and all the others think I must have asked my brother not to come, and that I was ashamed of them."

"It was, indeed, uncomfortable for you," I said. "But how about the wedding, Pirotou?"

"I am coming to that, sir," he replied; "there is not much to tell about the wedding. At the café I told my brother about Louisette, and, of course, he wanted to see her. I said that she and her mistress would be at church next day, and he promised to meet me there. He came; and when Mme. Dalbert came in, followed by Louisette, I whispered to him who they were. "She is pretty, is she not?" I said; and he nodded. I saw, however, that his eyes never left Mme. Dalbert, and that when we left the church he still stood watching her, and at last went away without giving me an opportunity of introducing him to Louisette.

"Next day I met him again at the café, but this time he was accompanied by friends of his, officers whom he had met accidentally. When he saw me coming, he left them and came forward to meet me, knowing that I should be uncomfortable among these friends of his.

"'Did you say that Mme. Dalbert was the name of the lady where your Louisette lives?' he asked me; and when I said that was so, he continued: 'This is very awkward, very awkward! That you should be engaged to her maid! Whatever shall we do? These friends of mine are going to a shoot at Mme. Dalbert's and want to take me with them. You would not mind?'

"Of course I laughed at the idea that I should mind, and gave him a message for Louisette.

"Two days afterwards I met him again, but his manner had changed. I asked him about Louisette, but he explained that as he had gone there with these friends he could not speak to the maid. 'I said nothing about you, either,' he added; 'I am sure you will not misunderstand——'

"All this seemed very strange to me, but I said nothing, and he continued speaking while stroking his moustache.

"'Mme. Dalbert is a very charming woman,' he said.

"I did not reply; indeed, I had never noticed her, for my eyes had always been fastened on Louisette.

"'If this engagement of yours were broken off,' he inquired, 'should you feel it a great sacrifice?'

"I could only answer that we had waited three years for one another, and that both of us had desired nothing so much in the world as our marriage.

" He frowned and chewed his moustache, and I soon went back to my work. For one reason and another, I did not see him for a week afterwards, and then went up to his room at his hotel, a fine big room on the first floor. He was in a great state of excitement, and paced the room impatiently. At last he came to a stand before me, and said : ' Can I trust you ? Have you courage to bear it ? '

" ' What is it ? ' I asked anxiously, seeing as I did that something had happened, and wishing to be worthy of his trust.

" He turned his head away as he spoke. ' The fact is that I have fallen in love with Mme. Dalbert and have spoken to her, and she returns my love. But I am so, so sorry for you, old man,' he continued, laying his hands on my shoulders.

" ' Why should you be sorry for me ? '

" ' Great Heavens ! Surely you understand ? Now that we are engaged you cannot possibly marry her maid ! It would be too absurd, too humiliating, that you should come to our house as a servant.'

" I shivered with cold, and I think my face turned pale, for he seemed to relent, and said : ' Well, well, let us wait and see if something cannot be done ; perhaps the matter can be arranged—— ' "

Pirotou stopped abruptly in the midst of his story and two great tears stood in his eyes. He winked desperately to keep them from falling.

" What about the wedding ? " I said, after a pause.

" Well, sir, the fact is, there has been no wedding," he said, looking on the ground. " Perhaps there will never be a wedding. I try to be patient, but my brother never writes, and Louisette has not written for a long time. Perhaps they have persuaded her that it would not do. Perhaps they have forced her to give me up. I know nothing about it ; except that they are now in Paris.

" It was hard for me, sir, for we had loved one another so long and waited so patiently, but in his case it was just a fancy for a pretty face. But there was no way out of the difficulty. I could not humiliate my brother, you know. He is older than I am, and he is all that I have in the world. And then, sir, remember—he is an officer ! Still, it is very hard ! "

With these words, as the tears came again to his eyes, the unhappy Pirotou moved away to the window.

MARCEL PRÉVOST
B. 1862

A YOUNG GIRL'S DIARY

WHEN I was going up to my room, last Monday night, mamma kissed me, and said, in the severe tone which she reserves for communications touching my marriage: " Juliette, two gentlemen will dine with us Thursday. Consider it settled. You know what you must do."

I considered it settled, certainly; but mamma was mistaken in one thing—I was in absolute ignorance as to what was expected of me. What is expected between a Monday and a Thursday of a young girl who is to be inspected by two suitors for her hand? One cannot change one's face or figure, and there really isn't time to learn a new language, one of those tongues which possess, so mamma says, such a powerful attraction for marriageable men! Nor have I even the time to order a new gown. I have decided, therefore, to remain just as I am, and to present to those gentlemen on Thursday evening the Juliette of Monday, with her pink and white complexion, her five feet four of stature, and the two poor little living languages which she murders atrociously.

Who are these gentlemen? I have a faint suspicion. Mamma will not tell me their names, for she fears my preliminary criticisms. Usually I sit upon her candidates so thoroughly beforehand that she dares not exhibit them. " They are charming men," she declares; " charming, that expresses it. Much too good for a madcap like you. One of them is no longer young; but the other is not yet thirty." That mamma of mine has such an adorable way of putting things! She regards my suitors collectively, offsetting the faults of the one with the good qualities of the other. Would she like to have me marry all of them at once, I wonder?

Papa gave me more information. I do anything I choose with papa by a walk to the Champs Elysées in the morning, or a stroll on the boulevards about five o'clock. I walk along with my hands clasped around his right arm, clinging to him, my large grey eyes raised to his white beard as if in adoration. People nudge each other as we pass, and then how papa straightens up, and how happy he is! In these moments, if I were not a good girl, I could have my allowance doubled; or buy all the diamonds in the shop windows.

It was after one of these strolls that I questioned my dear old papa about the two musketeers who are to open fire next Thursday. Immediately he grew grave and answered:

"They are charming fellows—charming, that expresses it. Much too good for a——"

"Madcap like me. Agreed. Why do you let mamma put things into your head, you, who have such sound judgment? It is shameful!"

Now, nothing irritates papa so much as the discovery of mamma's exaggerated influence over him.

"Put things into my head! Put things into my head, indeed! I will not permit you to say that your mother put things into my head. I can judge men at a glance. The duke" (papa was a prefect under the Empire) "used always to say: 'Givernay—he is my hand and eye.' Do you know that, little one?"

I should think I did know the saying of the duke. At the age of three I had already heard it told so often in the family that I never said "papa" without immediately adding "hand," "eye."

"Why, papa dear, you know very well that I am of the duke's opinion, and that is the reason I want you to guide me a little with your experience. I am not a judge of me myself, and suppose both these gentlemen should please me next Thursday?"

Evidently this contingency had not been thought of. And, nevertheless, suppose I should be smitten with both of them, with the one who is no longer young, and with him who is not yet thirty? Papa's eye, celebrated by Morny, grew large and round. He looked thoughtful.

How amused I was!

"These two gentlemen," said he finally, "are certainly both capable of pleasing. However, I know one of them better, and therefore am disposed to favour him. He is a companion of the Imperial, Monsieur de Nivert, forty-three, cultured and high-spirited."

"What does he do?"

Papa wrinkled his brow and racked his brain in an endeavour to think what Monsieur de Nivert could possibly do; after which he concluded, pitiably enough:

"I believe he doesn't do anything!"

And then he immediately resorted to mamma's mode of defence; he considered the two collectively.

"But on the other hand," said he, "the other gentleman is a young man with a brilliant future. He is Judge of the Exchequer, and not yet thirty. Just think of it! Gaston Salandier will be director-general of a great administration some day, or a minister perhaps. And then he is very good-looking."

Poor Monsieur de Nivert! It seems after all that his most brilliant qualities are possessed by Monsieur Salandier! This freak of Dame Fortune begins to make me sympathetic.

"But," said I, after a few moments' reflection, "it seems to me that mamma was hesitating among four possible matches for me, and not between two."

Papa smiled.

"Yes; but after thoroughly considering the candidates, we have decided that two only are worthy of the prettiest girl in Paris. For," he added, kissing me, "you are the prettiest girl in Paris."

Poor papa, I wish I could have a husband like him. And just think how desperate mamma makes him!

Let us sum up the situation: Fate decrees that I shall become the wife of a serious young man, or of a middle-aged fashionable man of the world. Let me think a moment. No; I have never seen even the picture of the brilliant Judge of the Exchequer, who may, perhaps, be minister. But I think I noticed Baron de Nivert at a club entertainment. It seems to me that he has not much hair, but, by way of compensation, as mamma would say, he has a small stomach—oh, quite small. On the whole, he is not distasteful to me, for the baron, if I remember rightly, is very elegant and stylish in his dress.

Well, the die is cast! Idle nobleman or plebeian with a future, it is one of you two, gentlemen, who will wed—in January—Mademoiselle Juliette Givernay.

It is over. The presentation took place last night, and I must jot down the story of that memorable evening for the amusement of my old age.

Well, last night, at five minutes to eight, when my maid had assured me that all our guests had arrived, I made my appearance in the drawing-room. Entering a room is my strong point. I don't think I have often failed at it. I walk straight ahead, gazing steadily before me over the eyes of those present; I do not see, nor do I wish to see any of those who are looking at me. I choose, on the contrary, as a point of direction, some old lady settled comfortably in an armchair, or some inoffensive old friend of papa's, or simply mamma. Invariably all conversation ceases at once, and all eyes are centred on me. What wonderful tact I possess, and isn't it a pity to be compelled to exercise it in such a limited sphere?

Besides my parents, my suitors, and myself, the diners yesterday were Count and Countesse d'Aube, nobility of the Empire, whose combined ages would make a century and a half—insufferable bores, but fine people withal; Madame Salandier, the mother of the young Judge of the Exchequer, bourgeoise, with a protruding forehead, round eyes, and a ridiculous toilet, quite out of place in our society.

At table Monsieur de Nivert sat on mamma's right and Monsieur Salandier on her left. I found myself seated between Madame Salandier and Monsieur de Nivert. Madame Salandier immediately began talking to me in quite a patronising tone that quickly irritated me. She extolled the serious character of her son, whom she proudly called "my own." "My own" retires every night at ten. She also offered me a few cursory glimpses of the qualities she expected her future daughter-in-law to possess—her deportment, economy, and domestic habits—"with occasionally a reception or an evening at the theatre, of course; that is necessary in the position which 'my own' occupies."

In the meantime "my own," quite at his ease and stroking from time to time his pointed beard (he is really very handsome), was holding forth on the reduction of the public debt.

Papa, mamma, Monsieur d'Aube, Mademoiselle Espalier and even old Madame d'Aube, who is as deaf as a post, listened with open mouths, and Madame Salandier whispered in my ear:

"Listen to him. Not a minister is there that knows as much about it as he does——"

I looked at Monsieur de Nivert. He met my glance with one of discreet irony, and immediately we felt like comrades, two exiles from the same country who had fallen among barbarians.

Monsieur de Nivert is not handsome, but it is astonishing what an immense advantage he has gained over his rival by simply not saying a word about the public debt. In pouring me a glass of wine he paid me a neat compliment upon my gown, noticing that there was something really graceful and out of the common about it. And then we began to talk of "chiffons" in a low tone, while "my own" continued his harangue for the benefit of papa and mamma, who do not know how to add up the household accounts, and of Monsieur d'Aube, who is an old imbecile, and of Madame d'Aube, who is deaf. The handsome judge, however, is not stupid if he is pedantic. In a few moments he saw that he was boring us.

"This conversation," said he, "must be quite tiresome to Mademoiselle."

"Oh, no," I replied artlessly; "I was not listening."

And I had the joy of seeing a look of dismay spread over the countenances of my parents and the good Espalier, while Madame Salandier glared at me like a bonze who has just seen a street arab of Paris make a face at his Buddha.

Monsieur de Nivert smiled.

A little piqued, I think, "my own" replied:

"Indeed, such a conversation is beyond the depths of the young girls of our continent. In America they willingly take part in such discussions. Is there not some State in the North where women have the right to vote?"

"Do you hear, Juliette?" said mamma.

Did I hear? I should think I did! He wearied me, this economist bent on matrimony, and I let him see it very plainly. I took up the accusation of frivolity implied in his sentence, but I took it up as a banner. Proudly I declared my right—the right of a pretty woman, to be ignorant, frivolous, and whimsical. I argued the advantages of frivolity over seriousness, and of spirit and dash over dignity.

Oh, papa's expression and that of the two relics of the Empire and the mother of "my own"!

"My own" seemed perfectly amazed at discovering a young girl capable of giving him a retort that took the wind out of his sails.

Nivert alone encouraged me with smiles and whispered bravos.

The dinner ended in confusion.

In the drawing-room, in order to serve the coffee, I became a very proper young lady again; but the company had not regained its wonted composure. Madame Salandier could find nothing better to say than to ask:

"Isn't Mademoiselle Juliette going to play something for us?"

"Certainly," said mamma.

"Ah," thought I, "you want some music; well, then, you shall have it. Wait a moment."

I seated myself at the piano and played—and I played without stopping. I played everything that I could remember, for striking upon the little black and white keys soothed my nerves a little. Ah, you want some music! Well, listen. Take some Massenet, a little Mozart, some Serpette, some Wagner, and some Beethoven, some Lecocq, and some Berlioz, some Tchaikovsky, and some Nimporteki, one after another, haphazard, pell-mell; one hour and three-quarters at the piano without stopping. After which I turned round and looked at my auditors. They resembled a plantation after a hail-storm—they were simply annihilated. They took immediate advantage of the lull in the storm and fled. I was still caressing the keys with my right hand, and they trembled lest I should begin again. In a few minutes the drawing-room was empty.

Mamma came toward me:

"Will you tell me now, Mademoiselle——"

But I stopped her short.

"Listen, mother. You know that I am usually very amiable and seldom nervous, but this evening I am very nervous. Don't worry me, please. We will talk to-morrow as much as you like."

And I ran lightly up to my room.

This morning, on coming down to breakfast, I expected to find my parents with long faces, but oh, what a surprise! they smiled upon me, they kissed me, and were as sweet as could be.

The key to this mystery? It is this: papa rejoined the baron at the club last night about midnight, and Monsieur de Nivert said to him:

"My dear Givernay, your daughter is adorable! You will, I hope, permit me to call upon the ladies again as soon as possible."

But what is even more surprising is, that an hour before breakfast a letter came from Madame Salandier, in which that former chestnut vender declared that "her son had been deeply impressed by the wit and grace of Mademoiselle Juliette," etc., and finally asked if my mother could receive her on Monday to have a serious talk with her.

My friend Pepita was evidently right when she said:

"Little Juliette, there are two classes of men that you must trample upon in order to make them respect you—servants and suitors."

WOLF-SOLANGE

Marcel Prévost

THREE of us, with our packs on our shoulders and staff in hand, had tramped all the afternoon through the forest—that wonderful forest of Tronçais, covering half of Saint-Amand and half of Nevers. The little village of Vigne, nestling on the bank of the Cher, marked the end of our day's tramp, and having dined with our friend, a modest country doctor, we were seated at his door, peacefully smoking.

About us, over the blue forest that shut in the horizon, the darkness was slowly gathering. The flight of the swallows streaked the sky, and in a little tower that rose above the roofs of the village a clock was striking nine.

A woman, still young, dressed in a bright red flannel skirt and white blouse, came out of one of the houses near the doctor's, and went down to the river. On her left arm she carried a baby in long clothes, and with the right hand led a little boy, who himself had a still smaller boy by the hand. Arrived at the river brink, she seated herself on a large stone, and while the two little fellows undressed and ran into the water, splashing and shouting with laughter, she began nursing her latest born.

One of us, a painter, remarked, " There is a picture that would take in the *Salon*. She is well set-up, that young woman, and in a beautiful light ! And what a fine splotch of red that skirt makes against the blue background ! "

A voice behind us said, " Are you looking at Solange, Wolf-Solange, young men ? "

It was our host, detained a moment in his office by a patient, who now rejoined us.

And when we asked who this Solange, Wolf-Solange, was, and how she got her strange surname, he told us this story :

" Wolf-Solange, whose real name is Solange Grillet, *née* Tournier, was the prettiest girl in all the country of Tronçais ten years ago. To-day, the hard work of the country—and she has had five children—

has worn her out a bit, but in spite of her thirty years, she is still looking as you see her.

"At the time of the adventure to which she owes her surname, she was living with her parents, small farmers of Reiu-du-Bois, a few miles from here, near Lurcy-Lévy. Although poor, she was much sought after by the young men, even by the rich. But she paid no attention to their advances, except those of a certain Laurent Grillet, whom she had chosen, as a little girl, when the two of them tended their flocks in the pastures of Reiu-du-Bois.

"Laurent Grillet was a foundling, and his only fortune was his hands. Solange's parents had no notion of marrying their daughter to a poor man, especially when her hand had been sought by wealthy suitors. So they forbade Solange to see her friend. Of course the little girl met Laurent just as before. Living in the same neighbourhood, with the forest close at hand, they had every opportunity for meeting. When papa and mamma Tournier discovered that neither their scolding nor their schemes had any effect, they decided on a grand stroke. Solange was put out to service at Vigne, on the model farm of M. Roger-Duflos, our deputy.

"You suppose, perhaps, that our two lovers no longer saw each other on that account? Not a bit of it. They saw each other at night, instead of sleeping. As soon as it was dark, they both left the farms where they worked and walked toward each other by a cross cut shorter than the main road. Meeting, they stayed together until the first light of day in the sheltering forest.

"This was in 1879. The summer passed and the autumn. Then came winter. It was a terrible winter. The Cher was filled with ice and then froze over solid. The forest of Tronçais bent under its weight of snow like a heavily laden roof.

"All the roads became well-nigh impassable. The forest was deserted. Little by little, abandoned by men, it was reconquered by the beasts. And, a thing that has not happened since that terrible year, the wolves came.

"Yes, young gentlemen, wolves. They disturbed the outlying farms of Lurcy-Lévy and Vigne. They were even encountered in the streets of Saint-Bonnet-le-Desert, a wretched village close to the forest. It was necessary to organise bands to hunt them, and a price of fifty francs was placed on a wolf's head. I myself saw three, two of them huge fellows, prowling on the other side of the Cher, one morning when I went out in my buggy to see a patient at Saint-Amand.

" Neither the winter nor the wolves prevented Laurent and Solange from meeting each other. They continued their nightly expeditions in the face of a thousand dangers. It was the dead season in the country—the time when the peasants are no longer at work. Every evening Laurent left Lurcy-Lévy, his gun under his arm, and walked with a quiet step through the forest, all black and white. Solange, too, left Vigne about nine o'clock. They met a little way from here, near a clearing which cuts the forest road and is called *La Decouverte.*

" Well, one evening Laurent Grillet, on reaching the rendezvous, slipped and fell on the ice, breaking his right leg and spraining his right wrist. Solange tried to lift him, but she could not ; she could only drag him to a great elm and prop him up against it, wrapping her own cape about him.

" ' Wait for me here, my poor Laurent,' she said ; ' I'll run as fast as I can to Vigne to the doctor's, and he'll come and take you back in his buggy.'

" She started off, but had not more than passed the first turn in the road when she heard a gunshot and the cry, ' Come to me ! '

" She hurried back and found her friend trembling with pain and fear, his hand clutching his gun as it lay on the ground. She asked, ' What is it, Laurent ? Was it you that fired ? '

" He answered, ' Yes. I saw a creature with red eyes and a strong smell. He was big like a big dog. I am sure it was a wolf.'

" ' And you fired at him ? '

" ' No, I can't raise my gun on account of my arm. I fired along the ground to make him afraid. And you see, he's gone.'

" Solange thought a moment. ' Will he come back ? ' she asked.

" ' I am afraid he will,' replied the young man. ' You must stay here, Solange, or I shall be eaten by the creature.'

" ' Of course,' answered Solange, ' I'll stay. Give me the gun.'

" She took it, threw out the old cartridge and put in a new one. And they waited.

" An hour went by, or two ; perhaps more. The moon, still invisible, had risen above the horizon, because the sky at its zenith reflected a faint glow that grew every moment more intense. Laurent had fever ; he shivered and moaned. Solange, as she stood leaning against the tree, chilled through and through, began to feel drowsy.

"Suddenly a kind of snort, a growl, as of dogs surrounded, in the night, made her start. In the darkness, growing gradually brighter, she perceived two red eyes that looked at her. It was the wolf. Laurent tried to rise, to seize the gun, but the pain made him fall back with a cry.

"'Raise the gun, Solange,' he said. 'Don't shoot too quickly. Aim between the eyes.'

"She lifted the gun to her shoulder, aimed, and fired. But the recoil swerved the gun aside and the beast was unharmed. It disappeared, however, down the road. A little while after, they heard it howling in the distance and other howls answered it.

"The moon rose higher. Suddenly it passed above the dark mass of underbrush and lighted the whole forest as the lamp on a gate lights the road. And then Solange and Laurent saw a terrible sight: a gunshot away, five wolves were seated on their haunches like dogs, across the road, and another, more courageous, was slowly advancing.

"'Listen,' said Laurent to the girl. 'Aim at the nearest one. If you can bring him down the others will eat him and leave us in peace for the time.'

"The wolf kept advancing by short steps. Now his bloodshot eyes were clearly visible, the bones of his back and of his whole body, his dull coat, and the long tongue hanging out of his mouth.

"'Take a good aim at the hollow of his shoulder, and fire.'

"The report sounded. The beast leaped to one side and, without a cry, fell dead. The rest of the pack galloped off and disappeared in the underbrush.

"'Run quickly, Solange,' cried Laurent, 'and drag him as far from the road as you can. The others will be back in a little while.'

"She went, but he called her back.

"'You must cut off his head for the prize.'

"'You have a knife?' asked Solange.

"'Yes, in my belt.'

"It was a knife with a short handle and large blade—a hunting-knife. She took it, ran to the beast, and plunged it into his throat, the hot blood gushing over her hands, her clothing, her face even. She severed the head from the still quivering trunk, then dragged the body by one leg over the slippery snow as far away as she could, and came back with the shaggy, bleeding head.

"What Laurent had predicted came true. The wolves, at first

terrified by the death of their companion, were drawn back by the scent of blood. They returned, the whole five. By the light of the moon, the young people saw that terrible group coming nearer over the echoing snow, saw them leap on their fresh prey, pushing each other aside; saw them quarrelling over it, tearing it in pieces, devouring it, till there remained not so much as a tuft of hair, not so much as a single bone.

"Meantime, the boy began to suffer more than ever from his broken leg. Solange, whose strength was completely exhausted, struggled vainly against fatigue and drowsiness. Twice the gun she held fell from her hands. The wolves, having finished their repast, began to approach. The young girl fired one shot, then two into the pack, but her numbed fingers trembled so that she shot wild. At each report the pack turned tail, trotted off down the road a hundred yards or so, stopped a while, then came back.

"At last the poor children understood that it was all over; that they must die. Solange let go the gun. Not for one instant did she think of trying to save herself, of abandoning her wounded friend. She lay down beside him under the same mantle, she put her arms round him and laid her cheek against his, and both of them, their flesh chilled by the cold, their blood burning with fever, waited for death. Before their misty eyes rose strange pictures. They thought the sweet nights of summer had returned, when the forest, clad in its green robe, sheltered their peaceful meetings. Then, suddenly, the trees and bushes were stripped of their leaves and covered with a glistening mantle of snow and peopled with moving forms, red-eyed and open-jawed, that multiplied, that drew nearer, that were about to devour them.

"But, happily, neither Solange nor Laurent were destined to perish in this frightful way. Because Providence—I believe in it, young men—permitted that on that very morning I should return in my buggy from Saint-Bonnet-le-Desert, where I had been up all night with a sick patient. I had the reins, my servant had the gun and kept a sharp look-out down the road. Undoubtedly our bells alarmed the wolves, because we did not see one of them. But, in front of the elm at whose foot the two lovers were lying, my mare gave a start that attracted our attention. I jumped out and, with the aid of my servant, I got the poor children, numbed and unconscious, into the buggy. We wrapped them up as well as we could with all the rugs we had, and we brought also the bleeding head of the wolf.

"It was about seven o'clock in the morning when we got back to Vigne. The sun rose on a country of threaded glass and white velvet. The farm-hands of M. Roger-Duflos and half the people of the village, alarmed by Solange's disappearance, came to meet us. And it was in that great kitchen where we dined this evening, in front of a roaring beech-fire, that Laurent and his friend told us about their terrible night."

One of us asked, "And after that, doctor, were they married?"

"Yes," answered our host. "What had happened seemed to show the will of Providence so clearly that the least discerning were struck by it. After the adventure with the wolves Solange's parents consented to the marriage of their daughter to Laurent Grillet. The wedding took place in the spring, and the fifty francs' reward for the wolf went to pay for the bridal gown."

The story-teller ceased. Night had fallen. The sky of turquoise-blue with its first stars was reflected in the river. The masses of trees, ink-black and motionless, looked now like black mountains. We saw Solange, Wolf-Solange, dressing the two children and returning to her house, the baby asleep in her arms. She passed close to us and, in passing, smiled at the doctor, who smiled in return and said, "Good evening, Solange!"

PSYCHE

Marcel Prévost

LIKE a wounded animal seeking cover in its wonted haunts, Ludovic Ambrus fled from Paris to his estate at Hourquet, in the depths of the Gascon country, there to exchange his poignant grief for an anguish attended by the luxury of memories.

Wrapped at that time in the fogs of winter, Hourquet was the spot where he had passed his childhood, and where, two years earlier, he had brought his bride. He had returned thither with her the September previous, more a lover still than a husband. And now he came alone—Paris held his dead.

But the dead woman had left too many souvenirs in this honeymoon spot. Her sunshade and straw hat, relics of the summer, met his eyes in the vestibule; in the deep closets were hanging gowns, still fragrant with the perfume she had used. On the table lay a book, the place where she had closed it marked with an envelope bearing her name. A withered bouquet she had hung over a window-seat made one fear to open the window lest the flowers should shower down in dust.

Ludovic could not understand why these tokens of a vanished life did not cause the cruel heart-pangs that similar personal belongings, encountered in the apartment in Paris after Louisette's death, had given him. It almost seemed as if all the things Louisette had left at Hourquet suggested sleep rather than death. The Louisette of this place seemed still to be alive; she was only away and the things she had lately touched slept in her absence. By and by she would come back and all would awaken. She would come back. . . .

Ludovic was undergoing that crisis which follows all very painful separations. He would have given the remainder of his days to see his wife again, if only in a dream or a hallucination—even in aberration of mind. Every night he tried to evoke this dream by calling up the features, the dress, the gestures of Louisette. Alas! Sleep dissolved the beloved image. Ludovic would dream of morbid things; he would see himself wandering in a cemetery, talking with men in mourning garb; he would imagine himself composing answers to the letters of condolence from his friends. But the phantom of Louisette was persistently absent from these dreams.

"Is there not," thought Ludovic, "some way of compelling it? Has not modern science, with its power of causing slumber by powerful drugs, the faculty of conjuring up images during this artificial sleep?"

He asked this question of the only neighbour whom he ever admitted to his retreat—an old physician who no longer practised, and who occupied an unpretentious dwelling about two miles from Hourquet. Himself a widower of many years' standing, Dr. Séjour lived alone with his daughter, Martha, a beautiful and reserved woman of Junoesque appearance who, in spite of her twenty-seven years, did not appear to think of marrying. Intelligent but timid, the country doctor passed his life in ineffectual studies; for want of learning painfully arriving at results which, unknown to him, others had achieved before him.

"Friend," he replied to the question hesitatingly propounded by Ludovic, "do not give yourself up to the hope of a dream. I, too, experienced that haunting desire when, like you, I lost an adored wife. But, mark me, never have I seen her since her death. And if you have, as I believe, a healthy and well-balanced mind, you will never see your wife again. Believe me, it is better so. Let us do as the Scriptures tell us—leave the dead to bury their dead. Do not let us live in contradiction to Nature. Memory fades; time obliterates the images we call up. Let us be resigned to this. As for me, I have lived for my daughter and for my humble labours. You are not yet thirty years old; you will marry again and your life will readjust itself."

"Never!" replied Ludovic emphatically. His glance met the great black eyes of Martha Séjour. "I have a vague feeling," he said to himself, "that Martha, good and beautiful as she is, is not indifferent to me, that my sorrow interests her. But my whole being revolts at the idea of introducing her or any one, no matter whom, into the place which Louisette filled in my life."

He continued to yield himself up to the luxury of grief steeped in the memory of the dead woman. Although completely idle, he was not a prey to ennui. He meditated ceaselessly on sad themes. His days did not differ materially from his nights: the enervation experienced at night was deeper and less voluntary; that was all. He grew weaker physically, however, and observing this began to hope for death.

One night as he entered his sleeping-room to go to bed, with the lamp in his hand, he saw, the instant he opened the door, in the cheval-glass standing next to the window, the figure of his wife. Yes, for an instant Louisette was there, her image reflected clear and vague at the same time, in the half-light—Louisette, just as he had so often seen her last autumn, in a costume of some light material.

A second more and the image disappeared. The cheval-glass, when he approached it, gave back only his own reflection.

The apparition had not caused him the slightest fear. On the contrary, the presence which had at last benignantly appeared brought him serenity. He spoke to it, he thanked it, he begged it never to forsake him. He went to bed and slept peacefully. For the first time since coming to Hourquet he was unable to recall his dreams.

All the next day an impatient desire for the coming of night consumed him. Would he see Louisette again ? He had a strong premonition that he would. He went up to his room exactly at the same hour as the night before. He took the utmost pains to open the door with precisely the same movement, holding the lamp at the same angle. The shaft of light which entered the room by the open door reached the cheval-glass, revealing, as on the night before, the rapidly disappearing vision of the well-remembered light dress, the dear, smiling face of Louisette.

From that time the life of Ludovic Ambrus was concentrated on the moment of happiness accorded to him every evening by merciful fate. The days were insufferably long. He was like a lover who, having a rendezvous after sunset, could willingly insult the sun for still remaining above the horizon. The hours of anticipation were withering his heart ; he could no longer, as before, dream of Louisette in a sort of calm torpor. He went in search of distraction, to shorten the endless days. Spring drew near, and with it the labours of country life recommenced. He applied himself to working actively on his estate. He visited his neighbours, the doctor and Martha ; he received them at Hourquet. But while engaged in all these duties of real life, his soul was apart ; he really lived only in the ineffable moment when, every night, the face of the dead woman would smile at him from the dimly lighted mirror.

Spring came, and with it cool nights, warm days, and sharp showers, bringing the renewed youth of the earth. Ludovic became animated by a peculiar feeling. He experienced a passionate desire for that phantom which, up to now, had satisfied him simply by its fugitive apparition. He supplicated the dead woman as if she were a saint, a Madonna. He begged her to leave those regions whence she smiled, and, if only in a dream, brush lightly by him, let him touch her. Alas! again were the dreams inexorable. Louisette would not, even in a dream, vouchsafe him the kiss which he entreated. But she continued to appear every night, vivifying for an instant the lifeless mirror with her apparition.

The recluse of Hourquet wasted away. His neighbour, Séjour, expostulated with him.

"You must be insane to bury yourself in this manner with your grief. What a life for a man of your age! You will fall a victim to some nervous disease. Get away from here as quickly as possible; travel, get out of yourself."

Ludovic shook his head. "No, I am well here."

But he felt that Séjour was right; that in living only for a phantom he was slowly destroying himself. He was dying by inches of this longing; the endless repression was becoming unbearable. "And since I shall never love any woman except Louisette," he thought, "there is no remedy."

Towards the end of March the doctor and his daughter dined one day at Hourquet. Their host was seeing them to the front door when Martha found that she had forgotten a black lace fichu which she wore over her head and shoulders on the cool spring evenings. Ludovic went back to the drawing-room to fetch it. As he was long in returning, Martha went to help him find it, while Séjour lighted a cigar in the vestibule. For some minutes the fichu could not be found. Then Ludovic saw it on the rail of a chair where it had slipped half out of sight. He held it out to Martha. Was it she—was it he—or was it a force outside their own beings that threw them into one another's arms? Their lips met without having uttered a word. Forgetting all else, their lips still meeting in a long kiss, they were suddenly startled by a peculiar noise which caused them to draw apart. It sounded like the click of a ringed finger on glass.

"What was that noise?" murmured Martha.

"I do not know. . . ."

The voice of the doctor called: "Well, my children!" They joined him. Martha hid her flushed cheeks in the folds of the lace. Séjour pressed his host's hand. They departed.

Left alone, Ludovic locked and bolted the door behind them. The hour was at hand when it was his custom to go up to his room for the mysterious meeting. Anxious and uneasy, he awaited that hour, face to face with the lamp which glowed softly in the silence.

"Louisette will not come to-night," he thought. "I have been untrue to her. Oh, why did I do it?" He went slowly upstairs. With the accustomed movements, which he repeated each night like a religious ceremonial, he entered the room. The light of the lamp shone on the blank surface of the mirror. Was it true? Had Louisette fled?

He drew near to the cheval-glass. His own reflection confronted him, cut in two as by an iridescent blade.

Straight across it the mirror was traversed by a crack.

MADEMOISELLE HEUDIER'S HUSBAND

Marcel Prévost

I

I DON'T think I shall encumber this valley of tears much longer. There was only one interest in my life of an old maid, resigned, and, after all, happy enough, in spite of age and loneliness. Now this interest has gone ; it no longer exists, it never did exist ; it was a mistake. There remains my dog Moustache, my harmonium, and the preparation of my soul for eternity. . . . Hum ! it is pretty thin. If I were a young girl in some love trouble, I could at least find relief by writing my secret sorrows in a little copy-book prettily bound. . . . But one does not form new habits at forty-three.

I have loved and been loved from the age of fourteen till forty-three until yesterday at half-past two. Are there many professional beauties in Paris or London who could boast as much ? And never a quarrel nor infidelity, twenty-nine years of perfect love.

II

This is how it began.

My father was a humble Excise man, one of those who never attain a high post, because every time such a post is vacant another less timid or with more influence steps in. He vegetated all his life in the canton of Sarthe, where he had been appointed on his marriage, and where I was born and brought up.

It was there, at Givry, that I met " my husband "—his parents and mine and myself, we all called him that—little Lucien, who came and spent two months every vacation with his parents, our neighbours. He was the son of a Comptroller of Customs, a worthy man with a numerous family, who found it no easy matter to support on his poor pay a wife and five children. In comparison with the Letertes, my parents, with their small independent income and one child, seemed almost rich. My ready consent to the " marriage " with Lucien was therefore prompted by no interested motive ; besides, we were both fourteen—he was two months older than I. At that age money seems of little importance.

We were nice sweethearts, Lucien and I. . . . He was very timid and gentle; I did what I liked with him. I had made him believe he was my husband, and he accepted the situation.

To be my husband meant, between the ages of fourteen and eighteen, running at my heels like a little brother during his holidays. We kissed each other sometimes, which caused us about as much emotion as the knocks and slaps that we also exchanged. . . . (I begin to think, after forty-three years, that I must be of a cold nature; as for Lucien, until the time he left me, he was like a little girl, even more innocent than I.)

At eighteen we were parted. The Letertes, thanks to influence, had got an unexpectedly good post for Lucien. He went as travelling companion to a very rich Englishman, who, having spent his life travelling for business, now wished to travel for pleasure. He wanted a young Frenchman to keep him company, knowing that the conversation of the French is particularly charming and amusing. Lucien, in spite of the real sorrow he evinced in parting from me, seemed delighted with the idea of seeing the world. . . . Our plans for the future were not forgotten. "As soon as the old soap merchant (that was the Englishman—'Robinson's Soap') has given me enough money, I shall leave him and come back to you. . . ." How long would it take to make enough money? We were not sure, but evidently it would not be long, and our marriage seemed only an affair of months. I shared Lucien's enthusiasm, and there was laughter mingled with our tears when we bade farewell.

III

All that happened twenty-five years ago. Twenty-five years! It is long enough for an ordinary woman to found a family, and often to see another generation succeeding her own children. I had waited for marriage and family life for twenty-five years. I know if I confided this to any one they would not believe me; they would think me mad. All the same, it is the truth. For twenty-five years the only thing that has made life pleasant has been that I loved some one and that some one loved me. Fate has not been over kind to me. I lost my father, then my mother; the little money I had was reduced to half one day by the roguery of a lawyer; all the same I never lost hope, confident in the happiness that the future held for me. . . . Without having once in all those years seen Lucien ?

Yes, without having seen him again. I believed implicitly all that he wrote me, for during these twenty-five years I received letters regularly enough from Lucien, in which nothing gave the lie to our hopes of the future, and which all seemed to me stamped with the same affection that I put in mine. He was seeing the world during those years, my little Lucien : Egypt, North Africa, Russia, India, America—he travelled widely in company with " Robinson's Soap." . . . Now and then he passed through France, but so quickly, so hurriedly, that he never had the necessary twenty-four hours to spare to come to Givry and see " his wife." His wife, that is what he always called me in his letters. And I replied, " My dear husband."

IV

Yesterday, about two o'clock, when I was practising on the harmonium some music that I was going to play next Sunday, my little maid came and told me that a lady had called to see me. It was an old friend of my parents who had become a fairly important person in the scholastic world—general inspector of primary schools, I think. She had come back to Givry very well pleased to show her success to those who had known her as a young girl. We talked about half an hour, recalling in turn all our old acquaintances. At last she said to me :

" And Monsieur Leterte, do you keep in touch with him ? "

" Lucien Leterte ? "

" Yes ; the one who is married in England, in Derbyshire ? "

I managed to answer : " No, I have lost sight of him . . ." and I asked more details. She gave them to me readily.

Having been sent to England recently to study the organisation of the Board Schools, she had spent some days in the manufacturing districts. And whom had she met at Derby in the manufactory of "Robinson's Soap" but "my husband," Lucien Leterte, old Robinson's heir, married, and the father of three children. . . .

V

When I found myself alone I wept a little, then I laughed at myself for being such a fool as to think that any man could remain faithful to a memory for twenty-five years. It is true that I had given to this very memory all my youth and a certain beauty that might have found me a husband, perhaps. . . . I began to write in this tone to Lucien, reproaching him especially for the useless deceit of his letters. Then I began to think. Thanks to this deceit I have spent twenty-five almost happy years. I have been married for twenty-five years. What would those years have been without the illusion that Lucien has given me? Perhaps he understood that himself. That is what kept him from saying nine years ago when he married: "My poor Adèle, you must not think of me any longer. . . ."

So, courage!—and no more tears. For twenty-five years I have believed myself married; to-day I am widowed or divorced, that is all. And then . . . when I think of it, he has three children. If I were to write him a nice affectionate letter and ask him to send me one of them, one that I could bring up here, less luxuriously, perhaps, than in England, but as a little Frenchman, speaking the same language his father spoke when he was in love with me? Surely Lucien will not refuse me that, and to bring up this little one will perhaps help me to follow with patience the road that leads from my house to the cemetery. . . .

I am quite cheered at the idea of it. Come along, foolish old Adèle Heudier, take your glasses and your best pen and write to the heir of "Robinson's Soap."

A little courage and goodwill is all that is necessary to overcome cruel fate. You will be a mother as you have been a wife—in imagination.

THE BEGGAR CHILD

Marcel Prévost

It is a little story, very slight and delicate, so slight, indeed, so delicate, that I am afraid the very act of putting it into words on paper may destroy its fragile grace, its faint perfume. Why, then, when it was told us one evening in the midst of the complex luxury of a modern dinner, by the charming woman who is its heroine —why did it make upon us all so lasting an impression that it has become, in this corner of the Parisian world, one of those classic stories which are the inheritance of each group of society and to which an allusion is always understood and welcomed? Perhaps because it was like a ray of light shed for a moment on our frivolity and cheapness; perhaps because, just as a movement, a gesture is sometimes enough to reveal the whole of a beautiful form, so, too, sometimes it only needs a few sincere words to lay bare the whole of a pure heart.

We had been speaking of the mysterious impulses, already classified and named by science, from which so few people are exempt. These mysterious forces compel one man to count the flowers on the wall-paper, the volumes in a bookcase, everything he sees that can be counted. They impel another to set himself the task, as he walks along the street, of reaching a particular lamp-post before the cab coming up behind overtakes him, or, if a clock is striking, before the last stroke has sounded. They make still another go through a set round each night before retiring, arranging certain objects, and examining certain pictures and boxes. They are the slight maladies of our modern brains, germs of monomania and madness transmitted from one generation to another, until they finally become a part of human nature itself.

We were all confessing our weaknesses, our absurd superstitions, reassured by the confessions of the others, charmed to find them like ourselves, or even worse than ourselves. But one young woman had said nothing. She listened to us, a little surprise on her beautiful face, framed in its set bands of dark hair. Some one asked her:

"And you, madame, are you exempt from our modern aberrations? Haven't you the least little peculiarity to avow?"

She seemed to be searching diligently in her memory.

"No." She shook her head. "No!"

And we felt that she spoke the truth, for everything that we saw and knew of her, her gentle poise, her spotless name, set her apart from the worldly dolls who had just confessed their shortcomings. But evidently her modesty took fright at claiming an immunity so complete, when all those about her were confessing their troubles. She changed her mind:

"Really, I'm afraid I can't say that I am in the habit of counting the cabs, or that I look through my boxes every night before going to bed. But still, the other day I had an experience that seems quite like what you have described—if I understood you—a sort of impulse from within, a force that peremptorily commanded me to do a certain trifling thing, as if it had been a matter of life and death."

We asked for the story, and she told it with a charming air of excusing herself for occupying the general attention with so unimportant an experience.

"This is what happened, in a few words. It was five or six days ago, and I had gone out with my little daughter Suzon. She is eight years old, you know. I was taking her to her lecture, for, if you please, the little lady already attends lectures. The day was so fine that we decided to walk along the Champs Elysées and the boulevards to our destination, a house in the Rue Laffitte. We were going merrily along, chatting together, when a cripple, a mere boy, dragged himself in front of us and held out his hand without saying a word. I had my sunshade in one hand and was holding my gown in the other, and I confess I didn't want the bother of stopping and looking for my purse. So I went on without giving to the beggar.

"We continued our walk down the Champs Elysées, Suzon and I. The little one had suddenly stopped talking, and I, too, without knowing very clearly why, no longer had anything to say. We reached the Place de la Concorde without having exchanged a word since our meeting with the beggar. Little by little I felt growing up in my heart a sort of uneasiness, the feeling of having done an irreparable mischief, and of being menaced, on account of it, by some vague danger in the future. I always try to look squarely at what I have done; so as I walked I searched my conscience.

"'I, certainly, have not committed a very grave fault against charity,' I said to myself, 'in not giving to this beggar. I have never pretended to give to every one that I meet. I shall be more generous to the next, and that ends it.'

"But all my arguments failed to convince me, and my distress increased, became a sort of agony. Time and again I was on the point of turning round and going back to the place where we had met the child ; but, if you will believe it, a sort of false pride kept me from doing so in the presence of my daughter. We have sunk pretty low when we hesitate to do right because of what others may think of us !

" We were almost at the end of our walk, and had just turned the corner of the Rue Laffitte, when Suzon touched me gently on the hand to attract my attention.

" ' Mamma ! ' said she.

" ' What is it, baby girl ? '

" She raised her big blue eyes to my face and said gravely :

" ' Mamma, why didn't you give to that poor beggar in the Champs Elysées ? '

" Like myself, she had thought of nothing else since our meeting ; her heart was oppressed as mine was ; only, being better than her mother and more sincere, she confessed her trouble quite simply.

" I did not hesitate a moment. ' You are right, dear,' I said to her.

" We had walked more rapidly than usual under the obsession of our fixed idea, so we had still twenty minutes before the time set for the lecture. I called a fiacre, got in with Suzon, and the driver started toward the Champs Elysées, roused to his best speed by the promise of a generous tip. Suzon and I held each other by the hand, and I can assure you that we still felt very uneasy. What if the crippled boy had gone ? What if we could not find him again ?

" Arriving at the corner where we had passed him, we jumped out of the fiacre and looked up and down the avenue. Not a sign of the poor little fellow ! We questioned a woman who hires out chairs near by. She remembered seeing the boy. He was not, she said, one of the usual beggars at that corner. She did not know in which direction he had gone. Our time was short, and we were just about to give up in despair, when all of a sudden Suzon spied the little cripple, squatting under a tree, fast asleep, with his hat between his knees. Suzon went to him on tiptoe, and slipped a small gold piece in the empty hat ; then we returned to the Rue Laffitte. I know well enough it was absurd, but we hugged each other as if we had escaped a grave peril."

The young woman ceased speaking, covered with blushes to have talked so long of herself with everybody listening. And we, who had heard her reverently, felt as if we had breathed a purer air, had drunk from a stream of fresh water at its very source.

GEORGES D'ESPARBÈS

B. 1863

THE BUTTERFLY

THERE was unusual gaiety in the little dwelling. Aline had never laughed so gleefully as on that morning.

"I can't understand you!" her grandmother complained indignantly. "How can you be so frivolous only an hour before the competition?"

Aline only laughed the more. "Oh, Granny, Granny, you surely don't want me to go before the gentlemen with a face as long as yours! And, dear, just think what Queen Rose would say, the rose that we are all to paint, if I looked glum and solemn!"

There was nothing solemn or gloomy about Aline! Her hair shone like silk threads in the sun, her mouth was adorable in every mood, her brown eyes shone with youth and almost seemed to tinkle like little bells, their glances ringing music in the hearts around. In a word, Aline was a darling, dear to every one in the little Gascon town, where she taught painting to a class of schoolgirls. It was an old, shabby little town, and it wore Aline as an old coat is brightened up by some sweet spring flower. And Aline was as clever as she was pretty.

The competition for which she was entered had been founded by an obscure painter lately dead. His bequest provided an annual prize of 3000 francs to be competed for by youths and girls between the ages of fifteen and twenty-five, and the subjects chosen were to be landscape or still life, flower or fruit. Thus the good man had made sure that his name should ever be held in pleasant memory. This was the first year of the competition; a great man had come down from Paris to preside; and notices had been sent to every village in the county calling the young painters to come up. The town was keenly interested. "Fifty artists," they said, "coming to paint one little rose! Poor little rose!"

But Granny went on complaining. "I never felt being poor so much before!" she said. "Ah, if your poor, dear father had not been so fond of his dinner and his wine, you would have had at least enough to pay for a Sunday frock. But you keep dancing about there! Do stand still till I get a look at you! Deary me! Yes, there's something on my bonnet that will do for your hat!"

She trotted with her tiny steps into her bedroom, and Aline's hat was soon the brighter for a tulle rosette—a lovely little rosette fit for a fairy's cradle. "Now, what about your frock? Turn round. That's better! Now walk a little. It is badly creased here; wait while I smooth it. Now put out your foot. There; that will have to do." The girl still crowed with glee.

"Your shoes and stockings are all right. Don't laugh, you silly child. Be quiet! You get on my nerves! The competition is a serious affair; but you—you are as pert as a sparrow!"

The old lady's quaintness upset Aline again. "You might have stepped out of one of the old masters, you old darling!" she said. "But don't be afraid; I shall not laugh up at the hall; I shall put on my best smile!"

"How many kinds have you?"

"Two at least, Granny; one for home and one for company!"

"You ridiculous mite," said Granny, "whoever taught you——" But the cathedral bell boomed through the noonday air, and the fragile old woman raised her arms aloft. "The clock has struck," she cried, "and you are not ready! Your easel, brushes, box of paints; are you sure you have everything? What it is to have to think for two! Have you got everything?" And she sank excitedly on the sofa. "A kiss, sweetheart!" she said.

The sun without was calling Aline. The girl gathered up her things, and drew down her veil over firm lips which seemed to say, "These judges shall see what I can do!" In a moment the grandmother was alone, a pathetic, dispirited figure.

"After all," she said, "a rose cannot be so hard to paint! If only Aline could tell the flower how lovingly we care for our own flowers here in the garden, it would surely do everything it could to help her. How noble it would be of that rose to save her and me!" Alas, Granny spoke none too strongly; "save" was exactly the word. And then the 3000 francs would be only the beginning; the prize would lead to all kinds of honours. Aline, first among women painters of all the countryside; pupils thronging to the bright flowery studio—Oh, this prize would be far more than a fortune; it would mean a future!

Crouching in a corner of the sofa, with her hands clasped on her knees, the old lady murmured her dreams all through the drowsy afternoon. "Will to-day," she asked, "be the turn of our fortune? Will to-day repay me for taking to the peasant life and putting on this black apron and these clumsy shoes? How young I was when I lost family and fortune, never to dance or hunt any more, nor wear pearls, nor even taste sweets! And for ten long years my darling fairy and I have eaten nothing but scraps of bread!" The wrinkled lips moved feebly and Madame de Colainville almost slept, then muttered again: "And then one day she wanted to teach painting. Aha, I drew the line at that! Fancy a de Colainville earning her bread! And she—what did she say, the minx? 'Times are changed, Gran,' she said; 'the king is dead. We are just common people, you and I. Let me work like all the rest.' I had to give way to her. And how she has worked! Surely those judges must give her the prize: she is so good, so good." And then Madame slept till her darling's return.

In the evening Aline could not hide her anxiety; and when the old lady pressed her: "I have no chance," she said. "The model was a great, lovely Gloire-de-Dijon, a perfect flower; and I am sure my work was true; it looked a sweet little study. But the judge passed me three times without stopping to look, though he often stopped behind others of us. He seemed specially struck with No. 34. I was No. 9. I could have cried."

"Don't be silly, No. 9," said her grandmother sharply; "come and have supper. We may be poor, but there is a special supper for to-night. Your judge is a stupid. I should like to give him a bit of my mind!"

"Ah, but he was not the only one," Aline continued with troubled voice, while a tear hung on her lashes. "Other judges passed and they did not stop either. I hate No. 9! I hate her! She can't paint a bit!"

"Now, girlie, have some custard. I have no doubt at all that any king would delight in your rose, No. 9. You will have the first prize; don't fear. Our 3000 francs will buy food for a year! We shall be rich; oh, so rich! And you will live long and happy in the dear old place where you were born. Stop crying, Aline; stop it, I say! I never was so angry in my life! Judges fit to judge turnips, not paintings! What are their precious names?"

"Monsieur Duran is the chief; but he is too big a man, and is not likely to come. Then there are President Baconel, Monsieur de Saint-Felu, Monsieur Prades the florist, and Monsieur Lambeye the land-agent. I don't know the others; there are more."

"I have a good mind to go and see them this minute!"

"Ah, don't! Please, don't! They will meet to-morrow to settle who is to have the prize."

"Mark my words: you will get it!"

"No such luck for me. I know very well what will gain it—a sickly, washed-out rose, done by a pretty blonde girl third from me on my left. It seemed to fascinate the judges; I heard Monsieur de Saint-Felu congratulating her."

"Poor child!" said Granny. "Your silly little head is full of nonsense; nothing but talk, talk, worry, worry. To-morrow Monsieur de Saint-Felu will choose No. 9. There is the moon above the elm; little girls should be in bed."

Next day at ten, in a great bright room, the judges gathered before the fifty studies of the rose. They eliminated the worst, and it was not long before fifteen canvases were set aside as hopeless. Then twenty others, neither very good nor very bad, shared their fate. From the fifteen which remained, the judges chose first seven, and then from the seven, three. Between these it was indeed difficult to choose.

"For my part," said the land-agent, "I am quite sure that the greatest of our painters, if he were here with us, would vote for No. 22."

"It is weak in drawing," said President Baconel. "On the other hand, this very excellent No. 9 is too gloomy, too heavy. Perhaps I should rather say it is too simple and natural. It lacks something. Now, this No. 18 is a picture. I vote for No. 18."

The gardener and florist, with a peasant's diffidence, had no remarks to offer. Bending forward, with his great gnarled hands resting on his knees, he studied the three roses with breathless attention.

"The fact is," exclaimed Monsieur de Saint-Felu at last, "that all three are quite charming. In my opinion we ought to split the prize. Give no first prize; but, instead, give two seconds and one third. That is my view."

At that very moment a little white butterfly fluttered in at an open window, darted about above the heads of these elderly gentlemen, alighted on one of the roses, and caught its feet in the wet paint.

The gardener stood erect at once. "No. 9 has won!" he cried.

So No. 9 won the great prize; no one could question the butterfly's choice. Granny, all joy and pride when she heard it, clapped her hands and sang that a butterfly had brought to Aline fame and a fortune. The young painter tried to free her benefactor, but found him dead. Mounted in a bracelet-medallion, he still hovers on the wrist of Mademoiselle de Colainville; and when she paints, she gently invokes his aid.

LÉON EUGENIE FRAPIÉ

B. 1863

"THE MISSUS"

WHENEVER Dubour mentioned " the missus," every one in the office shook with suppressed laughter, for his large clean-shaven face took on such a ludicrous expression of obedience, compunction, and respect. How touchingly submissive that big man must be at home! He was generally known as " the good little boy." Not that the others were all masters at home! Oh, no! Vanard, for instance, had to light the fires because the maid used too much wood and madame could not think of spoiling her hands; and Bijou was forbidden to smoke, as snuff was much more economical. But once away from the domestic tyrant, none but Dubour maintained that attitude of respectful obedience, not one adhered so religiously to the home regulations. Dubour's housewife evidently made him regard her as infallible, and certainly held him well in hand. No wonder he was in such good health; not the slightest excess, not the smallest caprice did she allow him. Sometimes at luncheon he would sigh: " I have too much meat, but I would rather force myself to finish it; the missus knows better than I what I should eat, and she would scold if I left any."

Before going home in the evening he was often pressed to come and have a drink, simply for the pleasure of hearing his frightened refusal: " Oh, no, thank you, I can't; it is impossible. I am expected. I must not be late."

It was evident that, office work excepted, he did nothing without the approval and consent of his petticoated government. If, for instance, a subscription list happened to be brought round, for a funeral wreath or a presentation, he asked for it again the next day; then he always gave generously, but it was clear that the amount had first to be discussed with " the missus."

Dubour was no talker. Little was known about him and speculation was difficult, for he had entered the service late in life, after several unsuccessful attempts at business. At the end of two years the most inquisitive had extracted only a few bare allusions to his failure and to family sorrows ; details as to the awe-inspiring missus were entirely wanting, so that chatterers had to content themselves with feeble jokes, such as, " She must have a moustache," or, " Surely she is always armed with a poker."

Although holding merely a modest post in a government office, Dubour was always well, even fashionably dressed. This proof that he must still have a remnant of his former fortune added to the consideration which his forty years compelled. Moreover, his never-failing kindness and willingness to oblige had made him justly popular. But he was really too much " the good little boy."

It was partly owing to the affection his colleagues felt for him that they concocted the plot to make him late, and thus disobedient to the commands of his dreaded missus. They wanted to break through his ridiculous submission, and felt convinced that it only needed one determined effort to shake off the yoke. The cleverest attempts had failed one after another ; but at last Leflot proposed a sure plan for his birthday.

On that evening, five minutes before the office closed, Dubour's colleagues pressed round him with such beautiful flowers and such hearty good wishes that only a boor or a coward could have run away on the plea that it was time to go home. At the same moment Leflot ran out shouting : " I will just send a wire to your home," and gave no time for objection. Then bottles of champagne were brought out of a kit-bag and glasses were set out on the table.

" Silence," some one cried, " silence ! What has Leflot to say ? "

That conspirator, who had only pretended to run to the telegraph office, reported; " That's all right ! Your people will have the message in a minute or two ! "

Reassured on this point, and touched, flattered; and dazed by the many speeches and incessant handshaking, Dubour drank several glasses of champagne, and before he knew where he was, had become more than a little merry. Unprotesting, he accompanied his gay comrades to the restaurant and joined them at a dinner in his honour. There, as the hours fleeted past, the company nodded and grinned with glee. What a dressing-down poor old Dubour was in for ! And worse than the late hours was the fact that he had spent ten francs of his salary ; for every penny of it went every week to the missus.

Near midnight came the question how this good little lad was to be taken home. No one wanted to carry the joke too far, and every one felt that a reporter must go to witness the rage of the domestic tyrant. Yet it was difficult to find any one ready to take the risk ; for doubtless the virago would be waiting with a broomstick, and whoever should accompany Dubour might easily come in for some of its blows.

There was long and furtive discussion on this point, and at last Leflot was forced to volunteer. After all, he carried with him authority, logic, and strength, for he was at once head clerk of the office, a trained lawyer, and had formerly held the amateur championship in fencing.

The unlucky Dubour was perfectly helpless. The gorgeous bouquet dangled from his neck by a string ; a card bearing the legend " Leave till midnight " was pinned conspicuously to his coat ; the ends of his tie floated in the breeze, and fragments of song issued from his wavering voice. Leflot, still fairly sober, led his victim by the arm.

At last they arrived, and Leflot was struck dumb with astonishment. Dubour had stopped before a poverty-stricken tenement of flats, and the glimmer of the matches which they struck showed a steep, narrow, ill-tended staircase.

Dubour was instantly seized with his inveterate instinct of submission. He whispered " Hush ! " at every step, and muttered, " I'll slip into my room and shut the door ; the missus won't see me at all. Here we are ! "

The door of the flat was ajar and a narrow gleam of light came through. After a moment's hesitation Leflot, conscious of his standing at the office and other qualifications, stepped confidently in. There was no lobby ; he found himself at once in the dining-room.

O surprise of surprises ! Here, too, was to have been celebrated this happy festival, but the missus, worn out with waiting, slept in a chair beside the feast which she had prepared in vain. On a round table, covered with oilcloth, was a leg of mutton now quite cold. One place showed that a child had supped ; the other two, quite undisturbed, proved that the missus had gone without her dinner. Before one of these there stood a little bunch of wallflower in a glass, and a new pipe. How sweet, humble, homely a life stood revealed at a glance !

And the missus ? Dubour's little girl ; no more than twelve years old, yet a perfect housewife, with this serious little face, neat dress and blue apron. She woke as in a dream, yet seemed to grasp at once the whole pitiable story. Her first thought was one of courtesy to her guest.

" Please sit down," she said. And then, anxiously, to her father, " Have you dined, Daddy ? " Then a loving kiss, and one more from the little brother who had at last been put to bed and had sobbed himself to sleep, at not having been able to say the little verses he had learned for Daddy's birthday.

Dubour had taken his easy chair, and in spite of the fumes of wine, showed vast satisfaction in being home again. Sitting near, Leflot tried to construct a plausible explanation.

" I am sure you will understand," he said to the waiting child, " that this irregularity of to-night is due to an old custom of ours at the office. It is an old custom from which none of us can escape. I can assure you," he continued, glancing doubtfully at Dubour, " that he has—there has been nothing—nothing excessive." And so he stumbled on, hardly knowing what he said ; only conscious that all his special pleading was lost on the grave little maid before him.

Ah, but he was touched ! All these so-loving preparations had been wasted ; all this happy anticipation had been rudely shattered and changed to a solitary, anxious vigil. All the time, while he spoke those measured phrases in which he was so expert, his eyes were on the little gift bought with money saved, penny by penny, where every coin meant another self-denial, the little gift at which for weeks past she had gazed in the shop windows. Then he studied this mistress of the house, whom they had pictured as a termagant, and saw in her a child who ought to have been playing with dolls, but with rare devotion preferred this brand-new pipe to any toy. She was slight, with transparent complexion of a delicate flush ; her fair hair was done up in a tight little knot ; there she stood in the homely frock, smiling kindly to him, and apparently accepting the " custom of the office " and the " nothing excessive.". " Of course, monsieur," she said, " what must be, must be ; and Father isn't more tired than usual."

And all the time, while listening to the stranger and approving what he said, the missus was at work so quietly that it was hardly noticed. She seated her father more comfortably, gave him a cup of cold coffee, arranged his tie, and removed the flowers from his neck and the hateful card from his coat. Not one proof of the excesses which she so indulgently denied escaped her.

Seeing all this, Leflot was struck with a kind of fear. The child's gentle, simple mind was quite ready to agree with his argument.

"Certainly, monsieur, you are quite right." But there was also in her mind another faculty, though inarticulate, which judged matters from a higher standpoint. There was that clear calm vision of the housewife, which assures the well-being, security, and regularity of every family ; the directing love which watches and repairs and cares for all ; that recall to wisdom and temperance to which even the strongest and most favoured at times must listen. Without this strict and loving protection who can live ?

The dainty, kindly little housekeeper came downstairs with Leflot, to light his way ; serious, calm, and reserved, she thought of everything, without a trace of ostentation. " I beg your pardon," she said, " the lining of your pocket is pulled out ; you might lose your purse. Take care, there is one more step. At the end of the street you will get a bus ; it's not yet half-past twelve."

When the heavy door had closed behind him Leflot, the head clerk, lawyer, and fencing champion, still stood there gazing at the house with a sad and tender smile. He was conscious that he himself was only " a little boy."

A SIMPLE SOUL

LÉON EUGENIE FRAPIÉ

WHAT do I want, sir? I beg your pardon, sir. I'm his mother, sir. Yes, sir, his mother. Mother of my boy; him as was shot by mistake.

I beg your pardon, gentlemen, I'm a little hard of hearing. Were they sorry for it? Oh dear, yes, sir, yes indeed. They couldn't understand how it could have happened, and begged my pardon, and said that no such thing should ever occur again. Oh, they were very kind indeed, most kind and considerate they were. Terrible upset they were and said there should be handsome compensation.

Don't you remember about it, sir? It was this way, gentlemen. If I may make so bold, sir, do you mind if I sit down? I'm that tired, having been on my feet since nine, and running this way and that over half the town. I went to the police station down our way, and they sent me to the head office, and a gentleman there told me to try the solicitor in charge of the case. I forget his name, but he wrote it down, and his clerk—the gentleman was busy—told me to apply to the magistrate, and there the officer said I ought to come here, gentlemen. What with walking, and missing my way, and buses, I have been half over the town. But if you're in a hurry it is quicker to walk than to take those buses, especially when the heart is sad.

The accident? Yes, sir, I'm coming to that. There were burglars who had broken into a house, the family being away, and the police were on the look-out for them, and had an idea, the burglars not being in the house, that they had got away by the roofs; and as I say, they were on the look-out for them all down the street. It was a Saturday afternoon, a fine day of sunshine it was, and my Henry, being a slater by trade, was doing a job on one of the roofs, and the police, thinking the burglars were on the roof and seeing them, though indeed I was told in the following week that they hadn't seen any one but just fired to scare them, and so my Henry got the bullet through his head.

You may well say so, sir; it was terrible indeed. When they

brought him home to me he still had the bit of lilac in his coat. Oh, it was a sad, sad day!

He was a good boy, was Henry. Always lived with me and hardly ever went out in the evenings, and was as handy as a woman about the house. And then came this dreadful accident; it was just the week after I finished a new dress, black with red spots, to please him.

Oh, yes, every one was very kind in my trouble. One gentleman wrote out a petition for me, and it was sent in, and after a time a messenger came and took me to the President himself. Ah, he's a kind good man! Directly I went in at the door of his room he got up, and as soon as I began to speak he said: "Dear lady, I know everything, and I promise you that everything shall be done for you. You shall have a life-pension." Those were his very words. Only, he said that I must give the Government time. I was not in his room more than a minute. And since then I have waited, waited; it is almost a year now!

But how I have been worried about the boy's death ever since, gentlemen, you would never believe! Called to one enquiry after another, questioned this and questioned that! They were set on showing that the police must not shoot innocent boys, and set on finding out who were guilty.

Well, four weeks ago they found them out, Victor and another, and sent them off to gaol.

Victor has the heaviest sentence of the two; and begging your pardon, gentlemen, I have come to see you about him. They say you can do something—— It being our trouble and me being the mother I must ask you, gentlemen—— Every one in our street knows that the President was good enough to say, "Why, certainly, my good woman, you shall have all you want!" They all know me; I have lived there for upwards of forty years; and in these last months they have all been so kind! They nod so friendly when I go down the street, and the shopkeepers behave as if I was a lady almost, as if I was rich. Well, so I am, when the President has promised!

But Victor's friend—she is called his wife—came to me and asked if I could do anything. And I thought and thought, but could not see how I could help them——

Gentlemen, please let me make an exchange. Only an exchange. If you can do it, please let me not have the pension which the President promised, but let Victor have a pardon instead!

I'm a useless old woman, anyway. I am over sixty—so old that I need hardly anything. Money ? What should I do with money ? I do very well as I am, with three hours' work in the morning and five in the afternoon, at threepence an hour. And sometimes a special job like a dinner, with plates and dishes to wash until midnight, and extra pay. Don't you see that I have everything I need ? Besides, I am getting old and stiff, and if I should stop work I should soon not be able to do anything at all.

I'm not saying, gentlemen, that the people in our street will be quite as respectful when they find out that I shall have no pension ; but there, no one ever paid much attention to me before, anyway.

And Victor, he's not a bad man. It was only his carelessness. He was never in trouble before. And he told the truth in court ; he didn't lie like the others ; that is why he came off worst. He is sorry about it, truly sorry. Then he has promised to marry the girl as soon as he comes out. She has a baby girl now ; and Victor is just as old as my poor boy would be ; and I sometimes think that when they are married they may look in on me sometimes. There isn't a living soul to care for me.

Are you going away, gentlemen ? Office hours over ? I must ask your pardon for taking up your time so long. I have been on my feet since nine this morning and had no idea of the time.

You took notes, then ? On everything I said ? And you will really do your best ? I shall not need to come back, then, but only wait ? How can I thank you for your goodness ? Thank you very, very truly.

That door, do you say, sir ? I came through so many doors and passages that I am confused ; and my eyes, too, are getting weak.

You, sir, are the clerk here, are you not ? Now, please remind the gentlemen sometimes, so that they will not take too long in——

Oh yes, please, do take it for your trouble, though it's only a trifle. It is because I am the mother, you know.

PIERRE MILLE
B. 1864

MRS. MURRAY'S REVENGE

"MRS. Murray! Madam! I have to tell you—— there has been a terrible accident—— Mr. Murray——!"

The veteran servant of the Bank of Messrs. Murray and Co. of Singapore could hardly speak for emotion. His eyes were red; he had run up from the town, weeping, and had wondered all the way how to tell the dreadful news. He had arrived without having made up his mind. Under the blazing sun the steep road from the Bank, near to the docks, up to the Murrays' country house, had quite exhausted him. And now, under the pale brilliant sky, he looked afar over the native fields rich with intensive cultivation; over the homes of wealthy Englishmen, of very British architecture, though smothered in exuberant southern vegetation, like European girls dressed in tropical raiment for a fancy dress ball, and saw stretching far below him the immense seaport and harbour full of steamships and sailing-vessels, and further still, among all the little islands, ships in full steam and full sail, Chinese junks and Malay boats, all meeting there at the crossways of three worlds.

Mrs. Murray, very pale, came quickly to his cry. "Is my husband ill?" she said. Her book fell from her hand, and the cashier raised it with habitual respect. Her next words were in a very low tone. "Is he—— Is he dead?"

"Yes, madam," he said. But knowing that he had not told all, the confession brought him no relief. She, who had loved her husband deeply, stood beside the man wondering why she suffered so little. The name of "death" seemed quite meaningless. She might have wept, but it would have been sheer affectation; she could not conceive that her husband could be dead, because every impression she had ever received of him was one of life and joy and vigour. But all at once a dreadful thought struck her, and she whispered hoarsely, "He did not—take his own life?"

"No, madam," said old Jim Stevens. "He was killed. We found him by the open safe with a knife between his shoulders. He had evidently just opened the safe, as he did every evening since the illness of the head cashier, to put away the coin and takings of the day. But we found nothing in the safe. They must have taken everything."

"Who?" cried Mrs. Murray, with great excitement. "Do you know who?"

"Yes," he replied. "It was Weldon, the head clerk, and his friend Nathan, the little cotton-broker. It is they who did it. Nathan had called to see Weldon, and we suppose that one of them caught his arms and the other did it." And then, so as to finish his story, he added, "They have escaped. We have not been able to find them. They must have got away from the town."

All this time Mrs. Murray was thinking, in shame and distress, "I cannot feel; I cannot suffer; I cannot understand."

She could not even see her husband Alfred except through her accustomed view of him, and this dreadful shock had not disturbed her memory of the quiet, silent, powerful man of command, to whom she had given herself entirely as wife and housekeeper, and whose service was the joy of her life. She strove in vain to picture him lying prostrate and motionless in the little strong-room of the office, with a dark stain on his coat and on the floor. Yet she felt fierce anger at the horrid deed, and a great desire to act, to do something. And now she saw the open safe, and experienced for a moment the suffering and rage of the betrayed and dying man. If he had still lived he would have had no thoughts but those of the living; he would have made swift pursuit to regain the wealth with which he had been entrusted. This seemed so clear, so certain, and so luminous, that Mrs. Murray nearly cried aloud, "He is in my heart and brain; this is he who insists on action!" And indeed, the impulses of man or woman are sometimes so strong, that it is impossible to believe that they do not come from another.

Five minutes later she was swinging downward towards the city in a palanquin carried by two Chinese porters, straining the muscles of their goat-like legs, while the bewildered Stevens ran behind them. There was a great crowd around and within the Bank; the clerks in the office were talking excitedly, while a police-inspector was interrogating them individually, insisting on every detail of the afternoon's events, whether important or not, with an invariably careful and calm manner. The dead banker, almost forgotten, lay on a long bamboo lounge, with a handkerchief over his face. Flies had gathered in troops on the handkerchief; it was this which first struck home to the mind of his wife, and taught her that here indeed were death and dissolution. She fell to sobbing by the body, and all around kept an uncomfortable silence.

Suddenly she rose and quietly asked how much had been stolen. The question was put in such an unfeeling way as to be almost shocking, especially as the woman was quite free of avarice, and hardly knew the value of money. Some one replied that the books had not been fully examined, but that the booty of the thieves might amount perhaps to 300,000 dollars in banknotes, and in securities to perhaps twice as much again. The murderers must have booked their passage beforehand on one of the ships which ply from Singapore to Yokohama and thence to San Francisco. A steamer of this line was the only one which had left the port since the hour of the crime.

"We have telegraphed," said the inspector, "and shall ask for their extradition."

Mrs. Murray shrugged her shoulders. "I know nothing about all that," she said; "but I know that Weldon and Nathan are Americans, and that the United States are not in the habit of giving up their subjects. As for seeing them in their own country, you know very well that they have plenty to buy the jury with. We must go after them; that is all!"

The inspector started with amazement. "Go after them? But how should we do that? And why? That does not lie within our powers. We communicate with the foreign authorities and give them all possible information. My duty ends there!"

"I said nothing about you," she replied; "*I* am going after them. It is *my* husband whom they have murdered."

The dead man seemed to her like a leader fallen in the fight, whose place must be taken by the next in command. She told Stevens to have his body carried in the litter to her home, to watch over it, and to make every arrangement for the funeral, as she was going away that very night. To every one present she seemed to have taken leave of her senses; but they let her do what she would, because her force of will was positively formidable, and it was evidently useless to waste time in meddling with her affairs. They thought, indeed, that she would be unable to leave Singapore, and would be stopped by the practical difficulties of her project. But eagerly, swiftly, without a moment's hesitation, she forced her way through every obstacle.

All along the quays the long ranks of steamers slumbered, silent and cold, with great funnels and tall naked masts, while hordes of coolies were incessantly throwing coal into their bunkers. Of all of them only one was under steam ; it was a long, swift, narrow vessel of cunning aspect, its steel hull painted a dazzling white. It was loaded with grapes, peaches, and a whole cargo of other fruits, destined for an Indian port. This was the product of the ingenious enterprise of a Yankee ; and the ship had been built for great speed, in order to transport undamaged these perishable goods.

Mrs. Murray chartered the steamer, and having purchased its cargo, unloaded it at any price it would fetch on the Singapore market. She raised money by pledging her house and jewels, and emptied her current account at the Bank. At eight o'clock that evening she set out, armed with a copy of the inspector's report, and accompanied by two of her husband's clerks to serve as witnesses. The people of the town were standing all along the quay, gazing with silent curiosity, for it was generally believed that she had gone off her head.

The Yankee skipper had laid his course and pressed his engines to the utmost. He was eager for the chase. " There's a woman for you ! " he said ; " I guess she's as real as they make them ! "

She stood beside him, with every nerve bent on her enterprise, and questioned him about their course. She was a tragic figure in the white gown which she had not had time to change. She heard how they must keep free of Saïgon and pass round Manilla ; and the throbbing of the screw, shaking all the hull, was like music in her heart. And now the skipper had the fires banked up, skirted dangerous shoals, cut every corner ; he pored over the chart with her, and was amazed how tireless she was and never thought of sleep. At last, under the lee of Formosa, they saw the smoke of a great steamer, and knew that this was their quarry.

The two clerks, who had suffered pitiably from the sea and took little pleasure in their present mission, now came upon the bridge. The crew, who had gathered something of the object of their chase, were howling like dogs, while the skipper could not contain himself for joy, and spoke of using the little quick-firing gun in the bow, which was mounted there as a protection against Chinese pirates. The *Sunbeam* cut the water so swiftly that you would have thought it was about to leave the surface like a flying-fish. The roar of its syren cleft the air and spread far across the wide spaces of the sea. The *Swan of Japan* thought that a pirate was in pursuit, and held all the more swiftly on its way.

"Give her all you can!" shouted the skipper down to the engine-room. "We are gaining."

And indeed, they gained at last!

Two hours later the *Sunbeam* was within fifteen fathoms of the liner's quarter. On the latter, expecting an attack, women were weeping aloud, while the captain mounted the bridge with his megaphone. "What do you mean by pursuing an honest ship?" he cried. "Put down your helm or I will ram you and sink you."

The Yankee skipper, taking his own megaphone, began by showing him that an American can swear more roundly than any other on sea or land. To tell the truth, too, he did not find it very easy to explain why he had pursued "an honest ship," and only swore the more.

"Give me your speaking-trumpet," said Mrs. Murray. Raising it, she called across the waters: "You cannot sink us because we are swifter than you. I am the wife of Alfred Murray, who has been murdered by two passengers on your vessel, Weldon and Nathan, who booked with you under false names. I have come to identify and arrest them, and to get back the money they have taken. We want you to lower a boat."

The captain's voice came back to her, "You must be mad! In any case it is none of my business. You must apply to the authorities in Japan or in the United States. And now, go to the devil!"

"Stop and lower a boat," Mrs. Murray replied; "I will explain everything. If you do not stop I shall follow you to the end of the world. We are well armed. I do not say that we shall sink you, but we shall bring down any one who remains on your bridge, and shall begin with you. Please lower a boat."

At this moment Weldon and Nathan, white with fear, were to be seen climbing the steps of the bridge.

"There they are!" shouted the woman. "I know them. They want to buy you off. If they go up another step, I fire."

The captain of the *Sunbeam* was already at his gun, and a loud report followed. The passengers on the other vessel thought that their last hour had come; but their captain, to whom the whole episode was merely absurd, now brought it to an end.

"We are lowering a boat," he shouted, "but I may tell you that you will have to pay heavily for all this."

The boat came alongside the *Sunbeam,* and Mrs. Murray entered it with her two witnesses. As they did so, Weldon was heard to say in shaking accents, "It is all up, old man; we shall have to settle the bill, Nathan."

"True enough," the other replied. "Good-night and good-bye." Thereupon two revolver shots followed closely on one another, and the murderers fell to the deck.

"Oho!" exclaimed the captain. "So your story was true! I don't mind admitting that this alters the appearance of affairs." And while he gazed curiously at the two criminals, Mrs. Murray came on deck.

She pointed to her companions. "These gentlemen," she said, "have come with me——"

"Oh, my dear lady," answered the captain, "I have no need of witnesses! These wretched fellows have not gone out for nothing. Where is the purser?"

The purser came slowly up, shaking with terror. Shudders ran down his back all the time that he was searching the trunks of the two wretches. All the same, he recovered the whole of the money stolen from the Murrays, and in addition 15,000 dollars which represented the savings of the two murderers.

"Keep the whole of it, Commodore," said the captain, giving to the young woman in all seriousness the highest title in the American navy. "Keep it all; it will pay for your little expedition."

She handed him the inspector's report.

"Whatever do you want me to do with that?" said he. "We like to look after justice ourselves, especially in these latitudes, and you have had good reason to do so, in all conscience. But you are very pale; will you have a glass of champagne?"

The poor woman was, in fact, at the end of her strength, and now that her end was attained, collapsed altogether. The champagne quite knocked her over; she had to be carried up to the *Sunbeam.*

The steamship passengers, fully satisfied now of their safety, shouted, "Hurrah for the lady commodore!"

But she heard nothing. During the whole of the return journey she lay in her cabin in utter prostration, and weeping bitterly. She felt that she had not done what it was her duty to do, that she ought to have stayed beside her husband's body, to have watched over him, to have buried him ; that she should, in short, have acted as a woman and have been a woman. Most of all, it was a real torture to her that she was not in mourning ; this fact was even a cause of the acutest physical distress. The sound of those two revolver shots made her head turn giddy continually. She seemed always to see before her those two figures with their writhing limbs stretched out in the noontide glare, those two faces on which death had fixed their last convulsions.

"And it is I who did it all," she told herself ; "can it be that I am still a woman ?" She suffered horribly from the sense that she had divested herself of sex.

And now they were steaming toward the quays of Singapore. The Yankee skipper signalled the news by semaphore, and shouted to surrounding boats the story of their success, of Mrs. Murray's courage, and of the death of the two fugitives. The mad, romantic, incredible tale intoxicated him, and he used the bombastic words of journalism, exaggerating all. He was more and more impressed by the sensational drama in which he had played a foremost part ; and while he admired himself, he admired more the indomitable lady.

"Listen to me," he said to her. "I want you to take back your money. I have said it before ; let me say again—you are indeed a woman ! And will you let me say this too. I hardly know how to say it—— But you know how men in love with an actress love and desire her with the strength of all the thousands of hearts who long for her. I want you ; I beg you to be my wife. The seas will be ours, if you like, from China to San Francisco ; ten years would be enough to capture all the shipping companies, so that not a vessel would ply on the Pacific without our permission. Or let us go to the States, if you prefer, and gamble with land and gold and all that is human ; let us found cities and reign as queen and king over great areas where everything shall be ours, where none shall live but by our consent, nor traffic except under our licence. We might pour the population into moulds of our own design, so that all human life should be stamped with the mark of our absolute will."

The woman stood with her face covered by her hands, trembling a little, and answered not a word. As the *Sunbeam* glided past the little island off the port, thousands of voices were raised in acclamation, and countless yachts, boats, and other craft surrounded her. All the ladies of the European colony were gathered at the Victoria Docks with huge bouquets of brilliant and fragrant flowers. It was a reception that could only be compared to apotheosis. Jason returning with the Golden Fleece, or Columbus bringing to Cadiz the glory of the New World, or Nelson coming to Naples and the arms of that terrible lover, Lady Hamilton, was not welcomed so splendidly as Alfred Murray's widow. The gangway was thrown out to the quay, and down it there glided humbly an unhappy woman, her face lined with fear, her hair nearly white, whose crumpled gown of white silk seemed to fill all her mind with shame. "For the love of Heaven," she said, "give me a black dress! I cannot show myself like this!"

The report spread that the unhappy woman, who had set out in madness, had returned in dementia. This belief was, however, unfounded. She was the same courageous little English wife who had lived obedient to her husband, securing his comfort in every way and controlling his household efficiently; who had never missed going to church, and had obeyed all the world's laws, respecting all that she had been taught to respect. And now her lord was dead, and she had broken the world's law by doing something immoderate, something unfeminine. She suffered mentally because she could not recognise nor understand herself. She was desperately conscious of inability to carry the enormous load of her renown. People struggled to get a glimpse of her; she was mobbed by her adorers; all eyes and voices reproduced the glances and the tones of the Yankee captain; every one took for granted that she was an exceptional woman, of formidable will, whereas in fact she was weaker than she had ever known herself to be. All her commonplace and tenuous will had been squandered in one swift act of violence. Yet henceforth people would always expect from her that which she could not give; she had left the feminine herd, and there was no more place for her in the world. No man would ask for her in marriage except it were one of brutal ambition such as this seaman, whom after all to have married would have been to have deceived, because she had no more spirit to bring him than that of a feeble and affrighted child. But still they spoke with enthusiasm of her courage and of the grand characteristics of her race; and with all her heart she desired nothing so much as to die.

Yet in spite of her prayers death was refused to her. When her lawyers had paid the liabilities of the Bank and had sold the home and business, and even the very name of the man to whom she had given her life, there was left to her a tiny income, just enough to eke out a miserable existence. She left the tropic scene and returned to England, a lonely mourner estranged from her sex. It was in those unhappy days that I saw her in a London boarding-house of mean aspect, where other poor, melancholy, dull women were passing their declining years. Mrs. Murray looked exactly like any one of the others, so that her story, when recited by a friend, who had compassionately looked in upon her, was received with incredulity. As for herself, she holds all those memories in horror, and cannot be induced to speak of them. Little wrinkles have gathered round her eyes, her nose is sharp and white, and the saddest thing of all, I think, is the delusively youthful flush of her cheeks, the thousands of tiny injected vessels of her skin. It is as if her form were withered and her soul were dead.

HENRI DE RÉGNIER
B. 1864

THE SIGN OF THE KEY AND THE CROSS

AS I walked through the streets of the city I kept thinking of one of the stories which Monsieur d'Amercœur had told me. Without having named the place where the circumstance occurred he described it minutely, so that I seemed to recognise everything. The old city, noble and monastic, crumbling in its dismantled ramparts beside the yellowish river, with, beyond, the mountains piled against the horizon ; the narrow streets, half shade, half sunshine, the old walled-in houses, the churches and numerous convents, each with its chime of bells—all was familiar.

I seemed to find it again exactly as he described it, this city, an old pile of stones, sombre or luminous, wrapped in warmth and solitude, and the dusty ossification, retaining for such of its monuments as were yet standing the skeleton of past grandeur. In the centre the houses were crowded in a compact mass, still vast, outside of which the buildings were scattered, while over all a sleep or torpor seemed to hover, broken suddenly at times by a tolling or a merry clang of bells.

The streets, paved with flat stones or hardened with gravel, cut across each other oddly to open into squares where the markets were held. The flocks of the country-side gathered there to go away dispersed, according to their sale. The auction and the church service were, turn about, the sole occupations of the inhabitants. The place remained rustic and devout. The quick trot of the sheep pattered over the pavements, which echoed with the sandals of the monks. Pastor and flock jostled each other. The odour of the shearing mingled with the smell of woollen cloth. The air was redolent of incense and tallow ; of shorn and tonsured ; of shepherds and priests.

I arrived at the angle of two streets. A fountain was flowing into a time-worn basin. I remembered the fountain ; Monsieur d'Amercœur had praised the freshness of its water. The street to the right ought to lead to the Close of the Black Friars. I followed its windings, which led into the very heart of the city. A few poor shops displayed their wares. Rosaries hung beside horsewhips. The street suddenly grew wider. The high frontage of an old mansion appeared. I had seen several others of the sort here and there, but this one was particularly noticeable. It was built on a battered stone masonry. The windows, high above the soil, were grated. In former times they must have used those foundations for the present building, which was of severe architectural design. At the corner of the structure the street turned abruptly and descended by steps, gradually encircled the back of what proved to be an ancient castle—a stronghold, with its blocks of stone laid into the living rock.

I recognised the mansion d'Heurteleure. The street ended ; before me I saw an avenue of poplars. Old stone sarcophagi, now empty, stood in rows amid the long grass where a pathway had been worn. To the right stretched a wall with a low door at the side. I started as I perceived it. It opened into the herb garden of the monks, the portal of whose convent could be seen at the end of the walk. I paused and approached the little mural door. It was massive and iron-bound. The keyhole was shaped like a heart.

Continuing, I reached the convent porch and rang. The porter admitted me. Immense corridors led to vast halls. We ascended stairs, my guide gathering up the skirts of his frock as we mounted. We met no one. From the chapel, which I did not enter, came the droning chant of psalms. I was shown through several cloisters, one of them charming, square, full of flowers, and habited by doves, grouped on the cornices like a natural, graceful bas-relief. From a church spire, visible in the distance, the horologe was ringing the hour. A great yellow sunflower was looking into the deep water of a well and reflecting there its golden disc, like a monstrance.

Nothing had altered since Monsieur d'Amercœur visited the city. The same aspect proved the duration of the same habits. The cracking of horsewhips still mingled with the clicking of rosaries ; the convent bells clanged their chimes together as of yore, when Monsieur d'Amercœur, in frock and cowl, his bare feet sandalled, his staff in hand, came knocking at the door. He asked to see the prior, which office was at that time held by Dom Ricard, whose tomb I was shown among the anonymous sepulchres surrounding it. The prior had preserved powerful links with the world from which he had retired, keeping one hand open there for alms, and lending it, at need, in exchange for delicate enterprises, which might be aided by his prudence and wisdom. Monsieur d'Amercœur explained to him the meaning of his dress, the motives for his coming, and the details of his mission.

After twenty years of high service in the army, a gentleman of the country, Monsieur d'Heurteleure returned to settle. He married shortly after Mademoiselle Callestie, a poor girl of good family and great beauty. The wedded pair lived at the d'Heurteleure mansion. The nobles of the city frequented the house, the most assiduous in his visits being Monsieur d'Aiglieul. He had served under and was related to Monsieur d'Heurteleure, who was very fond of him. Life at the mansion was very simple, no pomp, very few domestics; the dignity of rank was upheld by the vast proportion of the apartments, the width of the stairways, and the general aspect of antiquity.

Whether they grew weary of the dull existence in this old town after the excitements of a military life, or were seized suddenly by a spirit of adventure, or from whatever cause it might be, Monsieur d'Heurteleure and Monsieur d'Aiglieul disappeared one day, no one knew whither. Time passed. The searches were fruitless. Some mystery was hinted at. Madame d'Heurteleure wept. All sorts of singular suspicions were afloat, which finally reached the Court, where these two gentlemen were still remembered. One day the double disappearance was mentioned in the hearing of Monsieur d'Amercœur, who determined to solve the enigma. He was empowered with full authority to act, and at once he set about it.

His first care was to assume a monastic frock, certain with this attire to penetrate everywhere, through half-opened doors as well as through the fissures of conscience, and Dom Ricard helped him to the best of his power. For a while his researches were without result; but aided by the disguise of his costume and his apparent calling, his inquiries were patient and diverse. He hovered about the d'Heurteleure house, scrutinised the people and the habits, studied the life. He listened to and weighed all the still vivacious rumours. In vain. He wished to see Madame d'Heurteleure. He was told that she was ill. Every day he passed the house; following the street which rises around the sub-basement, he reached the front, pausing sometimes to slake his thirst at the fountain. Returning, as he descended the steps, he examined the enormous foundations of stone and solid rock, longing to apply his ear and listen to their mystery, for it seemed to him that the flanks of the old castle contained the phantom of the secret, which he had come to evoke from silence before it passed into oblivion. At last, discouraged, he was on the point of giving up. He would have taken leave of Dom Ricard but for the old monk's urgent advice to remain. The venerable prior enjoyed the society of this sheep, so dissimilar to the members of the flock which his wooden crook conducted in the monotonous paths of the Order.

One day toward five o'clock in the afternoon, Monsieur d'Amercœur went out by the old portal and strolled amid the tall grasses of the avenue. The moment was melancholy and solemn ; the trees threw their shadows across the funereal path, the lizards ran over the warm stones of the antique tombs and in and out of their fissures. With one hand Monsieur d'Amercœur held up the long monk's frock, with the other he held the key to open the heart-shaped lock of the medicinal garden, where he loved to wander. He wished to visit it once more before he went away, to hear once more the soles of his sandals scraping over the gravel, while his frock brushed the borders of boxwood. The symmetry of the plots pleased him ; their squares contained delicate plants and curious flowers ; little pools nourished aquatic specimens which plunged their roots into the water, flowered, and mirrored their bloom. At the intersection of the paths stood porcelain urns painted with emblems and pharmaceutical designs, with serpents twisted about the handles, and these urns contained varieties rare and precious. Above the walls waved the tops of the poplars ; from the kitchen gardens off to one side, separated by high green trellises, came the sound of a rake, the striking of a spade against a watering-can, the little sound of shears clipping the young shoots ; in here all was silence ; a flower bent, flexible, under the weight of an insect ; swallows darted about ; dragon-flies flitted across the greenish water ; heavy plants and delicate vines twined and intertwined.

Monsieur d'Amercœur was going toward the door of this odd little enclosure when, at the end of the avenue, he saw approaching a woman dressed in black. She walked slowly with faltering steps. By some inner revelation he knew at once that this was Madame d'Heurteleure. He slackened his own pace, so as to meet her at the moment when he stopped before the door. Arrived there, he put the key into the lock. At the sound the lady started and hesitated. He stooped as though trying to turn the key. She wished to profit by this moment to pass ; but found herself face to face with him as he suddenly turned. She stood with one hand pressing down her palpitating heart. He saw a face pale and lovely, though haggard from grief and insomnia, with troubled eyes, half-parted lips. Then he entered quickly, closing the door and leaving in the iron heart of the lock the key.

The next day he was meditating in the little cloister when a messenger came to tell him that a veiled lady desired to speak with him. She was admitted. He recognised Madame d'Heurteleure, and invited her to be seated on a stone bench. The doves cooed softly on the capitals of the quiet cloister, their murmurs mingled with the sighs of the penitent. She sank on her knees, and with bent head and hands folded in his wide sleeves Monsieur d'Amercœur listened to her dolorous confession. It was a horrible and tragic story. Why relate it to him? Because her secret seemed to have been laid bare. When she saw a monk holding a key to open that heart-shaped lock, she felt as though he meant to force open her conscience. Their meeting seemed like a decree of fate, his gesture a mysterious allusion to the deliverance of her soul imprisoned in the horror of its silence.

Her marriage with Monsieur d'Heurteleure was loveless. She esteemed, while she feared his noble character, the hardness of which intimidated her confidence and discouraged her tenderness. Years passed. One winter Monsieur d'Aiglieul appeared and called frequently. He was handsome and still young. She yielded to his love. Then followed days of joy and terror; a dread of discovery and an agony of remorse. Monsieur d'Heurteleure seemed unaware of their perfidy, though he grew suddenly old and another deep line was added to those already furrowing his brow. He was as usual often absent. One evening Madame d'Heurteleure retired to her room about midnight. She felt depressed. Monsieur d'Aiglieul had not appeared and he seldom missed a day. As she was combing her hair before a mirror she saw the door open, and her husband entered. He was booted, but his boots bore no trace of outdoor mire; his coat looked dusty, a long spider web hung from his sleeve, and in his hand he held a key. Without speaking he went directly to the wall of the chamber where a nail fastened an ivory crucifix, which he tore off and broke upon the floor, while in its place he suspended the heavy, rusty key. Madame d'Heurteleure gazed for a moment without comprehending, then all at once her hands clasped her heart, she gave a cry, and fell unconscious.

When she came to herself the whole affair was clear to her. Her husband had allured Monsieur d'Aiglieul into some trap. The old mansion in its invisible depths contained dungeons, chambers of eternal oblivion. A cry, his, vibrated still in her ears. It seemed to come from below, deafened by the piled-up stone, piercing the superimposed arches, reaching her from those lips for ever separated by the thickness of the walls. She tried to get out; the door was fastened, the windows were padlocked, the domestics occupied another part of the house and were beyond her call. The next day Monsieur d'Heurteleure came to bring her food. Each day he came. The spider's web still hung from his dusty sleeve, his boots creaked on the tesselated floor, the great line on his forehead deepened in a pallor of sleepless misery. He went away silently, and to her tears and supplications he replied only by a brief gesture, showing the key hung against the wall.

During those tragic days the wretched woman lived with her eyes fixed on the horrible key, which grew larger to her vision, became enormous. The patches of rust looked like red blood. The house was still as death. Toward evening a step was heard. Monsieur d'Heurteleure again entered bearing a lamp and a basket. His head had grown white, he did not now so much as glance at the unhappy being who grovelled at his feet, but he never failed to stare greedily at the key. Then at last Madame d'Heurteleure understood the desire which gnawed, which was devouring him—to see his rival in death, to gloat over his vengeance, to feel of the corruption that had once been flesh and blood, to take down that key he had hung on the wall in place of the Sign of Pardon, the ivory emblem of which he had shattered to substitute an iron symbol of eternal rancour. But alas! vengeance never is satisfied, always she craves for more; frenzied, insatiable, she feeds on her own vehemence to the very dregs of memory, until the end of life.

Monsieur d'Heurteleure felt that she guessed his morbid longing and that added to his torture. The adamant pride was streaked with veins of blood. One night when Madame d'Heurteleure slumbered, stretched on her bed, she heard her door open softly and saw her husband on the threshold. He carried a lamp with the flame turned low, and walked as lightly as a shadow without a sound, as though the sombre somnambulism of his fixed idea had made of him an imponderable phantom. He crossed the room, reached up, took down the key, and went out again. There was a dead silence. A fly awakened by the light buzzed for an instant and then ceased. The door remained on the latch. Madame d'Heurteleure bounded up. In her bare feet she slipped into the hall. Her husband was going downstairs; she followed him. At the ground floor he continued to descend; the stairway plunged into gloom, but she could hear along the subterranean corridors the steps which preceded her. They were now in the ancient substructures of the castle. The walls sweated, the ceilings were vaulted. A last stairway twisted its spiral into the rock. At its base the light of the vanishing lamp still glimmered on the slimy pavement. Bending forward, Madame d'Heurteleure listened. A grating sound reached her and the light disappeared. At the foot of the stairs she found a circular chamber. An opening in the wall revealed a shallow bay; she still crept on, until, at the end of the passage, by feeling her way, she recognised a door very slightly ajar. She pushed it open. In a sort of square hole, vaulted above and tiled below, Monsieur d'Heurteleure was seated beside his little lamp. He was motionless, staring with wide-open eyes. He looked at his wife without seeing her. A nauseating odour came from the cell, and beyond the shadow spread over the tiles lay a fleshless hand already greenish in hue.

Madame d'Heurteleure did not scream. Should she waken the wretched somnambulist, whose frenzied sleep had drawn him to this tragic dungeon? Was she capable of inflicting this degrading shock upon his pride? No. The vengeance of the outrage was just. She felt pity for those wild eyes, which stared at her without seeing her, for the tortured visage, for the hair blanched by such poignant anguish, and it seemed to her best to protect the secret of this nocturnal adventure, so that he might never discover his self-betrayal. He must, she deemed, be allowed to satisfy his terrible craving in the eternal silence of the tomb, without ever knowing whose unseen hand walled him in face to face with his sacrilege.

Monsieur d'Heurteleure still gazed blankly at her. Very calmly she knelt and clasped the greenish palm which stretched its fleshless fingers over the tiles, and then from the outside she closed the door. Walking away on tiptoe, she slid the bolt of the vault which closed the passage. She ascended the spiral stairs, the subterranean steps, the stairways of the upper house, and on the rusty nail of her chamber wall she suspended the tragic key, which balanced itself an instant, and then hung motionless to mark an eternal hour.

The doves passed to and fro as they flew below the arches of the little cloister. The hour rang out simultaneously from all the belfries in the city. The miserable woman sobbed and offered Monsieur d'Amercœur the great key, letting it fall at his feet. He picked it up; it was heavy, and the patches of rust were red like blood. He walked away. Madame d'Heurteleure, still kneeling, supplicated wildly with her hands joined convulsively. He descended toward the little garden, which embalmed the centre of the cloister with its fragrant flowers, which grew in beds equally divided by boxwood. Great roses engarlanded the well with its stone circle; their thorns clung to the monastic frock as he bent over to drink; the water spurted out. A tall, golden sunflower mirrored its honey-laden monstrance. A dove cooed faintly, and Monsieur d'Amercœur, returning to his still prostrate penitent, murmured in her ear the words of an absolution which, if it lost nothing in heaven, gave at least on earth peace to a tortured soul.

GEORGES RENARD
B. 1864

JACQUES BRULEFERT'S DEATH

I WAS on my way to the village, toiling up the old, paved road on a slope, known for miles around as the stiffest climb in the neighbourhood. It was a hot August day, and as I stopped to take breath, old Sauvage, the owner of the "Rising Sun," an inn most discreetly perched at the top of its thirsty summit, came up behind me, and accosted me with a cordial "Good-day!" We went on together, glad of each other's company; and at last arrived at the very steepest part of the way, a sheer incline, abutting on a ravine, thickly clad with undergrowth, at the bottom of which flowed the river; and bordered by a green hedge, the only protection against a fall over its side. Right in the very middle of this hedge was a great gap, which seemed as though some massive weight had crashed through it.

"Has there been an accident here?" I asked my companion.

"Better than that," was his answer. "That hedge still wears the scars of war, like a disabled warrior. A terrible thing happened there."

I scented a story.

"Tell me about it," I begged; and, as we advanced slowly under the burning sun, he began:

"It was the 17th of December, in the year of misfortune 1870—a date I have good reason for remembering.

"On the afternoon of the day before, a troop of German soldiers had arrived among us. No one thought much about it at first: we had grown accustomed to such visits by then, for our village is on the road to Germany, and for the last three months, Heaven knows, we had seen nothing but Prussians and Bavarians, Uhlans and artillery-men, cuirassiers and foot-soldiers passing through—a never-ending stream. They did not stay long, but managed to consume everything they could get hold of; they devoured our corn, our oats, our cattle, and our sheep, which they were brutes enough to kill before our very eyes, and left us in their stead little scraps of paper with I don't know what sort of unintelligible stuff written on them. Afterwards they would go on down the hill, through the valley, and forward to Paris. At night, when the wind blew from the west, we used to hear dull, heavy sounds which were the voice of the cannon—Paris calling for help. But Paris called in vain, and in vain we hoped ; the *pantalons rouges* never came, and always, always there arrived fresh troops of Germans. I would wager more than a hundred thousand have been over the old, paved road where we are. But we could do nothing, and had to watch them go by in mournful helplessness, as you might watch the course of a river that had overflowed its banks.

" This time it was only an infantry battalion. It halted up there, in front of our place, by the church. But evidently something extraordinary had happened. The soldiers stood at attention ; their officers were in a group, gesticulating, shouting, swearing. I could hear them at it from the house. The commandant was the most furious of all. I can see him still—a long, lean old fellow, with a red scar on his white face, a great white moustache, with occasional reddish hairs in it, and the very oddest way of walking I ever saw—just as if he were walking on egg-shells, and was afraid of breaking them—and a way of swinging himself about that made me think of a poplar swaying in the wind.

" While he was raging up and down, a captain pointed out to him the house opposite to ours. And at once he seemed overjoyed ; he called out some order in his lingo ; four men came out of the ranks, and followed by them and the captain, he marched forthwith to the house pointed out to him, looked at its signboard, and read aloud : ' Jacques Brulefert, Engine and Machinery Mender ' ; then he opened the door and entered with the officer.

" I wondered what the Prussians could be wanting with Jacques, and said to myself : ' Look out for squalls ! ' for I must tell you Jacques hated the Prussians, and he was a hot-headed fellow. He had served with the army in Africa, and though now he was well past forty, had courage and daring and strength enough for a much younger man ; he was not tall, nor by any means a beauty. By much fighting against Bedouins he had got almost as swarthy as they are, but he was as agile as a cat, and dexterous as a monkey, while he was as sound as only an old Zouave like himself could be.

" Ah, there was no lack of fire in him, eyes or heart, I can tell you ! His rage had known no bounds ever since the campaign had begun. You should have heard him storming against the Emperor in the big room at the inn, for a coward who couldn't even die when he ought to, and against the townsfolk, who were cowards too, and the Germans who could only fight three to one. He banged on the tables as if they were Prussians. He was mad about it all. Why, I myself, sir, as true as I'm here speaking to you, I saw him cry like a child when he heard that Bazaine had surrendered Metz.

" At every fresh disaster (and, Heaven knows, there were enough of them) he wanted to be off, wherever the fighting was, and take his share of it ; he said that the others had got the very job he wanted, and he would have gone, over and over again, in spite of his age, if he had not had to stay and take care of his wife and his little boy, a lad of ten years. So he stayed behind, but as if he felt disgraced, and ready for any desperate deed. Every time the Germans came through, he shut himself up so as not to see them, and if by chance some of them were billeted on him, he would rather pay to send them to the inn, than himself lodge the sauer-kraut gobblers, as he called them.

" So I said to myself, when I saw the two Prussian officers going in to friend Jacques : 'There'll be a row, I warrant.' And I wasn't far out, as you'll see. They had hardly been inside for three minutes when I heard a great uproar of doors banging and shouting. Then out came the commandant, as red as a cock's-comb, and shouted out some rigmarole to the four men who had stayed outside ; they rushed in to the workshop, and I knew that they must have had orders to fetch out Jacques. But not a bit of use was it, for while they were turning the house upside down, I saw a man suddenly leap out of the loft, and run for dear life along the road. It was Jacques ; and he went like a runaway horse ; but a few minutes after, a Prussian showed his ugly face at the very window Jacques had jumped out through. You can imagine his looks when he saw Jacques had been under their very nose all the time. And the officers, too ! They swore like anything, and the commandant looked as black as thunder.

" *He* didn't jump out (it was too far from the ground for that), but he rushed down the staircase with his men, called up the others, and set them like dogs on the track of the runner. Ah, so he did—but there was no Jacques to be seen ! Every trace of him had disappeared ! He was nowhere to be found, and they searched everywhere in the bushes, the corners behind the church, and the little wood ! And bare and level before them stretched the road. Where the deuce could he have got to ? The night was beginning to fall ; in vain the men searched everywhere round; in vain the commandant swore and raged and fumed like a madman: the soldiers had to come back jabbering and empty-handed. All the village had assembled up there at last, looking as though they understood nothing, you can imagine, but bursting with laughter to see them so dumfounded.

" Everyone knew already what had happened. My wife had been up to Jacques's house to see what had been done, and she has a tongue of her own, you know, a regular woman. She found the poor wife frightened out of her wits, and crying with fear. It seems that the commandant had wanted Jacques to go with him at once, without a moment's notice. He wanted him to repair a great steam-engine he was escorting with his battalion, and that he had had to leave behind a mile back. The night before, the engineer had been killed as they came through a wood, by a *franctireur*; and he wanted someone to replace him in bringing along the machine which was stuck there. You can guess it was pretty serious for him. The machine was dragging along a great cannon destined for the bombardment of Paris. And the commandant had come to requisition Jacques for the job, as if he had been a Prussian soldier, at the least. He had come to the wrong shop this time. Jacques got white as a sheet, and said: 'Supposing I won't do anything of the kind?' The commandant told him, with a sneer, 'Then you'll be forced to,' for he spoke French like a schoolmaster, the great, lanky lout. But he did not know Jacques. With one bound the fellow skipped through the door behind him, and once out of their sight, got away as I told you.

" We thought that was the end of it. But there's no dealing with these obstinate folk. A few minutes after there wasn't one among us inclined to laugh, for the commandant announced to the Mayor that he would now spend the night in the village; and soon we each had our share of Prussians to lodge. And to see them there, strutting about in one's own house, stretching across the fireplace or the table, and talking a jargon no one could understand, while the very rifles they carried had probably shot down more than one brave fellow from our little village, was enough to take the laugh out of one for ever, I can tell you.

" Up at the inn, of course, we had the commandant and two captains to provide for gratis, and didn't feel particularly flattered by the honour. The commandant was striding up and down, and looking very furious. Suddenly I saw him stop and rub his hands. 'A bad sign,' thinks I.

And, sure enough, he calls his men and talks away to them, pointing every now and then to Jacques's house. I didn't know yet what he was up to, but I hadn't long to wait. Outside in the street we heard a noise, loud laughs, and the cries of a woman and a child; then our door was pushed roughly open, and a woman was just thrown into the room by four great ruffians, who pushed, and dragged, and hustled her in. It was that old wretch's idea. The cunning old thing said to himself: 'If you want to take the male, the surest way is catch the female.' And he had Jacques's wife arrested.

"As for the boy, a regular son of his father, as bold as a lion, he tried to resist; yelled and screamed, fought and kicked, and was trying to bite the hand which had grasped him cruelly by the wrist. Poor little lad! they wouldn't even let him stay in with us, but kicked him outside, and for a quarter of an hour or more we heard him sobbing with rage and cold out in the dark night. The mother was like a creature possessed. She struggled until she was in such a dishevelled state you wouldn't have known her, and screamed insult after insult at the commandant, calling him 'cad,' 'villain,' 'coward.' He cared no more than if he had been a log; but laughed mockingly at her, the heartless beast, and said, quietly, 'Come, come, behave yourself! You shall be set free when your husband returns. If he doesn't come back, so much the worse for you. You will be our prisoner, and will have to come with us. That will teach your man to refuse us his services.' And while the poor woman, over whom two soldiers mounted guard, was crying quietly in a corner of our big dining-room, the commandant and two captains, seated at the other end, ate enough for six, and drank enough for ten, because they knew they were not going to pay for their dinner."

By this time we had climbed the hill, and reached the inn, where I had invited Père Sauvage to drink a glass of wine with me, and it was over a venerable bottle in a cool corner of the big room, looking on to the sunny highway and the delightful view beyond, that he continued: "Well, the Prussians were gobbling at the very table we are sitting at now, and I was serving at the bar, when Jean Lacroix, the mason, came in. He had come to fetch a pint of wine; but he looked as though something was up; so when he made me a sign, I pretended that I had to go down to the cellar, and went into the kitchen with him.

" ' I've seen Jacques,' he said softly.

" ' Where ? ' I asked.

" ' Quite close. He has hidden under the road. I found him crouched up in the little tunnel that takes off the rain-water in bad weather. The Prussians must have passed over his head at least a dozen times when they were looking for him. Wasn't it a trick to play them ? But now he is cold and hungry. He whistled softly to me as I was coming in from the fields. He wants something to eat, some sort of wrap, and a little money, then he is going off to his Uncle François—who lives three leagues off. I wanted to tell his wife, and knocked at her door ; but there's no one there. What am I to do ? '

" I told him the Prussians had arrested her, and meant to take her off with them ; that she was up there in the dining-room, and that we must let Jacques know somehow ; but it was easier said than done, as one ran the risk of being caught in the act, and betraying his hiding-place. Then I thought of the boy, who was bold enough for anything, and an intelligent little fellow. It was a pitch-dark night ; he could creep along and hide himself in the ditches more easily than a man ; and then, once with his father, he would at least have some-one to defend him.

" ' He can't be far away,' I said to Jean Lacroix. ' We must find him, and send him.'

" It seemed the best thing to do, sir, and yet I have often thought, since then, that without meaning to, I was doing just what that old wretch of a commandant wanted. No one will ever persuade me that that wasn't the idea he had in his head when he let the child go : he thought he would get at the father through the child. What do *you* think ? Jean Lacroix was of the same opinion as myself, that it was the only thing to be done, and he went off to see after it all.

" The Prussians had done their dinner, and were smoking like a factory chimney. Jacques's wife was still crying silently in her corner ; she would neither eat nor drink ; and it was heart-breaking to see her so wretched and know that we could do nothing for her. The sentinels in the street could be heard calling ' Wer da ? ' (who goes ?), and no one was allowed to enter or leave the village without the commandant's permission. The officers and men came in from time to time to report to him. But on the stroke of seven, Jacques's wife sat up straight, and gave a loud cry. Her husband and her little boy were being brought in by the patrol.

"Jacques was quite pale and very calm, but his jaw was set, and his look ugly. When the commandant said, with a laugh: 'I knew we should catch you, my fine fellow,' he replied, looking straight into his eyes:

"'I was not caught at all. I knew that you had arrested my wife, and that she would be set free if I came back. So here I am. But all the same, you have acted like a coward.'

"The commandant grew quite white, then quite red, as if he were nearly choking; his hand felt for his sword, and I thought he was going to fall upon Jacques, who stood before him with folded arms. But he contented himself with swearing big oaths, which I didn't understand; but he must have been wild, to judge by his men, who were trembling in their shoes. Ah! if they had not had need of Jacques Brulefert and his skill, the poor fellow would have had a bad time of it. At last, when the commandant could control himself sufficiently to speak, he said:

"'You are going to sleep here, you dog of a Frenchman. Your tools will be brought to you, and to-morrow, off you go with us. The least attempt to get away, and you'll be shot at once.'

"Jacques did not flinch. He sat down quietly at a table in the corner, while four great Germans settled themselves at the next table, with their guns loaded and bayonets fixed. His wife brought him food and drink. He supped as though nothing was the matter, without saying a word; then asked for his tool-bag and a blanket; sent home his wife and the little lad, who didn't want to leave him; after which, like the old veteran he was, he rolled himself up in his blanket, stretched himself out on his table, with his box for a pillow, and went to sleep.

"The next day, at dawn, a whole company stood at attention in front of our door, sent to fetch away Jacques. He had already jumped down from his table, and stretched his limbs by a turn round the room, so he took a glass with me and was ready to go.

"He chaffed and joked his four guardians, who would not let him out of their sight for a single moment, but seemed afraid that he might vanish up the chimney. All the same, there was something very queer-looking about him. Sometimes he would stay for a whole minute staring and frowning, as if he was looking at something a long way off, and then he would suddenly rear up his head, as if he was defying some one.

"At about eight o'clock his wife and the child came to see him. The poor woman was crying so, that she was pitiful to see.

"'Listen, Catherine,' he said; 'you must promise me to leave the village at once, and go to Uncle François.'

"And when she objected, he spoke lower still. My own opinion is that the four soldiers didn't know a single word of French; but they may have been shamming, and anyway it was wiser to speak softly. So he whispered into her ear:

"'You see, I mean to try and escape on the way. But if you are still here, they will arrest you again to get me back. I shall not feel safe, unless I see you away. Go and get your things ready, and don't be afraid, dear wife. I'll get out of it, you'll see.'

"He kissed her affectionately, almost cheerfully, to inspirit her a little, and pushed her towards the door. The boy stayed behind, sobbing—naturally enough. But Jacques caught him between his knees and said:

"'Little man, you must be brave, and not cry; those cads are only too pleased if they see you cry. Think that I am going off to the war, and shall be coming back again. If by chance, though, things go badly with me, and I never come back any more, you must love your mother, my boy. You must love her for two. And when you are a big man, remember to be a good soldier, so that the Prussians may get back from you some of the harm they have done us. Now, laddie, don't cry, whatever you do.'

"And the little fellow nearly choked himself in his efforts not to cry, and said:

"'You see, father, I'm not crying now.' Only the words sounded very shaky, and two great tears ran down his cheeks. Jacques sent him off after his mother. Ah! he couldn't manage to look cheerful any longer, just then, poor Jacques! His voice was trembling when he said to me:

"'It's cold this morning, Père Sauvage. Let's have one more drink together—perhaps it's for the last time.'

"'The last?' I said to him. 'Why, man, it's not the first time you've been in the wars: you'll come back to us, never fear!'

"He smiled without speaking, but I saw he had got something planned out in his head.

"The commandant had just come out from his room, and he was no sooner downstairs than he gave the word 'March!' Jacques took his box and followed him outside. All the village was there, sir, to see him off, and everyone had a good word for him and insisted on shaking him by the hand: he had never had so many friends. He kept looking anxiously towards his house, but when he saw his wife come out holding the boy by one hand, and in the other her bundle of things, he seemed relieved. Only, as all the good-byes were being said, and everyone wished him *au revoir* and *bon voyage*, the commandant asked, roughly: 'Where is she going?' He was a sly old thing, that commandant, to be sure; and was suspicious about this departure of hers. But Jacques replied, as quiet as you please:

"'I shall be away some time, it seems. She is going to stay with our uncle as long as you need my services.'

"The commandant was quite taken in.

"'That's right,' he said, slapping Jacques on the shoulder. 'You are sensible this morning; and that's better all round, my lad. In a week you'll be back here. It's not so bad after all, is it?'

The wife and the child started off as he said this. Jacques followed them to the next turning with his eyes, threw them a kiss from where he stood, and gave a great sigh; but as soon as they were out of sight, sir, you would hardly have believed it was the same man: his expression changed as you might change your shirt, saving your presence. It was our Jacques at his very best; laughing and joking and snapping his fingers at the Prussians; whom he called old slow-coaches, telling them they never would get anywhere at that rate. A regular 'gamin,' sir, but a true Frenchman too, who meant to show these lanky Germans that there was nothing in *them* to frighten an old soldier of the African army.

"At last the column began to march. Jacques, who was placed in the middle, walking along quite gaily, called out to us, 'I shall see you again soon! You'll be having news of me before long.' I assure you, sir, he could not have gone off holiday-making more gaily, and more than one of the village folk were surprised, and didn't quite like to see him so soon going quietly with the Prussians. But I knew my man, and could have sworn he had in his head some trick to play them and their machine.

"The place where the Prussians had left it was not half a league away, upon the plateau above us; and, faith, we were curious to see this engine which had come from so far. ' Well,' said I, ' let's go along ; the Prussians won't eat us ' ; and five or six of us followed after the column that was taking off Jacques.

" Soon, in the middle of the road, we saw a great black object, guarded by a little detachment that had had to camp out round it. It was that brute of a machine : a traction-engine, it was called, I think ; and behind, on two great carts, themselves a mass of iron, was the gun and the carriage ! Ah, sir, if you had seen the creature ! A monster of a cannon ! Heavens, how is it possible such engines are invented ? Two men could have lain down in its mouth, and goodness knows how many tons it weighed ! It could discharge shells that would demolish a whole house from garret to cellar. And when we thought that a piece of that calibre could carry two leagues at the least, we said to each other, gloomily enough, that the Parisians weren't exactly going to have a gay time of it. Only you will guess a mass like that wasn't easily conveyed about ; it would have taken thirty horses at least just to move it. Steam alone could drag along such a monument, and just in the very nick of time the engine-driver had been killed, and the machine got out of gear. ' Ah ! ' we said to each other, ' what a pity Jacques got taken prisoner ! If only he could damage its inside a little, so that it couldn't be got to move.'

" But nothing of the sort ; he just gave a look to its works, and in a few minutes had put everything right, for he was a rare workman, I can tell you. Then, while they were getting up steam, we heard him giving a heap of explanations to the commandant. The old man was afraid of the incline it had to descend. But Jacques reassured him ; he understood quite well how to manage it ; he would slow down at the entrance to the village ; he would put on the brake ; he would shut off steam ; if necessary, he would reverse the engines. ' You needn't be afraid of anything,' he said. ' I'll answer for it all. It'll answer to my hand, an engine of that kind. Only, send some men on first to clear off the snow which is drifted up on the hill-side. That might make us slide down.'

" For I must tell you there had been a heavy snow a week before. Since when, though it had been trodden into mud by the passers-by, some still lay between the paving-stones, and as it had frozen hard during the night, the road shone in the morning sun like a mirror. The commandant had noticed it. ' You're right,' he said to Jacques, and some minutes after, the Prussians who had stayed in the village were clearing the highway with picks and brooms, like so many road-labourers, and spreading shovelfuls of earth from top to bottom of the incline.

"All this time Jacques was waiting. The machine was ready, he was seated on it, and smoking his pipe as calmly as if he had been at home. The commandant, however, did not yet feel quite safe about him. At the moment of starting he called a lieutenant and said something that I couldn't understand, though I heard him plainly. The lieutenant answered: 'Ja, commandant. Ja, commandant.' Then I saw him take a revolver from his belt, and climb up on to the locomotive by Jacques; and the commandant called to Jacques from his horse:

"'Understand, you engineer fellow, at the first attempt to escape, you'll be shot.'

"'You'll be shot' seemed to be the words that came most natural to him. Jacques shrugged his shoulders.

"'I've no wish to get away,' was his reply. But in spite of that, for greater security, the commandant had a double file of men posted alongside, to the right and the left of the machine; then he himself went to the head of the column, calling out first something in German, and then in French for Jacques, 'Forward, march!' The engine panted and snorted and tugged with all its might; the cannon jerked off with a clash of iron; and between the two rows of soldiers who accompanied it, it all proceeded slowly along the level highway.

"We had run on to the village to announce the approach of the wonderful machine, and all our folk, men, women, and children, were out in the road to see it pass by. Soon were heard cries of 'It is coming! It's coming!' and there it appeared, clearly outlined against the sky, all black and smoking. Lean this way a little, sir: you can see the place from here. It was about ten feet from our house. You can see, just where the cobble-stones stop and the paving begins. That's where the incline begins; there's a little slope before the big one.

"At that moment the commandant, who was prancing along on horseback, turned round to Jacques, and called out, 'Attention!'

"'Don't be alarmed,' sings out Jacques. 'I'm going to put the brake on.'

"Ah, sir, if I live to be a hundred, I shall never forget what happened then; no, nor will any one who was there, and saw it all.

Then I understood why Jacques had sent off his wife and the little one. Such a sight would have driven them crazy.

" Instead of slowing down, he put on all possible speed, jumped at the lieutenant, twisted his arms, so that the revolver fell out of his hands, and kept him fastened to the spot, shouting all the time, '*Vive la France!*' And the engine began to rush on down, leaping over the paving-stones; and the gun rushed after it, gun-carriage and all, making a very deuce of a noise. The commandant only just got out of the way in time to escape being crushed. He was yelling like a madman, and shouting out orders to his Prussians; which I expect meant: 'Stop him! Kill him!' But, all the same, they stood still, stupid with astonishment and terror. They might as well have tried to stop an express at full speed. The machine sped straight on, like a flash of lightning. The houses shook; the paving-stones were crushed under it, and sent out showers of sparks; it was a whirlwind crashing down the street with thunder and lightning. Jacques, clinging to his Prussian, looked a regular demon. Once more we heard him shout, '*Vive la France!*' Then, at the turn of the road, in a single bound through the hedge, everything rolled over into the ravine below. It was an awful crash. To have any idea of it, you must imagine a thunderbolt falling into the midst of this room. And then immediately there came a great silence. No one could speak; the women covered their heads with their aprons; we felt sick at heart.

" Can you believe it, sir? I can't think of it even yet, without creeping all over. And yet it's fifteen years now since then. I expect you'll despise me. But I can't help it.

" Well, to cut a long story short, the Prussians were more than six weeks over fishing up their big gun. At the bottom of the ravine was a horrible mess of twisted iron-work, dislocated wheels, ploughed-up soil, broken trees, and shattered stones. When at last it was all got up out of the débris, it was too late to be of any use in the bombardment—the siege of Paris was raised.

" Good old Jacques! That was what he had wished. And to think that we could never even give him a hero's funeral.

" He had been so completely crushed that nothing of him was found but a few mangled scraps of flesh some days after—one couldn't even tell if they belonged to him or the Prussian. Everything was carried off to the cemetery, almost without ceremony, for the Prussians were still in the village and furious after the smash. Later on we put up a little headstone over the grave, with the inscription, 'Died for his country,' under his name, then the date, and that was all. Thirty years hence, no one will remember who it was. The wife is dead, the house sold, the boy has gone for a soldier—now he is a sergeant in the line, and the Prussians will catch it pretty hot if ever he has a chance of getting at them. But he doesn't often get back to his old home; and with the exception of himself and a few old folk like me, who will remember Jacques Brulefert?

"I have it, sir: you, who are a scholar—you should write his story. It would only be justice to him. I tell you, spite of their great battalions, and their great guns, the Prussians would have had a bad time of it in 1870 if there had been many Frenchmen like our Jacques.

"And now, sir, I've been talking long enough. I must get to my work. Your health, sir!"

"*A la santé de la France, père Sauvage*, and the memory of Jacques Brulefert. I promise you to write his story."

"FERNAND VANDÉREM"

B. 1864

HIMSELF

"NO, sir, I am sorry that there is not an unoccupied table. But if you don't mind waiting five minutes, sir, there is a table, this one just behind you. You see, sir, they are finishing their coffee."

In no very good humour I looked all round the many tables of people dining in the dim evening about the garden, and the little lights of gilt candlesticks which made the tablecloths gleam in the twilight. A voice sounded close to me, "So it is you, is it?"

I turned and recognised my friend, Lacquin. Perhaps I should hardly call him my friend; for our friends, after all, are people like ourselves, are they not, who have to bear the same anxieties and sufferings and weaknesses as our own, and whom we love with that strange mixture of pity and tender devotion which we have for ourselves. No, I can hardly say that Lacquin was my friend, but he was something really very much more pleasant and soothing than a friend. I had struck up a kind of acquaintance with him the year before, when away on a holiday, and his frank, jolly, debonair way pleased me; there was something delightfully careless about his way of thinking and acting. He had no ambition, because he was in the happy circumstance of succeeding his father in a huge leather business. Of course, he had no bother about money, for the profits of the business were very large indeed; and then again he had no social worries, because, like myself, he could not stand the humbug either of a drawing-room or of a club. He was really a happy creature, being quite free from all those little torments with which people spoil their lives and stultify their minds. Now, that is the kind of man I love to spend my leisure with; a man like that is a great rest from those dreadful creatures whose faces are always white and drawn with the love of money or of notoriety, or of getting on in some way or other; he is a rest, I say, from those who are always chewing hatred and rancour as you might chew a poisonous drug.

"Well," he said, "how are you, after all this time? Share my table, will you not? I have hardly begun." "Thanks," I replied, "I shall be delighted," and ordered my dinner.

I found that Lacquin had lost nothing in this last year of that radiant good humour, and natural delight in life and wisdom of the man of the world, which had so attracted me. He was the same fine fellow, careless of all humbug and nonsense, the same brilliant talker, who never said a fatuous word, and was extremely well-informed on every subject. He was just the same as I had known him a year ago, only that he was even more genial and jovial, from the fact that he was in better health. But all of a sudden, when he was in the middle of a hunting story, he stopped and threw me a glance of pointed meaning, and then turned it on a big fair-haired woman who was followed by a big man with light moustache. The head waiter was just taking them to a table near our own.

" What do you think of her ? " Lacquin whispered, in a very confidential way.

I looked at her with the eye of a critic. " She's a bit of all right," I said. " Good deal of swank about her ! "

" I should jolly well think so," he said. " She's a high-stepper, isn't she ? Well, old chap, that's my wife."

" Good gracious," I said, " you don't say so ! The lady, as you say, is very attractive—" but here I stopped, not knowing exactly what he wanted me to say. I did not want to put my foot in it. The only thing I had ever heard about his marriage was the fall of the curtain, the divorce. When Lacquin told me one day that he lived alone and had been divorced two years before, I could hardly ask particulars, and he offered none. As usual in such cases, there was a moment of silence, and then we went on to another subject. But there is rarely much mystery about these unhappy affairs ; very likely she was a wanton trifler, or he was tired of her, or both, and they had agreed to separate. When I had met him in the country, I came to the conclusion that it was he who had been unfaithful, but I was far from sure of that when I saw her in the garden of the hotel. No, the fault,—if fault there had been,—had lain with those great blue eyes, those heavy eyelids, and that astonishing burden of golden hair. And then I saw her taking off her gloves with the languid and supple manner of women who never, even in public, can throw off the sleepy grace of the lover. I nodded so as to say, " Yes, she is lovely indeed."

Lacquin kept his eyes upon her until her gaze met his, and then turned quietly to me. " She's a beautiful woman ; I will say that for her," he said ; " but Lord, how I have suffered through that hussy ! She gave me three years of it ; three appalling years ! You know I am not difficult to get on with. Well, sir, in those three years I became a cruel, hateful creature, whom it is horrid to think of. I was like a wild beast. There was nothing ordinary about our divorce. From seedtime to harvest, it took no less than three years. By James, what a time it was ! "

I kept silence so as not to seem to invite the secret of his life. He continued, after a pause :

" After all, why should I not tell you the story ? I don't know the lady. I shall never know her again. She is nothing to me. She is no more to me than she was before her marriage, a pretty figure in the street, a certain Mlle. Legoin."

He moved a little on his chair and leaned his arms upon the table, evidently recalling the past. " Yes," he said, " it must have begun about five years ago. One day, about three o'clock, I came home much earlier than usual so as to give Marie a surprise—that is her name. I thought of taking her for a drive in the Bois, or spending the afternoon in chatting or playing with her—anything. I loved her more than I can say. I do not mean as you love a mistress, of whom you can never see enough, but with the ordinary good honest love of marriage, which in two years had never weakened nor been shaken. Quite apart from her beauty, Marie had really been very good to me. I had never cause to notice her attentions to others, and she had the prettiest way of trying to give me pleasure. No, in those days I had nothing against her. Possibly, it is true, I might have wished that she had been a little more intelligent, though, again, ' intelligent ' is hardly the right word. She might perhaps have had a finer insight, a finer judgment about the world and its people. But that is not what you have a wife for ; there are plenty of friends if you want serious talk. When you set up house together, all you want is to live quietly with a dear, good woman. Is that not so ? "

I nodded, and he continued :

" Well, sir, I got to the house and opened the door and came quietly up the stairs. I stole furtively into the drawing-room to give her a surprise. What do you think I saw ? Marie was standing close to the window reading a letter. At every moment she stopped to kiss it, and then read again with a mad joy, and then lavished on it kisses such as you can hardly imagine. Certainly she had never given me the like. In a few swift paces I was at her side, and tried to seize the letter. She crushed the paper in her hands and tried to hide it away, crying, 'O Henri, Henri, please don't.' But I had set my mind on having it, and after a moment's struggle it was in my hand, and I began to read: 'My sweet Beloved.' I could hardly believe my eyes! The pages, from beginning to end, were in my wife's handwriting! It was a love-letter which she had written to herself! It purported to come from a man who said here an infinity of sentimental and disgusting stuff. He had wept incessantly through the last twenty-four hours, and wanted to plunge his face into the river of her golden hair, and would suffer any torment to be allowed to bite her tiny coral ear. And here she was sobbing beside me with her head buried in her hands. 'O Henri, you are cruel, are cruel,' she cried. I was like one bereft of his senses. The most frightful and horrible thoughts swept through my mind like dead leaves driven by the wind. But I bent over her and schooled my voice to its tenderest and most kindly tones. 'Come, Marie,' I said, 'why don't you trust me? You know how truly I love you. Do tell me the meaning of this letter and of all its absurdities.'

"She had not a word to say, and indeed her voice was broken by great sobs. 'No, no, no,' was all that she could murmur. Then all of a sudden she made up her mind, rose and fetched from her desk an envelope addressed to herself in her own handwriting, to 'Mme. Henri Lacquin, 27 Rue Lafayette.' As well as she could speak for weeping, she implored me, 'Do not be angry, do not laugh at me. I wanted so badly to have a love-letter. And then—and then—I thought I would write one to myself.' Just imagine it, she had written to herself that she loved herself! What do you think of that?"

I could hardly say for the moment, and besides, her act appeared to me to have a certain charm about it. I told him so, but Lacquin interjected:

"Yes, that is just what I thought at the first moment. I took Marie on to my knee and into my arms and comforted her and kissed her and gave her a playful little scolding, chaffing her about her friendship with this ardent correspondent. Then I rang for the carriage, and we drove to the Bois. She was now quite happy and pleased, and often laughed with that sweet voice of hers which did me so much good to hear. 'I am a silly little thing,' she would say, 'am I not?' and I would answer, 'You are silly enough for two.' But then there was a change. When we were returning in the twilight she became very thoughtful, so thoughtful indeed as to forget my presence. I wondered what in the world she was thinking of, and then a thought struck cold to my heart. Of course, it was plain as the sun in the sky. She was thinking of Him! She must always now be thinking, quite naturally and inevitably, of Him and Himself alone, the unknown lover whom all her romantic being was for ever awaiting. On this there followed the certainty that she had no love for me. If she had loved me she could never have thought of writing that detestable letter, with its very unpleasant imaginations, so as to voice the lover who was so much desired but who still had never come nor written. Oh, it was horrible! My impulse was to tell her how I hated it all; but it seemed wiser to be silent, lest any incautious words should clothe this imaginary person with more reality than he had yet achieved.

"I could only study her face and wonder what those great eyes of hers were meaning. But in the evening after dinner I could not resist chaffing her as in the afternoon. I asked her whether He was dark or fair, if He was a good sort, if He smoked, if He rode in the Bois, and so forth. At first she was reproachful, pleading that I had given my word not to laugh at her; but soon she entered heartily into the joke and became radiant under the influence of the delightful game, which surely had long been the secret felicity of her life. She drew a picture of Him for me, describing in the minutest detail His character and appearance. I managed to laugh, though my heart was tortured to hear her so ready with an answer to every question about the man who was yet to come. I knew all the time that He was bound to come; He would certainly come and rob me of my Marie's heart.

"From that day forward this pitiful jest continued. Every morning I would ask her whether she meant to meet Him that day, and every evening when I came home from the office I asked how He was and whether she had any letters from Him. Of course you will say that this was a stupid and fatal thing to do, and so it was. But somehow I could not help it. The fact is that He was stronger than I. At home, at dinner, even in our own room, wherever I was with Marie, I felt Him always there. Try to imagine the situation. Realise what it was to be jealous of and to hate with all one's heart an intangible being who did not yet exist, but was unquestionably coming into existence, and who—I knew it with absolute certainty—must some day turn up and take away my wife, who was all the time waiting for Him, and had already saved Him the trouble of writing to declare His love."

Lacquin dropped his voice, saying with a bitter smile, "Aha, my voice has startled you. That is the voice, you understand, which belonged to those dreadful and horrible years. When I look back on them I become once again that insane beast that I was all that time. But let me finish. This life of hidden torture and suspicion went on for two years, until I happened one morning to make some joke about Him in very bad taste indeed. Marie no longer laughed as she had done before. Instead, her face darkened. I insisted on an answer, but she quickly put me in my place. 'My dear boy,' she said, 'surely this comedy has lasted long enough. For my part, I really find it rather dull. It may be your idea of humour, but will you try to understand that it is not mine?'

"So, all this nonsense no longer amused her! You can hardly imagine what an enormous relief her confession was to me. Anything said against Him, any joke at His expense, no longer pleased my lady. I knew what this must mean. At last He had taken to Himself existence, and had really arrived. She had a lover at last. In place of that awful suspense there was now the peace and relief of accomplished and final ill. From this time forward I had no interest in life but to get hold of the brute and to strike Him to the earth—the scoundrel who at last had found courage to appear in the flesh, instead of lurking as a cowardly fugitive phantom in the eyes of the woman I had loved.

"I need not go into all the miserable story: how I put detectives on their track, made out a case, and got my divorce. It is enough that my long martyrdom came at length to an end. For two years I had no longer loved my wife. I was now able to return to the good old way of living which I had followed before the nightmare of my marriage.

"By the way, there is one rather curious thing that I forgot to tell you. My wife had always described Him as having a short brown beard. This had always been a fixed idea with her. But see how wide of the mark we shoot when we try to foresee our fate. That man there is the man in whose arms I found her when——"

Lacquin nodded toward the man with the long fair moustache who was now dining with the late Mme. Lacquin. As I looked from him to her I noticed that her face was slightly turned in the direction of her former husband, and that it wore a pensive little smile.

"Surely," I remarked, "she is smiling at you! Can it be that it is you who have now become Himself?"

Lacquin's reply was given in a tone of derision. "Oh, dear no. That would indeed be a waste of her favours. No; it is not she who is destined to be my love, but another for whom I shall indeed be—Himself. There is some 'Himself' for every one in this world. Not one of us but is that incomparable treasure—to Someone!"

PHILIPPE MONNIER

B. 1864

THE FOOLISH VIRGIN

IT happened when we were seated round a table in a restaurant of a town of which I will not give the name. It was when we were happy boys, each with hardly a moustache, but with a grandiose future. When we laughed we made such a noise that the windows shook. It was awfully cold; it was winter, and the wind was scurrying down the streets. And it was then that she came in.

She was just one of those poor women who go round from door to door singing tiny songs, wearing a threadbare shawl, and carrying a guitar. Some of us knew her, and others did not know her, but we were all of one voice in crying, "Put her out!"

Our wish that she should not enter was due to the fact that we very much valued these evenings together, and did not want either the botheration of a beggar or the unpleasantness of looking upon unhappiness.

All the same, she came in. Shivering with cold, humble, simple, and poor, one of life's victims, she came in. She was certainly Italian, having that weird, wicked air of an old sorceress who is always ready to tell your fortune. You see, our old women, even the poorest of them, have always got something, a shawl or bonnet, which is a link with happier days; when they are almost starving they still make a point of keeping up appearances. But this poor old thing was a derelict of improvidence, and as useless as a broken pitcher. But you could see very well that tears were no strangers to her cheeks, for her pathetic face looked like marble polished by a stream.

Our disgraceful reception did not put her out. She came quietly up the room with that contrite little smile of hers and that look of aged resignation, as if she was quite accustomed to this kind of welcome. She took all our silly noise as a joke; and this was all the more courageous of her, because she was quite conscious that the charm of womanhood had left her long ago.

Young dogs that we were, we shouted all the more; we beat our feet and sticks on the floor, and whistled and made every kind of zoological noise. Really it was a tremendous row, and our only excuse must be that we were very young. The effect was overwhelming, and she suddenly stopped affrighted. Her hands were trembling, and her eyes, unseeing, opened widely, reddened by light and fatigue and tears. She was suddenly aware that we really meant that she should go, and what a helpless, lonely, poor old thing she was. She stayed quite still while you might count sixty, and then her poor little mechanical smile went out. Without a word she turned and went toward the door.

Well, we had gained our point and were alone. The wretched old woman had departed. But as soon as the door had closed behind her and she was out in the inclement night, we all became very silent and rather uncomfortable.

Then Blaise,—I can see Blaise as if he was here,—he had a wonderful voice and eyes lit up with spontaneous goodness. I remember that when he used to sit down in country inns the dogs and children from all around used to come to him. He has gone over to the majority, and on that day when we laid him under ground, I think we buried our youth with him.

He got up and walked quietly out; and then we heard him calling in that silver voice of his to the poor old lady; and they came in together, she with her hand on his arm. They were a picture, the two of them: he was young, in glorious health and joy of life; she was old and worn, and had one foot in the grave.

Partly because of the curiosity of the picture before us, but I think even more because we were thoroughly ashamed of our scandalous conduct, we gave them a rousing cheer. It was a far worse noise than we had made before. We clinked our glasses and raised a cloud of dust from the floor, and a waiter ran in to implore us to be quiet.

The old lady sat down with us, and Blaise did his best to serve her. He seemed happy, eager, and respectful. He called her "Madame," and fished for the best bits of lemon in the punch. But Blaise was always well-behaved to women, even to housemaids and peasants and beggars; we often used to joke him about it.

Of course I must confess that we were very young, and therefore rather coarse. Moreover, this unhappy person now seated with us had been dragged through the gutter, had fallen down into the pit of life, had lent herself to the most degrading uses, and at the last was gaining a crust here and there by a crazy song to the sound of her guitar. She had fallen very low, and I think we had fallen a good deal lower, but as soon as she had taken her seat at our table we became more collected in spirit, and felt that we had a certain bond with her. After all, she was a woman.

She bravely drank the punch, hot and strong as it was, so that it made her cough. She was a little frightened, as if surprised at kindness to which she had been so long unaccustomed. Her fingers were very thin, and she sat just at the very edge of her chair. It really made quite a jolly picture—all these happy boys crowding round the poor old singer. Then some one said, " Won't you sing ? "

And then she sang. She sang the music of old Italy, those melodies for ever sweet and fresh, which leave behind them joy upon the soul as a boat leaves its wake upon the summer seas. One could tell, too, that she had had the best of schooling in the art. I wondered even at what theatre she had burned the hearts of men. But now it was a tiny thread of a voice, like the voice of one of the kids you hear singing when you pass the day school. And these tender little songlets, coming from her dried and ancient lips, touched us with the strangest sense of I know not what. I suppose it was the first time that any of us had realised that nothing lasts in this world, that roses wither and birds fly to other climes, and understood, too, that this youth of ours was fleeting as the roses and the birds, and that even if we should remember it in days to come, it would be but as the echo of a song.

Poor grasshopper of forgotten summers ! She had sung all her life long through. Any one could tell that she had never known how to do anything else but sing. She had sung her breath and life away. Doubtless she had sung before kings and princes, in great halls shining with fair women and lights and jewels. Doubtless she had been worshipped like a goddess. No doubt that when she was young and lovely the applause and the gaze of men went up to her like incense. All summer she had lavished her trills and smiles, and had laughed in the insolence of beauty and the carelessness of the morrow. Her radiant and prodigal youth had been spent on every comer, and every drop from her flask of oil had been consumed in midnight revelry. Then, at last, had fallen the shades of night, and—there was no more oil. The cutting winds had come upon her, and no store was in her larder. With nothing but an old guitar she trailed the streets and begged a livelihood, and boys howled upon her when she came into the café.

I wonder whether she thought of all this, child of joy that she was, who had lived for joy alone and had survived it! O, foolish virgin, who had not learned to die when spring was dead! The myrtles had faded, the song of the birds was done, the laughter of happy couples had ceased from the countryside, but this touching old wretch had gone on, lost in the maze of years and the snows of winter, with no longer any excuse but her misery. She sang with so frail a voice that the noise of a cab would have drowned it. Hers was not the rich fruit of autumn, but the white peace of winter. As for us, on the other hand, we were boys rejoicing in the dawn of life, racing one another up the steeps of hope. All the sky was fair above us, and all our youth was laughing in the sun.

And here, all at once, we were touched by a fellow-feeling for this weird old crone, who had refused to take anything from life but just exactly those things that we ourselves were after, love and laughter, wine and song. She was actually just as old as we were, and our sister. She was just ourselves grown old. And she was a symbol, too, a moral of a kind, to show us at the beginning of joy's path what was its end.

Reflecting many things, we listened in silence with a rich and pleasing melancholy, while the lightsome and florid arias followed one another from her tiny voice.

Whence had come this child of Italy, whom chance had made our guest? What had been the unhappy story of her life? What had been the cost of those first years, when she had learned that sorrow was no longer her servant, but had become her master? If only she had been able to tell you! If only she had known! But the fact is that she did not know. She had never learned anything except to sing and to be pretty and to please her lovers; and the day had come when she could no longer please any one. To tell the truth, she was no more than a bundle of bones, and retained nothing of her former splendour but a pair of rather too gaudy earrings, which were doubtless the memory of an ancient love. Not so very long ago it was she who had graced the tables of others, but now it was only by grace of others that she was received at their table. Why was all this? Surely neither her heart nor her manner had changed. Surely it was not her fault. No; the world was visiting her age and ugliness upon her as if they had been sins.

Contemplating her white hair and all the misery of this playmate who had grown old and could no longer play, we could not but think of other aged women, as, for instance, of our mothers. They were not in the least like this. They were not tossed about at the mercy of fate, but lived in venerable repose. They were comfortably and decently dressed, and were firmly established upon their honourable record. Look into the eyes of any one of them, whether rich or poor, and you will see the same profound and chaste tranquillity, the same sweet and recollected mother's love. But this poor old grasshopper, on the other hand, had no son to dream of or to bless ; even lads like us were men to her, not children.

That was plain enough when she had finished singing, and, thinking to please us, ventured on certain jests which are supposed to appeal to careless manhood. This was quite the saddest thing of all. Her risky playfulness and double meanings were infinitely sadder than those old-world love-songs of hers, or than her miserable life itself. None of us said a word in reply, and the poor old thing was evidently thoroughly ashamed of herself, for she looked round us with so pitiful a gaze that I thought she would break down.

And now she sat quite motionless, her hands clutching at her guitar as if she were afraid that it would be stolen. She was like some wild creature not quite sure that any kindness was not a trap. She said not a word, and was intently awaiting some horrible jest to be sprung upon her. A few minutes ago, when we were hissing and jeering at her, she had smiled from force of habit ; but now that we were altogether friendly she was every moment on the watch. Her eyes and head were lowered, and she sat silent before an empty glass. It was then that Blaise spoke to her with his honest and good-hearted voice. He clothed her with his interest and sympathy. He tried to assuage this horrible fear of hers.

For some time she was unable to reply. It seemed to me that she could find nothing, though she raked in the ashes of her memory. But those bright eyes of his, and his honest smile, and that voice which always touched one like a caress, began to do their work. And when she spoke, it was not of her loves or her successes, nor of the sand or mud which the flow of time's river had washed upon her shores, but of the days when she lived at home a little girl, and herded geese along the green hillsides. This was what she treasured—the fact that she had been loved, that her nurse had put her to sleep cuddled in her arms and singing to her. This alone had survived the shipwreck of a life.

This fact of love was the luminous and lovely truth. This was what came to the memory of this ancient hag of the gutter.

As if no time had flowed away, and as if everything which separated her from blissful childhood had been nothing but a dream or an illusion, she told us boys a thousand absurdities of those days so long ago, which came quite fresh and sweet from under the ruins of her memory. There was a boy who had made her such a clever bird-trap. That day when her brother went away on horseback to the wars, how his sword shone and how brave his plume! And you should have seen those Corpus Christi processions, especially one when she had led the way, a tiny white-robed child, candle in hand. And then she told us of her first communion in the parish church, which smelt that day, oh, how sweet, of branches and of herbs.

Strange, simple soul, had she ever since then received the Sacred Host? And had Its merciful miracle worked in this queer old body any cleansing or renewal? Not many months could pass before again the priest should bring to her the Blessed Sacrament, to where she lay in some hovel or infirmary. And then, this flighty songful soul, forgetting all her sins and all the wearisome paths of error, would go all white and clean to heaven. God would forget those passing adventures of hers. Indeed, would she herself remember them? Had not her forgetfulness and unconsciousness of evil already brought her back to that white little girl, candle in hand? I tell you that in this restaurant, where we ourselves were quite far enough removed from the realities of life, we felt a sudden unity, we young men, with this ancient child. She spoke a language which we altogether understood. We had exactly the same feelings and had the same stories to tell. Our hearts came together with hers, and we drew our chairs nearer; and we were very happy indeed, let the wind blow never so wild and cold outside.

All of a sudden she smiled rather wonderfully. Something had come into her memory and had evoked a whole world of long-forgotten images. It was a song; might she sing it? Of course we said "Yes" and "Hurrah!"

Doubtfully at first, but soon with growing certainty, she sang this song to us. It had nothing in common with those gay lyrics of hers all flowery with spring and love, which were, after all, the songs of her profession. It was an old, old peasant chanty, so good, so elemental, one of those dear old grandmother songs which you may find in any land the world over, and which teach you how like all peoples are. God knows when or where she had picked it up. She had forgotten it, and across this great space of time had recalled it, with us—and may I not say, perhaps because of us?

As she sang she slowly swayed and nodded, moving her head to right and left, her trained voice doing it every justice. There were no more trills or flourishes; she only remembered the countryside of long ago. This ancient ditty had some kind of refrain, and Blaise soon joined in it with a sweet tenor. All of us followed him. And then, at the end of this chorus, we were silent, while her thin, feeble, but now joyous voice renewed its antique strains.

The old girl was smiling all over. She was happy and calm. We had all of us found our real point of contact. There was no longer the poor old wandering beggar and a few smug youths; all our spirits were united in one sympathy and intention. It is the fact that there are eternal realities which bring all men together, whether they be learned or simple, rich or poor, strangers or dwellers in the same house, and these are the things which lie at the root of all humanity and at the source of every life and being. Why do we not, in brotherly fashion, seek those things which are the same for all of us, instead of seeking, as we are so apt to do, every possible point which may distinguish and separate and make us envious?

And now the singer was ready to go. She was warmed and comforted. She could take out into that dark winter night a new peace and happiness. Not the drinks we had given her nor the contagion of our youth, but our sympathy had done her good. We had really subscribed for her a little of our hearts.

She got up to go—and when in this city shall we see her again?—and one of us took off his hat and took it round the table. We threw in everything we had, copper and silver, the coins which by some miracle remained in our trouser pockets, and the cash had a jolly tinkle and laugh as it fell into the hat. The old lady was in an ecstasy of delight, and I verily think believed she had got to heaven.

Many years have passed, and yet I remember that hat going round the table. It collected little, and there was nothing very noble about our impulse. But when I look back on our unprofitable youth, wherein there was so little good of any kind and so many scandalous extravagances, I sometimes think that this absurd boyish act of generosity is after all the thing which it is pleasantest to remember.

ANDRÉ GODARD
B. 1865

THE NONA

COUNT RAYMOND DE VILLEMÈRE woke at last from the heavy stupor of unconsciousness which had lain so long upon him, and slowly stretching his limbs, murmured, "Thank Heaven, I am safe!"

But his eyes suddenly met those of the doctor, fixed upon him with an expression of profoundest sorrow, as the old man exclaimed, with a deep sigh, "My poor, dear friend!"

The Count was startled by his alarming tone.

"If you will brace yourself to hear it," the doctor continued, "I will tell you the whole truth."

"Whatever are you talking about?"

"You have all the symptoms of nona."

"What do you say that I have?"

"It is a mysterious and dreadful illness, which begins with a period of deep unconsciousness. This is followed by an interval of brightness and apparent health, lasting for three hours. But at the end of that time the patient suddenly—expires!"

"Good Heavens!"

"Why trouble, after all?" the doctor resumed. "Is life really worth while? And you, I know, are a brave man, and need have no fear of death. Good-bye, dear friend! Good-bye!"

With these words the doctor left him alone, in order that he might settle up any business that might have to be done in the short time still left to him. The Count presently rose from his couch and began to dress with the most scrupulous care. After arranging his hair and putting the finest polish on his dainty nails, he got into a soft smoking-jacket, and, choosing a good cigar, sank down into the sofa-cushions to smoke and meditate. Ah, for all those many cigars which he might never smoke!

The Count was a brave man; the thought of death had no terrors for him; but he might be excused for thinking that fate had dealt with him in a particularly cruel and unfair way.

Yesterday he had been convinced that he was about to die ; and when he felt the fever taking hold upon him had called in priest and lawyer, and had burned all his correspondence. And when all this was finished, he lay back upon the pillows, believing in his heart that he would never wake again on earth.

He felt now as a criminal must feel who has been sentenced to death and has then been reprieved, but finds himself at last cheated of his hope, face to face with the gallows.

It was mid-June. The world outside was all brightness, colour, and joyous movement. The gay-liveried equipages of the wealthy passed in endless procession along the Champs-Elysées, and the streets were crowded with people enjoying life to the full. At this moment he felt in as perfect health as any one of them ; and yet, if he was to believe the doctor's verdict, long before to-morrow's dawn, all this gay crowd would for him be no more. The only procession left for him was the rumbling, slow ride in a sombre hearse, with the silent, black-robed mourners, ending at the newly dug grave, and the muttered prayers above it. All that he had loved in life, its dearly loved faces, its pleasures, its romance, its emotion, would be never any more.

And now, in the curling smoke of his half-consumed cigar, he seemed to be reviewing the whole drama of his life. Ancient memories of childhood came back with all the vividness of a dream ; and then he saw, following one another in swiftest images, the faces which had figured in all those many love-romances of his youth ; and at last he lived once more through that first sweet month which had followed his marriage.

Raymond remembered every moment of those wonderful days of cloudless bliss. What a gay and glorious holiday their honeymoon had been ! What fun they had had, and how jolly and bohemian they had been ! They had made quite a stir, and some of their escapades had come near to providing society with scandals. Everywhere they had gone his wife had been the centre of admiration, and he had rejoiced in her and had loved her more passionately every day. With what bitterness he reflected upon the stupid misunderstanding which had shattered their happiness ! A mad blunder on his side, the carelessness of high spirits on hers, and the Count and his little Countess had agreed to part for ever !

They lived apart, indeed, and met only as chance acquaintances ; but in their hearts they loved one another as passionately as before ;

and those who knew them best had least belief in their comedy of indifference. So it was to the Countess that the dying man's thoughts were turned in these last moments that he had to live. He *could not* die without seeing her once more! Surely at a solemn time like this, neither of them could persist in an attitude of relentless pride!

Raymond decided at least to make the attempt. After all, if it should fail, he had nothing now to lose by it. Rising hastily, he seized a telegraph-form and wrote a few words, then rang for his servant, and told him to send it off at once.

He took out his watch. Two hours still remained to him! There was yet time for her to come!

But would she come? Would this appeal, though sent in the hour of death, succeed in moving her woman's heart; or would her woman's pride, looking only on her private injuries, still refuse to relent, even at this awful crisis?

His heart was torn by the conflicting emotions of hope and despair, and in spite of his resolve to face with calm resignation everything that must come, his nerve began now to give way. As his few brief moments passed so swiftly into death, he found himself watching the clock with a dreadful fascination. One precious hour had flown! He sat at his desk and wrote to his mother, telling her all, and recalling a chain of tender memories.

He was brushing away the tears which could not be kept from his eyes, when the door-bell rang sharply, and before he had time to rise, his heart beating furiously with excitement, the servant announced the Countess of Villemère!

His face went dead white. "Odette!" he cried hoarsely, springing up from his chair.

But the visitor did not move a step. She stood just within the door; and as she looked at him a flame of anger kindled in her face.

"How dare you deceive me so cruelly?" she said, in tones of deepest indignation.

"Deceive you? How?"

"Your wire said that you were ill and dying, yet here you are writing letters, as well as you have ever been. Good afternoon!"

"Odette! Odette! Listen for one moment! Let me explain!"

She turned angrily to leave the room, but the Count seized the letter to his mother which was lying on his desk, and thrust it into her hand. "At least," he cried, "read this!"

She took the letter and scanned its earliest sentences ; then, unable to read any further, she threw herself weeping into his arms.

"My poor darling ! Oh, it is true, then, true ! " she cried.

He clasped her more closely, and for a long time they forgot all else, locked in the embrace of utter suffering and of bliss. Thoughts of their happy life together passed unspoken between them ; and passionate regrets for the wasted year of foolish pride thrilled their repentant hearts.

He drew her down beside him on the sofa, and with clasped hands they sat in silence, too deeply moved for words.

Once the Count ventured on a jest, evoked by the memory of an ancestor who had gone to the block humming an operatic air. "I suppose I should be proud," he said with a smile ; "doubtless I shall be a leader of fashion, and to-morrow all Paris will have this new disease." But Odette could not bear this ghastly humour, and when he saw that he had pained her, he spoke no longer in that strain.

After a time they fell to talking of the old happy days. They spoke at first hardly above a whisper, and with the sense of being in a death-chamber ; but gradually this excessive awe receded before the train of memories conjured up by all the familiar furniture of the room, and they began to smile as they recalled to one another details of their many adventures, and of those sweet times now gone for ever. A hunting picture made them think of the first day on which they had followed the hounds together ; and they seemed to hear again, as on that misty November morning, the cheery horn of the huntsman and the crisp rustle of dead leaves beneath their horses' feet. They handled the dust-begrimed little favours which brought them together in a cotillon of long ago, and remembered the tender gay coquetry amid the palms of the conservatory that evening.

How many wonderful mornings had seen them out early on horseback, cantering under the trees in the Bois, and enjoying existence like a couple of truant schoolboys. Then they would breakfast at the Pavilion, and return home by way of the Champs-Elysées. Then for a few hours they had to part, each to endure a round of tiresome social functions ; but in the evening they would meet once more, perhaps at the Opéra, but oftener quietly at home.

Living over again in memory those happy days, Raymond and Odette forgot all else, even the fatal shadow which had brought about their reunion, until the sound of the bell suddenly startled them into recollection. They looked at one another in terrible anguish.

The servant entered. " Doctor Darlois ! " he announced.

" What ! " cried the astonished doctor. " You are still up ? Why, I called to—— "

" You called to—what ? "

" As I seem to have made a mistake, I may as well tell you the truth. I thank God that I was wrong. I came round to convince myself that you were really dead."

" You are very kind," said the Count with a smile.

" Is he—going to live ? " asked the anxious little wife.

" Certainly. There is no doubt now. I don't understand it at all. He had all the symptoms of nona, as described by the highest authorities. Let me assure you that I am overjoyed to find—— "

No doubt it was indeed a joyful surprise to the worthy physician. But perhaps there was also in the depth of his heart just a tinge of annoyance at his failure in diagnosis.

" Don't you think, Odette," Raymond whispered, smiling, " that it would be a good idea to ask him to dine with us this evening ? "

MARCEL SCHWOB
1867–1905

THE WOODEN STAR

I

ALAIN'S grandmother was an old charcoal-burner, who lived in the heart of the forest. This forest was immemorially old, and so dense that its paths were merely clearings through the trees, which opened from time to time upon little green lawns surrounded by giant oaks ; or, again, upon a moveless sea of bracken, and above it the impenetrable interlacings of delicate twigs. Here, through the ages, these majestic trees reared their mighty colonnades, among which the fugitive leaves held counsel, their branches forming window-frames through which one looked upon an immense sea of green, with its deeps of heavily scented shade and its pale rays of light from the hidden sun. Here was all the magic of a bank of purple heath or a flaming river of gorse among the trees ; the wonderful filigree of glimmering lights and shadows ; the freshness of young pines and oak trees springing up in the natural clearings, and swaying lightly in the soft breezes ; the great forked mossy roots of the ancient trees plunging deep into their beds of red-brown pine-needles. Squirrels had their homes in the tree-trunks, adders in the rich earth beneath them ; myriads of insects darted and circled in the spaces, and the leafy galleries were filled with the songs of countless birds.

In the heat of midsummer the forest was alive with humming, like a mighty ant-hill ; and whenever there was rain, it continued for long afterwards a rain which was quite its own, falling slowly and aimlessly from the tree-tops, and dripping sadly on to the dead leaves. It seemed, indeed, to breathe and to sleep, at times even to snore ; and again, held in a profound silence, to be watching intently, without so much as the rustle of a snake or the warble of a bird. What was it for which the whole forest was waiting ? No one could say. This forest was like a feminine creature of moods and fancies ; now throwing out a strong line of birch trees, straight as the flight of an arrow, then ending it tremblingly in a cluster of aspens ; now advancing a step beyond her boundaries, right out into the open plain, and, again, repenting of such temerity, seeming to flee back to the cool, sombre depths of her ancient woods, into the everlasting night at her heart. All sorts of wild creatures lived in peace and unmolested within her boundaries; but there was something inimical to man in this tremendous palisade of inexorable trunks, stretching out on all sides like huge petrified lightning flares thrown up by the earth.

The forest was not unfriendly to Alain; but it had, in fact, hidden the heavens from him. The little boy had so far known no other light than the dim confused greenness which pervaded it, and in the evening he used to see the stack of charcoal glowing with little red points here and there. He had never seen the procession of gold and silver lights across the spangled night sky. His little life had been passed with the good old charcoal-burner, whose face, like the bark of a tree, had settled into the deep lines of patient and peaceful old age. He helped her daily to cut down branches, to pile them up into stacks, to cover the piles with earth and with turves, to see that the fire burned slowly and gently, to pull out the pieces into black heaps, and to fill the sacks of the charcoal-heavers, whose faces were almost indistinguishable in the forest gloom.

But Alain had many joys and delights of his own in this deep old wood. He loved to lie at mid-day under the tall bracken and listen to all the forest sounds, watching the tiny dancing circles of sunlight, and drowsily meditating upon the fact that his grandmother and he were neither green like the world nor black like the burnt charcoal, until he would fall asleep and dream that the old woman was a twisted oak tree, and that the trees were seated at table sharing their soup. He liked to watch the saucepan boiling on the fire, and would wait expectantly to sniff up its delicious smell; and he delighted in the gurgling of the water when he thrust his little stone jug into the spring, where three big stones held it as in a cup. Sometimes a lizard would dart across the foot of an elm like a wavy flash of green light, or in a hollow on the trunk of the tree a huge flaming toadstool would form.

Many such delights the forest had for Alain, and at ten years old he had a heart and mind filled with the dreams which it gave. In the autumn of that year a great storm swept over the forest. The mighty trees groaned and creaked, as the torrents of rain pelted down through their thick foliage, and squalls of wind came swirling among their tops; the noise of the tempest became deafening; it crashed through the wood, carrying destruction before it, and many veteran trees received their death-blow. The great trunks fell headlong to the ground, carrying with them masses of shattered branches, twigs, and foliage; the wonderful forest roof lay in fragments beside its fallen columns, and through these yawning gaps the unwonted daylight penetrated into its scared depths.

In the evening, when the storm had subsided and peace reigned once more in the forest, Alain went out into the glorious freshness which follows upon a long and fierce tempest, to dip his basin in the little pool of the spring. As he stooped down to the water he saw in it brilliant points of light, glittering, shaking, and dancing, as if in sparkling laughter. He thought at first that they must be sparks of fire like those which glowed in the charcoal piles; but when he tried to touch them with his fingers they did not burn him, and always escaped his grasp, glancing hither and thither, and returning defiantly to their first place. These were cold and mocking bits of fire. Then, leaning over further, Alain saw among them the reflection of his own face and hands. So he looked up above him.

There, through a great rent in the curtain of foliage, shone the radiant sky, no longer hidden or veiled by the forest. Alain had a sense of sudden confusion, as if he had been discovered naked, for from this vast distant blue vault thousands of bright eyes were shining steadily down upon him, twinkling and sparkling, piercing the distance with their myriad glancing rays. Thus Alain saw the stars for the first time in his life, and they smote his heart with a wonderful joy and an immense desire.

He rushed in to his grandmother, who was gently stirring the pile of charcoal, lost in thought, and asked her how it came that there were a lot of shining points of fire shimmering among the trees and reflected in the little pool.

"Those are the bright stars of heaven, Alain," she told him. "Above this forest there is the sky, and the people who live outside in the open country see it all the time. And every night God lights His stars in the sky."

"God lights His stars in the sky," repeated the boy. "And could I light stars, too, grandmamma?"

The old woman stroked his head with her hard wrinkled hand. "You are too small," she said. "We are all of us too small. Only God Himself can light His stars in the dark night."

And again the boy repeated her words, "Only God Himself can light His stars in the dark night."

II

From this time a certain restlessness tinged all Alain's former delight in his forest life. There was a jarring note in the sounds which had sung him to sleep, and the lacy bracken was no longer a protecting nest. The sunlight seemed to die off the mosses with disappointing quickness, and he grew tired of living in these gloomy green shades. He longed for light, for something far beyond the glistening of lizards or the heavy vividness of toadstools or the red glow of the charcoal. Before going to bed he stole out to the little pool and looked up to the glittering face of the sky. His whole soul went out in a great yearning to be beyond the dark gloom shut in by these beeches and oaks and elms, behind which were other beeches and oaks and elms, and always more and more of them, an impenetrable night of great forest trees. He remembered his grandmother's words, and his pride was stung by them: "*Only* God Himself can light His stars in the dark night." He thought, "I, too, might be able to light my stars if I could go into the open country outside the forest. Oh, I must go; I *will* go!"

Nothing any longer pleased him within the forest, which seemed to besiege him like an entrenched army; which held him as in a harsh prison, where tree-gaolers in ever-increasing numbers barred his escape, holding out threatening arms in all directions, rearing themselves like huge, terrible, silent ogres, supported by knotty buttresses and by forked barricades, and with enormous unfriendly hands. The forest now seemed to him to be hostile to all that was not part of itself, to anything that was not one with its own dark and gloomy heart. It would soon close up again the rents which the storm had made and by which the light had entered, and the little pool would once more become shrouded in darkness, unable to see or reflect the dancing lights of the sky.

But Alain dreamed of stars which were always dancing. And one night, while his grandmother was asleep, he escaped from the little hut, taking with him some bread and a hard end of cheese.

The charcoal piles gave out a few quiet glimmers of dying light. What a miserable light beside the living sparkles of the sky! In the night the great oaks were only like huge shadow forms blindly groping in the dark. These grim gaolers were, like his grandmother, asleep, but they slept standing at their posts, each trusting to the others to keep watch, and Alain knew that they would remain thus silent and still until the first fresh breath of dawn stirred among their leaves. But by that time he would already be beyond their power. When all the birds chirped out their warning, Alain would already have slipped through their hands, out into the open plain where they dared not follow him. They might threaten as much as they liked from a distance, this army of dark giants, but it would be in vain; they could only gather themselves together in ever thicker ranks, spread out their forked palisades and their silent tentacles, thrust forward their great heads or their horrible club-like branches; but at the edge of the plain they became powerless, held in a sudden enchantment, dazzled into stupor, as it were, by the light.

Once safely out in the open, Alain dared at last to look round. The great black giants seemed to look after him sadly. Then he looked up. Surely a miracle had appeared in the sky. The whole vault of heaven was studded thickly with stars, twinkling and flashing, dying out and rekindling, growing larger and smaller, shining red or gold or steely-blue or silvery-white, uniting and separating again. Sometimes they shone with piercing radiance, painful to the eyes, but again took on a softer light, then became misty and blurred, shone clearly again, and glanced through the air with the sharpness of a stiletto. Alain began to discover all sorts of figures among them—houses, carriages, animals—and the light gleamed first on one feature and then on another. Now it sparkled on the roof, now on the doorway, now on the end of the carriage-pole, and then it disappeared from all, and in the changing brilliance all the forms he had seen became confused.

The boy stretched out his arms into the night, longing to seize these lights and to shape them into new forms of his own. He wanted to find out what their fires were like, and whether there were up there great piles of blue charcoal studded with points of flame.

He looked about him over the plain. Flat, bare, and formless it stretched away to the horizon, with no stir of life amid its low vegetation. In the distance wound a slow-moving river, showing only as a vague white ribbon upon the plain; and Alain crossed to this river that he might see the stars in it. Here they seemed to be flowing with it, to have become fluid changing things, now distorted in shape, now round, and again divided into a crowd of fine glittering lines. Sometimes they came to the water's edge, strayed into a backwater, and died, stifled among the bunches of weeds.

All night long Alain walked up and down the river bank. The coming dawn threw a shroud of pale grey over all the stars, shot with pink and gold. Alain sat down under a small tree with silvery quivering leaves, and munched his bread, drinking from the running stream. He was a little tired; but he walked on all day, and at night slept in a hollow in the steep river-bank. The next morning he started walking again.

And now the river became much wider and the plain more colourless; the air was damp and salty, his feet sank in the sand, and a tremendous murmuring sound seemed to fill the space in front of him. White birds were sweeping and circling, uttering shrill and mournful cries. The water turned yellow and green, swelled up and became foamy. The river's banks gradually disappeared. Soon Alain could see nothing but a vast stretch of sand, across which in the distance ran a long dark streak. Here the river was stopped by a barrier of foam, against which its wavelets seemed to dash themselves in vain; it spread itself out into a great flood, sweeping over the sandy plain as far as the eye could see.

Alain saw tufts of sea-pinks and of dry yellow reeds dotted over the sands. A ceaseless tumult was all about him. The fresh salt breeze played over his face. The water rose and fell in perpetual rhythm, the white-crested waves breaking on the shore like dark yawning mouths closing down to swallow it up. As they fell they cast up along the sand a line of slime and bubbling foam, and amid it all sorts of strange and beautiful fragments; shining shells perforated with tiny holes, wonderful fossil flowers, bright crinkled cornets, weird, soft, transparent things which moved with quaint and rapid motions, indeed an extraordinary mass of debris. The low roar of the waves was sad and soft; they did not groan like the forest trees, but in another voice of more gentle complaint. But they, too, must have been jealous and insensible as the forest; the light could never penetrate into the deeps of the rolling purple billows.

Alain ran along its margin, delighting to draw his feet through the wet foam. The sun had set, and for a moment red flares from the western sky took fire in the shining waters and glowed there. Then night covered the ocean's face and reigned supreme, silencing the rolling of the waves, and in the sky above the stars shone out. But the ocean did not mirror the stars. Impervious as the forest, its cold dark heart resisted their radiant beauty by the ceaseless movement of its surface. The mountainous waves heaped themselves up, and in the same moment were again dissolved ; they advanced in armies at a furious gallop, only to fall in a moment utterly lost to view.

A dancing light appeared at the base of a jutting cliff, and Alain advanced to examine it. At the water's edge were a group of children, moving busily about, examining the treasures left on the beach by the sea ; one of them was carrying the unsteady light. Alain joined them, and saw that they were gathering up little star-shaped things full of wonderful lights and colours—rosy, violet, shimmering blue, spotted vermilion, touched with phosphorescence. They looked like the palms of unearthly hands, with shrivelled fingers curling round them, or like fleshy leaves of some sea plant, endowed with life and movement, or like starry beasts which belonged to the deeps of a dark firmament.

" Sea stars ! sea stars ! " the children shouted gleefully.

" Ah," said Alain, " stars ! "

The boy who held the light turned to Alain. " I will tell you the story of the stars," he said. " On the night when Our Lord was born, who is the children's God, a lovely new star was born. It was a great big blue star ; it followed Him wherever He went, and He loved it. When wicked men killed Him the star wept tears of blood, and three days after His death it died too. It fell into the sea and was drowned. At the same time a great many other stars drowned themselves in the sea for grief at His death. The sea, being sorry for their unhappiness, would not let them lose their beautiful colours, and every night gives them up to us in this sweet way so that we may keep them in memory of Our Lord."

" But can I not light them again ? " asked Alain.

" They are dead," said the boy. " They have been dead ever since Our Lord died."

When Alain heard this he turned away, his head bent down, and left the little band of torchlight seekers. He had no desire for a dead, drowned star, whose light was put out for ever ; he wanted to light a star, even as God does, to rejoice in its brilliance, and to see it rise through the clouds, far beyond the shadows of the forest which shut out the stars, far from the deep glooms of the great sea which drowned them. These children might collect dead stars if it pleased them, might keep them and cherish them, but he had no use for them. He had no idea where he should find his own particular star; but he was certain that he would find it. It would be wondrous lovely; he would light it himself and it would belong to him; perhaps, even, it would follow him everywhere, as the glorious blue star followed Our Lord. God, who had so many stars, could not grudge this one to little Alain; he wanted it so badly. How astonished his grandmother would be when he went back home and the whole terrible forest was lighted to its darkest corners by his star! He would say to her then, "It is not only God who can light the stars. Here is a star which is all mine. Only Alain lights this one, to shine amid these old trees. This is my star, my own star of fire!"

The dancing light of the children's torch moved hither and thither, reddening as the night grew misty, until it died away in the darkness, and with it the shadowy forms of the children. Alain was alone again. A fine drizzling rain began to fall, chilling him to the bone, and shrouding him in a delicate network of tiny drops, which filled all the vast space about him. The unceasing sea now murmured gently, now grew to a deep roar, while at times a huge wave would dash with a loud report against the cliff, and, scattering into spray, would rise like a great foam-spectre into the black night. Gradually it settled down into a low monotonous plaint, like the sighs of a sick person whom sleep evades, or the gentle strife of light breezes. Then all became still for Alain.

III

Day followed day, and Alain watched the rising and the setting of the stars; but still he had not found his own star. He had reached a countryside where everything was dried up, and the autumn grass had turned yellow over the fields, while the vine leaves were reddening on the stems before the sour and thickly clustered bunches of immature grapes. Long lines of poplars stretched across the plain, and clumps of oak trees made dark spots upon the bleached meadows of the gently sloping hills, while the steeper hills were crowned with dark, gaunt pines. On the vast uplands the trees stood in open and formidable array, amid which the little clusters of fir trees made by contrast quite a cheerful note.

Across this barren plain a clear, pebbly little stream wound its way, leaping gently down a hillock, its bed half dried up below the first of its falls, then making itself two arms to encircle the base of flower-covered ruins of old wooden houses. The water was so transparent that the backs of the shining, speckled fishes, lying in close, motionless groups on the bottom, were clearly seen, and the pebbles made a bright mosaic of its bed. At night Alain saw cats crouching on both its banks, intent on catching fish.

In the distance, where the stream became a river, a charming little town nestled on its low banks, whose tiny houses had pointed roofs and many grated windows, and wonderful chimney-pots painted blue and yellow. There was an old wooden bridge and an old monastery, a great ruddy, shadowy edifice, with the sign of Saint George in the act of thrusting his lance into the jaw of a huge red sandstone dragon.

The shimmering green river swept in a broad curve about the little city. On the one side of it, in the distance, rose great snow-capped mountains, and on the other side the pleasant hills, up which the streets of the town sloped gently, each bearing its own signboard painted in colours—the "Helmet Road," the "Crown Road," the "Swan Road," and the "Wild-Man Road," which was near the Fish Market, with its great stone lion, from whose mouth issued a fountain of crystal water. There were homely inns, where jolly-faced girls poured out the sparkling wine into tankards of pewter. In the centre was the town hall, where the magistrates held their courts of justice, arrayed in a cloak of fine cloth over a shirt of unbleached linen, and wearing the gold ring of office on their second finger; and in the narrow streets surrounding it one might see stalls full of inkhorns and parchment for the use of the lawyers and their clerks. The women of the little town had wonderful blue eyes in patient faces full of love and gentleness; they wore veils of tulle over their heads, and sometimes the mouth was covered with a band of fine white linen; the girls, in their white dresses, with slashed sleeves and gay-coloured girdles, carried distaffs, upon which they seemed to be spinning their long golden hair, and the little children had glorious red locks and the fairest of skins.

Alain passed under a low, thick-set arch into the Old Market, a rambling square encircled with small houses, hunched up under the slated roofs like old women squatting over a fire. The parish church, with its monstrous gargoyles bearded with heavy mosses, was built about a great square tower, tapering away into a long pointed spire. Close by was the barber's shop, whose thick bulging windows, round as bubbles, were flanked by green shutters, on which were painted in red, designs of scissors and lancets. In the centre of the square was the well, its kerb worn away by the steps of the thousands who had used it, its opening guarded by a dome-shaped lattice of iron against the barefoot urchins who were always playing about it, some running, some engaged in a game of hopscotch, and one fat little boy with a treacly mouth sobbing quietly by himself. Alain tried to talk to them ; but the children ran away and stared furtively at him, without answering a word.

The night dew began to fall through the smoky air, and candles shone in the thick window-panes with deep ruddy light. Doors were fastened, shutters closed, and the bolts were drawn. The signboard of the inn creaked on its iron support, and through the half-open door Alain could see the light of the great log-fire, could sniff up the good smell of the roasting joint, and hear the wine being poured out ; but he was afraid to go in. Then a woman's gruff voice announced that it was closing time, and Alain slipped into a narrow by-street.

In this inhospitable town he could find no shelter from the cold night air. The forest at least offered the hollows in its cloven trunks and the river the little pits in its banks ; on the plain one could creep into the furrows of the stubble-fields, and by the sea find shelter in the angles of the cliff ; even the parched countryside of yesterday had given him a ditch under a hedge to sleep in ; but this sullen, bleak-hearted town, with its many rows of tightly closed doors, had not a friendly corner to offer the little wanderer ; even the stalls were all dismantled and stowed away. In every direction it raised hostile barriers across his path, throwing out suddenly posts or planks from side to side of the winding passages and alleys. Without any warning a house would thrust out its turrets into the street, or another overhang it darkly with its gables, so that the ways of the town were everywhere dark and forbidding ; its buildings, like gloomy sentinels, cast over all an inhospitable silence and a thick pall of night. Alain trudged up and down and found himself wandering in circles, till he arrived once more in the Old Market square. All the windows were dark and shuttered up, except one small round window, where the light of a candle still flickered feebly.

This gleam of hope shone out from beside one corner of the church tower, and Alain found a door opening upon a spiral staircase which led right up to it. He plucked up courage and started to mount it. Half way up a cresset was burning, casting a dim light on to the staircase, and when he reached the top he found a weird-looking door studded with bronze nails. He stopped to take breath, and from within came the sound of an old yet piercing voice speaking in short, broken phrases. As he listened Alain's heart began to beat rapidly, and he felt as if he must choke. The strange old voice was talking about the stars! Alain put his ear to the iron-bound keyhole and waited, entranced. The voice went on:

"Stars which are baneful and of bad influence for the night, for this hour, and for those who inquire of them, write:—Sirius, showing blood red; the Great Bear, hidden by clouds; the Little Bear, veiled in mist. The Pole Star is brilliant and of warlike aspect. To-night, Tuesday, Mars red and fiery, in the eighth house, the house of the Scorpion, signifying death by fire, battle, slaughter, and consuming flames. At this third hour, injurious in its essence, Mars is in conjunction with Saturn in the house of fear, signifying death, calamities, and failure in all undertakings. Mars and Saturn are in union, signifying fire during the night and alarms while men sleep. The aspect is contrary, for the Bull enters into the Upper Circle and the Scorpion into the Lower Circle. Jupiter in the second house is in opposition to Mars in the eighth, signifying the ruin of all wealth and glory and might. The fiery Mars rules over all the buildings and life which belong to Saturn, signifying the city in flames and deaths by fire. In the third hour of this night of Tuesday, God is about to turn His eyes from His stars, and to deliver the souls of men to the flames."

As the voice of the old wizard finished dictating these words, the door was burst open by excited little hands and feet, and Alain drew himself up on the threshold, indignant, erect, and with blazing eyes.

"It's a lie!" he cried. "God never forgets His stars. Only God can light His stars in the dark night!"

An old bent man in a long sable robe, who was stooping over an astrolabe made in the form of an armillary sphere, raised his head, blinking his red eyelids like some ancient night-bird startled from its hole. A thin, pale little boy, who was seated at his feet writing down on parchment the horoscope, dictated by the old wizard, dropped the reed from between his fingers. The flames of two great wax candles waved and flared up in the draught. The old man stretched out his arm, showing at the end of his furry sleeve a hand as skinny as the hand of a mummy.

"Oh, unbelieving and untutored child," he said, "in what dark ignorance you live! Listen, this child here will teach you. Tell him, my child, what is the nature of the stars."

The thin, pale little boy recited as out of a lesson-book:

"The stars are fixed upon the crystal vault of heaven, and revolve so quickly on their own axis that they become ignited by their own motion. God is only the prime mover of these orbs, and the first cause of the revolution of the seven spheres; but since this first moving the sphere of the stars obeys only its own laws, and rules according to its inclination the events on this earth and the destinies of men. Such is the teaching of Aristotle and of Holy Church."

"It's a lie!" reiterated Alain. "God knows all His stars, and He loves them. He has shown them to me in spite of the big trees in the forest which used to hide the sky, and He has made them float along the river and dance so jollily over the great plain: and I have seen, too, the stars that drowned themselves when Our Lord died, and soon He will show me my own star."

"My child, God will show you your own star. So be it!" said the old man.

Alain was not sure whether he meant what he said. He heard nothing more, for at that moment a sudden gust of wind blew out the candles. He groped his way along the wall to the stairs, and, growing bold, seized the little copper lamp with its floating wick, and bore it off, thinking he would punish the horrid old man for his lies about the stars.

The whole place was in black darkness, but Alain came safely out into the street by the light of his lamp. The night sky was covered with a lattice-work of stars, crossed by the finest airy threads with sparkling knots, and with a network of limpid fire hung upon it. Alain raised his face toward this radiant spectacle. The stars seemed to laugh at him with their sparkling, frosty laugh. There was no pity for him in their glance; indeed, they did not know him, since he had been all his life hidden from them by the horrid thick forest. These lofty and dazzling gems of beauty could only laugh at him, small as he was, with his flickering smoky lamp; but they would laugh, too, at the old wizard, with his lies and his extinguished candles. He looked at them again, wondering whether they laughed in pleasure or mockery, and thinking that they must be happy because they danced so joyously. Did they know that some day Alain would light one of them, and had God told them, perhaps, which it was to be? Surely, one night, this little star would come down to him and he would only have to pick it like a ripe fruit ; or, if it would not let him touch, it might fly in front of him with its wings of fire, laughing with him and making him laugh, till the gloomy old forest should be sprinkled all through with tiny lights which were just sparkling gleams of laughter.

Alain had reached the old bridge, which trembled on its carved pillars as he walked. Between its great girders the water could be seen. Half way across was a watchman's box covered all over with blue and yellow tiles, but the watchman had deserted his post, or he would not have let Alain pass with his lamp. The boy walked very quickly past it, not daring to let the light shine into its dark opening. Across the bridge were the humbler streets, whose houses had none of the coloured coats-of-arms, nor the carvings of dragons and monsters for waterspouts and window-frames, nor of snakes about the doorways, nor of hideous, unshining suns at the gable-ends, which decorated the prouder houses of the other side. These little houses were quite simply made of squared planks, without even tiles or slates on their roofs.

Alain raised his lamp above his head in order to see the road. Then, suddenly he stopped, trembling all over. There was a star right in front of him, hardly higher than his head!

It was a dark star, indeed, for it was made of wood ; but it was perfect in form, and was nailed to the end of a pole which projected over the roadway. Alain let the light fall on it and examined it. It was already old and cracked, having waited a very long time ; perhaps God had forgotten it in this out-of-the-way little town, or perhaps, rather, He had just let it stay there, knowing that Alain would come. The house was a poor one, with no shutters, and within its lower windows Alain saw strange figures made of wood, with stiff straight gowns, dull round eyes, rigid lips, and crossed hands ; all stood upon a plank, as if to look out of the window. There were an ox and an ass, too, with straight, spread-out legs, and there was a cross with a pitiful figure nailed to it, and then, over a wooden manger, there was a little star just like the one in the road.

Alain knew now that he had found it at last. This was his star, made out of wood from the forest, and waiting to be lighted. It had been waiting for Alain. He put his lamp to the star, and the red flame licked the wood until it crackled. There were little glimmerings of blue, and then the star really took fire and flared up, a wonderful sphere of red. The child clapped his hands and cried, "My star at last! My star is burning!"

Then he heard a coming and going in the house. The upper windows opened, and Alain saw little scared heads with long untidy hair, the heads of children in their night-dress, who had waked and were looking out to see. He ran to the door and went into the house, exclaiming, "Children, come and see my star, my star on fire! Alain has lit his star in the night!"

But the flames spread rapidly and sparks were thrown around; the dry wood took fire, then the thatch caught, and flames raged upward from the house. There were cries of fear, cries for help, loud wailing cries. The house had become a furnace. Its structure fell, huge flames roared upward through the smoke, there was a dreadful confusion of red and black, and all soon ended in a fiery pit full of burning embers.

Then, the bell of fire's alarm tolled heavily.

At that very same moment the old wizard in the church tower was aware of a new red star in the sky. It mounted in what he called "the Heart of Heaven," which is the House of Glory.

ANDRÉ LICHTENBERGER

B. 1870

THE SNAIL

MAMMA had gone out for the whole day. In the morning a party of ladies and gentlemen had called for her in a grand carriage to take her out. M. de Veler was driving and M. de Thilanges blew great resounding blasts on the coach horn. It was all very jolly indeed. Of course Trott stayed at home; he was much too small to go with them! Mademoiselle had been asked instead to come and spend the day with him so that he should not feel lonely. Trott would much have preferred to have been left alone with Jane, but then who would ever have thought of asking a small boy about his likes and dislikes?

Mademoiselle was seated on a rustic bench at the foot of the garden reading an English book. She wore spectacles on her very imposing nose, and never moved a muscle of her face. With automatic regularity she turned over the pages of her book. Trott had tried to amuse himself in ever so many ways, but nothing seemed to come right all day; and at last he went to the corner where his own tiny garden was, to see if it needed any attention. He found it in a terrible state of untidiness; it was nothing but a wilderness of pebbles, rubbish, weedy-looking turf, and twigs—all of which made the garden look very far from beautiful. All the same, it contained one redeeming feature—there was a small rose-bush growing in the centre. Trott had not planted it himself, yet to him it was a superb achievement of gardening, and sometimes it even grew roses. To-day, as it happened, one had just budded out. Trott looked at the rose from every point of view with the greatest pride and delight. Oh, it was a ravishingly beautiful rose!

Suddenly Trott's eyes grew as round as saucers and were transfixed with horror, his mouth formed a round O! and his face crimsoned. What was this ghastly sight before him? Climbing over his lovely rose was a snail, a villainously ugly snail, that left behind it a slimy track. It turned its head from left to right, drew in its horns, put them out again. It didn't seem to be much embarrassed by Trott's gaze.

For a moment or two Trott watched it, and then he called out in a shrill voice, " Oh, Mademoiselle, please come here ! "

Mademoiselle lifted her big nose from her book. She then closed the book, put it under her arm, and in four strides was beside Trott.

" What is the matter ? "

Trott pointed one finger at the snail in disgust ; he hated creeping things.

Mademoiselle fixed her eyes on the creature.

" Why, it is only a snail ! "

Trott was not in the least convinced.

" This mollusc is harmful to vegetation," Mademoiselle continued ; " you must destroy it."

Trott was pleased to have such permission, but a shiver of repulsion went through him at the thought of touching the animal.

" Mademoiselle, won't you do it for me, please ? "

Mademoiselle looked at him sternly.

" Why should I kill it and not you ? " she asked him severely. " It is on your property, and you ought to defend your own possessions."

Trott sighed deeply. He knew that whenever Mademoiselle spoke in that final way it was no earthly use for him to protest. He put out his hand, then drew it back again. At last he touched the shell with one finger. What a stroke of luck ! The snail was afraid ! It had withdrawn itself altogether into its house. Nothing further happened. Trott began to breathe more freely. But all the same he did not like these creatures ; in fact, he hated them. What was the poor boy to do ? Ah, what a splendid idea ! he would throw it over the garden wall into Madame Ducrieux's flower-beds. Trott lifted up his arm ready to throw.

But Mademoiselle seized it just in time.

" You must never seek your own good at the expense of other people," she said sternly. " This mollusc would eat your neighbour's plants. It would be wrong for you to throw it into her garden."

" Then what am I to do with it ? "

" Crush it under your foot," she answered.

Trott looked at the snail in great perplexity. Crush it under his foot ? Pah ! The very thought of hearing the shell crack under his foot and then of feeling beneath his sole the soft body of the animal sickened him. There must be other ways of killing it ; why, he might even throw it down a well. Yes, that would be ever so much better.

Trott began to put his plan into execution. But still he was not satisfied. After all, the poor snail had not done anything very wrong. Would it not be wrong to kill it for no offence? It had been wandering about in an aimless way, and perhaps it had been very happy indeed walking about and dining on his beautiful rose tree under the golden sun. Yes, but it was destroying the tree; it was eating it, and ought to be punished. But why punish it? Surely the snail had a right to eat if Trott had. It was only eating its natural food. It had not been crawling about the rose out of spite or to do it any harm, but simply because it was hungry and had to find food for itself. Would Trott be justified in killing it for doing this?

But still, didn't people kill cows and sheep, calves and the poor little lambs that bleat so sadly, as well as the lovely birds that sing joyously in the woods? They were much more interesting than a snail, and no more wicked than this creature. Perhaps, though, they killed them humanely. Then so would he! Trott lifted up his arm to throw down the snail. But again he lowered it slowly, though he still held the enemy in his hand.

Yes, it was true that all these animals were killed, but that was in order that they might be eaten, and human beings had to have them as food. Trott remembered how once he had seen his father box the ears of a little street urchin who had stoned a bird to death. How angry papa had been then! And yet the birds pecked at the fruit and spoiled it; cows and sheep browsed on grass and pretty flowers. It was only the other day that Trott had seen a cow root up at least fifty marguerites at one time. In spite of that, though, it would have been very wicked to kill the cow, and the snail was guilty of no worse crime than the cow.

Poor Trott, perplexed by all these difficult problems, began to feel very restless. He felt very much inclined to cry. It seemed to him that he would be committing a very great crime if he made the snail the scapegoat of his anger. And yet at the same time he knew he could not leave his flowers to be at the mercy of this ugly brute. What was he to do? His mind was in a ferment.

Then at last some ideas began to shape themselves into something definite. It was wrong to kill a sheep for nothing, but not to kill it to eat. It was wrong to kill a snail, but——

He faced the creature in terror. No, truly, such an idea was impossible. Mademoiselle was watching him from a distance and grinning at him. She had let her book slip down upon her knees, and her open lips showed the yellow teeth that looked like an antique set of dominoes. She was laughing at Trott while he was in trouble. What was to be the end of his cogitations?

Suddenly Mademoiselle jumped up from her bench as if some one had pricked her sharply with a pin. She uttered one shrill cry and ran forward, leaving her treasured book where it had fallen on the grass.

What had happened to rouse her like this? Automatically, with a swift and unexpected movement, Trott had thrust the snail into the back of his mouth, then, closing his eyes tight, he had swallowed it.

"Oh, Trott! for shame! How could you do it? What a disgusting thing to do! You naughty boy! Oh, how horrible!" The words of Mademoiselle fell over one another in her haste.

Trott stood still in the midst of this outward storm. He was far too much engaged by internal troubles to listen to her. He was inwardly in a very uneasy state. He could hear a curious sound—surely the snail must be walking about inside him! The thought made him feel horribly queer!

But no, it was all over now; he must have digested it by this time. So Trott went back to his garden, and, with an increased tenderness, he looked at his rose, his heart beating high with pride because he had protected its beauty so carefully, yet without making a needless sacrifice of the life of its lowly enemy.

TROTT'S CHRISTMAS

André Lichtenberger

"IT'S Christmas Day!" Trott was only half awake when something whispered this to him, but the whisper wakened him completely. Last night he had lain in bed for hours, thinking to-morrow would never, never come; but now that it was actually here he jumped quickly out of bed and ran over to the fireplace to look inside the two little yellow slippers that he had purposely left there. When he saw them he gave a little shout of joy, and for a minute stood looking at them in delight: a drum, a sword, a gun, four boxes of soldiers, two picture-books, a box of chocolates, and other smaller things overflowed from his shoes—and they were all for Trott! Turning his head, he found that his pretty little mother was watching him from the door, and in his happiness he ran up to put his arms around her. She stooped to kiss him, and said gently:

"You won't forget that it's the child Jesus who gave you these toys, will you, my dear?"

Trott had seen pictures of the child Jesus and knew Him quite well, and he could not help wondering how any one so small could carry such a heavy load, and how He could still look rosy after He had climbed down so many chimneys. A feeling of awe stole over Trott, and he thanked the child Jesus from the depths of his heart. He hurried somewhat over his prayers, nevertheless, and resumed the enjoyment of his new treasures.

Jane, Trott's English nurse, opened the shutters. It was a beautiful day, and the bright sun of Nice peeped in at the window; the sea was a brilliant blue, and the very air seemed full of joy. Such a beautiful and sparkling Christmas made Trott's happiness all the greater. He felt he could hardly stand still to be washed and dressed, and he had to be coaxed to eat his breakfast. But at last he was sitting on the floor beside his mother's chair playing with his toys. He examined them on this side and that, and admired them greatly in every position. Suddenly he said:

"How I wish poor papa were here!"

Mamma gave a little sigh in reply to this. Papa had gone away in a big boat, and at that moment was sailing, far away, on the other side of the round globe.

A bell rang, then Jane came in, carrying a large bouquet and an even larger toy, Punchinello. She handed the flowers to mamma and Punchinello to Trott, saying, " They're from M. Aaron."

Mamma uttered a cry of delight, blushed, and hid her face in the beautiful flowers. But Trott felt displeased, and eyed his Punchinello askance. Trott didn't like M. Aaron. M. Aaron was very rich ; he was handsome and fairly young ; he had always been kindness itself to Trott, had taken him out driving in his carriage with mamma, had brought him sweets, and called him his fine boy. All the same, Trott did not like him : he took his dear little mamma away from him too often, and frequently, when Trott came home from a walk he would find M. Aaron sitting close beside her, and he would be sent away with Jane very quickly. And beside all this, M. Aaron was a Jew. Trott knew that the Jews were the people who had put the poor little child Jesus to death when He had grown up. Trott remembered a picture which showed Christ hanging upon a cross, and near Him was a man in fine clothes who was very much like M. Aaron. Trott knew that M. Aaron went to Mass, but in spite of this he was still a Jew. Teresa, the cook, said so, and Trott agreed with her. . . . What right had *he* to celebrate Christ's birthday ?

Mamma spoke at last :

" What a lovely Punchinello, Trott, darling ! Our friend, M. Aaron, spoils you terribly ! "

" I don't like Punchinello," Trott answered sullenly.

Mamma was astonished, and began to praise its good points. Trott scowled while she spoke, and then replied : " It has an ugly hooked nose like M. Aaron's, and I don't like it." Mamma laughed at this and made fun of Trott, but he felt hurt and ignored her remarks. In revenge he put the Punchinello in the corner, with its ugly nose facing the wall, and every now and then he looked at it threateningly.

But Trott's bad temper did not last. Eleven o'clock struck. Since it was a feast-day, Trott went to church with his mother. Dressed in his coat with the velvet collar, his fine yellow gloves, and his new cap with silk ribbons, he carried mamma's prayer-book and walked along by her side. At the door of the church a gentleman spoke to them. It was M. Aaron. Mamma thanked him for his present.

Trott refused to open his mouth. Mamma made some excuse for her boy, and then, to soothe M. Aaron's wounded feelings, invited him to her house to tea. Trott was furious, he had never heard of such a thing happening before. M. Aaron seemed delighted; putting his hand up to his mouth, he said something to mamma in a low voice which made her laugh and even blush slightly.

They entered the church. Trott sat down and listened attentively to the singing, the liturgy, and the sermon. The priest told the story of Christ's birth in the stable where the cow and the ass were kept; he spoke of His grievous death, and he begged the congregation, in honour of the feast, that each one should try to give happiness to his fellow-beings, especially to the poor and humble.

Trott drank in the words of the preacher, and his mind was disturbed by conflicting emotions: he felt his hatred for the Jews and M. Aaron become intensified, and yet he felt a wonderful tenderness for the child Jesus, and he wished to show this in the way that had been pointed out to him. But there——! Trott was too unimportant to make other people happy; every one gave things to him, but he had nothing to give. Who could find any one humbler than Trott, and who was so poor that he could not help him better on Christmas day?

When he had reached home Trott began to meditate on this serious matter. His mother spoke to him, but he did not hear her, and she, too, fell into a reverie. At last a sound broke in upon his dreams and made him lift up his head; it was the voice of a little girl who always stood on the beach beside a grey donkey, ready saddled, on whose back Trott was sometimes allowed to ride. No, Trott told her, he would not go out to-day. The donkey began to bray its morning greetings to him, and the little girl struck it sharply to silence it. The sight of the blow made Trott most unhappy, and suddenly a light came into his mind. Was it not the little Jesus Himself who was showing him a humble creature he could succour? This poor beast was the only friend of Trott who was not feasting to-day; he was the only one who had no reason to be happy. Now, Jesus was born near an ass and a cow. Trott knew no cows, but he did know a donkey—a donkey like the one that had witnessed the birth of Christ. And besides, perhaps this was that identical donkey! Teresa had told him how very old it was! Trott was all a-tremble now with joy, and yet felt a little abashed to think that he had ridden on the back of an animal which might possibly have been the first comrade of the infant Christ.

During luncheon Trott thought out his plan of action. After lunching, his mother left him in order that she might write some letters and prepare herself to receive M. Aaron. Trott slipped out at the front door and ran down towards the beach : he meant to look for the animal and give it some dessert from the dining-room table. The little girl consented to entrust her charge to Trott, and they returned to his home together, Trott leading the animal respectfully along, and, in spite of his impatience, not daring to hurry it even when it paused to chase a fly from its bald flank. Trott made the donkey stand still before the dining-room window, and said to it : " Wait a minute ! " then rushed into the room. Alas ! while he had been out Louisa had cleared the table and there was nothing left. Trott would have gone to the kitchen to ask for some bread, but he knew that good works must be done in secret. He was heart-broken. He went to the window and saw the ass waiting outside. Seeing him, it raised its head and came closer with short steps and an expectant air. It stood in front of Trott, and seemed to look at him first in astonishment then with reproach. What ! had he been deluding the unhappy creature with false hopes ? It gave vent to its disappointment by loud braying. The harsh sounds smote Trott like a cry of despair and of sorrowful reproach. Tears came into his eyes : had he nothing to give to this friend of baby Jesus ?

All at once Trott's eyes fell on the flowers which M. Aaron had sent and were now arranged in a vase on the mantelpiece, and again, as in the morning, Trott had an inspiration. He understood in that moment that it was his duty to please Christ by punishing one of His murderers and helping one of His friends at the same time Seized with an almost apostolic fervour, Trott took the flowers in his hand, ran to the door, down the steps, and stood still in front of the ass. For a moment it smelt the flowers, then it tried them with its teeth, and ate them greedily. Trott watched it in ecstasy, his heart beating with delight. So absorbed was he that he did not hear the window of the drawing-room open, nor saw his mother, who had heard the braying, put out her head to see what was happening.

" Trott, what *are* you doing ? "

Trott's ecstasy suddenly vanished. He raised his eyes. His little mother was frowning, and her voice was angry. Trott stood still, feeling vaguely that something was wrong.

" Come in at once, and bring me my flowers ! "

Trott went into the house and showed her sorrowfully a shapeless bunch of headless stalks. Mamma cried out:

"Oh, my poor flowers! Trott, how could you do that to them?"

Trott was greatly troubled to hear mamma speak like this.

"You have done it to revenge yourself on kind M. Aaron and to hurt me. Oh, you bad, naughty boy!"

Trott, overwhelmed with these reproaches, stammered out:

"I wanted to please the ass. Our priest said we should think about the humble people. I didn't know you loved M. Aaron so much."

But instead of appeasing mamma, the last sentence made her angrier than ever.

"I don't love M. Aaron. I have a great respect for him, and he deserves it. He's a very good friend." And mamma began to scold poor Trott so very hard that his heart felt like breaking, and the tears began to flow. Even then she did not soften. She sent him into a corner of the drawing-room and ordered him to stay there quietly, so that he should be kept from committing other follies, if that were possible.

It was too much. Trott hid his face in his hands.

"Mamma, mamma, you have never scolded me like this before,—not even when I broke the beautiful locket poor papa gave you when he went away."

The little boy broke into a storm of sobs. For a long time he cried; then, little by little, his tears ceased, but a horrible, sceptical idea took root in him. He no longer believed in good or evil. The child Jesus had deceived him; the ass was treacherous; he must ask M. Aaron to forgive him; he had hurt his dear little mother, and she had scolded him, oh, so hard! Another sob, which he could not repress, rose in his throat.

"Trott!" said a changed voice.

Trott dared not take any notice of it.

"My own little Trott!" said the voice, even more gently.

Trott turned his head a very little, looked over his shoulder, and saw that his mamma was smiling to him. His dear mamma was angry with him no longer.

"Come here and kiss me, Trott, darling," she said, her lips trembling a little.

Trott flung himself into her arms; she drew him up on to her knees and covered his face with kisses. Trott closed his eyes and was carried away with joy. When he opened them again he saw that his mamma's eyes were laughing. Would he ever again be able to hurt her without knowing? . . . No, surely not, for mamma began to laugh, and then, gathering up what was left of M. Aaron's bouquet, she said:

"Bah! since it is spoilt, it may as well be finished completely. Take it to your donkey and let him eat the rest of the flowers."

Trott hurried off in high glee.

"After you have done that," mamma called out to him before he had gone out at the door, "when it has been eaten up altogether, run and bring me my writing-case. I shall write to M. Aaron to ask him not to come to tea to-day because I have a headache. You shall take it to him yourself with the donkey."

That night Trott said his prayers as usual, with his little mother standing by his bedside. And when he came to the clause, "Lead us not into temptation but deliver us from evil," something warm fell upon his forehead. But Trott did not feel it, for he had fallen asleep already.

M. AARON, PHILANTHROPIST

ANDRÉ LICHTENBERGER

TO-DAY such a jolly thing happened. Mme. Ray came to see mamma to ask her to take a walk with her as far as the Winter Gardens. Mamma hesitated a little, saying, first, No and then Yes, and when she had finally consented, Mme. Ray said with her slightly American accent, " Let us take Trott with us."

First of all mamma said, " Oh no, he'd be so much bother," and then Mme. Ray answered, " I'm sure he won't ; he'll follow us about like a little poodle, won't you, Trott ? " And Trott had looked pleadingly at mamma while he echoed, " Yes, I'll follow like a little poodle ; really, I will, mamma." Mme. Ray began to laugh at his answer, and called him a darling, and this made mamma laugh too. He was hastily thrust into his blue jersey and his fisherman's cap with a big tassel. Then they set out in great style !

You can imagine how proud Trott felt as he marched along the road! With one hand he swung his beautiful cane, which had a bulldog's head in place of a knob ; with the other he grasped tightly a ten-centime piece that Mme. Ray had given him to buy a cake or some barley-sugar. It was a brand new copper coin, and Trott felt certain that for such a bright piece he could purchase a particularly large cake or an extra long stick of barley-sugar. From time to time he half opened his little fist to see how shiny his penny was. He felt tremendously happy. And all the time that he trotted along behind the two ladies he was murmuring to himself that he was not really a little poodle at all, but a big, strong man, whose business in life it was just now to take care of the ladies and protect them from any unexpected dangers. His companions were quite unaware of Trott's important position, but he realised it thoroughly.

Oh, what a stroke of bad luck ! There was M. Aaron coming out of a shop ! As he stepped out into the street he was in the act of replacing in his waistcoat pocket a beautiful purse made of gold meshes. He recognised the ladies at once, and showed his teeth in a pleased smile. He hastened forward to meet them, raised his soft hat, and bowed so low that he displayed the back of his shiny black head, just as though he were at the hairdresser's. Trott suddenly grew very sulky. His eyes had a malevolent gleam as he took in all the details: M. Aaron had on a pearl-grey suit; his collar was a dazzling white, accentuated by the blackness of his beard; he wore a flower in his buttonhole; his tie was of tartan; his boots were immaculate; and in his left hand, on which two enormous rings were sparkling, he swung a silver-headed cane. Mme. Ray looked at mamma in a quizzical way, as though she wanted to laugh, while mamma looked rather displeased, and was blushing a little.

Were they never going to say good-bye to this gentleman? It didn't seem like it, from the way they stood there talking about all kinds of things. M. Aaron gesticulated and smiled, scratched the earth with the end of his cane, and puffed out his chest; he looked exactly like one of the fat pigeons that coo and bow in front of the stable that belongs to the Cosmopolitan Hotel. At last they had resumed their walk. But M. Aaron, instead of taking the outer edge of the pavement, walked beside mamma and continued his conversation with her. Surely that was not the right thing to do!

Evidently Mme. Ray thought this as well as Trott, for in a few minutes she dropped back a step and walked with Trott.

Suddenly she said, "*Look*, Trott!"

As soon as she had said this she put out her tongue and made a fearful grimace at M. Aaron's back. Trott laughed out loud, and at this mamma and M. Aaron turned round sharply. Then very calmly Mme. Ray told them a little story which she said had made Trott laugh, and the little boy could not restrain his mirth. He knew that it would have been a very ill-bred thing for a small boy to do if he had made a face like that, but it was most amusing in a grown-up person. Really Mme. Ray was very amusing!

They spoke about many things which were of no interest to Trott, but having nothing better to do, he listened to their conversation in a dreamy way. He heard Mme. Ray ask M. Aaron for some details of a fête that had been held in aid of the St. Mary's Hospital for Sick Children. Poor little children! Sometimes Trott had seen them when he had passed very close to the hospital garden: they always looked thin and pale, and were always coughing. He hoped that people had collected a great deal of money for them.

M. Aaron shrugged his shoulders scornfully. He didn't approve of fêtes like that: they were an excuse for providing amusement for the idle rich rather than a source of profit to the poor children. At least half the money, he declared, was frittered away in needless expenses. It was an extremely silly habit to clothe charity in this garb of amusement. When people wanted to have a little excitement, let them take it openly; but, when they were busy helping the poor, they ought to take their work seriously and give themselves up entirely to it, without considering themselves or their own enjoyments in the least.

Trott had only half understood M. Aaron's speech; but one thing was clear to him, and that was that bad people had been spending the money that ought to go to the sick children. Well, that was very wrong indeed. While he was speaking M. Aaron had been gesticulating with his hands, and his voice had taken on a very agreeable tone, and Trott thought that he looked exactly like a picture in his book of Sacred History which showed King David dancing before the Ark of the Covenant.

"You make out an admirable case," Mme. Ray remarked rather pointedly, "but don't you remember, M. Aaron, that even St. Martin himself gave only half of his cloak to the poor people?"

M. Aaron laughed—he always laughed at everything! He went on talking, telling anecdotes, and making epigrams, and at last he said:

"St. Martin was wrong. In a matter of charity I maintain that one ought to give either everything he has or else nothing. That's my notion of charity."

Well, that *was* a splendid idea, Trott thought. He could barely tolerate M. Aaron before, but now he was full of admiration for him. Teresa had been most terribly in the wrong when she had called M. Aaron an ugly, miserly Jew—but then, after all, he had said that he would give either everything or nothing, and, who knows? perhaps he gave nothing.

Suddenly the sound of a whining voice reached Trott's ears. It came from a poor old beggar crouching at the roadside, his clothes in rags and mud-stained. A bristly beard hung from his chin, thin hair trickled down beside his hollow cheeks, and his gnarled old hands held out to the passers-by an extraordinary object that bore some remote resemblance to a hat. He was so dirty, miserable, and pitiable, that any one would have preferred not to see him; but nobody could have helped taking pity on him, all the same.

Trott was full of excitement; what would M. Aaron do?

M. Aaron didn't seem to notice him. He went on laughing and telling stories to the ladies as if he had not seen the beggar. In another moment he would have passed on without knowing he was there.

But no! Suddenly he stopped. He thrust two fingers into the very waistcoat pocket from which a little while ago he had taken his little gold purse; he fumbled in it for a second, threw something into the old man's hat which made him call out loud blessings on him, and then continued to walk on and to talk jokingly, as if what he had done was the most natural thing in the world.

Trott's whole conception of M. Aaron was completely shattered, and in his eyes M. Aaron's face seemed suddenly to have become surrounded by a halo. Everything he had—everything! He had given it all to a poor old man, with a slight, quick gesture, just like that, without seeming to pay any attention to what he was doing. And surely in that purse he must have had a great number of copper and silver and gold coins. There were very few people who would do that; it was safe to say, *very* few people!

Then a hot blush swept over Trott's face. He opened his left hand, and in it lay his bright copper. He had never even thought of giving anything to the beggar. And he knew that he did not really need any cake or barley-sugar; he wanted to buy one or the other out of sheer greed. And perhaps the poor man had never tasted either cake or barley-sugar! A great bitterness engulfed Trott's soul. He looked back; but the old man had disappeared, and it was too late to turn back altogether. It was impossible, Trott knew, and he was heart-broken.

An abrupt halt of the party arrested Trott's melancholy, and then he found they were all going into the Winter Gardens. M. Aaron pointed out the refreshment room to mamma, and asked her if she would come with Mme. Ray and take tea with him. Mamma refused. But M. Aaron persisted, still smiling.

What a good man he was! He was much better than St. Martin even, for he had given away not only everything that he had, but he now wanted to give what he had not got! He had forgotten that he had no money left, and he was offering to pay for tea for these ladies. Trott was moved almost to tears. As for Trott himself—still, he would try to repair his fault. Ten centimes! Well, of course a little boy could not buy much with that, but then perhaps a grown-up person might do something with a bright copper coin.

From somewhere about the height of his elbow M. Aaron heard a shrill little voice saying, " M. Aaron ! "

M. Aaron looked down in bewilderment. He could see a little fist held up above a little yellow head, and in the palm lay a shining copper coin.

" What is it, little man ? " he asked.

" It's to pay for the tea, sir, because, you know, a few minutes ago you gave all your money to the poor old man."

Mme. Ray began to laugh heartily ; mamma bit her lips. M. Aaron began to laugh as well, but he did not seem to do so very cordially. He stammered out a few words, such as " Good little chap ! " " Well-deserved lesson," " Taken literally," and patted the astonished Trott on the shoulder.

They went into the refreshment room, sat down at a little table, and M. Aaron ordered tea and a big selection of cakes. A white-capped waitress brought them a number of good things to eat. Who was to pay for all this ? Obviously it would have to be Mme. Ray or mamma, but M. Aaron didn't seem to be the least bit ashamed because of this, and to look at him any one would have said that it was he who was the host.

And, indeed, so he was. He put his hand into his waistcoat pocket and drew out the famous golden purse, where about a dozen gold pieces rolled about, and drew one out between his fingers.

Trott was dumb with astonishment, and his eyes nearly jumped out of his head. What was this ? What could he say now, and what had he said a few minutes ago ? What had he given to the beggar ? Perhaps it was only ten centimes ! Yet he had said that he would give everything or nothing ! M. Aaron was merely a liar. Trott threw him a look full of hatred and anger.

M. Aaron held out the gold coin to the waitress. Trott suddenly jumped up on his chair.

" Please, I want to pay for my own cake," he said to her.

Proudly he put his bright copper into the girl's hand. At least M. Aaron should not have the satisfaction of paying for Trott's tea !

RUDOLPH BRINGER

B. 1871

THE CAPTAIN'S LITTLE SECRET

WHEN it was learned by the town officials of Mondragon, a little place in the very heart of France, that Castagnol had just died at Tangier, and that he had bequeathed his immense fortune to his native place, so that it was absolutely necessary for some member of the Common Council to go at once to Morocco to take possession of this unexpected heritage—in this state of affairs there was no question as to Captain Lambounigue being the man who must go. Everything seemed to point to him as the proper man to make the journey.

In the first place, he had ample leisure, being a man enjoying a modest income, and wholly unoccupied. Then, he was a bachelor. Finally, he was an old sea-dog, who for more than thirty years had knocked about in all the countries of the world; and so this comparatively trifling journey could not alarm him.

It was only necessary to see Captain Lambounigue rolling about the streets of Mondragon to be thoroughly convinced that he was an old salt. In the first place, there was his costume, which he had never been able to abandon: his trousers with their legs flaring at the lower ends, his waistcoats of navy-blue adorned with gold buttons on which anchors were plainly to be seen. And the same emblem was embroidered in gold upon his cap. Even without this characteristic costume, his swaying gait and his continual tacking to and fro bore witness that the captain had far more often trod the deck of a ship than the quiet dwellings on shore. But if you heard him speak, doubt was no longer possible, for the captain never expressed himself but in nautical language, and his talk was richly embroidered with all the terms used by seafaring men.

Captain Lambounigue's story was a simple one, which he gladly told to everybody, and with which the youngest urchins of Mondragon were quite familiar. He had been born at a seaport, and was the son of a captain in the merchant service. As far back as he could remember he saw himself upon shipboard.

He had travelled to every country, sailed upon every ocean, visited all coasts, endured all tempests, escaped from untold shipwrecks, and he had always hoped to die on the sea, near which he had been born ; but a diabolical illness had developed in him, a disease hitherto unknown, but terrible, which was called " salingitis." Yes, the captain had become salted, like an ordinary piece of fresh pork, by reason of having so long lived in the sea-air. The medical specialists whom he had consulted had all assured him that he would not live for three months unless he succeeded in unsalting himself considerably !

That was his reason for settling at Mondragon, far from the sea. And there he hoped that the warm sunshine and the fresh breezes and the wholesale fragrance of thyme and marjoram which came from the little hills would at last freshen him and so prolong his life.

He bought a little country house on the banks of the Lez, and he provisioned and rigged it like a ship. His delight was unbounded when, one happy day, he took into his service his faithful Figaou, who was a living caricature of himself.

Figaou was a native of Mondragon, whence he had gone away when about twelve years old, not having returned until he was forty, after a past which was entirely hidden in mystery. Upon reaching his native place, quite penniless, with all his kinsfolk dead, and incapable of working at any trade, he had presented himself to Captain Lambounigue seeking employment as a house-servant. Figaou was lazy as a sloth, mendacious as a juggler, drunken as a Pole, untrustworthy as a breeze. In a word, he had all the vices ; but the captain received him joyfully, for Figaou, like himself, was an old sailor who had visited all quarters of the globe. He wore the pea-jacket and tarpaulin hat, he pitched to and fro as he walked, he chewed tobacco, he spoke the choicest nautical lingo, and he needed nothing more to make the captain consider him the pearl of servants.

So now it will be readily understood why the Common Council of Mondragon did not hesitate for an instant to commission Captain Lambounigue to undertake the delicate business of going to Tangier to take possession of the heritage bequeathed by Castagnol.

To tell the truth, Captain Lambounigue at first made a very wry face. This journey did not please him at all. He alleged the state of his health. His treatment had begun to operate. Day by day he could feel himself becoming less salt. Would not his malady become much worse if he suddenly went back to breathing the fatal air of the sea ? But they told him that the voyage was so short that it was scarcely worth talking about, and, besides that, they would give him, upon his departure, an ample supply of thyme, the fragrance of which he could inhale during his entire journey! Finally, they assured him that there was no one else who could go, for all of them were subject to sea-sickness, which would not trouble him in the least; and he knew Tangier and Morocco, and would be able to attend to the whole business. What could Captain Lambounigue say to all this? He accepted the commission, but without any enthusiasm, and when he went home in the evening he sank into an arm-chair and gave way to the blackest melancholy.

Ah, poor Captain Lambounigue was a prey to the darkest thoughts! Decidedly this journey was not at all to his taste. He sat brooding in his arm-chair for hours, and it became necessary for Figaou to inform him that his supper was ready. The faithful servant was at once impressed by his master's altered appearance, and, with his usual familiarity, asked him the cause of it.

"The cause, my poor Figaou," exclaimed the captain, "the cause is that we must weigh anchor and get under sail!"

"Get under sail?"

"Yes; for Tangier, and that at once."

"For Tangier!" Figaou repeated, his face growing noticeably longer. "But Tangier is far away, on the other side of the sea!"

"You are quite correct! It is two or three days' journey from here, and we shall sail upon the Mediterranean."

Figaou made no reply, but he turned pale. This voyage seemed to be no more pleasing to him than it was to the old sea-dog who had sailed over all the oceans.

"We were so quiet and comfortable here!" he said.

"Well, well! Do you suppose that this business pleases me? Still, we must go, all the same."

And three days afterwards they departed, very mournfully. At the railway station, indeed, in the presence of the Common Council, they bore themselves right gallantly, for the entire Common Council escorted them to the train. The good captain even squeezed the stationmaster's hand so vigorously that the officer could not help saying that the captain had a heart of oak and a hand like a vice!

But what a difference when they found themselves alone in their compartment! Leaning against the window, poor Figaou watched the disappearance of Mondragon, with its little hill, its ruined château and its dark tower, as though he never expected to see again his native place. The captain, buried in his corner, shut himself up in a mournful silence—he who generally could not keep quiet for more than half a minute.

When the tower disappeared at a turn of the railway, Figaou settled himself at the other side of the compartment and fixed his gaze upon his master.

"How calm and strong he is!" he murmured to himself with a deep sigh. "Ah, it is easy to see that he is an old sailor!"

They were silent, each absorbed in his own thoughts. Presently the train stopped and a guard called: "Tarascon!" Then the captain rose, as if moved by a spring, and handed his valise to Figaou.

"But we are not at Marseilles!" said Figaou.

"All the same, we get out of the train here."

"What? To go to Tangier?"

"Do not trouble yourself about that," said the captain with a confused air.

Figaou followed his master and with him installed himself in an express train which was just starting. Without trying to understand, he noted how they passed many railway stations. At last he understood, for, with all his faults, Figaou was by no means a fool. Instead of going to Tangier by water the captain meant to go there by land! No doubt because of the salingitis from which he suffered. And in proportion as they drew nearer to the frontier and, consequently, were farther removed from Marseilles, Figaou's heart recovered its wonted gaiety.

It was a long journey, a very long journey! All Spain to cross! But at last, one fine evening, they arrived at Algeçiras. To tell the truth, Figaou made a very ugly face when he saw the ocean in front of Algeçiras, raging and foaming. "We must cross!" he said to his master.

At the port the captain of a fishing-smack agreed to take them across the Straits of Gibraltar, a trifling distance, for a rather exorbitant price. Captain Lambounigue, however, made a very serious mistake: he paid the captain of the fishing-smack in advance and fully an hour before the time when they were to set sail.

An hour is a short time, but it was quite long enough for the fisherman and the sailors who formed his crew to find their way to a tavern and to get so outrageously drunk that, as soon as the vessel started, the three men rolled upon the deck and became insensible.

Captain Lambounigue, that hardy mariner, was already beginning to feel the approach of a frightful attack of sea-sickness; but the sight of the crew, quite incapable of the slightest effort, cured him as if by magic.

"Why, they are drunk, Figaou!" he said. "What are we to do?"

"There is nothing left for you, captain, but to take command! You understand that perfectly," answered Figaou, between two distressing hiccoughs. But Captain Lambounigue grew pale. At that moment the wind freshened, and the frail fishing-boat began to roll and to pitch in the most alarming way. Captain Lambounigue went close to his valet and said in a low, confused voice:

"Listen, Figaou! I have something terrible to tell you. I am no more a captain than the Great Turk is! All my life I have been only a simple Government functionary, the chief of an office in the Department of Agriculture; and, by ill-luck, I employed my many hours of leisure in reading accounts of voyages. That is what induced me to play the part of an old sailor! You are not angry with me? Heaven knows that but for the dangerous situation in which we are placed I would never have made this confession!

"Now you understand why I did not embark at Marseilles. Listen, Figaou, and tremble! While I lived in Paris I was never able to travel on one of the little boats on the Seine, I am so subject to sea-sickness! So do not count upon me for anything about a ship. Take command! I will obey you!"

"Alas, captain! I, too, have lied!"

"What do you say?"

"All my life I have been nothing but a bottle-washer in a pharmacy on Rue Réaumur, and I am seeing the ocean for the first time to-day! In order to get you to hire me I made believe that I was a sailor; but I am really no more a sailor than a lead soldier!"

"Then we are lost!" cried Captain Lambounigue.

Luckily the wind drove the disabled craft on the coast for which it had started, and some fishermen rescued three men who were dead drunk, and two others in almost as deplorable a condition!

Lambounigue and Figaou, having recovered from their fright, were able to proceed to Tangier; but neither of them was ever willing to go back to Mondragon, on account of the voyage. The little house on the banks of the Lez was sold, and Captain Lambounigue settled for the rest of his life in Morocco, where he still lives, the happiest man imaginable, for he and Figaou continue to pose as stalwart old mariners who have dropped anchor in every port in the world.

PAUL RENAUDIN

B. 1873

ASHES

THE door of the night café swung back on its brass hinges and two showily-dressed women came out, followed by several men. The little group stood in the boulevard, which was already becoming deserted, and continued the merry conversation begun at supper.

A little woman with a thin black lace veil over her head had been standing waiting for some time outside the brightly lit bar, and as the party came out she walked stealthily past them, keeping well in the shade. At last she glanced at one of them—a very tall man with a pale face; and from that moment her eyes never left his face.

As the merrymakers parted, she hesitated, and then quickly went up to the man whom she had been watching.

" Excuse me," she said, " but are you not M. Francis Vernier ? "

" What do you want me for ? " he asked.

" It's for little Annette Blaise," she replied; " you know, the girl who used to be a friend of yours. She sent me to look for you because she is dying, poor little thing."

The young man started. As the woman uttered the girl's name, old memories revived and he was touched for a moment. But the cab he had called was waiting by the pavement and his companion was already inside it. He drew a sovereign from his pocket.

" Well," he said, " give her this."

The woman looked at the money which glittered in his hand under the light from the street lamp.

" That is not what she wants, sir," she answered. " She is not in need, even though she has nothing of her own. What she wants is to see you. She may die any moment. It is for a dying woman, sir, and surely a rich man like you could have a little pity."

Then, in a lower tone, she added: " You need not be afraid; it is not blackmail. It is only a fancy of the poor little thing, who still worships you."

A painted face and large, flower-bedecked hat appeared at the cab door.

" What is keeping you, Francis ? " the woman asked.

" It is a troublesome woman," the young man said in excuse.

" But you look worried, my duck! Is she telling you some unhappy story ? "

" No, nothing of the sort."

" Then do hurry up."

He hesitated once more, but the woman came forward boldly.

" It is like this, Madame, and I know you will be pitiful," she said; " I am telling him about a poor, unfortunate woman who wants to talk to him before she dies. I swear that it is all out of friendship."

The scented lips, still moist with champagne and iced fruits, opened indulgently.

" Well, go on, dearie," she said. " It is lucky to do a good action, you know! Hurry up."

She pushed him away and left him standing alone with the poor woman on the pavement. A cab was passing, and he hailed it.

" Give the driver the address," he said angrily.

" Sixty, Rue Castagnary, Vaugirard," she answered rapidly, and got in beside him, looking very tiny and bewildered, yet very happy.

The woman began to think how happy she was soon to make her friend, and sat still, not daring to break the silence. When she had promised a week ago to find Francis Vernier among the crowd of gay lads who haunt the boulevards, and to bring him to the dying girl, she had never thought that she would be able to keep her word. " He is very tall and pale, and has a curled moustache and pretty, closely-set teeth. He looks like a marquis." How often Annette had described him, always adding some new detail, even to the little scar on his chin which had come back to her memory! She had told her about his favourite haunts also. But Providence, which often gives a last chance to the unfortunate, had taken matters in hand.

" Has she been ill very long ? " asked the young man without turning his head.

" Nearly a year, from what she says," was the reply. " I have only known her for about six months, since she came to live in the Rue Castagnary. Every one loves her, she is such a kind-hearted little thing; and then she saved my little boy's life, she took such good care of him. When that happened I vowed I would do anything in the world for her. Just think! For a whole week I have spent half my nights in looking for you, and people don't do that for everybody! And then when I go back I stay quite a long time with her. Oh, she hasn't got long to live now! Of course you will find she has altered a lot, sir. It is grief that has done that; and then, I am sorry to say, it is the life she has led as well. She has come down in the world since you knew her, sir. She came here with a hawker, a waster who used to beat her every night, and left her when she began to cough like this. She told me all about it, poor thing, though she is mighty proud."

All the time she was speaking the young man looked out of the window at the empty streets and avenues on the left bank of the river. This was a queer ending to an evening's amusement! He suddenly felt angry at the bad turn that fortune had played him; he resented being driven along with the poor woman by his side; he wanted to jump out of the cab or to bully the woman, and was haunted by a fear that he might be dragged into some awkward scrape and become ridiculous. All the same, he could not help listening to what his companion had to say. He had never forgotten Annette Blaise, with her great loving eyes, her vivid lips, her silken skin and warm heart, whom he had loved for a whole year, with the tenderness that one gives to a darling wife, in that little home of theirs where she lived between her sewing-machine and her crucifix. Since he had left her he knew that she had plunged into the vast maelstrom of Paris, following her star, for good or evil; he had been able to think of her without bitterness. But now that this wave had brought her, bruised and broken to his feet, how could he turn away his eyes and say that he knew her no longer?

"Is she really—dying?" he asked.

"Oh, I know enough about these things to know that she really is dying, sir. There are times when she would deceive you, when she is feverish and lively, but if you could hear her coughing all night long in the next room! And then, she is so thin; there is nothing of her!"

He tried to imagine her as he would shortly find her. But all the time it was the other Annette who came to his mind, the bright young girl who had come to him laughing and singing in all the joy of youth!

The cab stopped. Francis Vernier followed his companion into the passage of a humble house.

"It is Mme. Florent," she called out to the concièrge; "you need not trouble, M. Gaube."

They crossed a narrow and ill-paved courtyard, mounted a staircase without bannisters and with steps so narrow that they struck against the toes, and then stopped at the second flat. Mme. Florent knocked gently twice and listened. Francis heard no reply. The woman glided into the room while he waited outside. He could hear some whispering going on, and then he was aware of a stifled exclamation that made his heart beat quickly. At last, Mme. Florent returned.

" Come in," she said ; " I will bring a light."

The room was full of the stale smell of poverty and ill-health. He groped his way in, made out the bed from its whiteness in the gloom, and then spoke in quiet tones.

" It is you, Annette, isn't it ? You asked for me, so I have come, you see."

She sat up. He went forward, took her two burning little hands in his, kept them from playing nervously on the coverlet, and pressed them gently. His breath and hers mingled in the darkness.

Is it really true ? " she murmured. " Oh, you are *too* good ! I hope you will forgive me, Francis."

The lamp was burning behind him, on the mantelpiece. He could see her ravaged face, narrow temples, and the thin neck which showed from her half-opened night-gown. But in spite of this unhappy vision, her eyes shone, smiled and called to him as they used to do so long ago. It was his Annette.

He smiled a little sadly.

" Then you have been ill for a long time ? " he said. " And no one has been able to take care of you ? I will send you a good medicine to-morrow, to make you well."

" Well ? Oh, no ; it is too late. And, besides, I don't want to go on any longer."

Exhausted by emotion, she fell back on the pillow and closed her eyes. Francis looked down at the Annette whom he had loved. The blood was coming back to her cheeks now, flushing her dying face. But every feature was marked with the stains of her miserable life.

" Annette," he murmured, " I have been a bad man to you. Why did you not send for me sooner ? "

" Oh, I knew that you left me because you did not want me any more. I understood that at once. But it took me much longer to believe it. And then, later, I did not dare to send for you. If you only knew what I have gone through since then! When a woman is all alone with her—sin, she has to tread a long long path. But as for happiness and love, Francis dear, I have never had any one but you. I was really made to be an honest woman, you know."

A sob broke short her confession. With a sudden impulse the young man respectfully kissed the forehead of the unhappy woman.

"Annette," he said, "have you forgiven me?"

"Oh, I have always forgiven you, Francis," she answered, "because I have always loved you. Of course you have other girls; I have been only a tiny incident in your life; but you have been everything to me, you know, *everything*! When you first took me, you remember, in a room not much bigger than this, I gave you everything. I am not sorry that I did, because it is so good to be in love. Oh, Francis, how I have loved you! Only, when one gives everything, one doesn't give only one's own self; but much that belongs to other people as well. My mother and father, my sister and brothers; I have given a little of their happiness and their honour. It is because of that that God has punished me."

"Haven't you seen them since then?"

"No, never. While I was with you, I wrote to them twice, without telling you, lest it should annoy you. I never had any reply. That didn't surprise me, you know, because my father is very proud; I was just as if I were dead to them, and I knew that perfectly. Then when you left me, I wouldn't go back to find them for anything in the world. I too have my pride. And besides, to show them what I had become; to give them still more trouble and shame,—oh no! I would rather they should believe me to be dead. A little sooner or later, what does it matter?"

A violent cough shook her from head to foot. Francis gently laid her head on the pillow and told her to rest. But she continued eagerly:

"I found that death was too long in coming. I had counted up my savings, and found that they went quicker than I. Then, a week ago, I opened the window wide, and sat by it, and stayed there for an hour. Death is very good, very sweet, when life is too hard. You must see me when I am dead, Francis. Yes, you must see me when I am dead."

She sat up, leaning on her elbows, her eyes wide open.

"Only, Death won't get a beautiful Annette! I am no spotless bride! Oh, why did I make you come here? Go away; go away; *don't* let me tell you these horrors! You hate me; I know you do! It is my own fault! Go away and let me die alone!"

Anguish marred her face as she thought of her lost youth; and she fell back sobbing.

"Oh, Francis, should I have been dead if I had stayed your little Annette?" she asked.

Deeply moved, he raised the head of the unfortunate girl and encircled it with his arm, as he had protected it in days gone by against the remorse of his love. And in this dim room where they sat alone, with those pictures on the walls which brought back to his memory the days of their happiness; in this room which still held the perfume of her presence, he could have believed himself to be back again in that little room where, four years earlier, she had given herself to him, had been folded in his arms as she was now, and was sheltered by his love against the terror of her sin and against the judgment of God and man. In those lovely days he had known how to reassure and console her; but to-day he could find nothing to say. He stammered—he knew not what.

"Darling, don't lose courage. We shall bring you back to life and health; there is no doubt of it. You only need a little care. Now you shall have everything you want. And I will tell you what will make you better. Can you guess? I mean to find your father and mother, and tell them that you are in trouble and that they *must* forgive you."

The poor girl's face brightened immediately.

"Oh," she said, "you *are* kind! No, that would be too much; I shouldn't want to die any longer. But if only they could know that I was sorry, and that I had died better than I had lived; that is all I should want, Francis. I didn't dare to ask you to do this, but that is really why I wanted to see you so much, Francis. The other day Mme. Florent went to fetch me a priest. He was very kind and told me that God *would* forgive me. And I thought all the time about father and mother; perhaps they would forgive me too. Only, I don't know where they are now. But I will tell you exactly how bad a girl I have been. About a year ago I took my courage in both hands and said to myself: 'Mother must be very unhappy, and I must trample on my shame and go to see her.' Then I went to the Rue Foucault in Clichy, and blushed when I asked for Mme. Blaise.

I had even put on a thick veil so that the concièrge should not recognise me. But she answered: 'They left here three months ago.' Then I went away, thinking that everything was all over, and I cried—oh, I cried, in the street. Afterwards I got the idea that perhaps they had had some misfortune, and that my father might have died. I ran to the factory where he used to work. When the workmen came out they told me I had better ask the foreman. I found out then that my father was working in Billancourt. I ought to have gone there, don't you think? But it was already very late. When I reached home again I would not say where I had been. I cried and got a thrashing, and the next day I hadn't the courage. Oh, it was terrible, terrible!"

Her breath was exhausted and her voice became strained. He made her stop talking. Then he promised that he would go away to make inquiries, that she should have their forgiveness, and that she should be happy.

"Thank you," she whispered; "you're very kind. I am quite happy now. Stay here for another minute, so that I can believe we are back in the old days. Francis, you were always kind, and you haven't changed a bit. Perhaps I am making you feel miserable; I ought to have died without your knowing anything about it. But I was so terribly lonely!"

She whispered the last words very low. He watched her close her eyes, and she lay still for a long time with one hand in his. The April dawn began to quicken outside the little window. He gently disengaged his hand; murmured, "I will soon come back again"; left two sovereigns on the mantelpiece; and went downstairs, groping along by walls, the steps and the doors until he was out again in the street.

The strange new sensation which he experienced in this deserted district, with its mean and unfamiliar houses and its narrow streets brightened by a misty dawn, seemed to prolong the dream from which he was now emerging. First he took the turning to the right and then the turning to the left, at once eager to make his escape and yet indifferent. It was only when he had at last reached his own house and the room that he had left after dressing for dinner, that he could feel he had returned to his normal life and individuality. Then in one swift moment he lived over again what he had undergone in the last few hours.

"Heavens," he exclaimed, "I never expected such an adventure!"

He had no wish to think over what had passed, but undressed quickly, so that he might sleep the sooner. Suddenly, changing his mind, he wrote a telegram to his doctor, and laid it on his dressing-table for his man in the morning; then went to bed and slept soundly.

The doctor's report did not come until late in the evening of the next day. It was quite formal, and gave no hope. It was useless to take the woman to the hospital; she had only two or three weeks at most to live.

Francis Vernier threw the letter into the fireplace where the embers were still burning, sank into a chair, and covered his face with his hands. All day long he had kept himself from thinking about her story; or, if he thought about it, he told himself that she was wrong and that she would recover if she were only well-cared for, and poverty and grief were removed; besides, he would take all on himself and would fully pay his debt. His mind had always been busy with other things; he had had but little inclination to take responsibilities in life; he had felt that everything would happen in the way best for himself. But the doctor's verdict now struck his optimism to the ground. "Poor little Annette!" he repeated several times aloud. Deepest pity gripped his heart; and suddenly, astonished to think that he could have made her suffer, and surprised at this new bond between herself and him, he murmured: "But I *did* love you. How ever could I have deserted you?"

In this warm, scented room, with all its pleasant invitations, play-bills, memorials of bygone joys and loves, crowding the walls or laid upon his desk, the silence answered him.

"Whatever happens, she must have every possible comfort before she dies," he told himself. "I promised her that I would look for her parents, and I will set out to-morrow."

Immediately, so that his selfishness and natural indolence should not prevent him from carrying out the resolution he had made, he went over to his desk, sat down, took up a pen, and began to think how he could find the Blaise family.

But he went on dreaming about the task he had taken upon himself. Who were these Blaises whom he was about to track throughout Paris, urged on by this strange adventure? A household of ageing workpeople, with grown-up children, a daughter, and two sons who must now be men. Where did they live, and by what means? He tried to picture their looks and their home from the little that Annette had told him. But who would ever have believed that he would have to bother about people like that ? Of course, on that evening when he had taken her to the room he had engaged for her, half as a surprise and half because he felt that he had made a conquest of her—this little work-girl whom he had met accidentally on the boulevards two months earlier—he knew very well that some one was waiting for her elsewhere ; he had heard her whisper " Mother ! " in the arm-chair where she had thrown herself weeping. But they had loved each other so deeply ; no other souls had existed but just they two ; and she had proved only more desirable because she had yielded so tremulously.

He cut short his dreaming and thought over the ways of redeeming his promise. Should he go to a private detective ? No, that sort of thing was too ridiculous ! The simplest way was to make inquiries at the dyeworks at Billancourt ; perhaps to write to the managing director. He decided to do this, looked up the directory, and wrote two letters. If he were unsuccessful, at least he would have done all that he could.

Three days later a reply came, giving him all the information and the address he required : M. Blaise, employed by the Hallu factory for the last twelve months, 12, Rue des Peupliers, Billancourt.

So that was settled, and all he had to do was to carry out his mission. With the letter lying open before him, he began to think of what he should do, and for the first time the difficulty of the task came home to him. Yet it would make Annette happy. But, after all, the success of the whole affair depended on these people themselves ! The father would not compromise his daughter's honour ; she had told him so. Well, if they refused to acknowledge their own child, he would reason with them ; he had no doubt of success.

He became quite exhilarated at the thought of their imagined resistance. Then he reflected that he ought to go that very evening and watch the workmen come from the factory, and came to the conclusion that he would have to start very soon if he were to be in time.

The next day was full of engagements. He thought he would let Annette know what he had discovered ; then thought it would be better to announce the reconciliation when it had been effected, so as not to raise false hopes in her.

But now he hesitated, wondering what would be the most propitious hour. Ought he perhaps to go in the morning to Billancourt, and find the mother there alone ? Surely she would allow herself to be touched, for she was a woman and a mother. Yes, he would talk to her alone.

Or—should he simply write ?

But as soon as this thought came to him, Francis unmasked it. This was the third day he had wasted since he had undertaken this commission. " What a slacker I am ! " he said, took up his hat, and hailed a cab.

It was nearly six o'clock when Francis Vernier reached the corner of Rue du Vieux-Pont-du-Sevres. He got out of the cab and asked the man to wait for him until he should come back again. The sun was sinking into the gap made by the Seine, and shed its glow on the river, the high banks and the streets with detached houses ; the air was full of the sweetness of early spring. Many children were playing under the trees or in the tiny gardens, bright with wallflowers, which were before many of the houses. Women were gossiping at their gates, waiting for their men to come home. The evening meal was announced by the odour of cookery, wafted from the open windows and mingling with the perfume of the shrubs and trees.

Number 12, Rue des Peupliers, was one of these tiny houses, consisting of two storeys under a tiled roof, which could not hold more than two families at the most. A vine crept up the wall, and lilac-bushes showed green outside. Through the budding and still lace-like branches Francis noticed a young girl in one of the downstairs rooms laying the table for supper. Instinctively he began to count the plates—three, four, five. Was this their home ? He would have liked to loiter outside for a little to take stock of things, but fear of being noticed decided him, and he pushed open the gate. He walked down the garden path and knocked at the door. The girl came to open it.

" Does Madame Blaise live here, please ? "

" Yes, sir."

He could have answered for her before she spoke. She was very much like her sister, not so pretty, and with coarser features, but like her in that curious indefinable way in which family resemblances come out. When she fixed her steady eyes upon him he dared not raise his own ; it was with lowered eyes that he next spoke.

" Can I speak to her, please ? "

" She will be back from the laundry in a minute or two, sir ; I came out just before her."

" Then I will wait for her."

The girl took a chair from beside the wall and offered it to him. The polished sideboard, the folding-beds covered with chintz, and the cloth on the table, told of a certain comfort in this house ; it was by no means the wretched hovel of the thriftless poor, but the scene of real home life. The girl had removed the plates and put them back on the sideboard.

" Please don't let me interrupt your work, Mademoiselle," said Francis, noticing this.

" Oh, that is all right, sir," she answered. With a grace and simplicity which doubled the value of her courtesy, she added, " I was really too early."

Several minutes went by. At last, in order to escape the silence as well as to avoid speech, Francis said, " I will take a little walk outside while I wait."

He came back, and his eyes fell on a photograph on the mantelpiece in which two little girls were pictured with their heads close together, their hair mingling. They had the same smile and the same way of saying, " See how united we are, and how fond of each other ! "

He dared not stay in the room and went out again.

In the street men were coming home from their work, their bags on their shoulders. A boy of about sixteen or seventeen entered the Blaises' house with a round loaf of bread under his arm. And soon, in the distance, coming from the banks of the Seine, was a little woman, grey-haired, and loaded with a bundle of linen rolled up in a cloth. Francis followed her with his eyes until she reached the gate of Number 12. " She has no idea of the news I have to break to her," he thought. For a moment he let his mind wander over the day of a working-man, and his well-earned rest in the evening, with the father and the son coming in one after the other ; and he thought of the girl who had not returned for four years and whose place was no longer laid for her at the table. Then he retraced his steps and knocked at the same door where he had been a short while ago.

" You are Madame Blaise, are you not ? " he asked.

" Yes, sir," was the reply from the worn and worried-looking little woman.

Then suddenly he plunged into his story.

"I have been sent to you, Madame," he said, "by a lady who used to know your daughter Annette, and who is looking after her now. I am, unfortunately, the bearer of bad tidings. Your daughter is very ill indeed, and the doctor holds out no hope of being able to save her life."

Hardly had the name of Annette been pronounced than the wrinkled face of the little woman paled to her very lips, which began to tremble slightly, but she said nothing. Francis was more touched than he cared to be.

"She has not seen you for a long time, it seems," he went on.

Mme. Blaise lowered her head and shook it slowly. "No, not for a long time."

The young girl, who had put her arm protectingly round her mother, added: "My sister was just as if she were dead to us."

There was a silence in which only the old grief spoke: the true sorrow which this new blow had simply recalled and reawakened.

"It seems that she is most anxious to see you again before——" Francis stammered. "She knows she is dying. She has never dared to ask you to forgive her, has she? But I don't think you can refuse to give it to her any longer. I have been asked to tell you on her behalf that she is penitent and that she has asked to see a priest so that she may die a Christian."

A sob broke the silence of the lips which had for so long closed over their sorrow.

"We will go, mother, shan't we?" asked the girl, holding her mother close to her. "Don't you want to go now?"

The mother made an affirmative gesture, dried her eyes, and said, "Please forgive me, sir, but it's difficult to lose her twice over."

Francis Vernier waited to hear what questions they had to ask. But the two women were lost in thought. Sorrow did not rouse their curiosity, it was so familiar a guest.

Hastily he gave them her address, and was just about to go away when the door opened behind him and a man entered the house. He was tall, with hair and beard nearly white, and his eyes gleamed from his bronzed face. He bade the stranger good-evening, and looked at him slowly, steadily, and firmly. The same familiar look which had struck Francis a short time ago when he saw Annette's sister, now went to his heart as he looked at her father.

"Father," said the girl, speaking instead of Francis, "this gentleman has come here for some lady, to let us know that Annette is dying and that she wants to see us, to ask us to forgive her."

The man started suddenly ; then, instead of answering his daughter, he said to the visitor, turning his head aside : " She was taken away from us long ago. We gave up thinking about her. We are only poor people, but we have our honour like every one else."

Then, slowly, having made this confession, he looked at Francis. The latter gave a sign of assent.

" Doubtless," went on the old man, " girls ought to take care of themselves when they earn their living, and we ought not to make excuses for them. But youth is inexperienced, and it is the others who are the real wrongdoers and criminals, because they know what they are doing. If I knew who had dishonoured her, sir, whether he were a plain man or a lord, I would crush him like that ! We don't bring up our children in this house to live on their vices. There are plenty of girls on the boulevards, and there is no need to come and take ours."

Trembling, he shook his closed fist, and the stilted phrases he had used made his grief no whit less sincere nor his hatred less deep. He stopped himself suddenly as if to repress both these emotions. " You will excuse me, sir, won't you ? " he said. " I know I ought not to speak like this before you, but I have suffered so much ! "

He leaned on the sideboard and looked at the carpet without speaking. His daughter went over and stood beside him.

" You want us to go to see her, don't you, father ? " she asked.

He made a gesture of assent.

" Will you come with us ? "

He thought for a moment, then said, " No, go there by yourselves."

Then, turning to Francis, he said, " Monsieur knows where she is, I suppose ? "

" Yes, at Rue Castagnary, Vaugirard."

The man seemed to be searching his memory.

" I lived there myself when I was young, near the railway. It is a poor part of the town ! So she must be in great want, isn't she ? These things always end like that ! "

It was the old story over again, but it was his own. He went over it again to himself in silence, his forehead deeply lined, while the women made ready in the next room to go out. Behind him his two sons stood motionless. The setting sun shed its last glow in the room and lit up the walls with their customary brightness. But, though the men kept silent, they could hear the mother stifling her sobs in her haste to go away.

They were ready to set out. Francis suggested that he should take them to Paris in the cab which was waiting for him, so that they might see Annette the sooner. They accepted with some embarrassment.

" We have forgotten to thank you, sir," said M. Blaise, addressing him. " You must excuse us. It is even harder to show shame than grief."

The tears were falling from his bright eyes. Francis wished to show him his sympathy and held out his hand to him. The man took it and grasped it firmly. But their eyes did not meet ; Francis had looked the other way.

Outside, he took the two women to the cab, gave the address, paid the man, and cut short their protestations by saying that he had some business to transact at Auteuil and would return on foot.

He saw the cab disappear in the distance, carrying the mother and daughter to the child who was awaiting them so anxiously. So now his work was over, and it had all come about so easily and happily. Now Annette would die forgiven and contented. He needn't think any more about it ! But the part which he had just been obliged to play cut him to the heart. The man's handgrip burned his fingers. And they had understood nothing, suspected nothing. He thought of the stupid, easy solution, that any one of his own class would have proposed—a duel that would make no reparation at all, but might at least serve as a relief, and give one the sense of being a man of feeling. Before these poor people he had been able to look like an honest man ; but he had done so only under a mask. . . .

He had come back now along the quay towards Passy. He was thinking about Annette and about their love for one another. Well, of course he had not deserved the hard lesson that Fate had thrown in his way any more than other men had done, but he had deserved it as much as they ; and it went to his heart and his conscience. Then a furious longing came to him to shake off the lie which humiliated him, to see Annette again, to kiss her, and to ask for that forgiveness which he required much more than she. He found a cab and was carried away towards Vaugirard.

The darkened room was full of sobs. Annette, lying back on the bed, very pale, seemed to be waiting for death to come to her. Without taking any notice of the two women, Francis went to her and leaned over her bed.

" Annette," he whispered, " you are happy now, aren't you ? Will you forgive me for the wrong I have done you ? "

She opened her eyes, held out her arms, took the dear face between her two hands and pressed her lips to his.

Then, suddenly, he heard a cry behind him. The mother had seized his arm.

" Oh, it was you ! " she cried. " It was you who wronged her ! Out of my sight ! Go ! "

In his surprise he hesitated. But she placed herself between him and the bed, and repeated in a tremulous voice, " Go away at once ! Go away and leave her to her mother ! "

He drew back and went out without saying a word. He never saw Annette Blaise again, living or dead.

FREDERIC BOUTET
B. 1874

THE EXPERIMENT

MACPHERSON, the famous master of experimental physiology, tall, upright, his hands in his pockets, and his back to the fireplace in his study, leaned towards his listeners, Jeffries, the anatomist, and Moffat, the biologist, both men of world-wide fame ; his face, powerfully moulded and clean-shaven under his short, white hair, was bent on them in fierce resolution.

" I took the liberty of calling you here this evening," he said, in a level voice that dwelt on each word, " to show you a dangerous and astonishing experiment which I am afraid to carry out alone. An ordinary man would not have the courage to undertake it. But the results may be so important for the whole human race that I cannot hesitate. Will you come into the laboratory ? "

They followed him, silent and disquietened. They were friends of his—if he could be said to have any friends—and Macpherson had, that afternoon, mysteriously invited them to come at ten o'clock, and this in so abrupt and masterful a way that they had left everything in order to keep the appointment. His singular and daring genius always disconcerted them a little, and his lack of scruple in his experiments had already provoked some violent protestations and almost scandals. His preliminary speech now promised something very exceptional.

In the vast, closed laboratory, the high electric lamps poured down a harsh, white radiance. There, amid all the new, strange, scientific apparatus which was now familiar to them, the two men of science saw with astonishment an inexplicable bath. It had just been filled with hot water, for steam was rising from it. On one side, on a stool, sat a man clad only in a loose shirt and canvas trousers. He was livid, his shoulders trembled, and two pairs of handcuffs bound his wrists and ankles.

Towering above him, in a watchful attitude, was a young athletic negro, a servant of Macpherson's, who had been with him for years, and worshipped him with a dog's devotion.

"This man," said Macpherson to his visitors, "whom you see sitting here, tried yesterday in the street to murder me in order to rob me. Look at what he did."

He opened his waistcoat and shirt, revealing a long, deep wound over his left lung.

"But I caught him a blow under the chin, and knocked him out; sent him to sleep, as prize-fighters say. It happened just near my door, and I got my servant to bring the man indoors. I find he is Wilson, the notorious murderer. He has been practically condemned to death at two or three inquests, but the police have never been able to put their hands on him. Isn't it my plain duty to deliver him up and get him hanged?"

His words fell on a strange, heavy silence. The handcuffed man shuddered. Macpherson went on:

"But I have another idea. You know the applications I have made to the authorities for all condemned persons to be handed over to us for experiments in the cause of humanity. But there is so much silly prejudice that I have only discredited myself and my work by urging this most necessary reform. Well, now that chance has given me the power of life and death over Wilson, I have made a bargain with him. I won't give him up to the police, I will forgive the attack on me, and I will set him free and give him a thousand pounds, and arrange a free passage to any colony he may choose, if he will submit to a single experiment which, in all probability, will not end fatally."

"Whatever do you mean to do?" exclaimed Jeffries.

"I have discovered a serum," said Macpherson, "which I firmly believe can wholly take the place of human blood. It is, in fact, an artificial blood, possessing, I hope, vital qualities superior to those of natural blood. I say I hope, because I can't be sure until I have made a complete and definite experiment. This is where Wilson comes in. I shall open a vein in his arm in this bath. When his body is entirely bloodless, when, in fact, *he has been dead for several minutes*, I will inject my serum. It will, I feel certain, replace all the blood he has lost, and provoke the proper functioning of all his organs."

"What a revolution in medicine—if you are right!" said Moffat.

"Yes. If I am right," said Macpherson, "I may absolutely resuscitate Wilson. Of course, in every first experiment there are more chances against a successful result than there are chances for it.

But there is a chance of success. I am positively sure of my discovery. So I have proposed to this man, already marked for the scaffold and the rope, that he should take this chance, and be born again, perhaps to a new life won through a pleasant, painless death. Wilson will tell you he accepts my conditions."

The chained man made an effort to swallow the saliva in his mouth.

"Yes," he said at last, in a thick voice, "I accept them."

"But it is impossible, Macpherson!" cried Moffat. "I will take no part in it. You are either going to murder this man, or else let loose again on society the most dangerous criminal of our time."

"If I come out of it all right"—the eyes of Wilson lighted up with wild energy. "If I come out of it all right, governor. . . . Ah, heavens! I'll go to Canada or Australia, and live as straight as a die!"

"I believe him," said Macpherson. "After what he is about to undergo, he'll fear death too much ever to risk his neck again. As for my responsibility . . . I don't suppose Scotland Yard will worry over the disappearance of John Wilson. So there remains only, my dear Moffat, a case of conscience. Will you see the thing through, or go?"

There was a few moments of silence. Moffat grew pale.

"I'll see it through," he said at last. "After all, he only risks a quiet, pleasant death instead of a horrible execution in prison."

"And you?" said Macpherson to the anatomist.

"Of course I'll stay," said Jeffries. "If you have discovered the serum. . . . What a gain for the whole human race! It ought to encourage you, Wilson."

"When you are where I am, you only think of yourself," said the man, in a dull voice. "But I've a chance. . . . And there's breakfast in prison, hangman, bandage, and the drop"—he shuddered. "No. Give me the bath!"

When the man, his hands untied, was lying in the bath, held down by the grip of the colossal negro, Macpherson came to him, raised his right arm, bent it, and rolled up the shirt-sleeve.

"You are still willing?" asked the physiologist. "You will not try to get away when the experiment is begun? You won't be able to then, I assure you."

"Go on with it," said the man. He closed his eyes, his teeth chattered. Macpherson leant over, a lancet in his fingers. The patient gave a slight jump, and a little red stream ran down his elbow; but Macpherson had already placed it in the warm water.

"You know what will happen, my friends?" he said to Moffat and Jeffries. "The pulse will grow quicker, the arterial tension will diminish, the patient will have fits of giddiness, a keen thirst, and then syncope will follow."

He stopped speaking. With his thumb on the right wrist of the man, who was now breathing heavily, he measured the pulse. Then by means of an instrument with a tube and dial he registered the arterial tension. A strange excitement came over the two assistants, in spite of their professional experience. The negro, upright and watchful, was like a machine of obedience. Macpherson remained calm. As for the patient, stretched out in the bath, he did not pant any more now. With pressed lips and eyes closed he seemed dead already. And the water grew redder and redder.

"The pulse is quickening, and the pressure diminishing," said Macpherson.

"I am thirsty!" cried Wilson suddenly, in a broken voice.

His lips were moistened, and a little while after he groaned twice. Slowly the minutes passed, slowly and terribly.

"I can't feel the pulse," said Macpherson. "The pressure is lowered. The end is near now."

"I feel . . . so . . . giddy," stammered a horrible voice.

The man opened his eyes—large, dilated—and they stared from his waxen face without seeing.

"Take me out!" he cried suddenly, making a feeble movement. "I won't . . . won't. . . ."

"Syncope," murmured Macpherson. "It's the end."

"No! No!" The man's throat rattled as he tried to speak. He gave a desperate effort as though to escape, but he could hardly lift himself up in a convulsive, shuddering leap. The negro held on his shoulders, with his great black hands. Wilson fell back in the red water, and his livid head tumbled on one side, lifeless.

"Syncope," said Macpherson. "He has bled to death."

Jeffries ran to the bath.

"It's all over," he exclaimed. "Now let us take him out of the water, wait five minutes, and inject the serum. The poor devil!

He was plucky, all the same, and I should like to see him pull through. What a splendid thing it will be for you, Macpherson, if the experiment comes off ! "

The physiologist smiled strangely.

" The experiment has come off," he said.

The two men of science stared at him.

" Yes," continued Macpherson. " I have not told you the truth. The experiment I have just made isn't what I promised to do. All we have carried out is a study in auto-suggestion. . . ."

" Auto-suggestion ? " said Jeffries.

" Yes. Your meeting in this laboratory, this bath, my lancet, my talk were merely a fake to impress the patient. I wished to make an experiment in nervous impressionability, so to speak. This man has not been bled. He only thought he was, as you too thought."

The physiologist raised the reddened left arm of the subject, and wiped it, and held it up in the glare of the electric light.

" You see, there is no trace of bleeding. I only just scratched it with the tip of the lancet, and broke on the spot a pipette of warm red water. A simple apparatus fixed to the bath gradually tinged the water there. I dictated to the subject the feelings of being bled to death, and he reproduced these impressions, one by one, according to the indications given in my words, up to the profound swoon in which he now lies. It is a very curious experiment."

" It is more complete than you think ! " cried Jeffries the anatomist, who had stooped and examined the subject. " The man is really dead."

" Well, it was only a condemned murderer," said Macpherson.

But, all the same, he grew somewhat pale.

PAUL CLESIO

THE MUSGRAVIUS MONOPOLY

MINERALOGY has come to be considered the freehold of the Musgravius family.

Georges Musgravius, founder of the dynasty, has occupied for the past thirty years the chair founded for him at the French Academy. His eldest son, Jean Musgravius, is professor of mineralogy at the Museum. His second son, Henri Musgravius, lectures on mineralogy at the Normal School. One son-in-law, Pierre Donon, is professor of mineralogy at the Sorbonne, while another son-in-law, Charles Bonniguet, like all the other members of the family, teaches mineralogy, but holds a less important position, being only a lecturer in the Faculty of Toulouse.

The fact that her second daughter was thus condemned to live in the provinces was Madame Musgravius' keenest sorrow. It was a great grief and privation imposed upon her that she was able to see this one of her children only three times a year—on New Year's Day, at Easter, and for a short time during the summer vacation. For this reason, when it became known that a new chair was to be founded at the Sorbonne for lectures on mineralogy, Madame Musgravius at once thought that this place should by right be given to Charles Bonniguet. With this idea in view she arrayed her husband in his best frock-coat, tied a smart white bow under his chin, and, giving him elaborate instructions for the interview, sent him to the minister to ask him to confer the position upon their son-in-law.

The minister had been expecting the visit for some days, and had prepared in advance the arguments by which he intended to refuse to grant the petition of the old scholar. He happened to have a candidate of his own of whom he thought very highly, a young man of great merits and promising future, and he resolved that he would force this young man upon the Musgravius monopoly.

The minister felt nervous, and prepared himself irritably for a scene when the door of his room opened and Musgravius entered. He addressed him in an abrupt tone which quite startled the professor:

" I am charmed to see you, my dear sir, and, as your visits are rare, I suppose you have something to ask of me."

" You have guessed correctly, Monsieur ; I have been informed that you have decided to endow the Sorbonne with a new course of lectures on mineralogy."

" *I* have decided ? *I* decided !—pardon me, but you seem to credit me with unlimited power. The Sorbonne demands a new course of lectures ; the Superior Council is favourable ; I simply agree."

" You are no doubt too modest, Monsieur, but the important fact remains that the course of lectures has been decided on."

" Have you a candidate to propose ? "

" Precisely, Monsieur ; Charles Bonniguet, a young man of great merit."

" Your son-in-law ? "

" Yes, my son-in-law."

" Well, I will not deny that I have heard of the young man, but I do not wish to encourage false hopes, Monsieur Musgravius. This nomination is impossible, absolutely impossible ! "

" What do you say, Monsieur ? Has any one tried to injure Charles in your opinion ? "

" No ; no one has tried to injure him."

" He is a most distinguished candidate. His studies on cretaceous soils have even received notice from the Academy of Sciences."

" I do not dispute his merit."

" What, then ? "

" You have the right to ask me to be candid with you, Monsieur Musgravius. If we do not appoint Monsieur Bonniguet to the Sorbonne, it is not because we consider him in any way incapable of filling the position. No, our motive is more serious than that."

" What is your motive, then ? "

" Shall I tell you ? It is because he is your son-in-law."

" Because he is my son-in-law ? "

" Because you, your sons and your sons-in-law occupy every chair of mineralogy in Paris. You are creating a dynasty ! "

" Well, there are other examples, Monsieur."

" I do not wish to know them. I am the sworn enemy of nepotism. I have promised to fight it whenever I encounter it."

" The sentiment does you honour, Monsieur, but at the same time you commit an act of injustice and, pretending to war against nepotism, appoint an undeserving candidate."

"An undeserving candidate! Is it true then, as people frequently say, that you imagine it is only in your family that mineralogists are to be found?"

"I make no such claim. Charles was my pupil before entering my family."

"Ah, on that subject you may set your mind at rest, for the young man whom I am going to appoint has also been your pupil. I may as well cut the matter short by telling you his name at once to avoid further arguments. It is Paul Granjean, who is at present a private tutor at the Normal School."

"Paul Granjean?"

"Yes. If I am not mistaken he has just written a brilliant thesis?"

"Yes, Monsieur."

"The report I have received concerning him is excellent."

"He is very young."

"So much the better; he will have so much more time before him in which to aid French education. Now, you must admit, Monsieur Musgravius, that in default of your son-in-law, my choice is a good one."

"Ah, it will be a blow to my wife!"

"No one regrets that more than I do, but at the same time I cannot make appointments just to please Madame Musgravius."

"But we counted on that course of lectures! Charles has a right to it. I submit, since you tell me it is impossible; but don't you think that you owe us some compensation?"

"Is he an officer of the Academy?"

"He has been at Toulouse for the last six years; he has the degree of doctor, is thirty-five years old and is still only a tutor. Couldn't you make him a professor? There is no chair of mineralogy at Toulouse. Found one! You do not want me to go back to my wife and tell her that I have obtained nothing, absolutely nothing. Really this much is due me!"

"I see that you are philosophical, Monsieur Musgravius, and I promise you I will do all I can."

"All you can! That is rather vague."

"I must consult with the Faculty, the Superior Council."

"Ah, if you really did wish it, Monsieur!"

" Of course I wish it. Well, you may count on me."

" The affair is settled, then. May I say so to my wife ? "

" Yes, I promise that you may count on me, and Monsieur Bonniguet will be appointed professor."

The minister rose, as a sign that the interview was terminated. He congratulated himself on his victory, but was somewhat surprised at having met with so little opposition from Monsieur Musgravius. Holding out his hand to the old scholar, he said :

" You are not angry, Monsieur Musgravius ? "

" No, I am not angry, Monsieur. Your choice is, after all, very suitable. My wife can console herself. Paul Granjean is affianced to our third daughter."

JACQUES CONSTANT

THE BETRAYAL

"AT last, at last, Dmitri! Why do you frighten your Maroussia so? You leave directly after dinner without saying a word, and I have been awaiting your return, counting the hours, mad with anxiety. Where do you come from so late at night? What were you doing? Whom were you with?"

———

"No, I am not reproaching you, only I have been so afraid—I don't know why."

———

"No, don't joke. I know there are no wolves in Helsingfors, but there are men who are more ferocious than wolves. I know that the hospital of Saint-Vladimir is filled with wounded; that every night the soldiers fire upon people who walk through the streets after ten o'clock. It is dangerous to be out after that hour."

———

"Sleep when you are absent, exposed to danger? You know I could not do it."

———

"How did I pass my time? Crying, darling, and praying to God. Don't laugh, don't blaspheme, Heaven would punish us. As soon as I had put our little son, Sasha, to bed, I knelt before the image of the Virgin. My prayer was not in vain, for you have returned safely. You say you are thirsty? Have some of this vodka with water. Ah! I talk so much and I notice nothing! You are flushed, out of breath, covered with mud; you look gloomy and preoccupied, Dmitri, do you know that you have not even kissed me? And do you know that you went away without even kissing your son? Oh, bad papa! But—good God!—I hadn't seen it! You are wounded! Your right hand is covered with blood."

———

"Not your blood? What? You were attacked? You fought? You struck your adversary? Perhaps you killed him? Speak, tell me what has happened. You see that I had good reason for being anxious!"

———

"Some terrible mystery, and I must not know it! There are

things you keep secret from me now. Still, think, I must know what you are doing in order not to compromise you. In these days a thoughtless phrase, an imprudent word, is enough to condemn a man to death or to Siberia."

"I understand now. I will say that you came home to dinner, and went to bed at ten o'clock as usual. If only no one saw you come in! I can guess that something very serious must have occurred. Why do you hesitate to confide in me, your wife?"

"I annoy you? You would not have said that to me two years ago. What has become of our loving intimacy, of those pleasant evenings we spent seated in front of the fire, while Sasha rolled at our feet on the bear rug, holding out his little hands and calling to us in his childish voice? You smoked your pipe, you know—the one that was carved in the likeness of Tolstoy."

"Dmitri, you are crying. Oh, why did you ever join this society of the Invisibles?"

"Don't deny it. I know it. A letter fell from your pocket one day with that horrible black seal. What were you preparing for? I don't know; but I do know that every one lowers his voice and looks about him in terror when the name of this mysterious association is pronounced. Besides, since you have been associating with these people you don't laugh any more, and you seem plunged in gloomy thoughts. You read books that speak of a better condition of society, liberty and justice, but counsel crime."

"Oh, it is possible that I do not understand. I have never studied as much as you have; only it seemed to me that Christ had already said the same things more humanely, more lovingly. Don't be angry, Dmitri; if all the world followed the precepts of the gospel there would be less suffering and less iniquity. Laws were not to be changed by violence, but by love. He who strikes with the sword shall perish by the sword."

"What do I care about the universe, Dmitri? You and Sasha are all the universe that I have, and that is why I am afraid when you leave me. My happiness may be selfish—so much the worse. Swear to me that you will not risk your life! There are plenty of men who have neither wives nor children; let them sacrifice themselves first."

———

"No, all rich men are not bad. Look at that little toy horse over there that Sasha received as a present to-day!"

———

"Who? I dare you to guess. Well it was a present from His Excellency, Prince Ourivan."

———

"Yes, the Governor of Helsingfors himself. But what is the matter with you? How curiously you are looking at me. Don't you remember that my cousin, Fedora, is governess at the palace? We met her this afternoon when we were out walking, and she insisted upon my seeing the apartments of the Prince. She thought he would be away all day, but he returned sooner than usual and entered the great ballroom where we were standing in ecstasy before the pictures and tapestries. But far from seeming to be annoyed, he showed us the greatest courtesy. Sasha conquered him at once; he took him on his knees, kissed him and complimented me on his looks. He thought he was very big for a boy five years of age."

———

"Why do you object to my accepting the toy which the Prince offered me so graciously? A refusal would have annoyed him."

———

"He certainly looks more like an honest man than a cruel butcher. I imagine that a good many evil deeds are attributed to him that he is in no way guilty of."

———

"Killed? How? By whom? Oh, this must be the act of some member of your terrible society. Sooner or later the assassin will be discovered and he will be punished as he deserves."

———

"You say he is prepared for death and martyrdom? Then you know him? He is one of your friends? I am sorry for him. But —how stupid I am! This inexplicable absence, this secret which you dare not reveal, the blood on your hands!

"This man might have been a thousand times worse than he was, yet he was one of God's creatures and you had no right to take his life. Oh, my darling, I feel sure that a terrible misfortune is about to happen to us. He who strikes with the sword shall perish by the sword."

. . . .

"Yes, your Excellency, I am the wife of Dmitri Propopov, lithographer; but, judge, I swear to you that I do not know for what reason they have brought me before you.

"This morning, when I awoke, the police brutally invaded our little house and compelled us to follow them. In spite of our protestations they took us to prison—my husband, me, and even this poor little innocent boy who is smiling at you now.

"There must be some mistake, judge. I know you are good and just, and I am confident that you will set us at liberty."

——

"The crime that was committed last night?"

——

"Prince Ourivan assassinated? It is horrible! I saw him only yesterday afternoon. He was such an amiable, good man."

——

"I met him because my cousin is governess at the palace. He gave my little boy a toy. Oh, this is a sad misfortune for Helsingfors! I suppose the assassins have already been arrested?"

——

"Dmitri suspected? But that is infamous, your Excellency. A man so quiet, so honest as he is would be incapable of such an action."

——

"You say that the information you have received about him is bad? Doubtless there are some people who hate him because he is proud and will not associate with them, because he earns his living honestly and fears no one. Besides, think for a moment, your Excellency: the crime, you say, was committed between midnight and one o'clock. At that hour Dmitri was asleep."

——

"Am I certain of that? Why, of course, I was lying beside him."

——

"You say my testimony is suspicious! Of course I have no one to corroborate it. My house is isolated, and we know few people. No one saw him go out that night, that is certain."

——

"Excellency, this is my son. He was asleep at the time, and

besides, he is so little, he doesn't know. 'Sasha! Answer the gentleman! Do you love your papa?"

"Last night? Hush, Sasha, you're a bad boy. You do not know what you are saying."

"Judge, I will not allow him to annoy you any more with his babble!"

"It is false, your Excellency, it is false! The child has invented all that. You are crazy, Sasha!"

"I have no intention whatever of intimidating him, judge, but you can see yourself that he is lying. How could I have exclaimed: 'My God! It is midnight and Dmitri has not returned!' when Dmitri was sleeping beside me? Oh, God! I tell you he was sleeping, sleeping soundly."

"No, you cannot, you must not believe what a child says. Your Excellency will certainly not credit his statement. He is subject to hallucinations, to nightmares—and yesterday, now I remember, he was very feverish. He dreamed all that he has just told you. Oh, my God, believe me, he has no notion of time. Yesterday or last week are all the same to him. Silence, Sasha! Yes, yes, yes, you know you are ill. But he is repeating it again and with an accent of sincerity! Oh! Children are terrible, your Excellency knows, and could cause a catastrophe without knowing what they are doing. But do not believe him, judge, do not believe him!"

"Oh, heaven, we are innocent! Be just, do not hold us under arrest! You have no proof! You could not be so cruel as to base your accusation upon the denunciation of a child who is only five years old, and does not know what he says. On my knees, Excellency, I beg of you; you have a wife, children. Sasha, poor child, get down on your knees and pray the judge to give you back your father."

"It is all useless. We are lost. My God! I do not believe in Your goodness and mercy any more, since You have permitted a child to betray its own father!"

GEORGES JAPY

THE MIRROR

IT is really rather absurd to describe the Japanese as "the French of the East," as writers often do. For the fact is that these two peoples are in many ways utterly different.

In no respect does this inherent difference appear more clearly than in the innate vanity of the French baby-girl. It is said that these tiny coquettes will seize hold of a hand-mirror and gaze with insatiable delight upon the reflection of their own pretty faces; and that this ingrained passion for self-admiration grows stronger and more absorbing year by year. The French maiden of seventeen, we are told, likes nothing so well as the satisfaction of having mirrors all around her; and in the Palace of Versailles there is a room which for these young ladies contains all the bliss of Paradise. The walls of this great apartment are covered with mirrors reaching from the floor to the ceiling, and the floor itself is like a mirror, so highly polished is its surface. But such a room would be impossible in Japan, where feelings of this kind are unknown.

In the little village of Yowcuski, hidden away among the hills of Japan, such treasures as looking-glasses are unknown, and a girl cannot judge of her own appearance except by her lover's rapturous expressions. And a lover, as we all know, sometimes gives a rosier account of his beloved's charms than the mirror would afford.

In Yowcuski there lived a young man named Kiki-Tsum, who earned his living by pulling a rickshaw, for the convenience of any passenger who would hire his tiny vehicle and his swift, sturdy legs. One day this young rickshawman noticed a small pocket-mirror lying in the street, where it had been dropped by some foreigner travelling through the country.

Kiki-Tsum picked up this mysterious round object and scrutinised it with the profoundest interest. What could it be? He had never in his life seen anything at all like it. But as he looked, his interest changed to awe and reverence and wonder. A light-brown face, with deep earnest eyes and a mingled expression of fear and astonishment, looked out at him from the glittering jewel in his hand, and as he recognised the features he sank on to his knees in an ecstasy of devotion, exclaiming: " The image of my sainted father! This is indeed a sign from the gods to me! How else should it have come here?"

He took out his handkerchief and wrapped it round the precious object, and placed it carefully at the bottom of his deep pocket. On reaching home he meditated long as to the safest place where he could hide it away, and finally chose the bottom of a deep vase which was unlikely to be disturbed. He said nothing about it to any one, having a sense that this miracle of his departed parent's image, revealed to him in such unwonted guise, was a thing too sacred to be mentioned. He said not a word even to his dear young wife, reflecting that " the curiosity of women is notorious, and they are not always innocent of talking about things."

The excitement of his recent discovery lasted for some time, and Kiki-Tsum could not bear to be long absent from his mystic treasure. He used to leave work and come home several times a day, in order to feast his eyes and heart with a sight of it. But such unusual conduct could hardly fail to arouse suspicion.

Japanese wives are much the same as all other wives, and are never satisfied until they get to the root of anything which seems incomprehensible or out of the ordinary. It was in vain that Kiki-Tsum protested to his fair companion that his sudden visits at all hours of the day were due to his desire to feast his eyes on her own pretty face. Lili-Tsee was at first satisfied with his explanations and his kisses; but when this had gone on for many days her woman's heart told her that something deeper lay behind these continual irruptions of her husband. And then, too, he always came in with such a strangely serious expression!

So Lili-Tsee, like many another woman all over the world, determined to get to the bottom of the mystery, and began to study the actions of Kiki-Tsum. She soon noticed that he invariably went all alone into a certain small room at the back of the house, before leaving again for his work. She therefore turned her attention to this room. There was no rest for her until she could discover the secret hidden there, but for many days she searched and searched in vain. At last however, her diligence was rewarded.

One day Lili-Tsee opened the door of this little room suddenly, while her husband was there, and was just in time to see him replacing upon the shelf a tall blue vase which she used for drying rose-petals.

She accepted with apparent composure his explanation that he was putting the vase straight, as it seemed unsteady; but she could hardly contain herself until he had gone, and then she ran back to the little room, climbed on a stool, and hastily lifted down the vase. Out came the secret treasure, and Lili-Tsee turned it curiously about in her hands. Whatever in the world could this strange thing be? Ah——! Now, when she looked into it, the dreadful mystery was revealed!

Could she really believe her eyes? There, before her, lay the portrait of a woman! And she had always been so sure that Kiki-Tsum was the very soul of honour, affection, and goodness!

The blow was too cruel! Lili-Tsee was utterly prostrated with misery. She sat on the floor, rocking her lithe body to and fro in anguish, the fatal portrait lying in her lap. So, then, it was to visit this woman's picture that her husband came home at all times of the day. This was the explanation of it all!

Then the bitterness of her suffering flashed suddenly into anger, and she looked once more at the hateful woman. How could Kiki-Tsum admire a face like that, so dark and malignant as to be actually terrible? The eyes had a horrible look in them, which she had not noticed the first time she looked at the face, but which now made her shudder and forced her to put the abominable thing away.

But all the light had gone out of life for Lili-Tsee. The cruel picture fell into her lap, but she sat on, her anger rising to a great bitterness. When Kiki-Tsum reached home, there was no loving wife to greet him in the front room; no supper was prepared. He went through the house to seek her, and was greeted with a storm of reproaches which came as a cruel surprise.

"Is this the sort of love you have for me, then? Is it thus I am to be treated when we have hardly been married a year?"

"What are you talking about, Lili-Tsee?" cried the astonished husband, beginning to fear that his wife had gone off her head.

"What am I talking about? You should say, What are *you* talking about? To think of your hiding away portraits among my rose-petals! Here, take away your precious thing, and never let me see it again!" And Lili-Tsee burst into a miserable storm of weeping.

"I don't understand what it's all about," pleaded Kiki-Tsum, now utterly bewildered.

"You don't understand, don't you?" she cried, becoming hysterical. "Well, *I* understand quite well. You prefer an ugly, wicked woman like that to your own faithful wife. If she were only good-looking, it would not be so bad; but she is a vile, hideous creature, with a face full of every kind of wickedness. She might be a murderess, a cruel wretch, anything that is bad!"

"What are you talking about, Lili-Tsee?" asked the indignant husband, at last losing patience. "This is the picture of my sainted father, who is dead. I found it in the street some time ago, and I thought it would be safe in your vase."

At this shameless falsehood, as it seemed to her, Lili-Tsee's anger flamed up still higher. Her eyes blazed, and her words rose to a scream.

"Listen to that!" she cried. "Do you dare to tell me that I can't tell a woman's face from a man's?"

At this Kiki-Tsum lost his temper, and the altercation became a violent quarrel. The angry voices reached the street, for the door was ajar, and an old priest who was passing put in his head to see what was the matter.

"My dear children," he said benignantly, "what is the meaning of this wrangling, of such unseemly anger?"

"I am afraid, father, that my wife is out of her senses."

"My son, all women are more or less unreasonable," said the holy man. "When a man marries he is a fool to expect a paragon, and he must be content to abide by the bargain he has made. All wives are an affliction, and it is no good losing your temper with them."

"But she makes charges against me which are gross lies."

"They are no lies, holy father," cried Lili-Tsee. "My husband has a woman's picture hidden away in a vase of rose-petals."

"I swear to you," protested the poor Kiki-Tsum, "that I have no picture at all except the image of my father, of saintly memory."

"Come, come, my children," said the old priest magisterially, "let me see these pictures."

Lili-Tsee produced it. "There is only one," she said in a voice of cold sarcasm, "but it is one more than enough. Here it is."

The old priest took the mirror and gazed at it with rapt attention, finally saluting it reverently. "Dear children," he said, and his voice had an entirely different tone, "make up your quarrel, and let there be nothing but peace between you. Both of you are in error, and your delusion is quite incomprehensible. This picture is the sainted face of a holy and reverend priest, which I will take away with me. It shall be preserved among the most treasured relics of our church."

The holy man then gave them his blessing, and departed, taking with him the mirror which had been the innocent cause of so much trouble.

MARC LE GOUPILS

THE CROSS-ROADS

WHENCE she had come, and who she was, nobody knew at all. The county police had never set eyes on her, and concluded that it would be a waste of time to make too deep enquiry into a matter which could lead to nothing. The entry in the register of deaths was simply:

" An unknown woman. Age supposed about sixty."

She was not even one of those ordinary beggars who have a certain round, and are known in the larger villages by some popular nickname, and whose social position the police can specify at once. She was a gipsy, an inveterate wanderer, living on the road rather by petty thefts than by charity, perhaps a derelict from some ragged tribe, prevented from following her companions by some illness, or it might be by drunkenness.

The only important point was that her death was due to natural causes, and permission for the burial had been granted at once. The Mayor of La Maladrerie gave orders that the tramp should be buried, in accordance with regulations, at the expense of the community, in the district in which her dead body had been found.

The death of this poor woman had, indeed, been the most natural in the world, and no fewer than fifteen witnesses were ready to testify to this. She had died at about eleven o'clock, near a gate leading into a meadow, at the side of the road, in the sight of the stars, one summer's night.

If she had been a drunkard, which was neither an impossible nor an unlikely supposition, she was certainly not drunk on that night. This had been stated authoritatively by those who had seen her and who had, they said, examined her thoroughly. Had she suffered from illness? Of course, since she had died. But it was unanimously agreed that her illness amounted to no more than exhaustion. About what age was she? Fifty or sixty years, who could say? Besides, they had been unable to get a word out of her about it, she was already so far gone when help had come to her. She had babbled a few incoherent syllables; that was all.

She had reached the hamlet of Carrefour-de-la-Forge at about half-past nine.

At the same moment the blacksmith's wife, nicknamed Mistress Nails, had come out to close the window-shutters. She had noticed this tall old beggar at once, standing in the middle of the cross-roads; she had kept quite still, but she seemed to be holding herself upright with all her strength by leaning on a long, knotted stick.

Seeing a carriage coming along at a good pace, Mistress Nails had called out to the beggar to keep out of its way, but she had made no attempt to move, and the carriage, in order to avoid knocking her down, had been obliged to swerve sharply.

Mistress Nails called out to her husband, who was inside the house, "Come out here, Philip. Perhaps you should ask that woman what is wrong with her."

Philip Nails came to the door-step. His wife and he looked first far along the road, for at this late hour both were naturally suspicious of the multitude of thieves and drunkards who wander about at night.

As the unknown woman, evidently frightened, but still standing stock-still, was mumbling unintelligible sounds, he went close up to her, and indeed walked right round her.

Mistress Nails suggested that she should wake her children, who were in bed and fast asleep, so that she could find out if this were the same woman whom they had seen a short time ago, when they had gone out to bring the sheep home, and whom they had spoken of as sitting with her feet in a ditch by the roadside, at a little distance from the village. But, on consideration, she remarked that their testimony could after all serve no important purpose.

At last the blacksmith went up to the poor creature, and spoke to her familiarly, in a voice which sounded kindly also: "Hullo, mother, you don't seem quite as well as you might be!"

There was no reply. Encouraged by this step, Mistress Nails in turn came forward, and both husband and wife examined the beggar. She was indeed a dreadful sight, but only because of her poverty and misfortune.

"She's a deader, I do believe!" the housewife pronounced at last.

They could not think what to do. They were good people and very neighbourly, as people often are in the country, but they were by no means well off, and could not afford much in the way of charity. Besides, they did not consider that they had any clear duty to fulfil to strangers and tramps, whose papers the police are always demanding, and against whom complaints are often made by workhouses, relief-committees, and parish councils. Vagrancy involves many dread mysteries.

Now this tall vagrant—for she certainly was one—standing there at the dark cross-roads, looked a very suspicious character. But, quite apart from the question of sheltering her it seemed only right to speak to her kindly, and perhaps to do a little more than that if her case were urgent.

"Are you ill, my good woman?" Mistress Nails asked.

There was no doubt about that. The poor soul nodded her head painfully, and, trying to find breath, made an effort to open her mouth.

"Good Heavens!" cried the countrywoman, horror-stricken; and, like the good soul that she was, stepped swiftly to the help of her failing fellow-creature. She put her hand under one of the arms that held the knotted stick so stiffly. "We can't leave her here!" she exclaimed.

"By Jove, that we can't!" the blacksmith agreed. But something stronger than he, some vague feeling which he could not have explained, came over him, so that his approval was only half-hearted.

"Come into the house for a little, and rest," Madame continued.

The vagrant made an attempt to walk, but her feet seemed glued to the ground, and her half-raised stick fell down heavily.

"Philip!" cried the blacksmith's wife. The man came at her call and took the other arm. Suddenly, while they were carrying rather than guiding her into the house, he suggested: "Suppose we let her sit outside on a chair?"

But his wife either did not hear or did not understand him: the poor woman was gradually led into the house, and seated in a comfortable arm-chair by the side of the fire.

"Can't you see that she's dying?" the blacksmith said sharply.

"Well, she looks like it, sure enough," his wife replied.

"Hurry up and see that she gets warm, so that she can go away soon," he said.

His words seemed reproachful, and his tone signified that it may not always be wise to play the good Samaritan.

"I don't want her to come to any harm," the wife replied.

"Neither do I; I want to cure her," he answered. "Didn't I speak to her first? But all the same, hurry up and get her warm."

With these words he knelt on the hearth, thrust in a handful of shavings, and made the embers underneath the ashes smoulder brightly, while the woman hurriedly brought brandy from the sideboard.

In the arm-chair, her thin hands clutching its arm, the beggar was gasping for breath, with her wan, bony, and corpse-like head thrown back. Her stick had fallen at her feet; and, slipping from her shoulder and hanging in mid-air, was an old and dirty canvas bag, full of holes; the string that held it had caught on the chair-back.

The fire burned briskly. A foot-warmer filled with ashes had been placed beneath the beggar's feet, and Mistress Nails, holding a glass to her lips, made her swallow three-quarters of a glass of strong spirit.

"My word, if I had that medicine," said the blacksmith, "I couldn't help getting better!"

For a few moments the woman seemed to have recovered. She could lift her head, utter a few sounds, and make a few gestures with her hands.

The hamlet of Carrefour consisted of four or five houses built at the roadside, and from these the neighbours came to see what unusual goings-on were taking place at the forge.

They looked at the dying woman, and felt an embarrassed and hesitating pity when confronted with the miserable rags of the vagrant and her besotted face, which had been ravaged by want and the vices attendant on a life which knows no hearth nor home. She was hideously ugly. Now that she had recovered her senses, she rolled her haggard eyes about in her foolish face. One wisp of grey hair strayed from beneath a dirty bonnet with cord-like ribbons.

Still, one must always help the dying, and all felt this duty so strongly that nobody uttered an inhospitable word. Each inwardly thanked his lucky stars that the lot had fallen to others rather than to himself, and every one praised highly the charity of the blacksmith and his wife.

"Wasn't I right, Philip?" the latter remarked, warmed by these compliments.

For some time they began to hope that she was less seriously ill than they had believed at first. La Fillotte, one of the neighbours, had gone home to look for a bottle made of thick and wonderful glass, the contents of which, an elixir, seemed to be a sovereign remedy. The beggar looked at every one in the room, and put several of her helpers out of countenance.

The hope that she would get up, take her stick and bag, and continue her journey under the stars, was strong in every one. They made fun of the matter, and then moralised : " These beggars are so hardy ! They look as if they are dying ; give them a glass of spirits and they're all right again. It's impossible to kill them ! Curious life, all the same ! "

Gaffer Durand, a gardener, and the most optimistic of the company, went out to observe the condition of the sky. It was a beautiful night : it would not become cool until nearly morning. This was very fortunate ! For the unlucky woman, as well as for her hosts, who had plenty of troubles of their own, it had only been an alarming accident. In the house attached to the smithy voices rose in argument.

But optimism did not last long, and soon it became increasingly evident that the poor woman would die. Their uneasiness began to weigh on the observers. Making various excuses, several of the curious disappeared on tip-toe. A few remained, but looked as if they wished to follow suit.

" I wonder if I can put her out now ? " the blacksmith said. He spoke interrogatively and not affirmatively, because he wanted public opinion to show him his duty, and he also wanted to give it a clue to the attitude he hoped it would adopt.

" I'm a Christian, by George ! " replied Gaffer Durand.

Having said this, and Christian though he was, the gardener went away all the same. Yet, he added, in case he could help his neighbours, he would not go to bed just at once.

" My goodness, no, that woman's not going out," Mistress Nails declared in a firm voice. " We'll see what happens to-morrow."

The fire would have warmed any one but a dying person, for the evening was mild, and the room very hot. But there was nothing more to be done ; on the pillow which had been slipped beneath her dishevelled and livid head the beggar was dying, and her breath came in rattling gasps.

About a quarter of an hour went by. The blacksmith suggested to his wife that he should fetch a doctor or the priest. Both lived a long distance away; but, since he was anxious to escape from the wretched scene, he did not mind that. His wife did not like to show him that she was afraid to wait there alone. But she made out that it would be a good errand on which to send one of their officious neighbours and counsellors. Her husband agreed, and went out to speak about the matter to the old gardener.

Durand had not yet gone to bed. He was talking to some one whose gig had pulled up at his door, on the opposite side of the road.

"Hullo, blacksmith!" the gardener called out. "Do you know what M. Vassort says? He tells me that if that woman dies in your house Blosseville will have to pay the funeral expenses."

"Yes, that's the law!" the gentleman in the gig added, turning to Nails. "And I imagine that the Mayor of Blosseville won't be too pleased about it!"

Then, only slightly interested in the story, M. Vassort whipped up his horse and was off at a canter.

Thunderstruck, the blacksmith forgot both doctor and priest. All he could think of was the terrible mayor of the district—the great, the old, and harsh Pierre Desfossés, whose anger nobody liked to rouse. And then what might not happen? The magistrate and the police would perhaps call on him. He swore he would have nothing more to do with the matter. A superior mind had rid him of the unpleasant task with which he had unwisely burdened himself, and he made up his mind immediately.

"In that case," he said, "I can't keep her. You surely see, Durand, the condition she's in. I can't keep her."

"I know, of course, what she's like," the gardener answered evasively.

But the blacksmith persisted. He wanted the other to realise that he was sending the wretched creature away only when she was dying, and he could do nothing more for her. But he saw something else, too; he wanted some assistant, or rather an associate, in a painful and delicate task. Gaffer Durand, greatly annoyed with himself for having suggested in any way the removal of the vagrant, followed him regretfully.

The blacksmith went back to his house with a firm step.

" I can't have her any longer," he declared.

Pushing open the swing-door, which at once began to close of its own accord, he put a stone against it to keep it open.

Briefly he stated the case to his wife; and she, without any false sentiment, approved of his resolution. The shrewd wife thanked Durand for giving her husband such good advice.

" One can't do these things all alone," she said to him ingenuously.

But they were obliged to set to work at once, for the poor woman could not last much longer.

" Fetch Gaffer Durand's wheelbarrow," she said; " it is better than ours. You can't carry that poor wretch: you'd choke her!"

Since it was all-important for their business that the beggar should be alive, they went off quickly. It was not from any religious scruple, nor from any superstitious fear, that these three peasants would not touch a corpse, but from a wholesome respect for the mysterious legislation which governs irregular deaths.

The wheelbarrow came at last, and both sides of the swing-door were fastened open.

The dying woman was carried out to her strange hearse by the three accomplices; her head lay on the pillow which the soft heart of the blacksmith's wife could not take from her, and her legs were made to rest on one of the handles of the barrow. Her eyes were already sightless and staring, and her breath came in slow gasps.

Once having cleared the door, the procession stopped short in the middle of the cross-roads. Where should they lay down this gloomy burden, which was certainly living, but was as certainly unable to give advice? It was a difficult problem.

Four districts meet exactly at the cross-roads: Bonnebosq, La Maladrerie, Blosseville, and Bretteville. The first two own none of the houses in the hamlet of Carrefour; old Durand had the only one in Bretteville, and all the other houses belong to Blosseville.

To which of these districts did the pauper belong? She had been standing on Bretteville soil, on the high road, when first discovered, and in the blacksmith's house she had become a denizen of Blosseville.

Gaffer Durand had no difficulty in finding that Blosseville had a right to rid itself of her, since she was not yet dead. He volunteered this information, but yet he would not permit that she should fall to the lot of his parish.

None of the neighbouring houses opened their doors, but the discussion was helped out by people at various windows.

"But, after all, it's quite an easy matter," Durand argued calmly. "Where did the woman come from? From Bretteville, of course. But where was she going? To La Maladrerie or to Bonnebosq? I am not finding fault with you, you know, but perhaps it would have been better to have let her find her own way."

The entire Blosseville portion of Carrefour warmly approved of these wise remarks. It was a man from Blosseville who had made the mistake, and the Brettevillian was showing himself a good neighbour, trying to redeem the false step his friends had taken.

"If you carry her only about fifty yards farther," said a voice from somewhere, "she'll be in Bonnebosq or La Maladrerie."

Her custodians hesitated between the two parishes, but the blacksmith's wife at last decided for the former, because it seemed to her that "the poor thing was looking more towards Bonnebosq" when she had first seen her. This argument seeming conclusive, they considered that she belonged to Bonnebosq.

Then they hurried off, the blacksmith pushing the barrow, his wife and Durand following. At fifty yards from the cross-roads they lifted the dying woman carefully, and laid her down as gently as possible beside a milestone; they then turned back, Mistress Nails carrying her pillow under her arm.

After they had walked a few steps in the peace and silence of the night, they heard a rattling sound.

"It's *her*!" said the woman.

"Very likely!" answered Durand.

"She has not long to live," the blacksmith remarked.

And they went on walking.

When they reached the cross-roads, the woman said, "Well, after all this, I'll bet it's past eleven."

At that moment a trap, coming swiftly out of the darkness, crossed Carrefour. The driver had to rein in his horse to keep him from running into the barrow, and he swore loudly. The pedestrians bade him good-night: he was Michael Leloup, the Mayor of Bonnebosq.

When he had gone by, the blacksmith laughed at the thought of the face Master Michael would wear next day when he found that a vagrant had died in his parish. But his laugh rang hollow: Master Michael Leloup, Mayor of Bonnebosq, was, like his colleague, Pierre Desfossés, one of those coarse peasants whom one is afraid to cross in any way.

A sound, the meaning of which was immediately clear to all, made them stop short: Michael's horse was shying violently in the road. What awful luck! The animal was afraid and refused to go past the milestone at the foot of which the poor woman was gasping her last breath.

Soon a storm of oaths broke out in the darkness, and a few minutes afterwards Master Michael, leading his horse by the bridle—for it had narrowly escaped throwing him into a ditch—came back to know why this dead, or dying, woman was lying at the roadside fifty yards from these curious specimens of Christianity who were wheeling a barrow at this unusual hour! This was indeed a pretty state of things.

They would have tried to lie, to say that they knew nothing about it, declare that they had left the vagrant where they had found her, had not the blacksmith been incriminated by the wheelbarrow, whose handles he still held. And, above all, the three were frightened by the authoritative voice of the doughty peasant who addressed them. They betrayed themselves at once in the confused and contradictory account that they gave of the incident.

Master Michael Leloup was neither more nor less sentimental than the inhabitants of Carrefour, and what angered him was the bad trick they had tried to play on him. He then asked if they were absolutely certain that she was dying. They replied that they were.

"Then you were going to make a fool of me! And you would have done if I had not passed!"

"You mustn't get in a temper like that, Master Michael!" the woman said. "There's no sense in that. We'll take her away again to please you. Come along with the barrow, Philip. Come on, Durand."

While this conversation had been going on with the Mayor of Bonnebosq, the other people of Carrefour had come to their windows. The smith now turned back with the barrow, and his wife and Durand went with him.

"She's not dead yet," said the smith, when they had nearly reached the milestone.

They could, indeed, hear her groans come out at long intervals.

This time, in their hurry, they dumped her on the barrow as if she had been a bundle, and Mistress Nails carried the pillow under her arm, without placing it under the poor creature's head again. The smith spat on his hands; then, lifting the barrow by the handles, trundled it along.

Master Michael, back in his trap again, waited until the procession had reached the centre of Carrefour.

"Now then," he said in a tone of relief, "good-night, every one!"

Without more ado, he urged on his horse with a click of his tongue, and disappeared.

The vagrant was once more at the spot where her strength had failed her, and our three burden-bearers were at their wits' end. But the whole of Carrefour was in an uproar about the dispute.

"Is she any better?" one of the neighbours asked hypocritically; he had been the first to slink out of the way.

"She's soon going to 'pass away,'" was the reply.

"Are you going to leave her there, in the middle of the road?" suggested one woman, who understood nothing of the whole squabble.

"That belongs to Bretteville," quickly replied Durand, the Brettevillian.

The vagrant, left alone in the wheelbarrow during this argument, continued gasping, a shapeless mass in the dim light of the starry night.

No one left his house: let the smith and his wife, who had taken the trouble to get mixed up with other people's concerns, and this old Durand, who had not got out of it in time, finish off the work they'd taken in hand! But from one window to another passed questions, replies, suggestions, denials.

"I can't hear her any longer."

"Yes, I can."

"It's a sad case of poverty."

"You should say a case of laziness."

"She was fuddled."

"They say she wasn't."

"Where are they going to put her?"

"Good! I thought I could hear the sound of horses' hoofs! What if it were the police? It's really a matter for the police."

And they made comments on the law about which they had heard a vague rumour. Some said it was iniquitous, others that it was very wise. But all agreed that it was the duty of the government to bury these folk, and, also, that the police should patrol the roads better.

But they also laughed at Master Michael's outburst of temper and at his way of taking care of his own parish. They approved of it and said he was a good mayor.

Doubtless the whole affair would merely have amused these country-people, wakened at such an unusual hour, if it had not been for the persistent gasping that came from the darkness of the cross-roads.

" Her bag ! We left it in the house," said Mistress Nails, who had gone in for a moment. She threw the bag down upon the barrow on top of the poor woman.

" Well, good people," she continued, " it's time we decided what to do. For a quarter of an hour, Gaffer Durand, she was in Bretteville. She'll be dead in another five minutes, as sure as I'm standing here ! "

Durand took off his cap and scratched his head for a moment.

" Do you know," he said finally, " what I think we ought to do ? We ought to dump her down on La Maladrerie—it's a rich enough parish, surely ! If you think this bad advice, say so ; and, if they don't like it, they must get rid of her as best they can ! "

La Maladrerie had no supporter in the hamlet to fight out the vexed question, and it therefore met with no objection.

The blacksmith entered at once into Durand's scheme, and he elaborated it.

" We'll put her at the gate of M. Petitjean's paddock," he said ; " she'll be best there."

He did not explain why she would be better there than in any other spot, but nobody took the trouble to ask for the reason.

" Come on ! " said Durand.

He now spat on his hands, in his turn, and wheeled the barrow along with a determined step. But he began to suspect that nobody was following, and so turned round.

" Well, really," he grumbled, " you must come with me."

" Oh, of course ! " answered the smith half-heartedly.

It was only right : the treaty silently concluded between Bretteville and Blosseville demanded, in this act of mutual defence, that they should remain firmly welded to the end. The smith and his wife followed the barrow.

" Is she still alive ? " some one asked.

" Oh, Lord, yes ! " said Durand testily. " You may be sure she's still alive ; very much so ! "

In order that every one might judge of the truth of this assertion, he brought the barrow to a standstill. They could hear that persistent, heavy, choked breathing.

Then the barrow went on its way, and, turning towards Carrefour, it was swallowed up into the darkness along a road bordered by thick hawthorn hedges. It rattled along, going farther and farther away, for several minutes ; and at last they heard it coming noisily back, rattling emptily along the stony road.

Durand and his fellow-conspirators went straight back into their houses. After he had cleared the door of his house with the barrow, old Durand could not restrain himself from saying, for the benefit of the inhabitants of Carrefour, who were waiting for it before going to bed :

" My goodness, no ! I don't know whether she's dead or not. But, anyway, she doesn't make a sound now."

The windows closed immediately, and the Brettevillians and Blossevillians went to bed and slept soundly, while at the gate of M. Petitjean's paddock, on the La Maladrerie soil, leaning against a post, was the body of the poor woman who had come from nobody knew where ; and her wide open eyes stared stupidly at the stars.

A. LE HETRE

TRAMP AND POET

"WHAT time is it, Bastide, my good clerk?"

"Five minutes to two, judge."

"Let us enjoy those five minutes, Bastide! It is so hot! Whose are those tomatoes upon the window-sill?"

"Those are some of the fruits of my garden, sir. This morning I pulled up one of my plants by mistake, the finest of them all, the one I had saved from the insects; and so I brought the poor tomatoes here, that they might ripen. It must be owned that monsieur the judge's room is so freely exposed to the sun——"

"That it seems made expressly to ripen your love-apples! You are right, Bastide. What the deuce are we going to have to-day? Some fine domestic drama?"

"Alas! sir, nothing but a simple tramp, but we must not be down-hearted."

"I still hope, Bastide, I still hope! In the meantime let us examine Jean Clochepin, tramp by trade. A tramp! Good heavens, what a trade, and in such weather! Go and bring in this hero; it will be a charity to put him in the shade."

The judge let his arms drop along the sides of his chair. He had laid his cigarette close to his pen-rack; there rose from it a fine, silky smoke—a dainty keepsake from some invisible fairy's hand.

The judge saw in front of him, through the wide open window, the dazzling blue sky of a July afternoon, and the light tower of the college, which sprang up like a rosy stalk. A bee, that had rested upon a tomato that had burst open with a juicy laugh, bore away with his humming a faint echo of the snoring of the drowsy town.

At the same hour the sergeant and the substitute whom he had picked up dozed over their beer at the Café Tivoli. The professor of mathematics went back to his classes after having repeated to Mme. Graubjac, the proprietress, for the thousandth time, as he himself said, that her profile was growing more and more Grecian. The judge addressed verses to this lady, madrigals and sonnets, wherein he lamented her hard-heartedness. All this, however, was merely post-prandial playfulness. The judge loved poetry, cultivated figures and rhythms, and in his court this was his only consolation and the secret of his even temper.

Weariness fell from the city walls with the grey dust of the plaster. The evening, with its quiet hours, was coming, when those good, motherly voices in the belfries would counsel folks to go to sleep. The judge longed to escape to some calm retreat—with a book of verses.

" Move on there ! Quicker than that, you ! "

The magistrate drew himself up. In front of him, under Buzenat the gendarme's black eye, and preceded by the clerk Bastide, the tramp entered ; a tall, slouching body, bearded, and very hot. He had taken off his rusty felt hat, which looked like a mushroom. Two sea-green eyes shone under his bushy eyebrows, and his solidly planted nose projected over a red moustache. His beard foamed and flamed. He was dressed in an old suit of grey clothes, the colour of the roads.

The judge inspected his man with a glance. Then he let him approach without looking at him, affecting to be occupied with his papers and with the reports of the officers. This carelessness in regard to prisoners was the judge's favourite procedure.

He suddenly raised his head, looked at the man, and asked :

" Your name ? "

" Jean Clochepin, monsieur the judge, at your service."

" Thanks ! " said the magistrate scornfully. " Jean Clochepin, you have already had dealings with the courts."

" That is true," said the tramp, bowing his head.

" You need not flatter yourself upon that account," said the judge. " For some days your movements have thrown the peaceful hamlet of Saint-Pierre-le-Fenille into a state of terror. You must have threatened the people or the crops, either by gesture or by words, or else the men would not have driven you away with pitchforks and pointed you out to the police."

The tramp replied in a calm voice : " Pointing out their field to them, I said to three peasants who refused me a piece of brown bread : ' Still, you have fine rye this year ! ' There was no anger in my gesture or my words. That field, monsieur the judge, was very beautiful. I love the dusty green of the rye. The ladies whom I saw last year all wore that shade of green."

Crac, cric, crac, went the clerk's impatient pen. One might have thought that it was a cricket learning to chirp. The judge bent down toward the worthy officer:

"You need not take anything down, Bastide. Do not fatigue yourself."

Then, turning to Jean Clochepin again:

"As to the ladies," he said, "you addressed unsuitable words to a young woman of Peyrilles, near the fountain. It was in the evening toward nine o'clock, fifteen or twenty minutes past nine—this type is not very clear. Nobody knows what might have happened if Grateloup, the postman, had not chanced to pass that way."

"It is possible, monsieur the judge, that I may have spoken some words of harmless gallantry to this woman, who I thought was very pretty, and who bore upon her head, with antique grace, an old copper pail adorned with flowers. But I can assure you that my words were in nowise disrespectful. Tramps, monsieur the judge, look at young women as at the blue sky of our land; they look with joy, but without hope."

"A queer, good fellow!" murmured the judge, who had been regarding Jean Clochepin with interest. "A queer, good fellow, indeed—but perhaps one ought to be distrustful. The happy warrior may be a rascal. Let us be wary!"

The tramp was getting talkative. The judge checked him with a gesture:

"Have you any papers?"

"Yes, monsieur the judge."

He placed a dogwood stick against the table and drew from his waistcoat a thick, fawn-coloured pocket-book, frayed, worn, full of folds and pockets, crammed with papers and plants, bulging like a poacher's game-bag.

"Give me that."

The judge took the pocket-book with a sudden movement, opened it upon the table, unfolded it, spread it out. There were ferns in it, pressed flowers, some blue or faded rose-colour on a pale yellow background.

"Why, this is a perfect herbarium!" said the magistrate. "Wait, here are some pages!"

The judge had come to a dead stop. He was reading. Sombre at first, his face began to brighten. The judge swayed his head back and forth, with half-open mouth.

"Is this your own?"

"Yes, monsieur the judge," the tramp confessed, embarrassed. "You know how it is! The length of the roads, the loneliness of the inns, the open air, the smell of the meadows, the adventures ——"

The judge bent upon Jean Clochepin a face full of kindness.

"Will you leave me one of your poems?"

"If it pleases you, monsieur."

"Yes."

The judge glanced round the room: Buzenat, the gendarme, was stealthily drawing near the tomatoes; full, round-cheeked, swollen with rich juice, they temptingly diffused a warm and piquant fragrance in a wave of sunlight. Bastide, the clerk, his head upon his arms, was slumbering, a pleasant smile upon his lips.

The magistrate quickly drew from his pocket a five-franc piece and put it into the tramp's hand. The latter, having seen the movement, looked as if he would refuse the gift.

"It is the price of the verses," murmured the judge. "You are free."

And, rising, he himself opened the door for Jean Clochepin, tramp and poet.

GEORGES MAUREVERT

THE GOLD CHAIN

"*ESTÁ muerto!* He is dead!"

They believed him dead—impaled on the enclosure—killed instantly! From the entire amphitheatre a cry of horror rose to the dark-blue heavens.

The slender blade of Eusebio Moreno had bent into a circle and snapped like glass on the thick hide of the bull.

Miraculously spared, however, mute, haggard and ashy pale, the swordsman, his body caught between the sharp horns fast driven into the palisade, was trying desperately to extricate himself from his frightful position. The people grasped the situation and a stupefied silence at once fell upon the plaza.

The torero, Salvador Lopez, a wiry and nervous Castilian, nicknamed El Mico ("the Monkey") on account of his extraordinary agility and his small, dark and mobile face, leaped into the arena. He seized the bull by the tail, and the moment it succeeded in getting its horns out, with a supreme effort he pulled it back with so sudden and violent a jerk that the bull turned aside. Moreno cleared the palisade with a bound. He was saved!

"*Gracias!*"

He grasped Lopez by the hands and embraced him fervently, amid the acclamations of the multitude.

Already the bull was some distance off, attracted by the manœuvres of the chulos and banderilleros. Moreno, who had now selected another and well-tried blade, made signs to the men to drive the bull toward him. It was to be a battle to the death between the man and the monster.

The swordsman, an athletic Andalusian with a determined face, wished to try again the thrust that had so nearly cost him his life. Amid the breathless attention of the spectators he attracted the bull by calmly waving his muletilla, a cape attached to a rod. Right in front of the president's box he stood, with crossed arms, one foot placed upon the bench. The animal, a small Murcian bull, strong-necked, black and fiery, stopped in front of him, a sword's length off. His heaving breath agitated the blood-stained streamers hanging at his neck. From his muzzle ran thick slaver flecked with blood. With his round, red, fiery eyes he gazed at the swordsman as though hypnotised by the cold eye of his opponent. Fifteen thousand hearts beat high at the supreme and silent duel.

Suddenly the bull gave a long bellow, took one step forward and deliberately lowered his sharply-pointed horns. The arm of Moreno darted out like a flash, and a pale gleam of steel was visible. With lowered horns the animal staggered a moment, tumbled on his knees, then heavily sank to the ground at the feet of the torero, who stood impassive, his little sword still in his hand.

From the base to the summit of the amphitheatre a thunder of bravos went up. The vanquisher, splendid in his brilliant costume of red silk brocaded with gold, stood quietly wiping the bloody steel of his blade on the purple folds of his muletilla. Outwardly he was unmoved, but the delirious plaudits of the crowd filled his simple soul with the infinite pride of some barbaric king.

From every direction a frenzied tribute was poured on him. Hats, canes, fans, oranges, flowers and jewels flew toward him from all points of the circus.

A massive chain of gold struck him in the chest. The torero raised his eyes to the spot whence the gift had come and his face, up to this moment calm as a bronze statue, was irradiated by a flash of joy. Standing in a neighbouring box Lorenza Suarez, the beautiful interpreter of great tragedies, was wafting him showers of kisses with her clasped hands, her eyes aflame—Lorenza Suarez, the mistress of El Mico!

Moreno bent down and, amid the continuous rain of presents, picked up the chain and held it to his heart, bowing to the actress.

"*La oreja!* The ear!" shouted the crowd.

The president of the course, the Duke of Veragua, commanded that the ear of the bull be given to the victor. A chulo cut it off and, dropping on one knee, presented it to him.

"Don Eusebio!"

The swordsman turned toward the little chulo who had called him just as he came out of the plaza by a side door.

"What do you want of me, my boy?"

The boy carefully took a letter out of his pocket. " This is from a beautiful lady, Don Eusebio," said he timidly, his eyes cast down.

Moreno took the note and read :

" Follow the bearer. I am waiting for you and I love you.

" LORENZA."

Disguising his surprise and agitation, he asked : " And where are you to bring me, my boy ? "

" To a villa near the gate of the city, on the cliff."

" Palacio de las Rosas ? " queried Moreno, knowing that this was the name of the actress's villa.

" Yes, Don Eusebio. You know ? "

" Very good. I shall not need you. I can go alone."

" All right, Don Eusebio. You are expected about eight o'clock."

" Thanks, my boy. Here, this is for you."

He put several pieces of money into his hand. The boy disappeared.

Moreno enveloped himself in his cloak, drew over his eyes his broad-brimmed felt hat, and, passing through the suburbs, made his way toward the sea.

He arrived at the beach as the sun was about to sink into the Atlantic. All along the horizon the sky was of a putrescent green ; it almost seemed as if some cyclopean forge had overflowed and the fused metal, welling up, had circled the sky. Above the sun soared a long streamer of deep rose-coloured cloud, tingeing with its hue the white palaces standing near the sea. A profound peace brooded over the beach, broken only by the infrequent cries of gulls and the soft, rhythmic breaking of the waves upon the sand.

In the west the sun was very near its goal. All at once it plunged below the horizon, drawing with it the long red streamer. In its disappearance the cloud grew vividly red, like a pool of blood betraying a murder.

A lurid light seemed to haunt the swordsman, but he did not know whether it was a reflection from the sun's last rays or the effect of the flaming eyes of the bull, which he had so fortunately poniarded, and to whose death he owed the happiness of being loved by one of the most beautiful women in Spain. But remorse haunted him on El Mico's account. Still, when one reflected what Lorenza's love was—! Six months ago Garcia was the favoured one ; then it was Lopez, now it was he, Moreno. He would take his happiness, since it was offered to him.

He hastened on, leaving behind him the last villa. There was no longer anybody on the beach. At the extremity of the cliff, hidden by tall fir trees, stood the Palacio de las Rosas, which, by a whim of the actress, had been placed on the wild summit of the hill. He hurried on, longing now for the touch of Lorenza's scarlet lips, the intoxicating perfume of her hair.

"Bravo, Eusebio!" cried a mocking voice all at once. "Good! You are punctual at the trysting-place!"

A dark shadow flitted out of a niche in the rocks and advanced toward him. El Mico! He here, and at this hour? A terrible suspicion arose in Moreno's mind.

"Punctual at the trysting-place?" repeated he, in a tone which he endeavoured to make indifferent. "What do you mean?"

"You know very well, Moreno, you know very well. The note! Ha, ha!" El Mico burst into a bitter, sardonic laugh which reverberated weirdly along the cliff. "And the gold chain, Eusebio! Aha! Do you think I didn't see you when you picked it up? I know that chain well, for it was I who gave it to Lorenza."

"Mico, I assure you I did not know——"

"Ah! You didn't know, Eusebio? You didn't know? She sent you the chain—Lorenza—but it was I who sent you the note."

Moreno drew back a pace. "You, you?"

"I, myself, Eusebio! She loves you, the beautiful Lorenza—she told me so. And I—I hate you. Do you understand, Eusebio? I hate you like the devil."

He took a long knife out of his pocket. There was a sinister metallic click as he opened it.

Moreno drew still further back. "You want to kill me, Mico? And you saved my life a little while ago!"

"You saved mine a week ago. Now we are quits. And, besides, I didn't know then what I know now."

Moreno opened his cloak and bared his breast. "It is well, Salvador," said he gently. "Kill me, if you wish."

El Mico shrugged his shoulders. "I am not an assassin, Eusebio. I intend to kill you, but in fair fight, knife to knife."

"I have no weapon," said Moreno.

"That is nothing, Eusebio. Here is a weapon like mine."

He threw a knife at his rival's feet. Moreno crossed his arms upon his breast.

" I lied, Lopez. I am armed. But I will not fight with you. You may kill me if you wish."

El Mico came up to Moreno. " You say you won't fight, Eusebio ? I say that you shall !"

He spat in his face.

With a cry of rage Moreno threw himself upon El Mico, knife in hand. " You devil ! I'll kill you, Lopez."

El Mico stretched his arm out toward the cliff and said in a softened tone : " It is possible, Eusebio. But, first, come with me and let us pray to the Virgin."

He went toward a simple white statue concealed in one of the clefts of the rock. Trembling all over, Moreno followed him. The two men knelt in the fine sand, side by side, and prayed. El Mico rose first and withdrew a few paces. An instant later Moreno stood up.

They had thrown their cloaks upon the sand and were now face to face in their sumptuous apparel of the arena.

In silence the fight began, deadly and merciless. The first stars were piercing the faint blue of the sky ; the silver crescent of the moon hung in the west. The pallid gleaming of the thrusting knives mingled in the fragrant twilight with the scintillations of the gold and silver spangles on the clothing of the combatants. Like a tiger El Mico circled rapidly around Moreno, with frequent feints, offering false openings, and ready to profit by any unguarded movement. Suddenly, with a loud cry, he leaped in the air—then rolled upon the sand, his throat pierced by the blade of his foeman.

Moreno dropped his poniard, closed his eyes with a groan, placed his hands on his breast and fell a few feet from his adversary. For a moment there was no sound, save that of faint moans suppressed by the pride of the dying men. A gentle breeze arose, wafting in a smell of seaweed.

" Eusebio," said Lopez in a broken voice, " it's all over. I am dying."

" And I, too, Salvador," said Moreno, trying to raise himself on one arm

" Will you forgive me, Eusebio ? " asked Lopez in a stifled voice.

There was a painful silence.

" I forgive you," said Moreno at last.

With an agonised effort Lopez dragged himself over to his foe, leaving a red trail behind him. " Eusebio, in ten minutes I shall be a dead man. Will you receive my confession? You can repeat it to the priest for me."

Something like a grin flickered on the face of the other man. "I need a priest myself, Lopez."

"Less than I do, Eusebio—less than I do! I know how I struck you. If you were destined to die you would be dead now. Listen, I beg of you."

His voice both implored and inspired hope in Moreno.

"I listen, my son," said he gravely.

"My father, bend toward me—I am very—weak——"

In a voice that could scarcely be heard, broken by moans, he whispered his solemn confession to the man who had given him his death wound. They were surrounded by a dark stain which spread from moment to moment over the rock.

"Bless me quickly, my father," pleaded El Mico.

"Die in peace, my son."

With his right hand Moreno made the sign of the cross over the dying man.

With a supreme effort Lopez raised himself on his arm.

"Now I can die!" he cried. His voice was stronger and clearer. "I lied, Eusebio Moreno! Do you hear? I lied! I know the thrust I gave you; in an hour you will follow me. No one will find you here on this lonely beach. And you—you cur—you stealer of my love—you shall die burdened with my sins and your own—*unconfessed*—ah——!"

A crimson surge burst from his lips. He fell back dead.

SUICIDE

GEORGES MAUREVERT

SAN ROMANO! What a heavenly place! Here one fully understands the words of Flaubert, "There are some places in this world so beautiful that one has a desire to press them to his heart." What a pity that San Romano resembles an exquisite fruit whose taste is so bitter that we dare not eat it with impunity, since it causes death.

Unfortunately, the joyous peace that lies over the scene does not reign within the hearts of the people. On every side you meet sorrowful faces from whose lips these strange words seem to fall, "Oh, had I only placed it upon seven! The accursed *rouge*! Ten times in succession it won and I played *noir*!"

They pay little or no attention to the scenic beauty of San Romano. They are Œdipus in the struggle with the Sphinx Zero. The earth to them seems but as a gigantic *roulette* and the sky a slate of *trente et quarante*, for this is the Kingdom of Mammon, the Residence of the Demon Chance.

I, also, was a subject of his for a few months, lost a small fortune and became somewhat grey. One day, I wakened with only twelve francs in my pocket, and I owed the landlord fifteen. So I examined my pistol carefully and made sure that it was well loaded with six bullets, for these would certainly suffice to blow out a brain like mine.

I opened the window. "My last morning" was glorious—the heavens, azure blue; the waves, a shimmering green; and the air, heavy with the fragrance of the orange and the violet. I strolled down to the shore so as once more to breathe in the refreshing salt air; then I took a short walk and found that I was hungry. Before returning to the hotel, I bought a paper, the *Anti-San Romano*, a sensational weekly edged in black like a mourning letter.

During breakfast, I hastily turned the pages. The heading, "Suicides of the Week," drew my entire attention to it. "Here will also my death be reported within the next few days," I thought without much emotion. I even had a desire to thank the writer of my obituary in advance.

One notice, marked with a heavy black cross, attracted my attention and I read, " Yesterday, the body of Joshua Jacobson, an American, was found hanging from one of the palms that grow upon the terrace. The sum of three thousand francs was in his pockets—naturally ! "

Joshua Jacobson, I had known him well—I might say that we had gambled away, side by side, one franc after the other. During the previous evening in the Casino, where he had lost his last penny, he had grasped my hand with much feeling, had looked sadly into my eyes and, smiling, said in a low voice, " I am ruined, utterly ruined ! Farewell, my friend—" and went out and—hanged himself.

Still, how was it possible that three thousand francs had been found on him, and what the devil did that " naturally " mean ?

After a few moments, light began to dawn upon me. How stupid not to think of it at once ! Of course the proprietors of the Casino had had the money put into his pockets so that we should not think his suicide due to his losses. That was self-evident. Then I began to wonder how much money would be placed in my pockets if I should carry out my intentions and take my life near the Casino. I think I had lost as much money as Jacobson. And then—suddenly an idea rushed into my head faster than the bullet I had intended for it. Excited, but with a light heart, I continued my breakfast. Then I went to the landlord, told him that I would pay him his fifteen francs that evening, " Provided," I added, with a sad smile, " that I am still alive."

" My dear sir, we trust you implicitly."

" Then," said I, " please lend me one hundred francs until this evening. I am expecting money from Paris."

" Certainly."

I spent the afternoon on the beach where, after careful deliberation, I planned the various steps of an advantageous suicide.

That evening at nine, I donned my best fitting dress-suit, tied my most elegant cravat and went to the Casino. I made it quite evident I risked my last coin, and should have been greatly chagrined had I won. I lost, and assumed first a troubled, then an angry, then a meditative mien.

An attendant, who knew me, became interested in my fate. In

low, sad tones, I told him of my ruin. He sympathised with me and sought to comfort me.

" You can still have your travelling expenses home, for the Casino makes it a point of honour to——"

" The way that I go needs no ticket," I interrupted with deep earnestness.

He looked at me, amazed. " You are not in earnest. You are not going to be a fool, I hope."

I remained silent and turned my back on him. Looking about carelessly after several minutes, I noticed the attendants of the Casino watching me. Towards eleven, the crowd of players arose. I went out among the last, hanging my head and looking thoroughly crushed.

The night was glorious. The moon bathed forest and sea in a flood of light. In the distance I heard violins. Deciding quickly, I directed my steps towards a great bush of rhododendron not far from the Casino, a place that seemed a fit setting for the joke I had planned. My hasty preparations were carried out in the presence of a marble nymph that seemed to smile, then—crack, crack, two shots rang out! I fell, not without care, upon a bench and waited. Voices in the distance came nearer and nearer, and shadows fell across my closed eyes.

" My God, it is he ! "

" How awful, pierced with two bullets ! "

Then the voice of the attendant whom I knew, " Hurry ! hurry ! before any one comes. Oh, the rascal, couldn't he have done this somewhere else ? "

He bent over me and I felt that he slipped something into my pocket.

I almost choked. I groaned twice, slowly opened my eyes, raised myself with great care and looked in astonishment at the crowd. Unconcerned, I took my hat and my still smoking pistol and arose.

The crowd looked on with increasing astonishment. They stared at me as if I were some strange animal.

" This is unheard of ! " I said angrily. " A man can't even kill himself without causing a sensation."

The attendant who knew me came toward me enraged. " My dear sir, I would—well, you— ? " he stammered, confused. " What do you mean by this farce ? I shall have you arrested for disturbing the peace."

" Disturbing the peace ! " I repeated bitterly. " That is well said ; that will become the watchword of the season." And I walked away, dignified but inwardly laughing at the crowd of people who had gathered out of curiosity.

I returned to my hotel and paid my debts out of the three thousand francs earned through my suicide.

The Bank made repeated efforts to collect the money from me, but it never entered my mind to return it, for I considered that it had been legally given to me. Furthermore, I believe that three thousand francs is not too large a fee for a suicide.

To vex them, I lived extravagantly for a few days upon the money and then went to Paris. Subsequently, I have heard that the sum bestowed by the Casino of San Romano has been considerably reduced.

A. ROGUENANT

A SILVER COIN

IT was close upon midnight when Hector Merot left his office, after finishing the reading of his proof-sheets. During the previous week, when an article to which he had devoted an immense amount of trouble, and of which he had been justifiably proud, had been altogether ruined by a printer's error in its most important sentence, he had resolved never again to omit this precaution. He insisted on seeing a final proof each night, before allowing the next day's article to be printed.

It was a sharp night in early winter, and the wind blew chill against him as he walked along the Rue Montmartre toward the boulevards. The thought of his empty rooms was comfortless, and he turned aside as he came to a café, and sat down at an outside table, calling for a hot drink. He drank it quickly, for it was near closing-time, and the lights were already being turned out in the café; then he laid beside his glass a small silver coin for the waiter, rose from his seat, and turned to look for his stick.

At this moment, Hector saw a man glide swiftly up, seize the coin he had left, and make off hurriedly down the street and round the first corner. Pulling out another coin for the waiter and calling his attention to it, Hector ran after the thief.

It soon became plain that the man he was following was by no means a professional hand, and that he did not even know the district through which he fled. He ran forward blindly, dodging up and down one street after another, scared out of his wits by the pursuit, and was not long in coming back almost to the spot from which he had started. This odd behaviour gave Hector a keener interest in catching him, so that he might discover the reason of the man's eccentricity.

Himself familiar with all the alleys and byways of the district, Hector was able by superior tactics and by his swifter pace to meet suddenly, at a street corner, the wretched creature who was trying to escape from him. There was a lamp just above them as they stood together, while Hector sternly exclaimed, " Give me back my money ! "

But then, as he caught sight of the other's face, his feeling changed utterly. The man stood silent and cowed, the picture of sheer hopeless misery. He was a young man, but thin and haggard, and his white face was made quite unearthly by the contrast of his dark hair and moustache. It was a desperately sad face, the most pitiable Hector had ever seen ; and the man's clothes were equally worn and wretched.

Without a word the unhappy fellow held out the stolen coin to Hector, while the look of despair settled more deeply in his hungry eyes ; and Hector suddenly felt that he himself was the criminal, standing before a silent accuser. Taking out his purse, he put the stolen coin into it, then, thrusting the purse hastily into the hands of the other, he turned away and passed quickly into the night.

Ten years passed. They were years of hard work and many struggles for Hector, but at the long last he had won for himself a recognised place in journalism and in the world of art. His critical pronouncements were undisputed. His articles on literature and the arts were read and quoted everywhere, and were eagerly awaited by his many readers. No other critic combined in such a high degree the qualities of sincerity, sheer ability and sound judgment.

Yet traces of those early years of trial still remained upon Hector, in spite of his present eminence, and were especially evident in that slight shade of sadness which had become so characteristic of him. This drama of humanity, which had been his life-long study, has so much tragedy in it, for those behind the scenes !

There was no mark of sadness about him, however, on a fair morning in May, the day of the opening of the Salon. Hector came briskly into the Restaurant Ledoyen, where many sculptors, painters, and journalists were gathered, and the more outstanding exhibits and their merits or demerits were being eagerly debated. There was quite a stir all round the room as he entered. In his usual careless yet cordial manner he shook hands with all who rose to greet him ; then, moving to the little table where he always sat, he joined the two friends who awaited him—Paul Nielssery, the young landscape painter, and Charles Zirtius, the clever artist in water colour.

These three friends were always happy together ; they shared the same tastes, the same love of art, and the same hatred and scorn of all that is base and unworthy.

"How happy you look to-day, Hector," Paul exclaimed. "Have you come into a fortune? Or where have you been?"

"I have been where all the world has been, of course," Hector replied. "I have been looking at the paintings and sculptures. There is one thing which is absolutely superb, a wonderful piece of work. It has given me an inspiration which will last with me for long!"

His two companions looked up with professional interest, and many at the nearest tables were silent, so that they might hear with their own ears the famous critic's verdict, which all the world would read in to-morrow's newspapers.

"There are some very good things in this year's Salon; but there is only one thing which in my opinion stands altogether above the ordinary. It is the kind of thing you only meet with once in ten years. I expect you know which I mean—Jean Meunier's 'Wreck.'"

The babble of satisfaction at the surrounding tables showed that Hector's admiration of the young sculptor's work was shared by all who heard him. The three friends went on with their meal, all of them in the highest spirits and enjoying themselves immensely; and general conversation was resumed throughout the room.

When they had reached their coffee, Charles Zirtius rose, and, crossing to the further end of the room, brought back with him a man of about thirty years of age, handsome and well-dressed, obviously a gentleman. His dark brown eyes, full of intense passion, and not without a note of tragedy, were now gleaming with quiet joy, so that they transfigured the fine oval face. Fame at last had lent her laurels to his brow.

"Hector," said Charles, "let me introduce my friend Jean Meunier."

Hector sprang up and seized the sculptor's hand, exclaiming heartily, "I must thank you for a morning of the very greatest pleasure. Your 'Wreck' is a wonderful piece of work; no sculpture that I have ever seen has so delighted me."

The youthful artist glowed with pleasure at this praise from the famous critic, and gladly accepted their invitation to join them over their coffee.

The fine dark eyes with their unearthly earnestness seemed strangely familiar to Hector, and he studied Jean Meunier's wonderful face as they sat and talked, but without being able to remember when or where they could have met. He ransacked his mind for all the possible meeting-places—cafés, clubs, the studios of many friends—but all in vain.

Convinced at last that he must have been deceived by a chance likeness to another person, Hector gave up the problem, and was soon far too deeply interested in the conversation of his artist friends to think any more about it. The room was now almost empty. Summoning the waiter, he paid for their dinner, laying the money on the table. One silver coin, destined for the waiter himself, was hidden by the rim of a plate, so that the man failed to notice it, until Hector called after him, " Here, take this ! "

Jean Meunier looked up swiftly at these words, and glanced from the coin to Hector, shivering as if deadly cold, while his face became ghastly white and his eyes gleamed with sudden terror. Immediately, Hector saw in a flash that face of hopeless misery which he had seen years ago under the street lamp, on that night in November. He turned to the young man with a gaze of friendship and understanding ; and as the little party rose from the table, held out his hand in friendship. Jean Meunier seized it, and the fervent pressure of his clasp held all the grateful devotion of a lifetime.

The intimacy thus begun grew closer day by day ; and at last the day came when Hector heard the story of the terrible straits from which he had saved the young sculptor when on the verge of despair, and when his little sister was at the point of death. This sister was now twenty years of age, and was the darling of her brother's life. She was a joyous, radiant, lovely girl, and filled Jean's home with sunshine.

Hector's steps turned ever more frequently to that happy place, and by degrees all melancholy vanished from his expression. Not many months had passed before a notice appeared in the papers : " A marriage will shortly take place between Hector Merot, the well-known art-critic, and Mlle. Hélène Meunier, sister of Jean Meunier, sculptor of that celebrated work, ' The Wreck.' "

MAURICE SAINT-AGUET

THE CROISSEY YEW

I

I AM going to tell you, monsieur, why I come every evening to smoke my pipe under the Croissey Yew.

My story goes back to the end of the year 1812. Brought up by an old uncle, the curé of a neighbouring village, and having already a footing in the Pope's army, I had escaped the requisitions of the Emperor; as an ecclesiastic the conscription had spared me. But almost at the same time my old uncle died, and the worthy man, from having given all he possessed to the poor, even to the shirt off his back, had nothing to leave to his nephew but the poverty from which he had drawn others. There was I, then, at twenty, free, alone in the world, without means, and full of disgust at my calling, but undecided as to all others; in short, in that state in which one is at the mercy of mere chance.

I have told you that I loved to dream, while waiting for the means of living; and I often came to this spot to rebuild the "Château en Espagne" I had reared the night before, and which had crumbled in the interval. But I had wearied of standing at the foot of this colossal yew tree which covers in and freezes us with its shade, and which stands on the edge of the precipice expressly to shelter the spectator, and I had established a sort of dwelling-place in its branches, where I succeeded in making myself believe that I was isolated like an eagle on the watch, and secure from discovery as the most confirmed misanthrope or dullest philosopher could desire to be.

One evening I was at my post. The moon was rising. Suddenly I heard something below me: it was the voice, or rather the sob, of a woman, saying:

"The last time!"

Then I heard something which sounded to me extremely like a kiss, followed by the voice of a man, replying:

"Come, come, Louise; a little courage!"

Another voice, that of a young girl, soft but decided, then said:

"No, no—not the last time—I will not have it so, I tell you!"

Considerably mystified by this stray fragment of conversation, I peered through the branches, and perceived in the moonlight a young man in the dress of a workman, having in his hat the bow of ribbons and the fatal number. He was supporting with his right arm a young girl, who was weeping on his bosom, and giving his left hand to another and smaller girl, who was not weeping. It was she, doubtless, who had said, "I will not have it so." I quickly understood that it was the conscript's parting that was taking place.

"Poor Christine," replied the young man, smiling sadly; "your will goes for nothing in this matter, sister—I am not the master."

"But, brother, it is you who have reared me, you are the father of the family! You must not go away—besides, you are married, for you are betrothed to Louise—who does nothing but weep, as if *that* would do anything!"

And the pretty rebel, who in the moonlight appeared to be charming, fell to crying too. Louise replied in a voice broken by sobs:

"Christine—is unreasonable—isn't she, Eugène—unreasonable?"

'My poor dears!" replied Eugène tenderly, pressing them to his bosom.

"Well, then, Louise," cried Christine suddenly, "prove to me the strength of your courage! Since he will not listen to either of us—since he believes that we can do nothing for him—you see the quarry before us; it is deep and goes straight down from the brink—come with me!"

And, completely losing her head, she took the hands of Louise and drew her from the arms of Eugène.

"Are you both mad?" cried Eugène. "Can't you see that I must go with the others to fight for France?—for you?—for the cross? Louise, Christine, I shall return in eight years, and if I do not find my sister and my beloved one then, what will there be left for me? Do you wish me also to kill myself?—that I should not have the memory of you in my heart, to make me fight like a lion, to bring you back a pair of epaulettes? Let me go; one only has to serve one's time, and all is said."

"Oh, his time!" replied Christine. "There was Stephane, the mechanic, who went away with the others to Russia: *he* served his time—he died at Moscow—and his mother is in mourning for him.

The others, will they ever come back? His time! with their dog of an Emper——"

"Will you hold your tongue?" interrupted Eugène, clapping his hand over her mouth.

"No, I will not hold my tongue! Haven't you a colonel—he who enrolled you? Well, go to him, throw yourself on your knees before him and say, 'Monseigneur, I don't want to go with you—I don't want to be killed. I have a sister and a wife who cannot live without me, and who will throw themselves into the river if I am taken from them. Beat me, Colonel—put me in prison, but don't take me away for a soldier. Long live the Emperor!—he's a worthy man; let him leave me in peace and go wherever he likes. Look you, Colonel, I am a man, I am free, and I have no right to leave my sister Christine against her will—and she'll detest you, Colonel, if you compel me to go.'"

"That would be pretty conduct on the part of a soldier!" replied Eugène, who could not help laughing.

"Unfeeling, cruel brother!" she cried, in tears, throwing herself into the arms of Louise.

II

A moment of silence followed. I was deeply touched—so absorbed in the situation, that I forgot my own. Presently Christine raised herself, and was apparently a little more calm.

"Heavens!" she said, "is there not a man—a comrade—who will replace you? Others have means. Oh, how I would love him!"

"It could all be done as you say," assented Eugène, "only to do it we need money—and that by to-morrow."

"Well," cried Christine, "I'll give all I have—my gold cross, my earrings, my neck-handkerchiefs, my lace collars, all my jewellery—to whoever will go in your place."

"All that would not make the price of a man," replied Eugène.

Christine reflected for a while, and then, seizing her brother's arm, said:

"But I—I am worth a man—more than a man; I am sure I am! I'll give myself; I'll say to some one: 'Go instead of my brother, and I'll be your wife! See! I'm good-looking—a little over-petted, but that's no harm. I'll love you so dearly, if you save my brother!'—

I swear it on the gold cross in which there is a lock of my mother's white hair! I'll cheerfully marry whoever will devote himself for you."

"Good sister, I know you would do all you say, but you are over-excited to-night, and do not see how utterly impracticable are all your dear follies. Let us get away from here," he added, laughingly, "for if you go on, I shall really become afraid of the precipice before us."

I could not catch what Christine said in reply, and presently I lost sight of all three in the shadow of the trees; but both my head and my heart remained filled with the charming girl, and I became lost in thought.

That evening, as they were seated at their supper without being able to eat a morsel, and gazing at each other through their tears, somebody knocked loudly at the door.

"Come in!" cried the young man, hastily drying his eyes.

An old sergeant appeared before them and said:

"Good evening! Does the conscript Eugène Livou live here?"

"Yes, sergeant."

"That's for you, then," said the trooper, throwing a letter on the table.

Eugène read, at first slowly, then devouring the contents. It was a release in form!

He looked up at the old soldier in bewilderment.

"It says that you have been replaced, conscript—that's all. But I can't congratulate you—because a little gunpowder would have made your moustache sprout. Different people, different tastes—if you are satisfied, all's said. Good evening to you."

He had turned to go, but stopped suddenly and cried:

"Thousand bullets! I was forgetting half my errand. You have a sister—Mam'zelle Christine—where is she?"

"Here, sergeant," said Eugène, indicating Christine, pale with happiness and surprise.

"This is for you, mam'zelle"; and he threw a second letter on the table.

"You'll drink a glass of wine, soldier?" asked Eugène.

"With all my heart, conscript."

While Eugène was preparing to ask the old soldier a number of questions, Louise, out of her senses with joy, kissed her betrothed again and again, half crying, half laughing, while placing fresh bottles on the table and filling the glasses.

Agitated, trembling, Christine sat, holding the letter and looking fixedly at the table.

"What is the matter?" asked Eugène anxiously. "It is that letter distresses you? Who has written to you? Let me see it, dear."

He hastily read the letter, which he had taken from her unresisting hands.

"Read it aloud," she said; "it is all the same to me—all the same!"

Eugène read out the letter:

"Mademoiselle, I demand nothing, I go without making any condition, I replace your brother; you have need of him, no one has any need of me. But I love you—have loved you ever since I saw your tears. I send you a ring which belonged to my mother. If you feel pity for me, you will take the cross containing a lock of your mother's white hair, which shone on your neck this evening in the light of the moon, and place it in a crack in the side of the great yew tree, high up, near the branches. To-morrow morning I will go for it. You will wait for me two years, and, if I am not dead, I will bring it back to you. Will you remember that you have made an oath on that cross? Adieu!"

"What does this mean? How could anybody know?" said Eugène slowly. "Do you understand this, sergeant?"

"Oh! a vedette near you? Bah! I have it! it comes from a novice—a youth who knows how to write, but, for want of practice, doesn't know how to tell a woman just what he means," replied the sergeant, laughing.

Eugène shook his head.

"Your hand, soldier," he said; "I'll not accept this substitute—my sister shall not be sacrificed; I'll go with you."

And taking up his release he was about to tear it up, when Christine stayed his hand.

"But if I wish it!" she said. "He has acted nobly. He is going away unconditionally; he is unhappy. I have no other means of keeping him—and—and I want to love him! For the rest, he has done well not to show himself—perhaps I might have regretted it too much. I will take my cross, as he directs; but I should like to know—Sergeant, have you seen him?"

" Yes, I've set eyes on him."

" Well, he's not hunchbacked or bandy-legged, is he ? "

" Thousand thunders ! Hunchbacks and bandy-legs in the French army ! " cried the sergeant, scandalised.

" Is he a good fellow ? " asked Eugène.

" That I can answer for," replied the old soldier heartily.

" Well, then," said Christine, detaching her cross with its black ribbon from her pretty neck, " tell him that what he has done was well done ; and, yourself, put this cross in the side of the great yew tree. Do not tell him anything about it : but do not lose sight of him, and try and return with him ; he is worthy of you—he has begun as a brave man, and he will continue as a brave Frenchman."

Eugène and Louise gazed at her without being able to speak. The grenadier rose, and received the cross, while tears sparkled in his eyes.

Christine then turned towards her brother and future sister. She was no longer the same : her character had suddenly become serious. She said to Louise :

" I, too, am betrothed ; my pledge is in the hands of a soldier of the guard."

Next morning, on setting off, my knapsack on my back, I found the cross hidden in the side of the yew tree—and I fancied I saw amid the close-grown branches the uniform and red epaulettes of a sergeant of the guard who was watching me.

III

A year later, the campaign of Saxony was finished : the campaign of France was going to begin. Eugène was married to Louise. The terrible requisition reached him as well as others, but this time he was not kept back. It was foreseen that the anxiety would not be of long duration ; and then it was so clearly evident that the defence of France was necessary ; lads ran away from their colleges to get to the frontier, and it would have been shameful in any man who, in default of a sword, had not seized up his ploughshare, shameful in the woman who still hung upon the arm of that man.

Eugène went this time, and joined the army in Champagne. At the bridge of Montereau, after having fought long at the outposts, he found himself without cartridges, and was defending himself as well as he could with his short infantry sabre against five Austrian grenadiers, when a lieutenant of carabineers sprang before him, crying :

" Conscript, go and find your sister and your wife ; leave those to die who have nothing to live for ! "

And the lieutenant cut down two whitecoats with his long sabre. But his horse received a bayonet stab and fell under him. He received two others and fell also. A French fusillade laid low the three men of the enemy ; and Eugène, who had sprung to the body of his rescuer, carried him to a neighbouring house and brought him back to life.

The soldier and the officer became friends and brothers in arms ; but the soldier could not understand the devotion of the officer, nor the sense of the words that had accompanied it. He was but the more proud, the more fascinated ; and then, the officer was so fond of him and spoke to him so kindly, that he was wholly at a loss how to repay so much goodness. When, at the end of the drama, the armies were disbanded, he said to him :

" Lieutenant, if you have neither father, children, nor family—if you are alone in the world—come to my home. I am only a workman, but my people will be very fond of you. I have a good wife and a pretty sister—you hear what I am saying, Monsieur Charles ? You will not disdain my family, even if you do not consent to make part of it ? At least you will not deny me the pleasure of showing them my preserver."

The lieutenant could only throw himself on Eugène's neck and thank him warmly. A week afterwards, Eugène, stifled in the embraces of Louise and Christine, tore himself free from their arms and, pointing to the friend he had brought home with him, cried :

" Here is a brave man who saved my life without knowing me, and exposed his own because he had no family to weep for his death ; but now he has one ! He is my brother ; he has said that he will not disdain my home—let it be his ! We will work together, and some day, perhaps, we shall be rich and my house more worthy of a lieutenant."

" A lieutenant ! " cried Christine involuntarily.

" Sister," whispered Eugène, " this one is worth more than the other."

Christine cast down her eyes and looked furtively at the officer. He was not ill-looking ; his epaulettes, his wounds received for a dear brother, and, above all, his determined efforts to please Christine and prove to Eugène that he did not despise his family, resulted, at the end of two months, in causing her to appear thoughtful, while blushes suffused her cheeks in answer to the expressive looks of Charles ; at which signs Eugène smiled.

One day he took his friend and his sister apart.

" I am very happy," he said. " You love my sister, Charles ? "

" I love her," replied the lieutenant, gazing on Christine, pleadingly.

" Do you love him, sister ? "

" Yes."

" More than you love me ? "

" In a different way," she answered simply.

Imagine my delight, monsieur ! for I was the lieutenant. I who had repented of having engaged the young girl's promise, and had wished to die, so as to release her from it. I who longed to win her free and voluntary love ! I fell on my knees before her.

" Will you be his wife, Christine ? " asked Eugène.

" No," she replied, sadly, but firmly ; " no, I have given my promise to another. I am betrothed."

" Folly ! " cried Eugène. " Betrothed !—to a man you have never even seen—who asks nothing of you—who is ugly, perhaps, and as old as I am ?—a man, in short, who has never cared to show himself, and who by this time is dead, no doubt ! "

" Dead ! If so, he died for you, Eugène. Have you forgotten the year of happiness you owe to him, of which I am the price ? The bargain is sacred. If he is dead, the pledge returns to me, and I will wear mourning for him as for a husband. If he is not dead, I will wait."

" But have not the two years passed ? "

" Though that may be, I will still wait for him who, poor and friendless, trusted in my promise. Oh no, let him come ; let him return me my gold cross—and, if he pleases, set me free ! "

Eugène was losing patience, but I restrained him by a gesture. I was still kneeling at Christine's feet.

" Christine, Eugène," I said, " it is time that you should know all. It was I, my friend, who replaced you ; I who, hidden in the great yew tree, overheard your tearful parting ; I who accepted Christine's pledge ; I who love her and who ask her, on my knees, to restore to me my mother's ring."

" You ! you ! " they both cried at once. Christine had already drawn from her bosom the ring and the letter enclosing it; but suddenly she paused.

"Do not deceive me," she cried. "Can it be possible? Ah, you have agreed together, you and my brother! He has told you the secret! Where is my gold cross?"

"What!" I exclaimed, "do you refuse to believe me? Is not my voice that of truth?—my soldier's word?"

"The cross! the cross!" she repeated.

"I have it not," I replied sadly. "I have it no more! It was the old sergeant——"

"Where is he?" asked Christine.

"He is dead—he died at Leipsic," I replied hopelessly.

"No—thousand thunders!—I'm not dead," cried a voice behind us; "and I've arrived just in the nick of time, or I'm a Prussian! Lieutenant, don't you recognise me?"

"What! you are still living?" I cried, throwing my arms about him.

"As you can see for yourself! I've come from the hospitals at Leipsic; but while I've been grunting there—thousand bombshells!—changes have been going on, it seems. The Little Corporal—but enough of that for the present; we'll talk about it some other time. What we've got to deal with is Monsieur Charles's affair. Look at him, mam'zelle—though he had not courage to speak to you under his Jesuit's cassock, he knew how to fight under his tonsure. I saw him slip your cross out of the old yew tree, kiss it, and put it under his uniform—where I have mine now; but that's not the same thing. I followed him everywhere. He went under fire—thousand cartridges!—as if he were entering a ballroom! At Dresden, owing to his education and his dare-devilry, he was made a sub-lieutenant. At Leipsic, in a tussle on the bridge, I saw him dash right upon the crowd of white-coats, and I said to myself: 'What is he about? Does he want to get himself wiped off the roll?' Then I took the liberty of laying hold of the tail of his coat, and saying to him: 'Lieutenant, are you forgetting that you have a pledge to return to somebody—down yonder?'

"That told him that I knew all about the business, and he said to me: 'I've seen you somewhere—yes, I remember. Here is the pledge you speak of. Take it to Croissey; it weighs on my conscience. I have no friends, and I would not tempt fate by buying a wife—I leave that to the Turks. To give her back her liberty I am going to get myself killed. Fly! Save yourself! Let the old moustaches return to France—they have need of one another!' I wished to take an oath; but, bah! he was gone. As for myself, I got jammed between a gun-carriage and the parapet of the bridge; and that laid me up in bed for eleven months, with a dozen poultices to keep me company. But here I am, at last, and—no disrespect to my lieutenant—I find him still a bit of a conscript where women are in the case."

"How could I win her trust in me?" I said, looking beseechingly at Christine.

"Forgive me," she cried, throwing herself into my arms; "forgive me for having been too faithful to you! I will love you twice as much."

"The cross! the cross!" cried Eugène, mimicking her voice.

"Here it is!" replied the old sergeant delightedly.

Christine took it with transport, and, holding it, between our kisses said to me:

"May it render them sacred!"

We are now old married people. The sergeant died at Waterloo. Eugène and I have prospered by labour: we conduct the manufactures of M. de V——; we live in the little white and rose-coloured house you see in the midst of the foliage of the island yonder, and every evening I come to smoke my pipe under the Croissey Yew.

SAINT-JUIRS

NICETTE

"YOU are a dead man!" said the doctor, looking intently at Anatole.

Anatole staggered.

He had come gaily to pass the evening with his old friend, Dr. Bardais, the illustrious *savant* whose works on venomous substances are known all over the world, whose nobility of heart and almost paternal goodness Anatole had learned to know better than any other living soul; and now, without the least hesitation or preparation, he heard this terrible prognostication issue from those authoritative lips!

"Unhappy boy, what have you done?" continued the doctor.

"Nothing that I know of," stammered Anatole, greatly agitated.

"Tax your memory, tell me what you have eaten or drunk—what you have inhaled?"

The last word was a ray of light to Anatole. That very morning he had received a letter from one of his friends who was travelling in India; in the letter was a flower plucked on a bank of the Ganges by the traveller—a strangely formed red flower, the perfume of which—he now recalled the fact vividly—had appeared to him to be singularly penetrating. He hastily drew forth his pocket-book and produced the letter with its contents and handed them to the *savant*.

"No doubt is possible!" cried the doctor; "it is the *Pyramenensis Indica*! the deadly flower, the flower of blood!"

"Then,—you—really think——?"

"Alas! I am sure of it."

"But—it is impossible!—I am only five-and-twenty years of age, and feel full of life and health!——"

"At what hour did you open that fatal letter?"

"This morning, at nine o'clock."

"Well—to-morrow morning, at the same hour, at the same minute, in full health, as you say, you will feel a pain in your heart—and all will be over."

"And you know of no remedy—no means of——"

" None ! " said the doctor.

And, covering his face with his hands, he sank into a chair overcome by grief.

In face of the profound emotion of his old friend, Anatole understood that he was really condemned.

He hurried from the doctor's house like a madman. His forehead bathed in cold perspiration, his ideas all confused ; going he knew not whither, he sped on and on amid the darkness of the night, taking no heed of the loneliness of the streets he was traversing. For a long time he pursued this blind course, until at length, finding a bench, he sank down upon it.

How many hours had he still to live ?

The persistent and distressing sound of a racking cough brought him back to consciousness ; he looked in the direction whence it came, and saw, seated upon the same bench, a pale and weak little flower-girl—a child not more than eight years old, who, as François Coppée says,

> Dies of the winter while offering us the spring.

That verse of the poet's recurred to the mind of Anatole ; he felt in his waistcoat-pocket and found there two sous and two louis. He was going to give the poor child the two sous ; but recollecting that he had only a few hours longer to live, he gave her the two louis.

This incident did him good.

He had been like a man stunned by a blow on the head ; his bewilderment was overcome now, and he began to reassemble his dislocated ideas.

" My situation," he said to himself, " is that of a man condemned to death. A man in that position may still, however, hope for pardon —many of that sort are pardoned in our days. In past times even, some have been saved from the axe or the cord, to devote themselves to some difficult or dangerous piece of work—the launching of a ship, for example, or, as in the time of Louis XI., to marry an old woman. If I were consulted in the matter, I should prefer to launch a ship. Unfortunately, I shall not be consulted during the short interval of time that remains to me. But, by the way, how long *have* I got to live ? " He looked at his watch.

" Three o'clock in the morning !—it is time to go to bed. To bed ! —waste in sleep my last six hours ! Not if I know it. I have certainly something better than that to do. But what ? Of course —to make my will."

A restaurant—one of those which keep open all night—was not far off. Anatole entered it.

"Garçon, a bottle of champagne—and ink and paper."

He drank a glass of Cliquot and looked thoughtfully at the sheet of paper before him.

"To whom shall I bequeath my six thousand francs a year? I have neither father nor mother—happily for them! Amongst the persons who interest me, I see only one—Nicette."

Nicette was a charming girl of eighteen, with blonde tresses and large black eyes; an orphan like himself—a community in misfortune which had long established between them a secret and complete sympathy.

His last will and testament was speedily drawn up: universal legatee, Nicette.

That done, he drank a second glass of champagne.

"Poor Nicette," he mused; "she was very sad when I last saw her. Her guardian, who knows nothing of the world outside his class of wind instruments at the Conservatoire de Musique, had taken upon himself to promise her hand to a brute of an amateur of fencing whom she detests—the more because she has given her heart to somebody else. Who is that happy mortal?—I haven't the least idea; but he is certainly worthy of her, or she would never have chosen him. Good, gentle, beautiful, loving Nicette deserves the ideal husband. Ah! she is the very wife that would have suited me, if—if—— By Jove, it's an infamy, to compel her to destroy her life—by confiding such a treasure to such a brute! I have never before so well understood the generous ardour which fired the breasts of the wandering knights, and spurred them on to the deliverance of oppressed beauty!—And, now I come to think of it, what hinders me from becoming the knight-errant of Nicette? My fate is settled—at nine o'clock—after that it will be too late; now, therefore, is the time for action! The hour is a little unusual for visiting people; but, when I reflect that, five hours hence, I shall be no more, I conclude that I have no time for standing on etiquette. Forward!—my life for Nicette!"

Anatole rose—and then, perceiving that he had no money, he gave his gold watch to the waiter in payment for the champagne—a watch worth five hundred francs.

The garçon took the chronometer, and examined it closely—weighed it in his hand, opened it,—and finally put it in his pocket doubtfully and without thanking Anatole.

It was four o'clock in the morning when he rang at the door of Monsieur Bouvard, the guardian of Nicette. He rang once, twice, and, at the third tug, broke the bell-wire. At length Monsieur Bouvard himself, in his night-dress and in great alarm, came and opened the door.

"What is the matter—is the house on fire?"

"No, my dear Monsieur Bouvard," said Anatole; "I am only paying you a little visit."

"At this hour!"

"It is pleasant to see you at any hour, my dear Monsieur Bouvard! But you are so lightly dressed—pray get into bed again."

"I am going to do so. But, I suppose, Monsieur, that it was not simply to trouble me in this way that you have come at such an hour? You have something of importance to say to me?"

"Very important, Monsieur Bouvard! It is to tell you that you must renounce the idea of marrying my cousin Nicette to Monsieur Capdenac."

"What do you say?"

"You must renounce that project."

"Never, Monsieur!—never!"

"Don't fly in the face of Providence by using such language!"

"My resolution is fixed, Monsieur; this marriage will take place."

"It will not, Monsieur!"

"We will see about that. And, now that you have had my answer, Monsieur, I'll not detain you."

"A speech none too polite, Monsieur Bouvard; but, as I am as good-natured as I am tenacious, I will pass over it, and—remain."

"Stay if it pleases you to do so; but I shall consider you gone, and hold no further conversation with you."

Saying which, Monsieur Bouvard turned his face to the wall, grumbling to himself:

"Was ever such a thing seen!—rousing a man at such an hour!—breaking his sleep, only to pour into his ears such a pack of nonsense!——"

Suddenly Monsieur Bouvard sprang to a sitting posture in his bed.

Anatole had possessed himself of the professor's trombone, into which he was blowing like a deaf man, and sending from the tortured instrument sounds of indescribable detestableness.

"My presentation trombone!—given me by my pupils! Let that instrument alone, Monsieur!"

"Monsieur, you consider me gone; I shall consider you—absent, and shall amuse myself until you return. Couac! couac!—fromn! brout! Eh?—that was a fine note!"

"You will get me turned out of the house; my landlord will not allow a trombone to be played here after midnight."

"A man who evidently hath not music in his soul! Frrout! frrout, prrr!"

"You will split my ears!—you'll spoil my instrument!—a trombone badly played on is a trombone destroyed, Monsieur!"

"Couac! prounn, pra—pra—prrrr——"

"For mercy's sake give over!"

"Will you consent?"

"To what?"

"To renounce the idea of that marriage?"

"Monsieur, I cannot!"

"Then—couac!——"

"Monsieur Capdenac——"

"Prrrroum!——"

"Is a terrible man to deal with!"

"Frrroutt!——"

"If I were to offer him such an affront, he would kill me."

"Is that the only reason which stops you?"

"That—and several others."

"In that case leave the matter to me; only swear to me that if I obtain Monsieur Capdenac's renunciation, my cousin shall be free to choose a husband for herself."

"Really, Monsieur, you abuse——"

"Couac, frrroutt, ffuit, brrrout!——"

"Monsieur, Monsieur,—she shall be free."

"Bravo! I have your word. Will you now allow me to retire? By the way, where does your Capdenac live?"

"Number 100 Rue des Deux-Epées."

"I fly thither!—Until we meet again!"

"You are going to throw yourself into the lion's mouth, and he will teach you a lesson you deserve," said Monsieur Bouvard, as Anatole hurried from the bedchamber and shut the door after him.

Without a moment's hesitation Anatole betook himself to the address of the fire-eating fencer; it was just six o'clock when he arrived there. He rang the door-bell.

"Who is there?" demanded a rough voice behind the door.

"Open!—very important communication from Monsieur Bouvard."

The sounds of a night-chain and the turning of a key in a heavy lock were heard.

"Here is a man who does not forget to protect himself against unwelcome visitors!" remarked Anatole to himself.

The door opened at length. Anatole found himself in the presence of a gentleman with a moustache fiercely upturned, whose night-dress appeared to be the complete costume of the fencing school.

"You see, always ready; it's my motto."

The walls of the swordsman's antechamber were completely covered with panoplies of arms of all descriptions; yatagans, poisoned arrows, sabres, rapiers, one- and two-handed swords, pistols—a regular arsenal—enough to terrify any timid-minded observer.

"Bah!" thought Anatole, "what do I now risk!—at most two hours and a half!"

"Monsieur," said Capdenac, "may I be allowed to know——"

"Monsieur," replied Anatole, "you want to marry Mademoiselle Nicette?"

"Yes, Monsieur."

"Monsieur, you will not marry her!"

"Ah! thunder!—blood! who will prevent me?"

"I shall, Monsieur!"

Capdenac stared at Anatole, who was not very big, but appeared to be very decided.

"Ah!—young man, you are very lucky to have found me in one of my placable moments. Take advantage of it—save yourself while you have time; otherwise I will not answer for your life!"

"Nor I for yours."

"A challenge!—to me!—Capdenac!—Do you know that I have been a master of the art of fencing for ten years!"

"There's nothing of-fencive about me, Monsieur!"

"I have fought twenty duels—and had the misfortune to kill five of my adversaries, besides wounding the fifteen others! Come. I have taken pity on your youth!—once more, go away."

"I see, by your preparations, that you are an adversary worthy of me and my long growing desire to confront a man so redoubtable. Let's see! what shall we fight with? Those two double-handed swords standing by the fireplace? Or those two boarding-axes?

With cavalry sabres, or would you prefer a pair of curved yatagans? You hesitate: can't you make up your mind?"

"I am thinking of your mother and her coming distress."

"I haven't a mother to be distressed. Would you rather fight with a carbine?—pistol?—or revolver?"

"Young man—don't play with fire-arms."

"Are you afraid? You are trembling!"

"Trembling! I? It's with cold."

"Then fight, or at once renounce the hand of Nicette."

"Renounce the hand of Mademoiselle Nicette! By Jove, I admire your bravery! and brave men are made to understand one another. Shall I make a confession to you?"

"Speak!"

"For some time past I have myself had thoughts of breaking off this marriage, but I did not know how to do it. I consent, therefore, with pleasure to do what you wish; but, at the same time, you must see that I cannot appear to give way to threats, and you have threatened me."

"I retract them."

"In that case, all is understood."

"You will give me, in writing, your renunciation?"

"Young man, you have so completely won my sympathy that I can refuse you nothing."

Furnished with the precious document, Anatole flew back to the dwelling-place of Monsieur Bouvard: he had a considerable distance to walk, and by the time he reached the professor's door it was nearly eight o'clock in the morning.

"Who is there?"

"Anatole."

"Go home, and go to bed!" cried the professor savagely.

"I have got Capdenac's renunciation of Nicette's hand! Open the door, or I will break it down."

Monsieur Bouvard admitted him, and Anatole placed in his hand the momentous paper. That done, he rushed to the door of Nicette's room and cried:

"Cousin, get up—dress yourself quickly and come here!"

"It appears, Monsieur, that I am no longer master in my own home!" exclaimed Monsieur Bouvard; "you go and come, and order as you please! To make you understand that I will have nothing more to say to you, I—I will go back to my morning newspaper, in the reading of which you have interrupted me ! "

A few minutes later, Nicette, looking fresh as dawn, arrived in the drawing-room.

" What is the matter ? "

" The matter," said Monsieur Bouvard, " is that your cousin is mad ! "

" Mad ? So be it ! " replied Anatole. " Last night, my dear little cousin, I obtained two things : the renunciation of your hand by Monsieur Capdenac, and the promise of your worthy guardian to bestow it on the man of your choice—the man you love."

" Do you really wish me to marry Anatole, guardian ? "

" Eh ? " cried Anatole, his breath nearly taken away.

" Since I love you, cousin ! "

At that moment Anatole felt his heart beat violently. Was it from pleasure at the unexpected avowal made by Nicette, or was it the agony, the death symptom predicted by the doctor ?

" Unfortunate that I am ! " he cried. " She loves me—I am within reach of happiness, and am to die without attaining it ! "

Then, taking the hands of Nicette feverishly within his own, he told her all about the letter, the venomous flower he had scented, the prognostication of his old friend, the will he had written, and the steps he had successfully taken to release her from the claim of Capdenac.

" And now," he said, in conclusion, " I have only to go home and die ! "

" But it is impossible ! " cried Nicette. " This doctor must have mistaken ; who is he ? "

" A man who is never in error, Nicette—Dr. Bardais."

" Bardais ! Bardais ! " cried Bouvard, bursting into laughter. " Listen to what my newspaper here says : ' The learned Dr. Bardais has been suddenly seized with mental alienation. The madness with which he has been stricken is of a scientific character. It is well known that he was absorbingly engaged in an inquiry into the nature of venomous substances, and latterly he had fallen into the delusion that everybody he met was under the influence of poison, and endeavoured to persuade them that such was their condition. He was last night transported to the Maison de Santé of Dr. Blank.' "

" Nicette ! "

" Anatole ! "

The two young persons fell into each other's arms.

RAYMOND SCHWAB

THE PRINCESS "JUST BECAUSE"

WHEN the little Princess lowered her head, any older persons who were looking down on her from above and had seen the shadow of her heavy hair on her forehead and of her eyelashes on her cheeks, the lines round her mouth, and the curve of her neck and her rounded shoulders, would at once have forgotten how slight her figure was and would have taken her to be grown up. Any one who had seen her sitting down would have come to her side to talk about all manner of things, for she had the look of one who understands everything. Looking at her in full face, she had the features of a woman of thirty whom suffering has not embittered but has somewhat broken. Yet, when she turned her head and showed her profile, it was easy to judge how very young she was from the concave line of her retroussé nose and the pout of her tightly closed lips. And those whom she deigned to allow to kiss her hand had noticed the groove which forms a natural bracelet on a baby's wrist. The creases in her fingers, arms, and neck were not set lines, but were rather dimples.

The Infanta's favourite attitude was one in which she stood up straight in her immense stiff skirt, her hands crossed at the back, and her arms hanging straight down. Sometimes, although not a hair would be out of place, she would raise her right hand with a tired gesture and would smooth her forehead with her palm, closing her eyes at the same time as though she were making an effort. And just as her profile seemed a contradiction to her grown-up face, so was her hand, which seemed full of vitality and independence, so that every gesture was complete and perfect.

The soul of this young girl was always very near to the very heart of things, and far from her fellow-creatures. Just as one recognises a friend by his voice, so with closed eyes she knew every month of the year by its particular odour.

When she came out of her room, she ran her fingers caressingly down the richly chased blades of the halberds which the guards lowered before her. The lady-in-waiting warned her to be careful of the sharp edges of the blades, and asked her what pleasure she could find in such an action. And when the Princess's uncle, Don Fabian—who was nicknamed "The Bully"—replied in his rude way, "She finds pleasure in it, Madame, because she is touching the weapons that destroy our enemies," the little girl let his remark pass without deigning to contradict it; she merely shrugged her shoulders disdainfully. But the old lady-in-waiting hurried angrily after her, grumbling out: "But why do you do it? Why?" And the little girl, answering as a little girl must do when surprised in some wrong action, yet certain of herself, said in a humble though obstinate tone: "I do it—just because!"

When it was noticed that she took an extraordinary pleasure in touching or looking at brilliantly coloured or highly polished objects, she was taken to the royal portrait gallery. The lady-in-waiting showed her the portraits of her ancestors in their gorgeous robes, and introduced them in passing; once she stopped in front of the picture of a child with a sallow skin and faded features, awkwardly represented in a costume whose colours had faded so that they mingled with those of the wooded countryside that served as a background. "You must love this child, Madame," she said, "because he was your brother." The little Infanta, following her lead, made the sign of the Cross, because, just as she had never sinned against etiquette, she did not wish to lose any opportunity of showing her reverence to God, the most powerful of all princes, Who rules the kings of the earth.

But suddenly she resumed her childish vivacity and ran toward another picture in which, from above garments of bright colours, there rose a very beautiful little face, which seemed to be continually changing, and always full of life. She stood there thoughtfully for some time and then, as if in an ecstasy, she said: "It is *here*, Madame, that it would more befit us to praise God and pray to Him."

The lady-in-waiting showed by a look of astonishment and a swift interrogation that she was paying unwarrantable honour to a mere court dwarf, a plaything dead and now forgotten even in name. But the little girl kept on looking from a distance in her dreamy way at the picture where the greens and the blues were so bright, and she murmured: "Because—because—"

No one understood her. They smiled when with evident joy she caressed French silks, soft and fluid as water; Moorish leather whose roughness had been obliterated by art and the hand of time; when she stood still in amazement to kiss rare gems and necklaces; and when she opened her eyes wide, careless of the amusement of her companions, on a wonderful piece of tapestry. Sometimes her maids of honour would hint at hereditary weaknesses which had afflicted her father's line, and at the manifold follies which in olden times had been committed by representatives of the dynasty. They dressed up her dolls in rich stuffs, captured from pirates and long ago sold by Venetian merchants to the Great Turk; every yard of material had cost several human lives and in their dull designs were flat-looking stains which were, perhaps, splashes of blood. And every time the Infanta undressed or dressed her dolls she wept.

She won much reputation in the court for her affectionate soul, because for six months she had carefully treasured the hair of a little dead peasant-girl who had been brought up at her own expense, because they had been born on the same day. Often she would spread it out on her hands like a skein, and would caress it with her fingers or curl and uncurl it; but she never kissed the hair. Once when the dead child's father threw himself on his knees before her to beg for some favour, she had him sent away spurned, and all day long she shrank from the thought of his eyes, where colour had been all dissolved in tears. She would allow no one to serve who did not excel in beauty and in dress. And they said that not all the beauty of the world would satisfy her longing.

No one ever asked her now why she liked such and such a thing; it had become a household jest among her footmen when courting her maids to say, " I love you for our little Infanta's reason."

" What's that ? "

" Oh, just because—! "

And they called her " The Princess Just Because—! "

The favourite resort of the princess was a little old ante-room which smelled so musty that no one would go past it alone. Even the palace guards were no longer ordered to inspect it, because the dreadful odour of mortality so unnerved them that more than once its horror had led to suicide. Many ugly stories were current about corpses in the walls, and about an unnatural gloom which was said to haunt this desolate chamber. Yet this queer child had some strange predilection for the ancient smell of the leather which lined its walls.

On her tenth birthday the little Infanta, robed in blue brocade, appeared for the first time at a royal ball and danced the minuet. She had been a dancer ever since she had learned to walk, and her appearance at the ball was one continuous triumph. When she sat out she was in an ecstasy far beyond thought, and no one could evoke a reply to even the most fervid compliment. She would only bow her head slightly, and no one could tell whether her fatigue was due to the dance, or to the emotion aroused by the applause, or to the unaccustomed delight of hearing music; for she had never before attended a royal concert. The conductor of the orchestra, touching the strings of his violin with an affected gesture, glanced boldly towards the Princess. Noticing this, the aged duenna remarked: "How music uplifts and carries away the soul!" The little girl rose in a temper, and without a word went back to her own apartment.

From that day forward she forsook the leather-lined ante-room, and no longer took delight in scents; she no longer caressed swords nor the richest stuffs of the East. Instead, the delicate tips of her fingers began to pucker, as if they had been kept too long soaked in water. The most brilliant colours no longer evoked any response from her expressive eyes. And when from time to time she looked out below drooping eyelids, it was noticed that those wonderful eyes were now growing pale, and it was soon whispered that her sight was failing. This went from bad to worse, yet still the court-physicians dared not tell the King that the little princess had difficulty in breathing, that her hands were only too like those of a paralytic, and that she would probably become blind.

And now "Princess Just Because—," altering her style of hair-dressing, no longer let her hair fall in heavy masses over her ears; but at the same time her voice became more powerful, and so sweet that it seemed to be raised in one long song. Until now she had ever been silent, but now her chattering never ceased, as if she were greedy of hearing her own voice and generous of it to others.

All that extraordinary delight which she had taken in the senses of sight and smell and touch, had now become transferred to the sense of hearing. She, who had always been so greatly admired for her elegance and courtly manners, her wonderful knowledge of the etiquette of the royal Court and of the proprieties before the Sanctuary, had now fallen exclusively in love with Sound. Music, as it seemed to her, welcomed and uplifted its hearers, and made a majestic and reverent accompaniment to all their thoughts. Above all, she loved the strains which had the honour of guiding her own steps, the music of her own minuet. She was insatiable in her desire for it, and ever moved unconsciously to its stately rhythm.

But now, when rather more tired than usual, she no longer moved at all, nor even opened her eyes; and even breathing seemed too great an effort. And one day, lying inert upon a regal couch, still robed in the blue brocade, but now without eyes for the treasures of art, she summoned the musicians to play her minuet. But even as the merry instruments were tuning up, the sweet child suddenly drew her last breath, and by virtue of her immaculate innocence, and her utter love of all beauty, went straight in the blue brocade to heaven.

Yet the music still pursued her through celestial space; she was still aware of the symphony now resounding through the palace far below. Angels bore her in their arms and guided her unaccustomed way, but though their voices joined in sweeter chorus than any ever heard on earth, she begged them haughtily to be silent, and bent forward from their arms to hear the music of her minuet.

When at last she arrived before the throne of God, the music no longer resounded in her ears. She found the Court far less gorgeous than she had expected from the churches in Spain, and became sulky and fractious as a peevish and ill-tempered child. All that they could do was to place her in a cloud as blue as her brocade, and there St. Cecilia played her the most touching melodies.

But the little Infanta had no desire for moving strains. She neither loved nor understood the saint. St. Cecilia, in an ecstasy, listened to her own music; she played only for her own pleasure, without caring about the unhappy maiden. "Princess Just Because—" did not understand these melodies, which came from the heart and hoped to reach the heart, these simple and yet subtle airs, so insinuating, which might make even princesses submissive to their sweetness; she wanted something less caressing, less direct, less heartfelt, but with more majesty and more reserve. She wanted the music of procession and of precedence, slow marches in time with the pacing of heralds and courtiers, or, better still, the dance music of royal courts, where one may hear the swish of silken trains, while the wailing strings evoke the dignity and grace of people of high degree. Above all, she wished to hear her own minuet; but, whenever she lilted a few of the bars which capriciously crossed her memory, St. Cecilia caught them up and wove them into a hymn inflamed by a devotion of which the little Infanta had no knowledge. Thus eternity stole from the blind and paralysed princess her last joy. The insatiable little creature did not indeed become deaf; but, stiff and solitary in her blue brocade, she heard the majestic symphonies of Heaven pass over her, as she lay there insensitive.

. . . .

HENRY KISTEMAEKERS [1]

B. 1851

IN EXILE

I HAD made up my mind to go down into my cabin when a rather elegant but melancholy-looking passenger—I had noticed him during dinner—approached me on the upper deck.

" A beautiful night, isn't it ? " he remarked.

" Extraordinarily beautiful ! "

" Do you land in Alexandria ? "

" Yes, to-morrow morning."

" We touch there about daybreak. As you will see for yourself, the picture of Alexandria as it takes shape in the golden and rosy glow of an Egyptian daybreak is a sight like some enchanting fairy scene. I know nothing so beautiful, so graceful as this city of Aphrodite, poised like a jewel casket on the edge of the desert. Truly Alexandria is beautiful ; it is like some hymn of light. There is only one spot in the world that is more bewitching, and that is Paris ! Do you know Paris ? "

" It is my native city," I returned.

" Just as I thought—I felt it. Even blindfold I can single out a Parisian in any crowd." He leaned over the ship's railing, watching the phosphorescent arabesques that formed in the wake of the boat. Then he murmured : " What a happy man you are ! "

He turned suddenly on me, his eyes flashing wildly, and fixed his gaze steadily on me. " You are an extremely fortunate mortal—you do not realise your good fortune. You have before you a man who adores Paris ; one who has Paris in his blood, in his veins—and will never see Paris again. Can you imagine anything more ghastly ? "

" Are you exiled ? " I queried. In a tone that was most matter-of-fact he answered : " Far worse than that. I am dead ! "

My features must have betrayed my sensations at such a confidence,

[1] Henry Kistemaekers and the brothers Boëx (J. H. Rosny) though Belgian by birth are so essentially French by residence, training, and sympathy, that they are seldom classed with the authors of their native country, and here they are included with the French, the Belgian section being devoted entirely to the authors of Belgian origin whose literary work has remained native in inspiration.—ED.

for he added rapidly : " Don't be frightened ; you are not confronted by a maniac. Don't look up at the rigging so anxiously ; you are in absolutely no danger, for I am the sanest and most peaceable man in the world. My story will prove it—of course, you must guess that there is a story to tell, inasmuch as I claim to be dead and you see me here alive in the stern of this boat. Have you five minutes' time to give to me ? " I thought it best to humour him and nodded assent, seating myself on one of the deck benches. He lit a cigar, placed himself opposite me, and began : " Have you ever heard the name Saint Mai ? "

" I know not only the name but also the works of that great master," I answered. " Are you going to tell me something about him ? "

" Exactly—about the famous Saint Mai, author of ' Heracles,' the thousandth performance of which took place last night ; about the creator of ' Marie,' and ' The Woman of the Sabots '—in short, of all those works that have had such tremendous success in the last ten years. I want to tell you about Saint Mai, who died without having tasted of fame——"

" Well, what about him ? "

" Only that it is all a mistake and that Saint Mai is alive. Don't look so surprised, for it is just as true that he is alive as that I am here before you. In fact, Saint Mai and I are one and the same person."

" Oh ! " I cried, and my voice sounded my alarm.

" True ! It was just about ten years ago that I began to vegetate. A concert of my compositions had been noticed with the most prominent indifference ; my opera, ' Marie,' had flattened its nose against the portals of the Opéra Comique, and bore the honour of having been the greatest failure since that of ' Carmen ' was recorded in the annals of modern French music. My portfolio was bulging with unpublished works, and I withdrew to a small corner of Brittany to ruminate over my fate and to economise in my expenditures. It was during this retirement that one fine morning I got hold of a Paris newspaper and discovered in it the announcement that I was dead ! A laconic despatch from some news agency brought the information that I had been shipwrecked in a bark. I have never been able to discover the motive of the news correspondent who reported me dead ; but as a matter of fact this incident decided my career."

" How is that possible ? "

" Let me proceed : When I read this news item the first impulse that arose in me was to run to some telegraph station and contradict the report. The nearest telegraph office was four miles from my place of seclusion. On the road there I pondered the matter and realised that it would cost me one sou per word to contradict the report, and that a telegram would have to be sent to each one of the ten prominent Paris newspapers. The total cost of all this telegraphing would have made a fearful hole in my meagre purse. As I considered these things I gazed out upon the ocean from the high cliff, and the thought flashed across my mind : It might be a very interesting thing to discover just how much of an event my death would be, and what would be said about me after my death. So I decided to wait until the following day before recalling the news.

" Without boring you with many details, let me assure you that I had a magnificent press. Some of my intimate friends tried to besmirch me with mud by spreading evil reports about my private life ; but they only succeeded in raising me in the estimation of those people who had not known me personally, and the latter praised me to the skies. Within comparatively few hours I was made the object of most tender consideration. I became the subject of laudatory magazine articles—they are not very difficult to write, for the formula is ready at hand and there exist numberless phrases that were coined at the time of Bizet's death and are still available as models. In short, it was unhesitatingly asserted that I had been a genius. My opera, ' Marie,' which had been a failure, was hurriedly put on the boards again and had a tremendous success. At the Paris Grand Opera, in the archives of which the score of ' Heracles ' had been slumbering, every effort was made to produce that work—and at its première it was frantically applauded.

" Meanwhile I was still in Brittany. I had come to realise my position and did not dare risk endangering my successes by breaking the silence. I was mightily convinced of the fact that the position of a dead composer was much easier than that of a living one—the dead composer finding a ready publisher for his works and eager managers to produce them ; and thus he achieves a success that living composers cannot dream of tasting until after their death. I am in a position to assert this !

" And now let me tell you the rest of my story. I had a nephew who was absolutely without morals, and I determined to press him into service. Carefully disguised and with precautions of secrecy of which you can have no idea, I hunted him up, this conscienceless young man, and made him a proposition. After much deliberation we arrived at an agreement that my death was to be declared a suicide ; the evidences were to be found in the letter that I had ostensibly written to my nephew on the evening before my death. In this letter I named him my sole heir. Other documents that gradually came to life confirmed this disposal of my property. At the point on the coast where I was supposed to have been wrecked my nephew found some of my belongings that the sea had thrown back, and among them was my portfolio containing valuable manuscripts.

" As my sole heir he was entitled to all the royalties of my works, and we agreed that he was to pay over to me three-fourths of the sums thus collected. Furthermore, I had named him as the heir to all my unpublished manuscripts and had stated that he was to publish them at his discretion. In this way it has become possible for me since my death to have written six operas, and I hope to write more. I wish to make the whole world gasp in amazement. I wish to make the universe marvel at the tremendous number of operas I had written before the breath of life departed from me ! To this end I work with a fiery energy—I am a corpse of most remarkable zeal.

" Since I have died I have allowed myself extravagances that were denied me during life. I own plantations in India, a palace in Rio, and a harem in Damascus. All these fancies cost money, and I have to work hard ; yet I am convinced that never before has a corpse enjoyed life so vividly.

" But alas, that all this happiness should be marred by a speck of discontent ! Each of us carries his own unhappiness in himself, and my misfortune is that I love Paris so dearly ; that I adore the city which I cannot see again without risking resurrection. And that is my continued nostalgia. Oh, Paris ! One cannot find you in Rio, nor in India, nor in Damascus ; not even in Paradise ! Apropos, do you happen to know little Evelinette, of the Theatre of Varieties ? "

" I should rather think I do ! "

" How strange ! And you see her occasionally ? "

" Very frequently ; she is quite my most intimate friend."

" Really ? " " Most assuredly ! "

" What a coincidence ! Has she ever spoken to you about me ? "

" Never ! "

He suddenly grew thoughtful ; then, after a short silence, he remarked : " You see, there are some disadvantages in being dead. That little minx Evelinette was my last love, my only one. And yet she has succeeded in forgetting me entirely ! "

J. H. ROSNY
(HENRY and JUSTIN BOËX)
B. 1856 and 1859

THE GARDEN

I was born for love, and more especially for that sacrificial kind of love wherein a man gives himself entirely into a woman's hands " for better, for worse," so that he is ready to live or to die for her. Fate has twice struck me down : the first time when my fiancée died from some sudden illness during our engagement ; the second when my beloved, after having seemed to love me very dearly, ran away with a mandolinist from Chile.

These disillusionments had been so cruel that I despaired altogether of my future happiness. They left me listless, without dreams or desires. I went into solitary retirement in a deserted cloister near Lyons, and spent every day in a huge garden where none of the trees had been touched for a hundred years. It was a perfect wilderness of birds and tiny creatures, and a thousand chances had enriched it with flowers and grass, strange newts and long, glittering, timid snakes. A stag wandered about with his graceful herd of hinds and fawns ; I cannot think how he came into that hermitage. He soon became a great friend of mine ; and one day when I was unable to go out, he walked up the steps leading to the ancient convent and moaned most mournfully ; he threw back his great antlers and gazed at me uneasily.

I roamed about this garden early in the morning, and at night when the sun seemed to set the trees on fire, and later while the clouds played their comedies in countless wonderful scenes. But I never found any pleasure in it. My heart was as withered as dead autumnal leaves. The sorrowful words of Ecclesiastes were ever in my mind. I was always nursing my grief amid the amazing scenery of this wilderness, where oaks, elms, and beeches made a virgin forest.

One morning, when I had gone to the far end of the garden, and stood beside the crumbling wall, I saw a door open and admit the startling figure of a girl. Her dress was scarlet, embroidered with gold, and hung in heavy folds about her ; she wore a dazzling emerald necklace ; her hair, fastened by tiny pearl combs, fell in waves of light over her shoulders, and was as silky as a spider's web. Her eyes were of a delicate river-green, her complexion pink and white, her cheeks finely rounded, her lips were sensitive and her form was supple ; and all this beauty made her look like a fairy, a nymph, a sylvan queen of story in the lovely old garden.

She seemed to be frightened and threw me a timid glance. I was too much overcome to be able to move, but I still knew how to show proper respect to this fair divinity.

" Please take no notice of me," I said sadly. " This garden is altogether at your service, if you will only let me stay here ! "

She smiled, and I saw that I had quite reassured her.

" I thought it was quite deserted," she said, speaking in a voice that made me think of running, crystal water ; " I have often spent hours here without meeting anybody."

" It used to be deserted," I answered, " and we may still call it so."

We then fell a-talking of the old trees, the stag, and the newts, and to me there was a great charm in our conversation. This young fairy was so fresh and sweet ; she loved books and living nature equally ; she was as much at home in fields and woods as when deep in the romances of George Sand, Lamartine, Bulwer-Lytton, and Alfred de Vigny. She chose her words carefully and well, and there seemed to be something whimsical even in her silence. Every now and then she had a far-away look in her eyes, and at last I noticed that she seemed to be gazing right beyond the old wall.

" What are you looking at ? " I asked.

" Well," she answered, " it is just this : *I have left my body in my bedroom.* I am a little bit worried about it, because I am always afraid it might want to go out *alone* ! "

I saw, of course, that her mind was disordered, but this only aroused my deeper interest.

She came back again ; at first after fairly long intervals, then nearly every day. I was sure there was nothing wrong in this, and as for the future, how could I foresee anything when I didn't care a hang about my life ? First spring, then summer, passed by, and a pleasant autumn began to dry up the flowers and verdure. Then, one September morning, I discovered that the unhappy exile had awakened the love that slumbered in the poor mad girl's heart. It was the first vivid emotion that I had experienced since I went into retreat, and it roused my pity and my fear. I wanted to wean my kindly friend from her love, but I saw that she was growing paler and thinner every day; and thinking over our many conversations, I knew that she had a loyal heart, and that, like mine, it was made for lasting love and unswerving devotion. Then my heart was torn, and I bitterly repented my rash conduct.

" Why should I not make reparation to her ? " I asked inwardly. " Why should I not give the rest of my gloomy life into her keeping, poor soul ? "

I had hardly conceived this idea before my veins ran molten fire. I could see the resurrection of the love I had believed was dead, and I felt once more the breath of hope. And why not ? Lucienne's trifling delusion was a secret known only to herself and to me. She lived with a doting aunt and several faithful old servants; there was no legal hindrance to our marriage; my destiny was all that was at stake, and that was a dull one with no promise of living joy.

It was nearly twilight. The huge stag had ceased to bell in the gathering shadows, and clouds like celestial flowers strewed the sky. We could see amber, ruby, and sapphire lights breaking through the mists, scattering them and filling them with fairy dreams.

Lucienne drew closer to me, and together we looked upward beyond the branches. My heart was full of a great tenderness. My lovely companion, with her hair as beautiful as the twilight and her soft white face lit up by the seductive evening glow, brought back to me the days of my joy and youth.

She seemed sad and uneasy, and very much on the alert. With all gentleness I took her little hand in mine.

" Lucienne, my little Lucienne," I murmured, " why should we not watch the twilight together until the end of our days ? "

She became paler still and began to tremble, then her hand closed in mine and she spoke as if in a dream.

" Don't you know," she said, " that I care for nothing in this world unless I can share it with you ? "

She leaned close to me, shyly and nearly fainting. I pressed her to my heart, and as my lips met hers I felt that I had found the happiness I had lost before.

I am now married to Lucienne. We did not give up the old garden, and it has become the garden of Eden. My charming wife has healed my wounds and repaid me a hundredfold for my lost joys. Even her queer delusion endears her to me. Often, after we have been walking together under the oaks or beeches on a fine night, while the owls fly past and the young rabbits run away in the moonlight, Lucienne begins to talk about "her body left in the house." And then I feel that I am wandering in the spirit-world, with the loveliest of spirits, until I hear a silvery voice murmur :

"Are you not growing anxious ? *It* has been left alone so long !"

And really for a moment I feel deliciously uneasy. We go back home, and when we are safely back in our nuptial nest and I clasp my sweet wife in a close embrace, I really feel that I have met her body again after having walked with her soul.

And the hallucination of this gentle being has become a kind of symbol, a misty, pleasant, and smiling allegory.

A LOST SOUL

J. H. Rosny

"NO," he replied, "I have got nothing to grumble about; Fortune has always been kind to me and lavish of her gifts. My misery is simply the product of my own imagination, and all that keeps me from being radiantly happy is an absurd fiction which seems more terrible to me than anything real could be.

"I suppose you remember how enthusiastic I was that evening when we first met little Léa Dambère? Everything about her made her so lovely that I have never been able to think of any other woman afterwards. Her movements were so winning, her lips so sweet and beautiful, her dark eyes were so wonderfully gentle and full of womanly kindness; and then she had countless different ways of smiling that wholly transfigured her, and a little trick of bending her sweet head under the weight of that glorious hair which made me mad with love.

"Now, as you know, I have always detested myself, and with good reason. I know that I look very gloomy and dull; I am awkward, coarse of feature, and of ashen complexion; I find conversation difficult, and succeed only in uttering the most dismal phrases; and, what is worse, I am incapable of paying those trifling attentions which compensate for many graver errors. With all this in my mind, I could not, of course, hope to make this incomparable girl my wife. I had to be content with admiring her from a distance and with seeing her whenever I could; but it was in the same way as we wait for a gleam of sunshine, or seek a welcome shade, or the murmur of a hillside rivulet. And there is no doubt whatever that my relation with her would have remained at this stage, if chance had not given me an adventurous opening.

"Her father had challenged a cheat at the gaming-table. There was a fearful scene, and they went for one another tooth and nail. I was privileged to intervene. I took Dambère's side, which happened to be the side of justice, and had the satisfaction of routing the card-sharper, who was an alien Spaniard from the Balearic Isles.

"This little affair determined the rest of my life. Good old Dambère was so pleased with what I had done that he became monstrously friendly with me and thrust invitations upon me. It was thus that I came to meet Léa and soon knew her intimately, with the result that my love was altogether engaged. I thought of nothing but Léa all through those terrible nights when insomnia hovered over me like a bird of darkness.

"But it was a lonely love, for I never dared to show it to the mistress of my heart. The most that I could do was to speak to her very gently, and for the most part to be silent in her presence. I never hoped to be able to win her love; but, by slow degrees, as I saw that she was indifferent to other men who courted her, I began to dream of marriage. For a long time I revolved this idea in my mind, and my ardour was unequalled except by my unfathomable humility. It is quite possible that I might have remained all my life in this state of indecision, if I had not accidentally betrayed myself while talking to Dambère. As soon as I had done so he became greatly excited and ran away to ask his daughter what she thought about the matter. An hour later he came back to me. You know how effusive he can be!

"'She's in love with you, my dear old chap,' he told me; 'and she is wonderfully happy!'

"I put these words down to the blindness of friendship. Nevertheless, they implied that Léa was quite ready to consent, and so made me as happy as if they had been really true.

"Our engagement was short and delightful. Léa was always ready to welcome me and to keep close to me, to the exclusion of every one else. She showed evident delight in listening to me, and my adoration of her was unbounded. Her whole manner showed wonderful kindness. I never dreamed that it was a proof of her attachment to me; and, indeed, I rarely spoke of love at all, for fear of evoking conventional avowals of affection.

"I trembled whenever I thought of that formidable wedding-day, and when it had passed and we were alone together, the evening began for me in a kind of fear. But contrary to every expectation, I found a joyfully-yielding wife; her lips were brimming over with tenderness as I held her in a close embrace. And when the summer dawn showed silvery through the window, I looked down on her smiling rosy face, and asked: 'So you don't detest me altogether, Léa?'

"'Are you blind, dear husband of mine?' she said. 'Do you mean to say that you have never noticed that you are the only man in the world at whom I ever look? Don't you know that my soul is filled with joy at your mere presence?'

"I was overwhelmed by this avowal of love, and for the first few days of our married life I replied to it by an intensity of passion. Then a strange sense formed itself within me, and at last became my dominant impression. It was, that I ought not to be loved by such a perfect being as Léa, and that the whole situation was absurd and wrong. In proportion as this impression grew, my tenderness for my wife diminished. When she drew me to her gentle breast I experienced not so much joy, as a curious shame, and a feeling of moral uneasiness. It seemed to me to be abnormal for her to kiss me; I felt as if, by doing this, she was committing some perverse crime against nature. And then, sometimes, I felt that vague kind of hatred that strikes us when we see a very pretty girl become the wife of a repulsively ugly man. Yes, it is no more than the truth, that in the end I hated her for being fond of me; I had to keep myself from reproaching her for her bad taste.

"What more is there to tell you? This morbid state of mind has become chronic with me. She has changed me into an absolutely miserable creature; for I have a burning desire for love, a fanatical need of adoration, yet it would be impossible for me to transfer my love to any one but Léa. She seems to me to be the only beautiful and interesting woman alive; she sums up for me all grace, sweetness, and pleasure. I cannot love her because she is in love with me; and yet I should be carried away by passion if only she could feel nothing but friendship and affection for me. But she goes on loving me more and more as the years go by, and it looks as if I should never find a cure for my disease."

The Belgian Story-Tellers

THE art of the short story as it has been developed in Belgium is fairly illustrated by the examples brought together in the following pages. It will be noticed that, though all these stories were written during the last fifty years, they present remarkable contrasts. There are in fact few periods in the history of European literature so rich in originality and diversity of style. After dwindling into insignificance during the seventeenth and eighteenth centuries, when the Belgian provinces were placed under foreign domination, national literature burst out in every direction, and asserted itself with a vigour and authority which, in ordinary circumstances, could never have shown themselves among a young people. This alone should be a sufficient proof that, if politically the kingdom was new, its spirit was as old as that of any great European nation.

When, in 1850, Decoster for the French-speaking part of the community, and Gezelle for the Flemings, succeeded in freeing Belgian literature from French and Dutch influences, they took up the thread where Commines, Froissart, Van Maerlant, and Ruysbroeck had left it. They expressed a spirit which had never ceased to exist since the early Middle Ages, but which had had no opportunity during the last centuries of manifesting itself. They tapped old sources of knowledge and inspiration which had for a long time remained hidden to the world ; they were helped in their work by the accumulated energy of centuries of silence.

THIS long interval, during which the Belgian soul remained unexpressed, accounts for most of the characteristics of Belgian contemporary literature, for its richness, for its contrasts. Elsewhere, in France for instance, we could not find such glaring opposition as exists between realists like Eekhoud and Hubert Krains and symbolist writers such as Rodenbach and Blanche Rousseau. Still less could we discover authors like Lemonnier or Franz Hellens who pass constantly from one mood to another. This strange mixture of sensuality and mysticism is foreign to the French modern spirit and taste. French originality is held within bounds by a strong classic education. Mediaeval dreams have been regulated by a rationalist religion, mediaeval violence has been tamed by criticism and irony.

The French as a rule wonder at these wild outbursts of physical and spiritual energy through which the Belgians endeavour to express their aspirations. They look upon Lemonnier's novels or Verhaeren's poems as upon strange elementary forces, which it is impossible to master or classify. They generously recognise the power of Belgian writers, but they feel in their works a want of measure and of balance, and some Englishmen of French education will share this feeling.

OTHERS will, no doubt, derive some pleasure from the extreme diversity of subjects and talents which may be found in Belgian contemporary literature and appreciate the popular spirit and the deep sincerity which characterise its production. There is a striking analogy between the Belgian modern movement and some writers of the Elizabethan period. The subjects differ, of course, but the temperaments are to a great extent akin to each other. Pre-Shakespearian writers indulge in the same excesses of language, the same outburst of congenial vitality and, at the same time, display a delicacy of feeling, a sense of mystery, which has never been equalled abroad since the Renaissance, but which manifests itself over and over again in the works of Belgian modern writers.

Charles Decoster

CHARLES DECOSTER (1827–79) is at present considered as the founder of Belgian modern literature. Before his time, Belgian letters were entirely in the hands of uninspired writers, imitators of the French, especially of Victor Hugo. It is typical of the conditions prevailing in the middle of the nineteenth century in Belgium that, outside a small group of friends, Decoster remained practically unknown. He led an obscure life, making his living by journalistic work in the Brussels papers, and by occupying a small post as a State employee. It was only twenty years after his death that, thanks to the efforts of Camille Lemonnier, justice was rendered to Decoster, and that a monument was erected to commemorate his national epic, "The Legend of Thyl Uylenspiegel" (1867), which Mr. Geoffrey Whitworth translated into English in 1918. The story of "The Three Princesses" is taken from an early work of Decoster, "Flemish Legends" (1858). We have tried as far as possible to preserve in the translation the archaic form of the original.

Camille Lemonnier

CONSIDERED from a purely critical point of view, the works of Camille Lemonnier (1845–1913) do not reveal the same originality and are sometimes unequal. Out of the forty novels which he published from 1869 to 1910, a certain number will not survive him. But from the point of view of the development of Belgian literature, the action of Lemonnier has been considerable. He was the first Belgian writer to make a living by his writings and to reap some Parisian success. Though strongly influenced by Zola and his school, he succeeded in preserving his national temperament, and fought obstinately for the recognition of a purely Belgian literature. His headquarters remained in Brussels, and the best of his works, such as "Le Vent dans les Moulins," "Le Petit Homme de Dieu," "La Vie Belge," have been devoted to the exaltation of his country's spirit and beauty. Lemonnier was also an art-critic, and it has been said of him that "he wrote with a brush." His power for description and his sense of colour are characteristically Flemish. Lemonnier was the forerunner of an important group of Belgian poets and story-tellers who gathered round Max Waller (Maurice Warlomont), the editor of *La Jeune Belgique.* This group included all the most prominent Belgian modern writers, not excepting Maeterlinck and Verhaeren. Though deeply divided as regards ideals and methods of expression, the contributors of *La Jeune Belgique* agreed on one point: the right of Belgium to a national literature, distinct from France, finding in the country and the people its main source of inspiration.

Eekhoud and Rodenbach

GEORGES EEKHOUD (*b.* 1854), faithful to this programme, describes the people of Antwerp, his native city, and of the surrounding countryside, as in "The Little Servant," in "Mes Communions," "Le Cycle Patibulaire," etc.; he studies types of outlaws and vagabonds. He has published also several excellent translations from Marlowe and Beaumont and Fletcher, and essays on the Elizabethan dramatists. Georges Rodenbach (1855–98) is better known for his works of verse, such as "Les Tristesses" and "Vies encloses," than for his prose works. Though born in Tournai, he was brought up in Bruges and felt the charm of the "dead city" so keenly that he devoted all his talent to it. He went to Paris early in his life, and became there the recognised poet of Bruges. "Lace of Bruges" is his best effort in the short-story form, and essentially characteristic of his genius.

Eugène Demolder

EUGÈNE DEMOLDER (*b.* 1862) was also one of the first promoters of *La Jeune Belgique.* Together with Lemonnier and with a great number of Flemish writers, he is strongly influenced by his admiration for the artists of his country. His "Contes d'Yperdamme," "Récits de Nazareth," and other works are merely literary transpositions of the art of old Flemish masters, such as Peter Breughel, and of their method of interpreting the Gospel. Those acquainted with these works will remember that the events which they describe—such as the Nativity, the Massacre of the Innocents, the Adoration of the Magi, etc.—are not represented as happening in the past, in a far-away country, amidst Eastern surroundings, but as if they had taken place in seventeenth-century Flanders, in a landscape of ice and snow, among Flemish peasants and landsknechten in armour. Whether such interpretation is due to sheer ignorance or to the popular belief—so often expressed in folk-songs—that the Gospel story is eternally true, ever present, and intimately mingled in the people's every-day life, Demolder adopted it with delight, emphasising the humorous effects of anachronism while preserving the reverent treatment of the old masters.

THE dramas and essays of Maurice Maeterlinck (*b.* 1862) have gained for him universal celebrity. His first contributions to *La Jeune Belgique* were, however, in verse, and it is interesting to recall here that it was through the short story, "The Massacre of the Innocents," that he drew upon himself for the first time the attention of the Belgian public. This story at once stamps its author as a Fleming, not only on account of the influence of Peter Breughel, which is as evident here as in Demolder's works, but also the painter's methods are substituted for the writer's, the story being told through a series of pictures, not through a connected and logical narrative.

Maeterlinck

While most of the Belgian poets are of Flemish origin, the story-tellers are generally Walloons. But the latter, far from being absorbed by France, as might be expected, deal almost exclusively with their local surroundings. Hubert Krains (*b.* 1862) describes in a realistic and somewhat sombre vein the life of the peasants and small "bourgeois" of the country near Liège.

Hubert Krains

PROMINENT representatives of the group of Walloon story-tellers are Georges Garnier (*b.* 1868), Maurice des Ombriaux (*b.* 1868), and Louis Delattre (*b.* 1870). All three were born in Hainault and, like most Belgian prose writers, prefer to deal with the life of the country-side. They express the lighter side of the Belgian spirit, but, in spite of their dry humour, never lose an intense feeling for the landscape in which their pictures are framed. A Walloon can laugh at the human comedy better than a Fleming, but he shares his northern brother's delight in nature, and grows poetical when placed before some beautiful scenery.

A Group of Walloons

PERHAPS the most delicate prose-writer now in Belgium is Blanche Rousseau (Mme. Maurice Belval) (*b.* 1875), author of the delicate little fairy story, "The Little House in the Midst of the Woods." She has only published four or five books, but every one of them is full of poetry and of the most refined sense of the pathetic and humorous side of life. Her tales are symbolic without being forced, and she has succeeded in renewing the art of legend-writing. The symbol with her is never cumbrous, and, though entirely original in their subjects, her stories seem as natural and genuine as any familiar fairy tale.

In concluding these notes, it is scarcely necessary to add that the editors of this "library" have not attempted to do more than illustrate the national genius of Belgium in the field of the short story, and it may be claimed for this brief section that it is at least representative of the style and character of the Belgian story-tellers, though by no means representative of the general body of Belgian literature, in which the short story holds a less conspicuous place than in the literature of most other European nations. E. C.

*** All the Belgian stories, with the exception of those by Maeterlinck and Rodenbach, have been expressly translated for this volume by Mrs. Tita Brand Cammaerts.

CHARLES DECOSTER
1827–1879

THE THREE PRINCESSES

I

Of the three noble virgins and of their great beauty

IN the year of our Lord Jesus Christ 690, lived three lovely maidens, issue in the male line of the noble family of the great Emperor Octavian.

Their names were Blanche, Clara, and Candida.

If they had consecrated to God the flower of their virginity, it must not be thought that 'twas for lack of lovers.

For each day a large gathering of people assembled to see them pass to church, and each one said to the other, " Behold their fair eyes, behold their white hands."

And many a one, too, gazing upon them with longing, added lamenting, " Must these sweet virgins make a vow to God when there are eleven thousand, yea, more, already in His Paradise ? " " But not so dainty as these," replied one aged and asthmatic man behind them, as he drew in the perfume of their robes. And walking thus, this aged one, espying some youth spitting in the water or stretched upon his belly on the grass warming his back in the sun, would deliver him a kick, saying, " Up—wilt thou not see the most beauteous flowers in the world ? "

II

How a young Prince of Arabia doted upon the youngest, and what came of it

Many would have persuaded them to wed, but failing of their purpose, pined and faded visibly.

Among these was a Prince of Arabia, who with great ceremony was baptized, and 'twas expressly for the love of the youngest maid. Moreover, not obtaining what he would, either by prayer or force, one morning on the threshold of the door he pierced his heart with his dagger.

The maiden, hearing this noble lord cry out, descended in great haste, and caused him to be laid upon her couch, whereat he who was not yet quite dead, greatly rejoiced.

But when she stooped above him to bind and dress his wound, he found a little strength, kissed her lovely mouth, sighed as one relieved, and gave up his soul in great joy.

But the virgin was ill pleased with this kiss, for she thought it taken from the rights of Jesus her Divine Spouse. Nevertheless she let fall a tear or so for the sake of the noble knight.

III

In which is seen how Satan pursues those maidens who desire to fly the world

Oft were there many lovers before the virgins' house, some singing plaintive songs, others seated proudly upon the backs of brave prancing chargers, others in silence sad gazing the livelong day up at the windows. And ofttimes would they fight among themselves and kill each other for jealousy. At which the maidens were right troubled. " Ah," said the eldest to the youngest, " pray for us, Blanche, thou well-named one, white of soul and white of body, pray for us, dear one, Jesus hearkens willingly to the prayers of such maids as thee."

" My sisters," replied the youngest, " I am more unworthy than you, but I will pray if you desire it."

" Yes," said they.

Then these three virgins cast themselves upon their knees and thus the youngest prayed :

" Sweet Jesus, we have surely sinned against Thee, else wouldst Thou allow the Evil One to stir these miserable men to love by our beauty ? Yea, we have sinned, but wretched that we are, 'twas all against our will, Lord. Ah, pardon us, for we are sorely grieved. Thou wishedst us to be Thine, and all that is ours for Thee we have kept, our youth and beauty, melancholy and mirth, wishes and prayers, body and soul, thought and deed, all. In the morning, at midday, and at night—at every hour and moment—do we not think of Thee ? When Thy bright sun arises, O Beloved, and also when in Thy heaven gleam the bright stars, they can see us praying and offering to Thee, not gold, incense, nor myrrh, but our humble love and our poor heart.

'Tis not enough, we know it well. Alas, teach us to do more." And pausing here all three began to utter piteous lament.

"Sweet Jesus," said the youngest yet again, "we know right well the will of these men. They think that they are proud and fair to look upon, and that thus they should win our love, but they are neither fair, nor good, nor proud as Thou art, Jesus. Therefore Thine are we, Thine will ever be, and never theirs. Wilt Thou love us just a little still, for Thou alone art all our comfort, all our joy, in this sad world, Jesus. Thou wilt not forsake us. The earthly husband leaves not the spouse in danger, nor eke the bridegroom the bride. Art Thou not better than they all, and wilt Thou not protect us from the enemy's snares? If Thou dost not wish it, do it not, but then might they rob us of our virginity, which is Thine. Ah, rather, Dear Beloved, make us to pass all our lives withered and hideous, then into Hell descend in midst of devils, flames, and sulphur, and there abide till Thou shalt judge us pure enough at last to receive us into Thy Paradise, where we may look upon Thee and love Thee eternally. Have pity upon us. AMEN."

And having thus spoken, the poor maiden fell a-weeping and her sisters likewise, saying, "Pity, Jesus, pity."

IV

Of the voice of the Divine Bridegroom and of the fair knight in silver armour

On a sudden heard they a sweet voice saying, "Take courage." "Hearken," said they, "the Bridegroom deigneth speak to his brides."

Then was the chamber filled with a perfume sweeter than that which rises from finest incense burning in a censer.

Then the voice spoke again. "To-morrow morn," it said, "at sunrise leave the town, mount on your palfreys, and still riding go your way straight forward, not caring for the road. I will protect you."

"We will obey Thee," said they, "Oh, Thou who makest us the happiest among all the daughters of men." And rising, they embraced each other joyfully.

Meanwhile, as they were listening to the voice, there came to the place a fair knight in silver armour. Upon his head was a golden helmet, on which fluttered like a bird, a plume brighter than flame. His steed was white as snow.

None had perceived his coming, he seemed to rise from out the ground among the crowd of wooers, who, seized with fear, ventured not to look upon him.

" Ye evil men," said he, " Avaunt, remove your steeds. Know ye not that the sound of their hoofs disturbs these ladies' orisons ? " Thus having said, he departed riding towards the East.

" Ah," said the wooers one to another, " Saw ye that silver armour and that plume of fire ? Surely 'twas the angel of God, come down from Paradise to seek these ladies." And the most wanton muttered, " He did not forbid us to stand here on foot before the door, therefore can we do it modestly."

V

How, according to Divine command, the three virgins adventured on their journey

Upon the morrow, before the dawn of day, came many, but having left their chargers in their stalls. The sun having risen, they beheld the three virgins, according to the command of God, each mounted on her palfrey, thus issuing from their home. Thinking that they were going into the neighbouring meadows to inhale the fresh morning air they followed, singing joyous carols in their honour. While still within the town, the steeds moved with a stately tread, but leaving it, they quickened their pace.

Then did the lovers try to follow on foot, but finally one by one they fell upon the road, exhausted. Having gone for several leagues, the palfreys stopped. And the three virgins, seeing that they were now delivered from their troubles, resolved to proclaim the wondrous aid of God and to build in His honour a fair church.

Where ? they knew not. But the matter was already plain in Paradise, as you shall see anon.

For no sooner were they seated on their palfreys again than, led by the Spirit of God, these beasts galloped away. And they leapt across rivers, went through deep forests, passed through towns whose gates opened before them and closed again behind them, sprang over walls. And fear struck the heart of every one as those three white horses and those three fair ladies passed by him, swift as the wind.

And thus sped they on a thousand leagues and more.

VI

Of the diamond hammer and of the foundations which were uptorn out of the earth

At Haeckendover in the Duchy of Brabant the steeds stayed their course and neighed, and would take no further step neither forwards nor yet backwards. For 'twas that spot which God had chosen for His church. But the Virgins, gathering that the palfreys were a-weary, went on foot as far as Hoy Bout and there judged that 'twould be well to build the church.

Therefore they assembled the most sturdy workmen, masons, and artists in so great number that in one day the foundations were raised two handbreadths at the least.

At seeing which the maidens rejoiced much, believing that their work was pleasing unto God.

But on the morrow morn, behold all the foundations torn from out the earth.

Thinking that some traitorous heretic fortuitously there lay buried, who at night had shaken the sacred stones of the church with his accursed bones, went they to Steenen Berg with all these masons and there accomplished like work as at Hoy Bout.

But the morrow saw again the foundations torn from earth.

'Twas because the Lord desired to be adored at Haeckendover only. And He had sent His angels in the night, with diamond hammers from the storehouse of Paradise, and had made them to destroy the work of the three virgins, who, grievously troubled and full of woe, fell upon their knees, imploring and praying God to tell them where He would be adored.

VII

Of the youngest maiden and the beauteous angel

On a sudden beheld they a youth of celestial beauty, clothed with a robe of the colour of the setting sun. Benignly he looked upon them. Knowing him to be the angel of God the three maids prostrated themselves with faces to the earth. But the youngest, most full of hardihood, as are children, ventured to raise her eyes to that fair messenger and seeing him so well looking, gained courage and smiled.

The angel took her hand, saying to her and to her sisters, "Rise and follow me," which the virgins straightway did.

Thus came they to the spot where standeth now the church, and said the angel then, "Here is the place."

"We thank thee, sir," replied the youngest maiden gleefully.

VIII

How the three virgins beheld a green isle, and of the fair flowers and birds which were there

'Twas the thirteenth day after Epiphany. Much snow had fallen, and 'twas freezing hard on account of the bitter wind which blew. And the virgins beheld before them amidst the snow, as 'twere a green isle. And this isle had a girdle of silk thread of purple hue. And all within the isle was springtide, blossoming roses, violets, and jessamine, whose perfume is as balm. Without was winter blast and fearsome cold.

Towards the centre, where to-day standeth the high altar, was seen an evergreen oak, all in flower, as if 'twere truly Persian jessamine. Amidst the branches, redwings, nightingales, and finches emulated one another in singing the sweet songs of Paradise. For they were the angels, who decking themselves in feathers warbled thus in praise of God. A sweet nightingale, the loveliest singer of all, bore in its right claw a parchment strip whereon was writ in letters of finest gold: "Here is the place, chosen of God, divinely shown unto the three virgins, wherein that they might build a church unto the glory of our Lord and Saviour, Jesus Christ."

Great was the joy of the virgins, and the youngest said unto the angel, "Herein we see that God a little loveth us. What behoveth it us to do, Sir Angel?"

"It behoveth you, fair maid," replied the gentle messenger, "here to build a church, and choose unto that end twelve of the finest workmen, neither more nor less; God Himself will be the thirteenth."

Having thus spoken, up to high heaven mounted he again.

IX

Of the church of Haeckendover and of the wondrous mason who worked thereat

Thus the three, in greatest haste, chose out from among all the twelve fine masons, who straightway laid the foundations of the church where had been the purple-hued silken thread.

The work advanced now so well that in truth it was a joy to see how fast the stones rose one upon another. But lo, the miracle was that at the hours of work there were ever thirteen masons, but at the hours of dinner and of payment, only twelve.

For the Lord deigned to work with them, but not to eat nor to drink—He who hath such fine broth in His Paradise, such sweet fruits and wine from the fountain of Saphir, the which is a fountain wherefrom floweth ever wine yellower than would be molten gold. Neither suffereth He lack of money, which is a pain reserved for us, needy, wretched, and necessitous of nature.

Thus it befell that soon the bell was placed as is ever done whenas a church is perfectly completed. Then entered the three virgins, and falling on her knees the youngest said :

" By whom, O Spouse Divine and Well-Beloved Jesus, must this Thy church raised in Thy honour be dedicated ? "

Whereto the Lord replied, " Myself will dedicate and consecrate this church unto Myself. Let none come to consecrate it after Me."

X

Of the two Bishops, and of their withered hands

Ne'ertheless two venerable Bishops then in Haeckendover, seeing the new church, desired to bless it—naught knowing of the words of Jesus to the three virgins, else had they never done a deed so bold.

But terrible was their punishment. For while the one was busy blessing the water, on a sudden he became blind. The other held the holy water brush with arms aloft to bless the church, and these were withered and all power to move bereft them. But lo, the Bishops who had sinned were full of contrition, and prayed the Lord that He would deign to pardon them.

And they were pardoned for that they had sinned in ignorance.

And thereafter came they ofttimes in devout pilgrimage to Haeckendover.

CAMILLE LEMONNIER
1845–1913

THE FEAST OF SAINT CATHERINE

TWO little children came and went in the corridor with an air of mystery, watching the clocks, for it was customary not to celebrate the grandmother's saint's-day until a few minutes before dinner.

Outside in the streets, the snow was spreading a white cloak, and the flakes bounded in the air like shuttlecocks from invisible battledores. None of the poor folks who ventured out in such weather along the side walks could have suspected that something was being plotted that day within the house; it wore its accustomed appearance, there was not a tile more on the roof, nor a curtain more at the windows; but inside it was not the same thing. Every one wanted to laugh, and yet appeared as if nothing were the matter; there were whisperings behind doors, and sudden silences. Some one went upstairs quickly, then came down again on tiptoe; and quite quietly, as if by enchantment, in the most secret corner of the house bouquets and cakes arrived.

"Tick-tack" went the kitchen clock, but one could have heard more easily still the tick-tack of the two little children's hearts. How long these hours were! Up to mid-day it was nothing: one waited, one was patient, and then sometimes the confectioner was late, but the afternoon seemed as if it would never end. Then there was rage against the wretched clock!

The two children were very small; even if they climbed upon a chair they could not reach its face, otherwise they would certainly have pushed on the hands with their little pink fingers. At last, however, it seemed to have made up its mind to move a little quicker. The tick-tack became more frequent, and finally when night fell one could not have told which beat more irregularly, the pendulum of the clock or the hearts of the two children. For my part, I think it was the hearts of the children.

Without any one knowing how it happened, the fire was found alight in the big room, as it was on Sunday afternoons, and the grandmother had just settled herself by it in her red plush arm-chair, worn out at the place where her arms rest. Then evening fell, the servant closed the shutters, and the light of the lamps made stars in the shadows inside the room.

The front-door bell had tinkled many times that day, and people had come in carrying *things* in big paper wrappings and baskets. What things? The children knew all about it, but it was a secret which they would not have disclosed for anything in the world. Lids of hampers were raised, paper stripped off, and four little hands beat together, while eyes gleamed; and the grandmother, shut in her room, coughed as hard as she could, pretending she had not heard.

Tap! tap! tap! It was her walnut cane. Then every one scampered off so as not to be found in her way, and the grandmother, who heard doors slam in every direction, passed on murmuring, "All right . . . all right," in a voice which said, "Go on. I have seen nothing. I know nothing." She even tapped her stick on the ground a little harder than usual to warn every one of her coming. Thus the day passed until the moment when the hand pointed to six o'clock.

Then one might have seen every one in the house going to that mysterious corner where the presents were hidden; and long before getting there a smell of violets and vanilla gave notice of the presence of extraordinary things. Voices buzzed confusedly, plates clattered against one another, people came and went on tiptoe. The two little children looked like fat red peonies then, their cheeks were so flushed, and their eyes blinked hard in the effort to remember the verses which had been taught them.

The father, an old servant, and several neighbours were there too—only the mother was absent, having gone before them to the grave; but it is not at all sure that her soul was not fluttering at that moment around the lips of her children.

Then they set off, the children first, the father following, and behind the father came the old servant in her turn, carrying in her hands a pot of mignonette or a little rose tree in bloom. They wound through the hall, crossed the dining-room, and the sound of their feet stopped suddenly before the drawing-room door—only for a moment it is true—for the father turned the handle and the children rushed into the room, holding out their little arms and mixing up their verses.

How four candles had lighted themselves upon the mantelpiece was no more known than how the fire was made. On the table the special Sunday lamp was burning, yellow and bright beneath its glass shade ; and in the cupboard the glasses faintly rang, as if to remind one that they would also like to take part in the merrymaking.

Although the door has creaked as it opens, the grandmother has not turned her head, but the two little children raise their voices so high that she pretends to awake, and passes her hand over her face. Then a slight trembling passes over her whole body. She wants to speak, but cannot, but two happy tears run slowly down her cheeks, and in her turn she holds out her arms to them. No doubt it happens that her dress makes acquaintance with the cream from the tarts, but who would think of a little spot on one's dress at such a moment ? Bouquets and cakes are placed upon her knees and each one, as he offers his gift, kisses her on her dear cheeks, which quiver like jelly.

When every one has finished, it is the old servant's turn ; she offers her flowers, then wipes her mouth on her sleeve, and asks to be allowed to kiss the grandmother like the others. While she presses her fat, honest face against each cheek, you can see her laughing and crying at the same time, and the two little children show their white teeth and shout, " Long live Saint Catherine ! "

Is it the light from the hearth, the reflection of the curtains, or the brightness of the candles which suddenly sends, as it were, a pink fire over the face of the grandmother ? No ; it is the joy of her heart, and a new youth seems to have begun for her with this hour which brings her good wishes and kisses. The lips of little children make old grandmothers young again. And she admires the cakes and bouquets, and claps her hands.

" Really, is to-day Saint Catherine ? " says she. " I had not thought of it ! "

She does not notice that her best cap with ribbons and lace betrays her. " Why, then, have you made yourself so fine, grandmother ? " And everything in the room seems to be in admiration of her flowered silk dress.

Then the table is laid, courses are left out so as to come more quickly to the cakes. Letters in sugar run all over the almond icing and the cream, and all together make up the wish, " Long live Saint Catherine ! " From the cellars now come old bottles covered with spiders' webs, and the glasses fill with a golden wine which seems to reflect the happiness in every one's eyes.

The grandmother raises her glass up high, and thanks big and small for this happy day. No one present but is touched, and while all look at her, the light of the lamp makes around her, as it were, an aureole which fades softly into the shadows.

Thus it is with her memory, for all this is but a vision of long ago; but each year brings back the feast of Saint Catherine, and sometimes it snows again as it did in the old days. Then I hear through the room the echo of her tap, tap, and I feel that I shall see her leaning on her stick, and coughing under the lace frill of her cap. Alas, it is only a thick branch which the wind strikes against my window-pane; but the little grandchild of former years has a grandchild now in her turn, and they go together through the quiet country to the cemetery where the beloved grandmother sleeps, and a voice seems to rise from the earth and to speak to them through the silence of things, saying:

"Really, is it already the feast of Saint Catherine? I had not thought of it, my children."

GEORGES EEKHOUD

B. 1854

THE LITTLE SERVANT

LITTLE servant from over there, unused to service, bearing in your countenance, in your hair, on your lips, and, above all, in the depths of your great eyes, the quivering atmosphere and dreamy sky of the dear country. . . .

Recommended and introduced by Master Martens, a thoroughly good fellow, the little servant crossed our threshold one morning. A man from Brabantsputte, one of those pedlars who carry the products of the slender village industries to Brussels every Monday, and relieved of their roll of goods return to their own clock-tower towards the end of the week, had piloted his little fellow-villager to our door.

In a somewhat choked voice, which she tried to steady, the little girl asked her escort to say a last farewell to her mother, her elder brother, and her little sister.

" All right."

The pedlar took off his cap, adjusted his pack on his shoulders, and went off, emitting his nasal and guttural cry.

After putting down her modest belongings, tied up in a red cotton handkerchief, she glanced round the kitchen with her large brown autumn-coloured eyes, and said simply, " I think I shall like being here."

In the tone in which this tribute was spoken I distinguished a touching expression.

I read in it an appeal to our indulgence, the wish to settle down, the courage of a fifteen-year-old heart which doubts its own strength. It seemed to say, " You look kind people, and if I am clumsy and slow at first, you will not be hard on me, will you ? You will be patient and remember that I am only a child, and that I have never been away from my own village before ? "

She added aloud, " Mr. Martens told me to do him credit and to be very good and polite."

Surely she was a credit to the girls of the Campine and to Mr. Martens' confidence. From the early morning she was at work, but, in spite of her activity, at dinner-time she could not eat.

Next day found her with red eyes and a drawn face.

" She is homesick, but this trouble, which shows a good heart, will not last," we said to ourselves.

On the following days she showed the same energy over her work, but she had no appetite, and her colour, fresh as a peony, faded.

On Saturday, his round finished, the pedlar Franske came to ask news of her. As he went off, she called out after him, " Be sure to tell them that I am very, very happy, and that I don't want to go back to Brabantsputte." And, as if proud of her strength of soul, she said to me eagerly, " You heard, sir, he will tell my mother how happy I am with you."

Good little thing ! I felt suspicious, however, of this.

I guessed that she had cut short the interview with the pedlar of Putte to prevent herself from being tempted to go off with him to her native paths through the pine trees, for when I went down to the kitchen again, she did not turn away quickly enough to hide the tears trickling over her long dark lashes, and drowning in a November gloom the September richness of her great eyes.

In the afternoon she scrubbed the hall. From my room I heard her giving energetic blows with the broom handle. She continued to make the pump groan and to swish pailfuls of water over the tiles.

That's a good thing, I thought. She is throwing off her depression. I should not be surprised if she began to sing to cheer herself up at her work. The song did not come, though ; instead, the prelude became tempestuous. At last the hubbub prevented me from working. I went down to entreat the over-zealous worker to use her implements—brushes and pails—more discreetly.

I paused on the landing. The poor thing was indeed lifting up her voice in the noise.

But what a sad song ! What a heart-breaking lament !

It was to stifle the sound of her sobs that the little servant had made such a to-do. Thanks to the noise I was able to go up to her without her having heard me coming.

" Well," said I, touching her shoulder, " is this the way you are settling down ? "

She dropped her things, covered her face with her hands, and through a fresh outburst of tears, she confessed to me her weakness—her sacred weakness.

" Forgive me, sir . . . when I think of home it is stronger than my will and power. I must cry out or I would choke. . . . It is as if they had tied a string to my heart and were pulling over there as hard as they could. . . . They are pulling, and they'll end by getting me over to them . . . otherwise they'll drag out my soul. . . . It's stupid, I know. And how they will laugh at me in the village! I can't help it. . . . And it isn't your fault either. Surely I am well-treated! Yes, indeed, only too well-treated here. . . . But, you see, if you were better still, Madame and you, if you were the Blessed Lord and the Holy Virgin themselves, I would pack up my things all the same. . . . So let me go back on Saturday with Franske, the pedlar. . . ."

There was no way of keeping her; in vain during the week did she strive—touched by our words, our sympathy, and care—to fight against her obsession. Several times she declared her resolution to remain, and to be sensible. But even at the moment of this elation, the tone and look and pitiful smile denied her words. On the very eve of the visit of her fellow-villager, irresolute, not knowing whether she should obey her head or her heart, she packed and unpacked her humble luggage.

"My mother promised to come and see me; very well, I'll wait till she comes and go back with her if it isn't any better."

"That's settled, then?"

"That's settled."

A minute after this decision the demented girl ran mechanically to consult the clock, and found the hours already too long which separated her from the appearance of Franske, the deliverer. No; it would never be any better! It was unnecessary to confess to us her lack of courage. We released her from her promise.

The last night passed, and she got up long before day. The pedlar never came very early, but this did not prevent the little country girl from trembling at the milkman's ring. All ready, with her bundle in her hand, she awaited Franske in the hall. Suppose he should forget to pass to-day! Suppose he had not sold his wares! Suppose he should be afraid of troubling us! Any amount of cruel suppositions tortured the poor little thing, too inexperienced to set out on her journey alone, and find the way to her beloved clock-tower.

There was another ring, and it was at last he to whom she opened. . . .

The fellow was not a little amazed at this sudden change of decision. He laughed at his protégée, and undertook to make her listen to reason.

The big fair fellow, with his deliberate way, knew the town better. For five years he had walked through Brussels every week, calling his wares in the most distant streets, and if the capital had not succeeded in seducing and corrupting him, it had at least ceased to frighten him.

The wise exhortations of the pedlar did not persuade the little one in the least. Rather than stay she would have clung on to him as one would on to a life-buoy. The fellow was quite embarrassed, and apologised for her. If he had not kept her in the half-open doorway, she would have gone without saying good-bye to us.

I laughed condescendingly. " Did you ever see such a silly little thing ? She ran away as if the house were falling down."

Pose, affectation, a mask, all that, my good friend ! In my heart I was thinking—I don't blame you for this desertion, my poor child. And your people will be wrong if they make fun of you. You are not the only one who pines far from your lair. I, too, control myself and set my face. Noisily I dig and delve to dull my senses. And if I stir and bustle about, it is in order that they may not hear the beating of my heart. Like you, little one, it is when I seem most active and gay that I am on the point of breaking down and admitting myself beaten. . . . Dear little girl, my sister in the holy religion of patriotism, do you remember the day when the boy from Brabantsputte brought you news of your village and of what was happening on the Dutch frontier ? I went by with an indifferent air to catch some scraps of your conversation, and inquired in a casual tone of those good people who had forgotten me, or who had never known me, but who are " from yonder," bear names like ours, speak the dear dialect, haunt the heather or the meadows where I spent my best, my only life.

As foolish as you, in my crazy affection, I am inclined to believe that the sun, and especially the stars of the Campine, are different from those here, unless, like myself, the exiled stars put on an enigmatical face and hide their unquenchable suffering under a mask of coldness and scepticism.

Franske said, " And the son of Widow Hendrikx of the ' Cosy Corner ' is going to marry Bella, the cobbler's girl. . . . The Marinckx killed their pig on Saturday. . . . And Bastyns is going away. And Machiels is coming back. . . . And Nand is. . . . And the band plays on Saturdays now at Laveldoms."

At this spoken village journal, interrupted by your simple exclamations, " Zou het ? Hoor je ! " (Really ? Just listen !)—at this monotonous rosary told by the pedlar—such intimate, touching recollections surged up in my heart. . . .

Oh ! I could have listened to this melancholy song for hours—for long, long hours—as I listened to the wind in the leaves, the lowing of the cattle, and the sound of the church bells. . . .

After the departure of this fellow my books seemed more dull, my friends more affected, my business more unbearable, and the town more stuffy.

Between ourselves, dear little one, I am as weak as you. The carnival of town life wearies me more and more ; my mask and city disguise begin to weigh terribly upon me. May the time soon come for me also to go back at all costs to my own countryside, if it be only to sleep close to the church, you know where, at the foot of its slate tower, with its crooked roof which calls over its curtain of trees on Sundays to the laggards who are about to miss the Elevation of the Host ; you know—the place where the youths confess their love, and talk in low tones so as not to tempt the dead.

GEORGES RODENBACH
1855–1898

LACE OF BRUGES

SPRING had thrown its green mantle over the fields beyond the city where, standing by itself, is the Sisterhood of Bruges. From a window of the little convent, Sister Ursula was watching the twigs and branches of the elms, clothed with young foliage, slowly swaying in the light breeze, with movements recalling those of infancy. The lawn was brightly green, and green as grass were the little doors in line along the cloister ; but elsewhere white was the only colour, as if green, the colour of hope, lived here together with the white of innocence. All around were walls of snowy whitewash, white as the linen-covered altar-rails ; at the windows were curtains of spotless muslin—everything was lily-white. Here and there went quiet sisters under their quaint head-dress, moving like the swans of the Bruges canals, and scarcely disturbing the silence more than the swans disturb the water.

Sister Ursula was a study in white, her ivory complexion reflecting the white of her linen cap. She had early lost her parents, and had spent the years of childhood in an Ursuline convent before coming to the Sisterhood at Bruges. Young as she was, she had no memory of hearth and home, nor echo of the voice of other days. And having thus lived always among strangers, she was full of thoughts to which she had never given utterance. Yet sadness had no place in her heart. She was habitually silent with the silence which came to her from this peaceful cloister, where footsteps fell soundlessly upon the pavement, as if the whole place were part of the church, or the church had thrown over the garden its mystic atmosphere, heavy with old chants, and dim with incense mounting upwards. This mystical silence was all the vaster and more profound for the incessant falling through it of the chiming of the bells from city steeples, like flakes of music falling one by one.

Sister Ursula was very happy. She lived in the spirit of the hour and the place, more and more absorbing the character of the Sisterhood, her little soul echoing the chiming of the bells, and becoming herself a cloister surrounded by white curtains, festooned with the pale blue ribbons of floating incense.

Ursula and five of her sisters inhabited a tiny gabled cottage, one of many which together constituted this religious house. Their days were taken up with various duties ; there was the Divine Office to say, and prayers, and all the housework to do, and a little manual work. In their case this was needlework, well suited to the delicate white hands of these innocent creatures. Most of them, indeed, were engaged in lace-making, which is the chief and oldest industry of their Order. It is a gentle craft, and not unworthy of hands weary of the rosary. In every one of these convents you may see from an early hour the sisters in their workroom, sitting in line against the wall, and holding on their knees the cushions over which their cunning fingers chase the bobbins.

Sister Ursula was known as one of the cleverest lacemakers, and her marvellous work well supported the fame of that precious lace of Bruges, which has ever adorned the robes of queens. She loved this work with all an artist's love. For her it was indeed an art, and her fingers played among the threads of her cushion as those of a musician on his harp. Often she would improvise, suddenly inventing a new design, perhaps a cluster of rose-traceries, great white ornate flowers, such as she had seen one winter's night in frosted pattern on her window-pane and all at once now came back to mind. Sometimes you might have thought from her expression that she was working with threads lent by the Blessed Virgin. What snowy wonders she made as if in play ! Sometimes an invisible spider's web like a net in which stars had been entangled ; sometimes an intricate scheme which seemed mere confusion, but finally became an ornament of finest filigree. Is not lace, after all, the jewellery of flaxen tissue ?

When working at her best, Ursula was carried quite out of herself. She scarcely looked at the pattern, and even delighted in making variations on it, and in boldly creating some new effect to change the everlasting spring of these virginal roses. She would add some swift movement of her soul to those immemorial patterns which were the pride of the Order and had been copied for centuries ; no one knows how they originated ; perhaps it was at the time of the folk-songs and by the same unrecorded impulse. These laces are no more than flowers treated decoratively, as the songs of the people are redolent of natural life. Indeed, so close is the analogy between lace and music that even at Divine Office in the church, as Ursula listened to the chant, she instinctively followed the movement of an anthem as if it had been a lacework of sounds in the making.

But a deeper and more spiritual joy also pervaded Sister Ursula's humble heart whenever she remembered, many times a day, that her work was destined for uses of worship and that her hands were actually serving God. Her work was given only to the adornment of churches and altars and to vestments for the celebration of the mass. Surely these hours of hers were spent in a form of prayer. Her bobbins passed through her fingers like the beads of a swift rosary, where the fingers rather than the lips are engaged in prayer; and her fabrics were a kind of story or litany recited in praise of God. For this reason she refused to take orders for lace except from religious communities and from priests, for the convents and parishes of the city, or for the sacristies of the countryside. She knew well enough that the wonderful lace of Bruges, renowned throughout the world, was bought and sold and carried far away, often to be employed to far less saintly ends. It might become the servant of coquetry and luxury, adorn garments of vanity, and even frame the sinful picture of bare necks and shoulders. It was in vain that any one applied to her for lace to be used for such profane purposes as these; she had never hesitated to refuse every application of the kind, wishing to see in her dearly-loved craft nothing but ornaments kept for God alone, and having no other purpose than His honour.

In spite of her modesty and against her will, her reputation as an artist had spread all around. She was known throughout Bruges and all the province as the most expert and cleverest exponent of the art. Her work was asked for by name, and was recognised by connoisseurs as if she had signed it. It was the very last word in lace, fantastic, intriguing.

The dealers were soon upon her track, and knocked often at the convent doors. Some came from far, and were from other countries, to secure specimens of her astonishing work. But Sister Ursula rejected every offer and all reward. She had entered religion. Her renunciation of the world involved the entire devotion of her labour to God; and the restriction of her lace to the adornment of divine worship and of those engaged in it was altogether in the spirit of her intention. She refused to be moved from this resolution, as if it had been one of the vows of her vocation.

But one day, when the sister-portress had called her to the parlour and she had come obediently, though annoyed and unwilling, expecting to see only one more of these incessant commercial buyers, she was surprised to find three visitors of a different kind. One was an elderly lady; with her was a girl, plainly her daughter, for she was like a youthful portrait of her mother; and the third was a tall and handsome youth with some strange charm about him, especially a certain candour and directness of gaze. He spoke for the others. He was about to be married, and was engaged to the sweet girl beside him. He wished to make her a present of some of the most beautiful lace procurable, to adorn the bridal gown. He knew that Sister Ursula's gift was unique.

The gentle nun was much troubled by this request. She meant at first to refuse, saying, as was her custom, that she only worked for churches and for religious communities. But somehow, she did not dare this time refuse abruptly. The young man had spoken with such confidence that his request would be granted, such touching certainty that love cannot but obtain all that it asks, and there was something so resolute in all his manner, that Sister Ursula sought in vain for her accustomed formula of refusal. She caught sight, as it were, of the word, and could even touch it, but for some reason she was unable to seize that uncompromising negative, which might have given her instant freedom, but seemed to escape each of her attempts and to hide or vanish with diabolical sport.

Without giving her any opportunity of refusing his request, the young man had asked Ursula to show them a few specimens of her work. She brought them several pieces arranged like a long scarf. The two women went into ecstasies, the girl examining the lace while the young man gazed upon her. He happened at one moment himself to take up the end of the fabric to study its detail, and the two young figures seemed to be linked together by this bond more insubstantial than a dream.

The two of them were so touching that Ursula could not watch them without emotion. The girl was of that pink and white complexion, a peculiarly Flemish attractiveness, which would soon fade under the shadow of the belfries and massive towers. With what loving confidence her great eyes turned toward her lover as she spoke, and how tender were his tones when he replied! He called her "Dorothy" in every phrase, loving to repeat her name in the language of love, which was still somewhat strange to him. He spoke her name with a sense of something precious in it, as though every syllable were a caress. And Ursula, too, felt herself carried away by the music of this voice, which seemed to her as though she could not but follow it, though it should be to the end of the world. She felt herself no longer able, nor even at liberty, to refuse the request which these good people had made. Indeed, even while he was speaking, she had found plausible reasons for giving way ; this was no dealer, she said to herself, and God would surely not be jealous. Surely the good God would be very pleased, inasmuch as the nuptial lace, which just for once she meant to give them, would still take some small part in worship, united as it would be to a great sacrament of the holy faith.

Eagerly the little nun set to work. She had set her heart on doing a supreme piece of work, on surpassing herself indeed, and began at once to design a pattern which should express a new and symbolic idea : two flowers springing from a single thread ; two birds cooing upon the edge of a nest. The bobbins flew hither and thither through the forest of pins. She seemed to be improvising. Rapt in spirit, she worked on her lace as a player on his instrument, while her fingers, now swift and now slow, moved over the lace beneath them as if over a keyboard or zither.

Nevertheless, deep in her soul she was dimly doubtful of her part in providing the garments of a bride. Sometimes her fingers lagged and the threads became entangled, especially when she remembered how they looked in the parlour—the gaze which taught her what love is, nay, the gaze of love itself. And how they must have loved !

But what, after all, is love ? Until now, she had known nothing of it but its name. She had never really thought of it, but now she knew that it made you happy. This charming, mysterious, and tragic influence, from which she recoiled as from a sin, had at last taken human form in the traits of the commanding young man whom she could not forget. Ah, how lovely it must be to be looked on so, by such a face as that !

Sister Ursula knew very well that she would never know this superhuman joy. She was vowed to God, and was even wedded to God, but it was in the black robes of mourning, instead of the shining white garments which this happy Dorothy would wear, garments which she herself was helping to adorn. Do not imagine that Ursula envied her. The homesickness of love was with her, yet not clearly recognised. She never dreamed of loving any one, for she had taken a vow of chastity, fortified by every ascetic practice. Yet love no longer frightened her ; the word haunted her mind, and her lips pronounced it. She began to love—Love itself.

And now, as she worked among her sisters, bending over the lace pillow, the bridal pair were often in her mind. She saw them as she had seen so many others like them, on the days when she went down to the town to make some trifling purchase, or to go to confession at Holy Saviour's, or to make the " Way of the Cross " in the chapel of Jerusalem. Hitherto she had never noticed them, but now they were obvious to her at a glance. She knew the devotees of love by their slower and closer movement, by their clear and happy expression, even by a light which seemed to surround them like the halo she had noticed round the moon. And springtime now came into the conspiracy, the season of love. A tender sweetness invaded the breeze. The poplars reflected in the canals swayed to the light airs, their reflections seeking and flying one another, and uniting in the trembling water. Even the leaves met as in a kiss.

And now Ursula saw the sparrows twittering on the branchlets of the trees and on the gables, courting and fighting in playful encounters. She could not fail to understand. She remembered the two lovers in the convent parlour, and other lovers whom she had seen at eventide along the quays. A thousand trifles which she had never before observed now became significant. For instance, this Minnewater, the great sleepy lake which surrounded the outer walls of the convent, on which the windows of her room had always opened, had often struck her by its silence, its reflections of the moving clouds, and the water-lilies as white as the soul of infancy. Yet she had never realised the meaning of its charming name, Minnewater, " the lake of love," or more exactly, " the lake of lovers." It was well named indeed ; for now Ursula, less innocent, was incessantly conscious of the happy pairs of lovers who wandered round the shores of the lake, happy as the lovers whom she had seen in the parlour. Even their reflections as they walked by the lake united in the water under the pale moonlight.

Leaning out through her window Ursula watched the night, enervated and shaken with a storm of feeling. Sleep was impossible, but she tried to pray. In order to quiet her anxious thoughts by the repetition of words, she opened her prayer-book and read : " Lord, give us grace that we may be so filled with Divine love that we may give You all our heart." Hurriedly and eagerly she recited prayers which always brought back to her the word which she wished to escape; and the name of "love" seemed sometimes lawful, transfigured, burning like Isaiah's coal from the altar, but quite as often profane and sweet and earthly, touching her lips with the warmth of human kisses.

So the hours passed away in feverish vigil, marked at intervals by the slow striking of the clocks from the towers of Bruges. At every hour there was a disordered concert of sounds, the great deep old bells of the parish churches mingling with the high silvery tones of the convent bells. Sister Ursula knelt at these moments and muttered the canonical prayer: "The angel of the Lord declared unto Mary——"

And now she trembled with a great emotion and shook from head to foot. She had never hitherto gone very deeply into the significance of her prayers. But now, all of a sudden, she was plunged into this intimate and mysterious meaning, in which the Divine mystery emerged from the accustomed words. Her love had at last attained to more than the idea of love; and she was immediately convinced that she had lost in purity what she had gained in womanhood. She was ashamed of herself, and was struck with dreadful remorse. She knew now that all these thoughts, which were no longer venial, could be traced back to her acceptance of the order for the bridal robe. Surely she could not work at that any longer! She feared this beautiful lace which she had begun, just as she would have feared any other sin. She threw it aside as if it had been some bad book which she could no longer read. She knew that the Evil One, seeking her destruction, had devised this so innocent-seeming stratagem. All the pains of hell were hidden in these folds of lace. Strange medium for so deadly a poison!

Penitently Sister Ursula called to her patron saint for help, and started a novena to her. Every day she visited St. Ursula's shrine in Bruges, and lit a candle to burn many hours before it, a tiny quiet flame symbolising her own obedient heart. Peace soon came to the poor little sister. There was a heavenly calm in this shrine, where Memling's genius had painted St. Ursula, with her eleven thousand virgin companions, accepting death rather than the choice of sin. What a lesson of chastity they taught, standing fearlessly before the brutal soldiery and offering their breasts to the arrows of martyrdom!

And soon these holy observances, the novena and many rosaries and burning candles, and chiefly the intercession of St. Ursula herself, brought back our nun to the quietness of virtue. Temptation ceased to annoy her, and a resolution which came to her was carried at once into effect. She would immediately complete and deliver the order which too long had led her into doubtful ways. Inward peace was hers again. The pure laces of the sanctuary and altar now occupied her hours, instead of that dreadful marriage-lace which she had quite forgotten. Happy, heavenly thoughts now made their home in her soul, instead of the risky guesses and dreams of days gone by. She never thought of all that now, except as a danger of the past, which she had happily escaped. Yet sometimes a skiff, entering harbour, sees in one lightning flash all the raging sea behind ; and this was Sister Ursula's experience one day when she was called to the parlour, and there found Dorothy, who had once been so charming and pretty. But what a difference there was now! The girl was thin, wan, greatly changed, and all alone. The nun recognised her voice rather than her features. For a moment Dorothy was silent, while Ursula trembled, wondering whether her own temptations had returned.

At last her young visitor was able to speak, with broken accents, while her poor little fragile body shook with sobs. She had not been married after all. No, there would never be a marriage. And so— this beautiful lace would not be needed ; she had brought it back, and hoped that it would be accepted for a veil for Our Lady. And was it not, in fact, for Our Lady that Sister Ursula always made her lace ?

The nun listened eagerly, and began to understand ; the mystery seemed to clear up.

Yes, poor little Dorothy's fatal mistake had been that of wishing to take to herself Our Lady's lace. Dorothy had tried to believe that just for once these votive laces might be appropriated to her own pleasure and her own wedding-gown. But all her delusive dream, that she had really been loved, had only been a devil's snare. She herself had not believed in it. She had never believed in it, but had only pretended to believe. The child confessed that she had known it was all a pretence, yet that she had been unable to resist it ; and that in all the miserable comedy she had only enjoyed one moment, that moment when they had come to tempt Sister Ursula, to teach her what love meant, and to show her their faces glowing with love. Dorothy confessed that she had been no more than the puppet of fate. She knew now that it was all over, and had come quite simply to return the pieces of lace, like a theatrical costume which has played its part.

It all seemed very natural and logical. Ursula did not even ask her why she had brought them back herself, and had not rather returned his gift to the young man. Doubtless, she supposed, he was no longer available; he had disappeared, invisibly, through the air. It must have been no other than the Tempter, Satan himself, who had taken that attractive form, and had enlisted this pretty accomplice only to gain access with her to this holy retreat, all in order to seduce one poor little nun, and by tantalising her with the vision of a kiss to infect her with desires which must lead to her destruction.

Poor little Dorothy had only been the hapless instrument in the hands of the power of hell. Even now she was completing her task by coming to show the picture of love's to-morrow, with its melancholy face, the culminating disillusion of this clutch at happiness, all the perils indeed which the nun had escaped by entering religion. Dorothy showed her all that she might have been and mercifully had not been, all those dire effects of the hurricane which lays the soul in ruins from which it can never recover. Ursula gazed on her, deeply affected. The child was so wan and frail; she held out the lace with the broken-hearted mien of a beggar who has only her hair to sell. With tears streaming from her eyes, Ursula seized her hands. "Poor Dorothy! poor little Dorothy!" she cried, and even then remembered how the lover had uttered this name. Sister Ursula gave Dorothy's lace to the sister-sacristan, after arranging it as a long veil to drape the statue of Our Lady on Sundays and the principal feasts.

Soon afterward came round the Feast of the Assumption, which is celebrated by a great procession, following on Benediction, through the streets of Bruges. In order to get a good view of the ceremony, Sister Ursula had taken her place on one of the quays near an Altar of Repose. Here for some moments the white procession was halted, a picture of snowy surplices, lilies, and candles, while the white swans assembled on the dark canal. The silvery jingling of censers was heard, and the sounds of a holy chant arose. Down from the high steeples the bells flung their huge clamour, to be lost among the fragrant herbs and flowers which had been scattered along the streets.

Sister Ursula, kneeling, watched the solemn rite. Immediately before her, surrounded by banners and statues, stood high the image of Our Lady, smiling under her long lace veil, Dorothy's veil, the veil of temptation, which, like Ursula's soul itself, after having fallen into evil hands, had come home at last to adorn the service of God.

EUGÈNE DEMOLDER
B. 1862

THE DAUGHTER OF JAIRUS

A WHITE monk came out of Jairus's mansion with Joe, the servant, and said: " I will go to the Prémontrés Monastery and see that the bells are rung."

" God receive her within the Paradise of Virgins," replied Joe.

" Amen," said the monk.

And pulling up his hood he moved away, gliding along the walls like a shadow, with arms crossed on his breast.

Joe was left alone and thought: " The bells toll for the dead to-day! . . . It is like fasting on Easter Day."

Do they pour wine in the organ pipes on All Souls' Day when they blow for the Dies Irae? But it is all the same to me after all, for I must stop to look after the house.

But what a fair! The bells will make the very heavens sad. To go and dance to the sound of the bells tolling for your dead! And indeed the festival was being prepared on the market-place of Yperdamme. From the balcony of the Town Hall, where presently the aldermen were going to appear, hung rich rugs from Smyrna. On every house front were fastened flags and banners. Tables were being laid before the doors of the inns, and heavy brewers' drays deposited full barrels.

At one end of the market-place were planted poles, decorated with garlands of flowers and shields, a platform was being erected, and the guild carpenters made the beams and planks ring beneath the blows of their hammers.

Further on, there was a merry-go-round with wooden horses, which was already practising to the sound of a clarionette and a horn. And along the principal street stretched a line of booths, with awnings and open stalls newly set up in anticipation of the buyers at the fair.

Amongst these preparations, which the people and the sunshine made for a brotherly festivity, the mansion of Jairus alone remained sullen, with its closed shutters, its rich portico ungarlanded on this joyous morning, and the melancholy lights faintly glimmering behind the windows of Ephraima's room. Oh, the gleam of those candles!

like a star of ill omen rising on a peaceful horizon, or some will-o'-the-wisp, with thoughts of death, lighted suddenly above the flower-beds of a spring garden. The townspeople of Yperdamme cast pitying glances at the mournful house, and cursed Death who had that day mown down the most lovely flower of their city.

At that moment the noble lord Zacharius arrived. He wore a large felt hat with a yellow feather, a grey doublet frogged with silver, and one hand upon the rich guard of his sword, with the other he twirled his moustache proudly. He tapped Joe on the shoulder.

"Your master?"

"My master, my lord Zacharius! He has gone to look for Jesus. My master's daughter is dead."

"Ephraima?"

"Yes, my lord—this morning. Market was just over. She still heard the finches and warblers which the peasants brought into the market-place."

"A week ago she was dancing the minuet at my castle! . . . So your master has gone to Jesus?"

"Yes, sir."

"Waste of time! How old was she?"

"Sixteen."

"She was very pretty. So sweet and dainty! graceful and with eyes like forget-me-nots. What a divine Magdalen she would have made in one of our performances!"

"Yes, sir."

"For she had hair like an angel. And all that mown down. Oh, the mournful harvest, the cruel harvest. I will write some verses on her death."

"Yes, sir."

"Unhappy Jairus! What is the use of all his wealth? His ramparts of sapphire and emeralds have not prevented Death from entering his house and stealing his most precious jewel! And now he has gone to look for Jesus?"

"Yes, sir; may he succeed in his undertaking."

"Ha! ha! I should like to see that. Poor Ephraima! Poor little girl! But I must go and meet my rhetoricians, who are coming here to act the story of Joseph sold by his brethren. I advise you, Joe, to see the performance which we are going to give presently, over there. Do you see? They are putting up the stage. There will be an orchestra, and two dromedaries which a travelling Asiatic merchant has lent us. You will see the King of Egypt in a velvet gown, surrounded by guards, then Joseph and his brethren, the story of the dreams. Madame Potiphar will recite some verses which I have written."

"Yes, sir."

But Zacharius, catching sight of a procession arriving on the market-place, cried out, "There they are! there they are! there they are! I must join them."

"Good-bye, sir."

The rhetoricians arrived on the market-place in carts decorated with laurel wreaths. They were very boisterous, and the opening of the stone bottles of Louvain beer resounded. Sturdy horses with beribboned manes drew them, making a great show beneath the windows, which were thrown open. The actors wore odd costumes, large swaggering hats, and light cloaks. Their faces were animated, and they showed, in between the festoons of foliage hung around their conveyances, merry, comic, hilarious countenances, greedy mouths, sunburnt cheeks generously flushed. Gross pleasure oozed from every pore of these vehicles, like the scum from cider moistening the joins of a fermenting barrel. And what strange things to swing about on the wheels of the carts!—drums, lances, beards, armour which gleamed in the distance, a gilded sceptre, a tin crown, and Roman draperies. All these things were scattered around the stage under the direction of my lord Zacharius. Curtains were hung over the laths and wooden bars, and all around was a crowd of curious children.

A nun appeared at Jairus's balcony.

"She is tired of saying paternosters," said Joe to himself. "Other years it was Ephraima who came out on to the balcony. Well, well! a fortnight's mourning and then she will be forgotten, for the earth swallows up more than the bodies of the dead!"

And he went sadly along a path close to the houses between the spread tables. Mine host, polishing a pewter mug at the door of his inn, stopped him, saying: "You look very miserable, Joe."

"Ephraima is dead!"

"I saw the Holy Sacrament carried into Jairus's house this morning. But the candle-light makes a wretched illumination at the fair! Especially as my inn is so close to the house of death! It makes you think about too unhappy things, Joe! . . . And then Jairus cannot let his fine purple flag, embroidered with golden lions, flap over the front of his house this year."

" Jairus has gone to look for Jesus."

" I saw Jesus curing a paralytic one day. What magic, Joe! I couldn't believe my poor eyes! But here comes the crowd. I must tap my barrels. There are the vendors of gingerbread and fritters. The market-place will smell good of frizzling butter and caramels and fat. Ha! ha! They will have to gulp down a lot of beer to float all those pancakes and waffles into their stomachs! Here is the Guild of St. George coming to the cross-bow competition with the banner on which you see St. George with lance in hand! They are passing under the belfry. What lovely weather! The sun is pouring on to the cross-bows! The weather-cock on the Town Hall gleams like a coin in the sky! A good omen for our purses, Joe!"

Mine host and Joe were chatting thus in the midst of the animation on the market-place when a great noise arose at the side of the stage.

It was a crowd of beggars quarrelling with the rhetoricians! A little while before they had been at the gates of the town, attracted by the profits of the fair. They moved, descending the banks with strange contortions like hunted toads, hopping and struggling along with their deformed limbs. Some leaning on crutches, one poor fellow with a guitar on his back, others, out of breath, crawling like snails, dragging their swollen limbs wrapped in muddy rags; then the blind, with red eyelids, knocking themselves against the passers-by; one wretch had only one foot, but to make up for it, bagpipes slung on his shoulder. Poor things, mangy musicians of the fair, dirty street-singers, they bore their deformities as a means of livelihood. Some of them were real monsters out of the Revelations: horrible were their contortions, for they were twisted like the trunks of oaks in their repulsive rags. All this scurvy regiment, propped up on their stumps, hunchbacked and with sores, like a group of monstrous snails or chipped gargoyles, sent out pitiful glances from under their weak eyelids.

" It was over there," began one of them, " on the high road near the Post Horn Inn. We were on the bank, poor wretched toads, with the dust of the road on our rags. One was turning the handle of his hurdy-gurdy; one offering to tell fortunes. Jesus appeared. It seemed to me that the birds were singing in the orchards of Hoogeland Farm as I had never heard them sing before. People were passing on the road going to the fair. I had been blind for many years. But at the approach of Jesus my eyelids became transparent, with a soft silver-white light, and as soon as He had touched these miserable red-bordered lids with His hands which smelled of incense—ah, my brothers ! I saw again, beyond His linen robe, over the crowd, and in the joy of the light pouring on my eyes through the flags of the fair, yes, I saw the windmills turning in the sky, and the meadows through which winds the Lys ! I was intoxicated as if I had drunk all the sky. And the treasures which God has collected for the poor in the magnificent casket of the firmament once again enriched my eyes. I danced with joy ! The crowd had stopped, and I saw others who had thrown down their crutches and their sticks and their ulcerous bandages, and who leapt in the full light of midday. Butterflies, my brothers, who had cast off the larva of misery. Oh, the holy blessedness ! "

The rhetoricians burst out laughing and exclaiming :

" Ha ! ha ! ha ! "

" This Jesus is a magician ! "

" He will be burnt as was the witch of Maldeghem."

" No, He will be crucified ! "

" Like a slave, on the shameful gibbet ! "

" This feigned Son of God ! He ! he ! he ! Who is no more the Son of God than you were blind or paralytic, crowd of mountebanks ! A few blows with a cudgel would have made the most lame among you run like hares—and the most dumb, scream like peacocks ! "

But under this hail of derision which beat upon the newly opened flowers of his faith, the beggar continued :

" Jesus will come here and will raise up the daughter of Jairus."

" Ha ! ha ! ha ! "

" Jesus will raise her up ! He has just cured Saint Peter's mother-in-law."

" Saint Peter's mother-in-law ! Ha ! ha ! ha ! "

" When Jesus had sown health and light around Him near Hoogeland Farm, He went away with Saint Peter and Jairus, who had come to meet him. He went to the house of Peter's mother-in-law, who was suffering from a fever, and the crowd followed them. The poor woman was lying in a recess protected by red check curtains. Oh, the quiet cottage. Fishing-nets drying at the door, a silent spinning-wheel by the fireplace, a few loose faggots on the hearth crackled beneath a saucepan in which some marshmallows were boiling.

" Jesus only touched the sick woman : she rose up with great gestures of gratitude, and having put on a white bonnet and a red skirt, such as the shrimp-fishers wear, she served the visitors with fresh cheese, radishes, and a jug of beer. They sat down on little wooden stools and ate, while the old woman drew down a yellow muslin curtain over the window, which bathed them in a warm, golden light."

But the angry rhetoricians would not let these poetic accounts be finished. They cried out:

"Cunning rogues! You are sly politicians."

Some waved lances out of their unharnessed carts, others made faces. One among them, dressed as a fool, imitated the gestures of the beggar. Then they shouted out: "Come and see our plays and mysteries. They are sincere and honest, entertaining, with beautiful costumes and attractive women. We shall represent to you the Seven Deadly Sins. You shall see Pride and Deceit. But we play our plays without pretending that we are descended from David."

"Or calling ourselves the sons of God."

"These intriguers always come to a bad end."

"The rope is ready for them."

"Go to Calvary and count the skulls of which the vultures have emptied the sockets."

In the meantime the distant sound of trumpets of the guilds entering the town could be heard. A light breeze made the banners wave, and the crowd was like the sea which breaks its sun-bathed waves between the breakwaters.

Beneath the flags everything was in movement.

A Jew came out of the crowd with a face like a goat, and laying his crooked finger under the nose of the beggar who had just been so happily singing the glory of Christ, he said: "He shall be killed, your Jesus. The soldiers shall cast their lots upon His garments, the people will spit upon His face, the red executioners will make His flesh bleed, and your eyes shall be torn out with pincers."

The people cried: "The Jew! the Jew! the Jew!"

"The juggler who spirits away our money."

"He has the beak and claws of a magpie."

A workman struck the Semite, who fled towards the rhetoricians, "Protect me, noble lords, against this mob."

Some of the actors drew their swords. The workmen caught up tools.

Mine host cried out: "Will you quarrel like this at a fair? Be careful of my windows. Be careful of my windows!" And the nun at the balcony of Jairus entered quickly, crossing herself, without closing the windows.

But at the Monastery of Prémontrés the bells tolled slowly for the dead. When bells proclaim the death of a young girl, they are particularly heartrending. All the sadness of faded springtime veils their hearts. For they are also feminine and virgin, and understand the sorrow of the poor Ophelias plucked by destiny in the harvest of the world. They weep for the unfinished flower garlands, for the lace neglected by pale hands, for the unopened loves. . . .

Then Jesus came while the actors and beggars and people were disputing among themselves. He was dressed in a long robe like the pilgrims, and a cape with shells; and He leant upon a big staff from the end of which hung a flask. A felt hat thrown back from His head remained hanging on His back. A supernatural light hovered over His white face, with its fair beard, which was gentle and glowing as a fountain of light.

Jairus, in gorgeous Eastern costume, opened a path through the crowd. The rich jeweller wore a silken turban with a diamond aigrette, a pink jacket with gold embroidered satin belt; his soft leather boots were tapped by a curved, ivory-handled sabre.

Jesus raised His hand to those who were disputing.

"Why make ye such ado? The maid is not dead, but sleepeth."

A great silence spread suddenly over the market-place of Yperdamme.

When Jesus reached Jairus's mansion, He mounted the steps, followed by Saint Peter, whose old sunburnt face and worn-out brown toga contrasted with the brilliant dress of the jeweller. It was a mansion, the corridor of which, decorated with splendid pictures by famous artists and paved with marble, seemed, like the resonant avenue with its chiming clock, leading to some oasis of happiness.

He mounted a staircase covered with gorgeous tapestries and reached Ephraima's room.

Jairus was in despair. He was shedding tears and kneeling upon every step to kiss Jesus's hands. He cried aloud:

"O Thou, Jesus, Who made the leprous woman fresh as a rose, Who with a spark of Thy power lighted again the dead lanterns of the blind, Thou Who madest the lame to dance in a ring, and gavest strength and suppleness to the cripple, Jesus, on this festive day on which Thy Father lighted the most splendid luminary which He ever made to glow above forest and sea, Jesus, give back to the cold fruit of my holy and lawful love, that warmth which clothed it with fair youth!

"My daughter is dead, but come and lay Thy hand upon her, and she shall live. O Son of David, to Thee I sacrifice my wrought shrines by the finest jewellers of Bruges, my tapestries wherein are woven in gold the lives of the Holy Martyrs, and my ceremonial collars. Take from their frames my most magnificent canvasses, carry away my Utrecht velvets and my Malines lace."

But Jesus entering the room replied: "Man, be it unto thee according to thy faith. But keep thy wealth, or divide it among the poor. It will not help to gain the Kingdom of Heaven."

The beggars and the rhetoricians had collected around the door of the mansion. In the distance, through the streets, crackers went off, and through the open window, with the clear blue air, came the music of the merry-go-rounds, turning yonder, their tinsel glittering like rounds of fireflies above the heads of the crowd in its Sunday best.

And all these sounds rose up towards Ephraima, whose hair, still moist with the pale sweat of the agony, fell on the pillow like an unbound distaff-full of faded gold around her waxen face and closed eyes. She lay with folded hands, like a figure on a tomb, and on the white silk which covered her slender body had been placed branches of box and a diamond crucifix. She lay immovable among the flowers of her satin curtains, and one might have said that at the sound of the tolling bells and the orchestras of the fair, on this sumptuous bed amidst birds, she floated down the dream-river which leads to Paradise.

But already her delicate hands were cold, her eyes like closed caskets, and one felt upon the brow, but yesterday bathed with the light of dawn, the hideous trace of the finger which condemned the flesh of this child to the branding of worms and the shame of death.

Candles were burning and a psalter with silver clasps lay on the table among the phials. The nun had put her hands into her black sleeves and dropped her eyelids beneath the white wings of her cap. Jesus approached the dead. He laid His hand upon Ephraima's brow, and in the alcove it was as if all the larks awakened. One had said that the spirit of the springtime, summoned by the mystic gesture of the Prophet, had come to hover over the daughter of Jairus. The dried-up streams when they take up their course flow softly from their sources, murmuring hymns of flowers and sky. Little by little, daisies once more freshly gem their borders. Goldfinches again come to quench their thirst in the water which mirrors the periwinkles. It is festival for all the dwellers on the rivers, and through the meadows once more the stream makes the radiant cords of its reflection vibrate in the light. Thus in her bed, which seemed enchanted, Ephraima awoke. The red blood took up its course through her veins and bathed her cheeks again with living colour. Her stiff hands slowly relaxed and stretched out towards Jesus as if she offered Him a lily of prayer gathered in Heaven. Her breast rose again. Then her eyes opened. And they seemed surprised. They were radiant and strange. Ah, when Jesus gave back to the blind the treasures veiled by their dark lids, He raised them up but to the light. They had retained a warm heart in their breast. But Ephraima's body had become cold, her flesh insensible to the caress of the air. From what sights had she been snatched away ? She had looked upon that which our ancestors see who sleep beneath the brass plates in the cathedral, the mystery of the tomb had been unfolded for her. She bore on her looks and gesture a gleam from beyond the sky. And about her as she woke there hung a soft white air such as surrounds the saints and martyrs when they appear on earth. The bells for the dead had ceased their sobbing, and from all the church towers of Yperdamme, with one accord, burst forth a wild and joyous peal. The crosses gleamed brighter upon the spires. The procession poured on to the market-place—banners fluttered above the white dresses of girls, and seemed like great butterflies over blooming flower-beds. The richly dressed aldermen were seated on the balcony of the Town Hall. Trumpets scattered around on every side through the blue air the red flourish of their brass. Already the crowd knew that Ephraima had been raised up to life. The beggars sang hymns. The rhetoricians, converted, waved their hats and feathers, and carried baskets of flowers to the door of the house where the miracle had been performed. Yes, there arose throughout all Yperdamme a mighty hymn of praise—a hymn of praise to life rising up to the sublime ball of fire which pours joy through space. It was he, the symbol of life ; and Jesus, standing before the young girl slowly called back to the joys of life, seemed to have descended from the sun. Jairus, with eyes red with weeping, kissed the Prophet's robe. The nun upon her knees murmured a litany. Beneath the brotherly look of Christ, Ephraima, having regained the splendour of her youth, spread out her arms amazed.

MAURICE MAETERLINCK

B. 1862

THE MASSACRE OF THE INNOCENTS

TOWARDS the hour of supper on Friday, the twenty-sixth day of the month of December, a little shepherd lad came into Nazareth, crying bitterly.

Some peasants who were drinking ale in the Blue Lion opened the shutters to look into the village orchard, and saw the child running over the snow. They recognised him as the son of Korneliz, and called from the window: " What is the matter ? It's time you were abed ! "

But sobbing still, and shaking with terror, the boy cried that the Spaniards had come, that they had set fire to the farm, had hanged his mother among the nut trees, and bound his nine little sisters to the trunk of a big tree. At this the peasants rushed out of the inn. Surrounding the child they stunned him with their questionings and outcries. Between his sobs he added that the soldiers were on horseback and wore armour, that they had taken away the cattle of his uncle, Petrus Krayer, and would soon be in the forest with the sheep and cows. All now ran to the Golden Swan, where, as they knew, Korneliz and his brother-in-law were also drinking their mug of ale. The moment the innkeeper heard these terrifying tidings, he hurried into the village, crying that the Spaniards were at hand.

What a stir, what an uproar there was then in Nazareth ! Women opened windows, and peasants hurriedly left their houses, carrying lights which were put out when they reached the orchard, where, because of the snow and the full moon, one could see as well as at midday.

Later, they gathered round Korneliz and Krayer, in the open space which faced the inns. Several of them had brought pitchforks and rakes, and consulted together, terror-stricken, under the trees.

But, as they did not know what to do, one of them ran to fetch the curé, who owned Korneliz's farm. He came out of the house with the sacristan carrying the keys of the church. All followed him into the churchyard, whither his cry came to them from the top of the tower, that he beheld nothing either in the fields, or by the forest, but that around the farm he saw ominous red clouds, for all that the sky was of a deep blue and agleam with stars over the rest of the plain.

After taking counsel for a long time in the churchyard, they decided to hide in the wood through which the Spaniards must pass, and, if these were not too numerous, to attack them and recover Peter Krayer's cattle and the plunder which had been taken from the farm.

Having armed themselves with pitchforks and spades, while the women remained outside the church with the curé, they sought a suitable ambuscade. Approaching a mill on a rising ground adjacent to the verge of the forest, they saw the light of the burning farm flaming against the stars. There they waited under enormous oaks, before a frozen mere.

A shepherd known as Red Dwarf climbed the hill to warn the miller, who had stopped his mill when he saw the flames on the horizon. He bade the peasant enter, and both men went to a window to stare out into the night.

Before them the moon shone over the burning farmstead, and in its light they saw a long procession winding athwart the snow. Having carefully scrutinised it, the Dwarf descended where his comrades waited under the trees, and now, they too gradually distinguished four men on horseback behind a flock which moved grazing on the plain.

While the peasants in their blue breeches and red cloaks continued to search about the margins of the mere and under the snowlit trees, the sacristan pointed out to them a box hedge, behind which they hid.

The Spaniards, driving before them the sheep and the cattle, advanced upon the ice. When the sheep reached the hedge they began to nibble at the green stuff, and now Korneliz broke from the shadows of the bushes, followed by the others with their pitchforks. Then in the midst of the huddled-up sheep and of the cows who stared affrighted, the savage strife was fought out beneath the moon, and ended in a massacre.

When they had slain not only the Spaniards, but also their horses, Korneliz rushed thence across the meadow in the direction of the flames, while the others plundered and stripped the dead. Thereafter all returned to the village with their flocks. The women, who were observing the dark forest from behind the churchyard walls, saw them coming through the trees and ran with the curé to meet them, and all returned dancing joyously, amid the laughter of the children and the barking of the dogs.

But while they made merry under the pear trees of the orchard, where the Red Dwarf had hung lanterns in honour of the kermesse, they anxiously demanded of the curé what was to be done.

The outcome of this was the harnessing of a horse to a cart in order to fetch the bodies of the woman and the nine little girls to the village. The sisters and other relations of the dead woman got into the cart along with the curé, who, being old and very fat, could not walk so far.

In silence they entered the forest and emerged upon the moonlit plain. There, in the white light, they descried the dead men, rigid and naked, among the slain horses. Then they moved onward toward the farm, which still burned in the midst of the plain.

When they came to the orchard of the flaming house, they stopped at the gate of the garden, dumb before the overwhelming misfortune of the peasant. For there his wife hung, quite naked, on the branches of an enormous nut tree among which he himself was now mounting on a ladder, and beneath which, on the frozen grass, lay his nine little daughters. Korneliz had already climbed along the vast boughs, when suddenly, by the light of the snow, he saw the crowd, who, horror-struck, watched his every movement. With tears in his eyes, he made a sign to them to help him, whereat the innkeepers of the Blue Lion and the Golden Sun, the curé, with a lantern, and many others, climbed up in the moonshine amid the snow-laden branches to unfasten the dead. The women of the village received the corpse in their arms at the foot of the tree—even as our Lord Jesus Christ was received by the women at the foot of the Cross.

On the morrow they buried her, and for the week thereafter nothing unusual happened in Nazareth.

But the following Sunday, hungry wolves ran through the village after High Mass, and it snowed until midday. Then, suddenly, the sun shone brilliantly, and the peasants went to dine as was their wont, and dressed for Benediction.

There was no one to be seen on the Place, for it froze bitterly. Only the dogs and chickens roamed about under the trees, or the sheep nibbled at a three-cornered bit of grass, while the curé's servant swept away the snow from his garden.

At that moment a troop of armed men crossed the stone bridge at the end of the village, and halted in the orchard. Peasants hurried from their houses, but, recognising the new-comers as Spaniards, they retreated terrified, and went to the windows to see what would happen.

About thirty soldiers, in full armour, surrounded an old man with a white beard. Behind them, on pillions, rode red and yellow lancers, who jumped down and ran over the snow to shake off their stiffness, while several of the soldiers in armour dismounted likewise, and fastened their horses to the trees.

Then they moved in the direction of the Golden Sun and knocked at the door. It was opened reluctantly ; the soldiers went in, warmed themselves near the fire, and called for ale.

Presently they came out of the inn, carrying pots, jugs, and rye bread for their companions, who surrounded the man with the white beard, where he waited behind the hedge of lances.

As the street remained deserted, the commander sent some horsemen to the back of the houses, to guard the village on the country side. He then ordered the lancers to bring him all the children of two years old and under to be massacred, as is written in the Gospel of Saint Matthew.

The soldiers first went to the little inn of the Green Cabbage, and to the barber's cottage, which stood side by side midway in the street.

One of them opened a sty and a litter of pigs wandered into the village. The innkeeper and the barber came out and humbly asked the men what they wanted ; but they did not understand Flemish, and went into the houses to look for the children.

The innkeeper had one child, who, in its little shift, was screaming on the table where they had just dined. A soldier took it in his arms and carried it away under the apple trees, while the father and mother followed, crying.

Thereafter the lancers opened other stable doors—those of the cooper, the blacksmith, the cobbler—and calves, cows, asses, pigs, goats, and sheep roamed about the square. When they broke the carpenter's windows, several of the oldest and richest habitants of the village assembled in the street, and went to meet the Spaniards. Respectfully they took off their caps and hats to the leader in the velvet mantle, and asked him what he was going to do. He did not, however, understand their language ; so some one ran to fetch the curé.

The priest was putting on a gold chasuble in the vestry, in readiness for Benediction. The peasant cried: "The Spaniards are in the orchard!" Horrified, the curé ran to the door of the church, and the choir-boys followed, carrying wax-tapers and censer.

As he stood there, he saw the animals from the pens and stables wandering on the snow and on the grass, the horsemen in the village, the soldiers before the doors, horses tied to trees all along the street, men and women entreating the man who held the child in its little shift.

The curé hastened into the churchyard, and the peasants turned anxiously towards him as he came through the pear trees, like the Divine Presence itself in white and gold. They crowded about him where he confronted the man with the white beard.

He spoke in Flemish and in Latin, but the commander merely shrugged his shoulders to show that he did not understand.

The villagers asked their priest in a low voice: "What does he say? What is he going to do?" Others, when they saw the curé in the orchard, came cautiously from their cottages, women hurried up and whispered in groups, while the soldiers, till that moment besieging an inn, ran back at sight of the crowd in the square.

Then the man who held the innkeeper's child by the leg cut off its head with his sword.

The people saw the head fall, and thereafter the body lie bleeding upon the grass. The mother picked it up and carried it away, but forgot the head. She ran towards her home, but stumbling against a tree, fell prone on the snow, where she lay in a swoon, while the father struggled between two soldiers.

Some young peasants cast stones and blocks of wood at the Spaniards, but the horsemen all lowered their lances; the women fled and the curé with his parishioners began to shriek with horror, amid the bleating of the sheep, the cackling of the geese, and the barking of the dogs.

But as the soldiers moved away again into the street, the crowd stood silent to see what would happen.

A troop entered the shop kept by the sacristan's sisters, but came out quietly, without harming the seven women, who knelt on the threshold praying.

From there they went to the inn of St. Nicholas, which belonged to the Hunchback. Here, too, so as to appease them, the door was opened at once; but, when the soldiers reappeared amid a great uproar, they carried three children in their arms. The marauders were surrounded by the Hunchback, his wife, and daughters, all with clasped hands, imploring for mercy.

When the soldiers came to their white-bearded leader, they placed the children at the foot of an elm, where the little ones remained seated on the snow in their Sunday clothes. But one of them in a yellow frock got up and toddled unsteadily towards the sheep. A soldier followed with bare sword ; and the child died with his face in the grass, while the others were killed around the tree.

The peasants' and the innkeepers' daughters all fled screaming, and shut themselves up in their houses. The curé, who was left alone in the orchard, threw himself on his knees, first before one horseman, then another, and with crossed arms, supplicated the Spaniards piteously, while the fathers and mothers seated on the snow beyond wept bitterly for the dead children whom they held upon their knees.

As the lancers passed along the street, they noticed a big blue farmstead. When they had tried in vain to force open the oaken door studded with nails, they clambered atop of some tubs which were frozen over near the threshold, and by this means gained the house through the upper windows.

There had been a kermesse in this farm. At sound of the broken window-panes, the families who had assembled there to eat gaufres, custards, and hams, crowded together behind the table on which still stood some empty jugs and dishes. The soldiers entered the kitchen, and after a savage struggle in which many were wounded, they seized all the little boys and girls ; then, with these, and the servant who had bitten a lancer's thumb, they left the house and fastened the door behind them in such a way that the parents could not get out.

The villagers who had no children slowly left their houses, and followed the soldiers at a distance. They saw them throw down their victims on the grass before the old man, and callously kill them with lance and sword. During this, men and women leaned out of all the windows of the blue house, and out of the barn, blaspheming and flinging their hands to heaven, when they saw the red, pink, and white frocks of their motionless little ones on the grass between the trees. The soldiers next hanged the farm servant at the sign of the Half Moon on the other side of the street, and there was a long silence in the village.

The massacre now became general. Mothers fled from their

houses, and attempted to escape through the flower and vegetable gardens, and so into the country beyond, but the horsemen pursued them and drove them back into the street. Peasants with caps in their clasped hands knelt before the men who dragged away their children, while amid the confusion the dogs barked joyously. The curé, with hands upraised to heaven, rushed up and down in front of the houses and under the trees, praying desperately ; here and there, soldiers, trembling with cold, blew on their fingers as they moved about the road, or waited with hands in their breeches pockets, and swords under their arms, before the windows of the houses which were being scaled.

Everywhere, as in small bands of twos and threes they moved along the streets, where these scenes were being enacted, and entered the houses, they beheld the piteous grief of the peasants. The wife of a market-gardener, who occupied a red brick cottage near the church, pursued with a wooden stool the two men who carried off her children in a wheelbarrow. When she saw them die, a horrible sickness came upon her, and they thrust her down on the stool, under a tree by the roadside.

Other soldiers swarmed up the lime trees in front of a farmstead with its blank walls tinted mauve, and entered the house by removing the tiles. When they came back on to the roof, the father and mother, with outstretched arms, tried to follow them through the opening, but the soldiers repeatedly pushed them back, and had at last to strike them on the head with their swords before they could disengage themselves and regain the street.

One family, shut up in the cellar of a large cottage, lamented near the grating, through which the father wildly brandished a pitchfork. Outside on a heap of manure, a bald old man sobbed all alone ; in the square, a woman in a yellow dress had swooned, and her weeping husband now supported her under the arms, against a pear tree ; another woman in red fondled her little girl, bereft of her hands, and lifted now one tiny arm, now the other, to see if the child would not move. Yet another woman fled towards the country ; but the soldiers pursued her among the hayricks, which stood out in black relief against the fields of snow.

Beneath the inn of the Four Sons of Aymon a surging tumult reigned. The inhabitants had formed a barricade, and the soldiers went round and round the house without being able to enter. Then they were attempting to climb up to the signboard by the creepers, when they noticed a ladder behind the garden door. This they raised against the wall, and went up it in file. But the innkeeper and all his family hurled tables, stools, plates, and cradles down upon them from the windows; the ladder was overturned, and the soldiers fell.

In a wooden hut at the end of the village, another band found a peasant woman washing her children in a tub near the fire. Being old and very deaf, she did not hear them enter. Two men took the tub and carried it away, and the stupefied woman followed with the clothes in which she was about to dress the children. But when she saw traces of blood everywhere in the village, swords in the orchards, cradles overturned in the street, women on their knees, others who wrung their hands over the dead, she began to scream and beat the soldiers, who put down the tub to defend themselves. The curé hastened up also, and, with hands clasped over his chasuble, entreated the Spaniards before the naked little ones howling in the water. Some soldiers came up, tied the mad peasant to a tree, and carried off the children.

The butcher, who had hidden his little girl, leaned against his shop and looked on callously. A lancer and one of the men in armour entered the house and found the child in a copper boiler. Then the butcher in despair took one of his knives and rushed after them into the street, but soldiers who were passing disarmed him, and hanged him by the hands to the hooks in the wall—there, among the flayed animals, he kicked and struggled, blaspheming, until the evening.

Near the churchyard, there was a great gathering before a long, low house, painted green. The owner, standing on his threshold, shed bitter tears; as he was very fat and jovial-looking, he excited the pity of some soldiers who were seated in the sun against the wall, patting a dog. The one, too, who dragged away his child by the hand, gesticulated as if to say: "What can I do? It's not my fault!"

A peasant who was pursued jumped into a boat, moored near the stone bridge, and with his wife and children moved away across the unfrozen part of the narrow lagoon. Not daring to follow, the soldiers strode furiously through the reeds. They climbed up into the willows on the banks to try to reach the fugitives with their lances—as they did not succeed, they continued for a long time to threaten the terrified family adrift upon the black water.

The orchard was still full of people, for it was there, in front of the white-bearded man who directed the massacre, that most of the children were killed. Little dots who could just walk alone stood side by side munching their slices of bread and jam, and stared curiously at the slaying of their helpless playmates, or collected round the village fool who played his flute on the grass.

Then suddenly there was a uniform movement in the village. The peasants ran towards the castle, which stood on the brown rising ground at the end of the street. They had seen their seigneur leaning on the battlements of his tower and watching the massacre. Men, women, old people, with hands outstretched, supplicated to him, in his velvet mantle and his gold cap, as to a king in heaven. But he raised his arms and shrugged his shoulders to show his helplessness, and when they implored him more and more persistently, kneeling in the snow, with bared heads, and uttering piteous cries, he turned slowly into the tower, and the peasants' last hope was gone.

When all the children were slain, the tired soldiers wiped their swords on the grass and supped under the pear trees. Then they mounted one behind the other, and rode out of Nazareth across the stone bridge, by which they had come.

The setting of the sun behind the forest made the woods aflame and dyed the village blood-red. Exhausted with running and entreating, the curé had thrown himself upon the snow, in front of the church, and his servant stood near him. They stared upon the street and the orchard, both thronged with the peasants in their best clothes. Before many thresholds, parents with dead children on their knees bewailed with ever fresh amaze their bitter grief. Others still lamented over the children where they had died, near a barrel, under a barrow, or at the edge of a pool. Others carried away the dead in silence. There were some who began to wash the benches, the stools, the tables, the blood-stained shifts, and to pick up the cradles which had been thrown into the street. Mother by mother moaned under the trees over the dead bodies which lay upon the grass, little mutilated bodies which they recognised by their woollen frocks. Those who were childless moved aimlessly through the square, stopping at times in front of the bereaved, who wailed and sobbed in their sorrow. The men, who no longer wept, sullenly pursued their strayed animals, around which the barking dogs coursed ; or, in silence, repaired so far their broken windows and rifled roofs. As the moon solemnly rose through the quietudes of the sky, deep silence as of sleep descended upon the village, where now not the shadow of a living thing stirred.

HUBERT KRAINS

B. 1862

CHRISTMAS EVE

I HAD gone, that night with my parents, to a farm at the end of the village where they were keeping Christmas Eve. The guests arrived in little groups. They could be heard far off, for it was freezing, and their sabots and hobnailed boots made a great commotion in the silent streets. When they opened the door, a blast of cold air entered the house. The women took off their broad-brimmed hats and shawls, the men unwound their mufflers, and all drew reddened hands out of their woollen mittens. Then they sat down around a big roaring stove above which the smoke of the pipes hung in a cloud.

They had put us, Marie and me, at a little table in a corner. We had before us a Liège almanac and a gorgeously illustrated Bible. After having gazed for a long time at the astronomer with his pointed hat who looks at the stars through a big telescope, we admired one after another the ingenuous prints representing the Seasons. Marie asked me explanations every moment, and, in order to understand better, bent her roguish head on my shoulder. I felt her soft fair hair tickling my cheek, her red lips smiled at me, and her blue eyes looked deep into mine with affection. We were about to pass on to the Bible when the conversation among those grouped around the stove suddenly stopped. " Sh ! " said Marie, putting her finger to her lips, " they are going to tell a story."

We folded our hands on the table, turning towards an old man at whom every one was looking eagerly, and who seemed to be considering, with his head propped in his hand.

At last he raised his slender body, and after glancing round with a mischievous look he began :

" Once upon a time. . . ."

At that moment the door opened, a head appeared at the opening, and a frightened voice cried :

" They have just found a dead man out in the country. . . ."

Every one was struck with terror, and we all rushed out of the house with the exception of a few women. The street was full of people running fast. The moon had just risen ; its thin crescent, with slightly iridescent edges, gleamed like a crystal in the depth of the sky,thousands of stars twinkled, and two rows of poplars raising their thin skeletons along the fields, cast weird mysterious shadows. Before us, the heads of the crowd moved up and down through a dull sound ; this monotonous murmur was sometimes interrupted by a strident call, answered by a frightened childish voice. In a quarter of an hour we were out in the open fields, and soon we saw a group of people in the middle of a roadway. They formed a circle, bending over the body of a man lying on his side. One who was kneeling by, from time to time took a match from his pocket, struck it on his trousers, and passed it in front of the dead man's face. Then the pale still face could be seen, the eyes white between half-closed lids, the pinched lips, wrinkles on cheeks and brow ; his hair was grey, and so was his long beard, which flowed down over his breast ; his left arm was folded under him, while his right hand lay on the ground palm upwards ; with his big body, which obstructed the whole pathway, he looked like a warrior of olden times.

" Does any one of you know this dead man ? " asked the one who had been kneeling by the body, as he got up.

" No ! " answered every one present in a chorus.

" He is a beggar," said some one. " Look, his clothes are all torn, there is his stick in the rut, and here is his wallet," he added, picking up something from the ground, which looked like an empty bag.

A strange silence followed these words, everything was still around us ; you only heard the irregular breathing of the people. The more timid remained at the back, immovable, quiet, and oppressed, from time to time craning their necks over their neighbours' shoulders to cast a rapid glance at the corpse. On all sides the country, bare and flat, stretched out like a desert.

Suddenly a man asked me :

" You have never seen a dead man, little chap ? "

" No," said I, " I have never seen one."

" Then you must touch him ; otherwise he will appear to you every night in your dreams."

For one instant I wanted to run away, but the fear of finding myself alone in the lonely fields held me back. I went up, trembling in every limb. If it had been in daylight very likely I should not have been so frightened, but to touch this huge immovable body in the dark, under the eyes of all those vague faces moving in the stillness around me, seemed to me something appallingly dangerous. I made up my mind, however. I put out my hand—but drew it back at once. Finally, with a resolute effort, I laid it on the forehead of the dead. God! how cold it was! I shivered from head to foot. A crowd of thoughts buzzed in my head, and for several minutes I saw nothing but a black mass melting into the earth. Meanwhile, steps sounded in the distance; we saw a little light swinging to and fro as it drew near, and soon a man with a lantern pushed his way through us up to the corpse, near which two workmen placed a stretcher.

The three of them together casually turned over the body, laid it on its back, and then put the lantern close to the face, which suddenly appeared brightly lighted as if illuminated by a fire. After having examined it carefully they announced that they had never seen this man in the country. They spoke low and very slowly; in the oppressive silence, among the terrified people, their words acquired an extraordinary solemnity; it seemed to me at times as if I heard supernatural voices coming from the depths of the earth. Then they took up the body by the shoulders and feet. The cold having stiffened it, the men groaned as if they were lifting the trunk of a tree. When it was on the stretcher they crossed his hands upon his breast, and after raising his head, which was bending backwards, they set off. A man walked in front, with the lantern in his hand; we followed in silence. Presently some one said that we ought to pray. An old woman, thin and bent, began to tell her beads. Our voices made a melancholy murmur, the sound of our irregular steps became rhythmic with the steps of the bearers, the light of the lantern reflected by the ice in the ruts threw occasional gleams upon us, and when the unevenness of the road forced us to separate a little, I saw the corpse tremble on the litter. When we arrived at the village hedges, some one cried out suddenly: "Wait!"

Every one stopped. Where was the body to be taken? The question had not yet arisen, and although every one was full of pity for the unfortunate man, and felt obliged by natural feelings of humanity to pay him funeral rites as decently as possible, no one felt inclined to receive into his house the dead body of an unknown man. So no one answered, and the bearers stood ranged to the right and left of the litter waiting in vain for the order to go on. Finally, the farmer with whom we had gone to spend the evening went up and said:

" There is an empty stable at my place ; you could put him there for the time."

The procession went on. We had arrived by this time under the poplars whose branches showed up against the sky where the moon continued her slow and calm ascent.

When we got to the farm, three dogs rushed out barking. The house door opened and women appeared on the threshold. Then there was a great coming and going. Lanterns ran here and there, for the stable had to be cleared of harness and farm implements which had been put there. During this time the body remained upon the litter, near the dung-heap. At last it was carried into the stable and placed upon a heap of straw which had been arranged into a sort of slanting couch.

A woman removed the spiders' webs which hung in a corner, another brought a crucifix and laid it upon the dead man's breast, while a third wound a rosary round his hands. Then we said three Pater Nosters and three Aves. Before leaving we all gazed at him : in spite of the slight bruise on the cheek, caused by his fall, the face was calm and noble, and his great height as well as his long beard made him as majestic as a bishop.

When we were once more assembled in the house we felt first of all an unutterable sensation of well-being. Enjoying the soft warmth of the fire we looked with delight upon our neighbours' faces, which now appeared glowing with life and devoid of all mystery, and every one secretly congratulated himself that neither he nor any of those belonging to him had fallen victim to an accident which might just as well have happened to us as to this stranger who had just been found, lifeless, in the open fields. Our thoughts soon clouded. The dead man obsessed us, we felt unable to speak of anything else ; but as we did not want to enter into melancholy conversation, every one was quiet, and a painful silence reigned in the house. We heard voices in the street : people, no doubt, who had collected together in front of the farm to discuss the event. Suddenly our host turned to a servant :

" Call the dogs in," said he, " for they will howl if they are left out in the yard."

The three dogs came in one after the other with their heads hanging : they slipped in between the chairs and stretched down quietly before the stove.

But who was this man whom no one had ever seen in the country ?

Where did he come from ? What had he thought of before he died ?

" He must have suffered terribly," said some one. " Did you notice how he had scratched the soil around him ? "

" Yes," said another, " the tips of his fingers were worn to the bone."

Meanwhile the voices outside had died away ; a great stillness spread over the farm, but soon the sounds of a violin and an accordion were heard in the distance ; other people, who had gathered like us to make merry on this Christmas Eve, were making music ; they were singing too, and fragments of verses rose here and there through the silence. This cheerfulness, which at other times would certainly have added to our merriment, now only plunged us deeper into our gloomy thoughts ; besides it did not sound genuine, a kind of vague sorrow was mingled with it, it had something funereal which suited well with our melancholy reflections on the fragility of human life. . . .

" You touched the body," said Marie suddenly.

" Yes," said I.

" With that hand ? "

She took it in hers, examined it curiously, then pushed it away with disgust.

" Come," cried the farmer in a cheerful voice, " we are not here to make ourselves miserable. The man is dead ; we may think of him as much as we like, we cannot bring him to life again. Besides, people die every day. The cemeteries are full of them. . . . Somebody had just begun a story," he added, " now is the time to finish it. While we are in good health let us enjoy life, for we too shall have to die one day or another."

Again the thin old man glanced round with a mischievous look, and said, after clearing his throat :

" Once upon a time. . . ."

But the farmer's words had impressed a little old woman, the one who had led the prayers following the dead body, and she murmured in a weak and trembling voice, ignoring the narrator :

" God grant that it be in a bed, without too much suffering, in the midst of our family, and after having received the Holy Sacrament."

GEORGES GARNIER

B. 1868

JACCLARD

WHEN Monsieur Bonchamps, the notary, left his house on the opening day of the shooting season, with his legs in new gaiters, his starched smock magnifying the ampleness of his form, his brightly polished gun under his arm, the villagers ran to their doors and followed him with their eyes until he disappeared at the end of the high road. Jangette, the lad who carried the game-bag round which hung a smell of game, due to the congealed blood which had remained in it from the previous season, walked behind him, like a choir boy following the priest in a procession, respectful and proud. The dog, Bok, ran on in front, with nose in air: a strapping little spaniel, with muscular chest, and the intelligent, keen, and gentle eyes peculiar to the race, thick glossy coat, with strong mouth and a straight, well-carried tail.

The spaniel was making his first appearance in public. Monsieur Bonchamps had bought him the week before from a breeder at Bessons. After having tried him in the woods and in the open, he had paid, not without much hesitation, 500 francs for him—so high a price that he had not ventured to admit it to Madame Bonchamps.

As he passed the last house on the high road, a peasant leaning on a fence, by a hedge surrounding a vegetable garden, greeted him cunningly, taking off his cap.

"Good day, sir, there's plenty o' game. You'll have good sport, sir."

The notary seemed disagreeably surprised; he looked at him askance and answered coolly, "Good day." Evidently this man, whose name was Pierre Jacclard, had leant out there to address him as he went by, and the whole of a recent incident passed through Monsieur Bonchamps' mind.

Six months previously, he had surprised Jacclard in Halines Wood, swinging a brace of hare in his left hand and holding his loaded gun under his right arm. It was catching him redhanded, and Jacclard threw himself at the notary's feet, swearing that it should be the very last time he would ever poach. But a sportsman never forgives any one who robs him of his game. The poacher was prosecuted. Jacclard was condemned. On account of former offences he was given three months' imprisonment. This sentence had enraged him.

"I understand that the keepers nab us," he said. "They earn their living by watching the preserves, it is their business to spy on poachers; but if the sportsmen themselves interfere, it's not fair-play."

To him, poaching was a fight, a battle of wits, of cunning and care, played frankly between the keeper who watches and the thief who hides; a contest just like the one between the sportsman and the game, the keeper being armed with the law, as the sportsman is with his gun. As he left the court, he flung at Bonchamps, who watched him being led away:

"I'll be even with yer yet, Mister Notary!"

It was said in so clear, calm, and decided a voice, with the expression of a man so sure of himself, that the threat remained a long time in Monsieur Bonchamps' ears. He was on his guard for several weeks, then, as time passed, he forgot the matter. And now this morning the man as he greeted him had the same bold, quietly mocking look which the notary had seen on the day of the sentence. The poacher was known as a rogue capable on occasion of playing a nasty trick. He lived, no one knew quite how, with his father and mother, both over seventy years of age. Old Jacclard was paralysed, unable to bend his hips to sit down. He slept on a mattress on the floor, and in the morning his wife hoisted him up by planting his feet against the wall, as one raises a heavy ladder. As stiff as a board, he went off supported by two sticks as inflexible as his old legs; he mounted the steep village street as if on stilts, with bent back. It took him an hour, in fine weather, to get over the four hundred yards which separated his house from the place he was going to. Half way he stopped to take breath, and the hostess of the Black Lion, according to a charitable tradition inaugurated the day on which he became crippled, brought him out a "Jack," a big glass of gin, which he swallowed, leaning against the wall of the inn. Arriving at last at his rock, he propped himself up against the smooth vertical side: upright, unable to sit or stoop, by dint of using a hammer with a very long handle he broke stones for mending the road. He was paid by the cubic foot, and in the best days he earned as much as 1s. 6d. He did not beg, but accepted the gifts which pitying passers-by put into his hand. During this time his son, Pierre Jacclard, poached in the river. Quick as none other, he caught barbels and pike with his hands, drew up the lines he had laid over-night, threw dynamite cartridges in the richest pools, and limed the trout in the streams; when evening came he set traps for hares and rabbits; he had even caught deer.

The best hotels in Liège were secretly supplied by him, on occasion he knew how to secure the peasants' discretion by a brace of partridges or a thick-backed hare. As for the boys who surprised him, he gave them spankings, halfpence, or cigarettes according to their age. But, unlike his fellow plunderers, if by chance the keepers turned up, he never resisted. When he hoped he had not been seen, he flattened himself upon the ground, tried to slip into the underwood with the swift suppleness of an adder, with the tricks of a Red Indian disappearing into the prairie grass. Otherwise he allowed himself to be taken with a good grace, giving himself up quietly.

Well on guard against any foolish movement of anger, he never once made as if to shoot, nor attempted to intimidate "authority." He took off his cap politely; he was nabbed, so much the worse! These are the disadvantages of the trade; and he submitted to them like a sensible fellow, preferring a fine and prison to the court of assizes and penal servitude. He went in for still another kind of business: on Sundays in summer he walked as many as twenty or thirty miles to play at skittles in the village fairs; and he always came back with money, forks and spoons, and hams. He carried off all the prizes with such ease and calm that the players began to know him, and shouted out when he arrived. You should have seen him then, cordial and pleasant, joking with them, playing tricks, making faces, confusing them, entertaining the society with chatter. And all the time so merry, with such a genial and cheery manner, with his cap over one ear, shoulders and arms like a young Hercules, red lips laughing through an auburn beard, that he ended by cajoling them: he entered the game after all, and was the last to leave at nightfall, grinning, rich with spoils, and jingling his money. Strong as an ox and agile as a squirrel, he never shirked a scuffle; he fought for pleasure, delighting in it, without anger or ill-will. One day, having been on a spree with a poacher from Houdémont, and being tipsy, he said to him, "As we are such good friends, we'll fight to see who's strongest."

The other agreed, and immediately, in the inn itself, they stripped off their coats and set to. The man from Houdémont, who was looked upon as the strongest in the country, got a sound drubbing, and it took him three weeks to get over it. From that day Jacclard's reputation was made, and as he also owned a cock and two chaffinches unrivalled in the "singing competitions," this well-built and uncomfortably sly rascal began to be regarded with deference. And so this morning his former anxieties came back to the notary; his cheerful, round, clean-shaven face, with red hanging cheeks, clouded as he climbed the hill. He seemed to hear the poacher coming out of court, "I'll be even with yer yet, Mister Notary," and he felt a discomfort which quite spoilt the "opening" day. However, it was a splendid morning, real weather for sport, a bright sun in the pink sky of dawn promising victory to the shrewd sportsman. The heat would increase presently, but a good breeze was blowing from the east, passing in long waves and sweeping over the country with a healthy freshness. When he arrived at last on the upland with his dog and game-carrier, he spied a large field of beetroot and wanted to go in at once, certain of raising some partridges.

But while he slipped a couple of cartridges into his rifle he saw his dog suddenly sniff and seize in his mouth something grey-looking, which he could not quite see. He was certain, at once, that it was a poisoned bait, and in a voice trembling with fear he called out, "Here!" The dog was afraid of having this unlooked-for titbit torn from him, and swallowed it at one gulp. The result was instantaneous: he beat the air with his paws and rolled over on his back. Monsieur Bonchamps threw down his gun, ran up bravely and plunged his hand into the dog's mouth, trying to reach the piece of meat, which had perhaps stuck in the throat; he risked being badly bitten, for the dog's jaws were working in convulsions. For three minutes he struggled, the notary kneeling by him, still holding the jaws open. But Bok bit him deeply in the thumb and he was obliged to let go. While the notary stood distracted at the sight of the dying dog, the game-carrier picked something from the ground, and, stammering with fear, said:

"Look, here's another of 'em. It's strychnine."

The bait he held out was made of two pieces of ham stuck together and dusted over on the inner sides with poison. Monsieur Bonchamps looked at the piece of meat, and then when he had seen it, when the truth appeared evident and palpable, he was shaken with the fury of a wild beast; he stammered, choked with a rush of blood to his head, only grasping one thing, that his 500 franc dog had been poisoned, that this dog was dying before his eyes, would be dead in ten minutes, and that the rogue guilty of this was. . . . Suddenly Jacclard's big body appeared fifty yards off on the upland. The poacher advanced cautiously, sly and defiant; his eyes full of mischief, merry and mocking. He behaved as if he had not seen the dog, and, as if he guessed nothing of the scene, said in his taunting voice:

" Well, haven't yer got any game, sir, to . . ."

Before he could end, the notary had seized his rifle, and without replying or making a sound, mad with rage, he aimed. Jangette, the game-carrier, screamed and flung himself flat upon the ground so as not to see. But the poacher awaited the blow, turned rapidly, made a great spring in the air, and received the shot full in the back. Suddenly there was a great silence, the silence of death; the game-carrier had stopped yelling and was hiding his face in a beetroot, not daring to look. Jacclard, fallen on his face, remained immovable; the dog had done struggling; and it seemed to Monsieur Bonchamps that all of a sudden the wind had ceased to blow, the blades of grass to tremble, and the sun to shine.

He was stunned, stupefied, like a drunken man, with his rifle smoking in his hand. Only then did he realise; the revelation was appalling; he had shot at a man, bang! the blow had brought him to the earth, it had been done in a flash of lightning! and now it was irrevocable, no human power could make this thing undone. He saw himself placed between the dead dog and this man lying on his face, whose trousers were becoming covered with red spots. The frightful horror that clutched his heart developed into a mad idea of a precipitate flight, a wild rush across the fields; but seeing the man move, he went towards him, overwhelmed with horror, shaking on his legs. He said, as needing to justify this shot which made a murderer of him:

" It was you who killed my dog."

The other chuckled on the ground without even dreaming of denying it:

" Me? Your dog? Yer'll have ter prove that; when yer do, I'll kiss yer dirty——" The notary asked again, looking at the red spots growing on the seat of the trousers:

" Are you—are you——"

" I dunno. I don't care. We shall see. All I know is, I'm hurt bad enough to have yer up for trial in court"; and gleefully, fiercely, jeering:

" Well, I said I should be even with yer yet."

MAURICE DES OMBRIAUX
B. 1868

ZIRÉ BUZETTE

FOR many years Ziré Buzette had coughed his soul out, one of those hard dry coughs which seem to shake and tear the chest, and makes those who hear it say: "He has not long to live."

It was true, for a long time already Ziré Buzette had not had long to live.

Plasterer during the summer, he was seen going out early in the morning with his bucket, chalk, blue, brushes and sleeves, coughing all the time.

"Poor Ziré Buzette," said every one, "to do that sort of work with his health. It is the lime eating away his lungs. No, indeed, he has not long to live."

"That miserable Ziré Buzette, how brave he is; nothing will induce him to go into the infirmary; he persists in working, and all the while the 'blue' is poisoning his blood. He won't last long, that's certain."

And Ziré went off to make the house spick-and-span with whitewash, cough-coughing on his ladder, with a face as white as his apron. He used to whitewash kitchens and rooms too, and he was well looked after out of sympathy. For pity, and because his prices were moderate, he was ordered everywhere, and his services were bespoken long beforehand. Even in the humblest cottages a piece of meat was put in the oven for him.

"That poor Ziré Buzette," said they, "he needs strengthening. He is worn to a thread. He won't last long."

In the farms he was made to drink a mouthful of good wine every day; he needed it too, not having long to live!

Yet Ziré Buzette still went on. So much so, that on Sundays, at the fairs, on the platforms made of four casks covered with boards, near the dung-heaps, he played the fiddle for the young people to dance. Still coughing, he scratched his Stradivarius between the clarionet and the trombone.

" Poor Ziré Buzette, he must be hard up to chill himself like that, sitting out during a whole evening with such an illness. He has no strength in his blood. It makes your heart ache to see him shivering and coughing. Ah no, indeed, he won't last long."

And so at every pause he was offered either beer or gin, or even champagne, as well as large slices of cake. It was the least one could do for this miserable wreck, who had not long to live. And he was liked as a musician ; it was he who led the little orchestra, and nobody could make one dance as he could. He played with such a swing and rhythm that the clumsiest legs, and even the beginners, went of themselves. The leaders of the parties arranged with him from the beginning of the year to be quite sure that he would not fail them. How he was spoiled ! How he was " treated " ! For his sake a cask of beer was placed on the musicians' platform. Good old Ziré Buzette must be well looked after, for he would not play much longer, and who would make them dance then ?

Ziré Buzette never refused anything, drank everything, ate everything, slowly, without ever hurrying himself. To see him thus one would not have said that he had not long to live. A regular gulf was Ziré Buzette.

" It's his disease," they thought. " Ah, he needs all that to keep him up, poor fellow. Yes, one may well say so, and in spite of that he has not long to live."

He had the mild, gentle, resigned expression of the violinist.

Ziré Buzette also went to the big houses of the neighbourhood to make the young folks waltz at christenings, weddings, or engagements. And everywhere he was treated above a workman or servant. There was always something extra for him ; an interest was taken in him. He was regarded almost as a friend. I know not what else to say, except that, in fact, he was the one who had not long to live.

In winter no whitewashing was done, and there were no fairs. To earn his living, then, and occupy his leisure hours, Ziré Buzette, still coughing, plied the trade of bootmaker. He was not, truth to tell, remarkably capable at this profession, I had almost said this art, but work never failed him. People ordered slippers from him. He mounted those which had been embroidered or woven by housewives or girls for petted husbands or to fascinate lovers. He also made the children's boots.

" Poor Ziré Buzette! Goodness, he must live. It is a charity, a duty. He will not last long."

Weakly, sickly, perpetually coughing, Ziré Buzette, who had not long to live, had nevertheless already buried two wives. His first had married him out of pity, it was said.

" Let us risk it, one might as well," she had thought; " it does not bind one to much. He will not last long."

She died of a chill.

The second had married him for his modest hoard.

" It is a good business," she speculated. " I have nothing, and as he will not last long, I shall inherit from him, and can find whom I like after him."

She died.

And now the rumour spread through the village that he was going to be married again, for the third time, to a girl who was only twenty years of age.

" Did you ever hear of such a thing?" said the gossips. " He will do for himself, poor Ziré Buzette, and he has not long to live in any case."

" There is another who has an eye on his house and orchard," said others. " What a shamefaced thing! She knows well enough that he won't last long."

" After all, why shouldn't he, if he likes? We should do the same thing in his place. He has no time to lose, for he won't last long."

Ziré Buzette had his little house and piece of ground surrounded by the property of the Brothers Blairaux, the richest people in the village. One was mayor, another farmer, the third treasurer of the Charity Organisation, and all three were bachelors. Big robust fellows, with powerful limbs, strong and wiry as a whip handle, they looked as if they were made to live a hundred years. They owned over a hundred acres of land, and bought more every year. It was said that half the village belonged to them. The farm, field, garden and orchard made a splendid place. It was the finest property in the village. It had cost them a great deal of money and trouble. They had had to buy a bit of land from one, a ruined cottage from another, a hut here, a bake-house there, pulling down, filling up, levelling; in order that the estate should be complete and the whole perfect, they only needed Ziré Buzette's cottage.

" He won't last long," they said to themselves. " We shall have it for nothing at his death."

But their wish finally became stronger than their reason. They wanted to have the estate at once, as soon as possible, for who knows if, after Ziré's death, his heirs will not make difficulties and, in the circumstances, exorbitant demands ?

After all sorts of advances, manœuvres, with numerous peasants' tricks, they entered into negotiations with the plasterer. But their cunning plans were of no use, Ziré Buzette would not hear of it. He shook his head with its pale face, and, coughing, said :

" Ask me anything, sirs ; but not to leave the house of my grandfathers. You know I have not long to live. Be patient. I won't go anywhere else for the short time that is left me. I will die in the house where I was born and where all my people have died."

He met the pressing entreaties of his neighbours with a gentle and polite obstinacy. There was nothing to be done. He remained resolute. They tried frightening him with threats. In vain. They withdrew their custom, and the Mayor engaged another musician for the village fair. Ziré Buzette felt wounded by this blow ; he coughed more than ever. All the peasants took his part ; all the village youth deserted the official dance and paid for Ziré Buzette's orchestra themselves. The first county magistrate was roundly abused.

" Treat a poor fellow, who has not long to live, in that way ! You must be heartless ! "

There was quite a hubbub. The incident was used against the Burgomaster at the elections, and it was suggested that Ziré Buzette should be among the candidates. He was sure to be elected, and as he had not long to live he would not give any trouble. But he had the good sense to refuse.

The Blairaux, to avoid danger, made peace with him. They increased their offers. But in spite of these being tempting, Ziré answered, still coughing :

" No, sirs, a house like mine is worth 8 per cent. At the price you offer I should lose . . . and, besides, I want to die in my father's house."

" Sell it to us and you shall keep the use of it during your lifetime," said the collector of the Charity Organisation, who thought that Ziré Buzette would not last long. The idea pleased the plasterer. They discussed the matter and finally agreed. Ziré Buzette was to retain the use of his cottage until his death, and the Blairaux would pay the rent once or twice at most, for Ziré Buzette would not last long.

And the whole village said :

" Those Blairaux are fine foxes. You don't catch them napping. They've bought Ziré Buzette's place for an old song, for he won't last long."

Every year Ziré Buzette got his rent. Each time the Blairaux rubbed their hands together, saying to themselves that they had paid the last annuity.

The Mayor died without having seen the orchard joined to his land. The two brothers looked glum when Ziré Buzette called for his due.

The farmer died, also without annexing the fiddler's little domain, and Ziré, who had not long to live, continued, still coughing, to draw his rent. The collector of the Charity Organisation threatened ruin to Ziré, who, everlasting in his state of dilapidation, went on coughing, and getting the money. He had already pocketed two or three times the value of his field. But in the village they continued to say :

" This Blairaux is a lucky fellow. He has got Ziré Buzette's house for nothing, for the poor fellow will not last long."

A mad desire to strangle the plasterer made his fingers itch every time he had to hand over the precious gold pieces. Unable to control himself he could not help saying :

" Ah, there you are. Are you never going to die ? "

" Monsieur Blairaux, how can you say such a thing to a poor man like me, who has not long to live ? " answered Ziré, pitiful and coughing.

He buried the third Blairaux and died, over a hundred years old. For over three-quarters of a century he had not had long to live.

LOUIS DELATTRE

B. 1870

THE NEWS

AT the beginning of April the weather changed, and in one night spring opened like a primrose in the wood.

Monsieur Quât, in his little house on the town walls, was very glad of it. He told his servant to go to the end of the garden, climb on to the big stone at the foot of the wall, and peep over to see if the fine weather had really come back.

It had. The servant vowed, in a voice as clear as her blue eyes and blonde hair, that the wind would remain in the fair quarter of the sky. And she moistened her lips.

Monsieur Quât was delighted to hear it, and he believed her. He had only to make the sign which she expected, and with her large, red, affectionate hands she brought him the clothes suitable for such a day. The trousers of the colour of café-au-lait—goat's milk which makes the coffee yellower—the black cutaway coat, with its perfectly darned moth-eaten places, the Indian silk comforter with a pattern of gherkins, the hat, brightened by a drop of oil, and the good solid stick, a sapling oak with ivory knob.

Monsieur Quât thus tinkered up, the servant took his arm to help him down the front steps, and led him to the middle of the road. He felt his feet while she, steadying him with one hand in the back, pushed a pebble out of his way with her sabot. "There we are!" she said. "I'm off," he answered, and bending forward, he started.

He walked with short steps, tapping the ground with his heels. His outstretched neck kept his head high, which nodded "Yes" all the time. For a long time already if Monsieur Quât wished to say "No" he has had to do so with great energy, for his neck trembles, and even so, he sometimes signs "No" awry.

To-day his head's "Yes, yes" quickened. His eyes twinkled in their nest of wrinkles and grey hair. The keen air moistened them with cold tears which made them look like some beautiful old jewels. "Yes, yes, yes . . ." and he gazed at the freshly cleaned blue of the sky, as if he drew from it something subtle which others could not see;

especially over there, between the rounded hills of Blanche Maison and Rond Chêne, where the silky air shimmers with such bright gaiety. His stick tapped the ground and Monsieur Quât went on and on.

A big drop trembled at the end of his nose. On the Place du Trieu where he arrived, the old man suddenly acquired the aspect of a child delighting in the things which belong to the whole world—without reserve or shame.

" Hullo, Father Quât," cries the wheelwright working on the road in front of his shop. He holds his pipe in one hand and in the other the adze with which he was just chipping pieces off some post. He is flushed with pleasure and with working in the wind.

" So there you are, the fine weather has come again ! "

" April air, my boy ; it is the April air," cries Monsieur Quât at the top of his voice without pausing, smiling, sniffing, tapping the ground with his stick.

" Good morning ! Good morning ! "

And on he goes. Now he is opposite the blacksmith's forge. The bellows roar ; the hammer strikes the red-hot iron rod with a hurried sound. The blacksmith cannot stop. Still, he laughs as he sees Monsieur Quât, only in little jerks, because he is hitting hard.

" Good day, Father Quât! Winter is over. Ha! ha! I know where the fine weather is leading you. Hey ! the good for nothing ! "

" Ha ! ha ! ha ! " and the old pink hoary head goes on. " Yes, yes, yes. . . ."

At the end of the square, in the little inn with a bunch of holly hanging over the door as a sign, Monsieur Quât is in the house of his sweetheart ! He is eighty years old, but she is not yet twenty. From the window of her house where she was sewing, she had seen him coming. She opens the door to him as he climbs the step. Held between her teeth some bits of cotton flutter in the wind, like spiders' threads caught on a hedge. Her face is serious and beautiful. The pleasure of seeing Monsieur Quât, absent during the whole winter, illuminated it frankly. She leads him to the low chair close to the dogs, settles him against the iron stove, and pours him out in a thick crystal glass, which could be filled by a finger's length, a drop of gin. Then she goes on with her sewing.

Gently, without haste, she tells him the village news which had not travelled as far as Monsieur Quât's house ; she tells him of those who have died and of those who have been born.

" Dear, dear ! . . . The things that happen . . . in my time . . ."

But Monsieur Quât lets his sentence drop halfway, tired with stringing so many words together. And then, he is so happy !

The time passes, and inside the house, as the pale gold of the sun rises along the walls, the smell of the simmering soup at the point of perfection is spread abroad. Monsieur Quât rises.

" You are going ? " asks the innkeeper.

She goes to the mantelpiece and from between the crucifix and the copper pot of sulphur matches she takes a folded newspaper, yellow, dirty, and worn at the edges.

" Take the news with you. You can read it at your leisure."

" Thank you," says Monsieur Quât. " Yes, yes. I will bring it back next week when I have finished."

He has started off again. By dint of little steps with his heels and taps with his stick on the ground, and of doing " Yes, yes," he has arrived home. He has eaten his soup out of his little plate decorated with faded flowers, with his tin spoon, worn on one side. Seated in his cane armchair, armed with his magnifying glass whose lens is so scratched that it seems to be covered with spiders' webs, he spells out the news. There is a great deal. What things ! . . . But soon the light is no longer bright enough. Monsieur Quât folds up the newspaper exactly in the old creases. He will read on, to-morrow.

" The things that happen ! " say his lips. While his gentle little, cheerful, faded soul murmurs like a suppressed song, " And what is the use of it all ? "

And yet he will go on reading the gazette to the end. And when he has finished, he will carry the paper carefully back to the inn on the market-place. So that after him, this summer, or next winter, in the village which sleeps like a lilac spread open in the sun, another inquisitive person may still learn the news of the world—the great world, yonder, far away.

He who has nuts, cracks them ;
He who has none, lacks them.

BLANCHE ROUSSEAU
(MADAME BELVAL)
B. 1875.

THE LITTLE HOUSE IN THE MIDST OF THE WOODS

GOTTE and Nanette lived in a little house in the woods. Gotte was young; Nanette was old.

" Alas, alas," said Nanette, " what will become of Gotte when I die ? "

" I will look after her," said Pierre. And that was why, on the day on which they carried Nanette to the grave, he went to look for Gotte and said to her, " Will you be my wife ? "

" Wait a little," said Gotte, " until I have made my dresses. First the black dress and then the white dress. We will see about it next spring." And she worked away busily at the black dress.

In Gotte's little house everything was neat, quiet, and poor. Nanette's stool in the corner by the hearth, the bread bin, the bed, and the little cupboard with its starched curtains. As for ornaments, there was a bunch of anemones or buttercups in a glass of water, and in winter the pot of ivy in the corner of the window-sill. We must not forget that there was also, on the chimney-piece, a sacred picture, and on the walls, a cuckoo clock and two everlasting flowers dried, in the form of a cross, on grey cardboard neatly framed. Then there was the work-basket, with the thimble, scissors, and cotton, and the little rattling case full of needles, for Gotte earned her living by sewing.

She had two friends, Pierre who gave her love, and her cat Jude who gave her friendship. Pierre was young and strong: his stroke felled the oaks, and he lifted Gotte in one arm, as easily as a child can rob a nest.

Jude, old and bald, could only miaow and rub himself against Gotte's skirts, or sit on his tail beside her while his big sea-green eyes, full of little floating seaweeds, watched her thoughtfully. But at night he slept on Gotte's feet. And every one knew him to be a real devil, all teeth and claws, if one wished to touch his mistress.

One day, as Gotte was sewing at the window, a knight passed, magnificently attired, and followed by a great pack of hounds. He looked at Gotte, and seeing her so charming, asked her name.

" I am called Gotte," she answered, blushing.

" Gotte," said the knight, " do you know that you are lovely ? "

" I have no mirror," said Gotte.

" Take mine," said the splendid knight, and he gave her his silver mirror, and Gotte saw that she was fair.

Next day he came again.

" Gotte," said he to her, " would you not like to be a princess ? "

" You are mocking me," said Gotte, laughing.

But at night she asked herself seriously :

" Would I not like to be a princess ? "

" It rests with you to become one," said the knight on the following day. And he bore Gotte off upon his steed. When Pierre came back to the little house he found it deserted, the fire dead, and Jude tied to the bread bin by a piece of string. And thus did Gotte become a princess.

She lived in a magnificent palace and had people to wait upon her, and costly dresses and jewels. But she did not sleep at night, for a voice cried in the park from nightfall until dawn. " I know that voice," thought Gotte. And she drew the sheets over her face, but she did not sleep. Tired with sleeplessness she rose, hid her lamp behind her hand, and went and looked through the curtains. And she saw Pierre wandering in the park, lamenting. The next day she called her husband and said to him :

" A man disturbs me, crying in the park at night. Give orders, I entreat you, to have him driven from the country."

And Pierre was driven from the country.

But next night other cries sounded in the park. And it was Jude who wandered, lamenting. Therefore the princess said to her husband:

" A cat wanders at night in the park and disturbs me. Give orders, I entreat you, to have it drowned."

And Jude was drowned in the pond.

But next night the princess, slumbering, heard a voice calling in her dreams. And the voice said, "I am the thimble; I am the thimble." And another voice cried out at the same time, " I am the needle ; I am the needle." And other voices cried out all together, " I am Nanette's stool. . . ." " I am the window. . . ." and " I am the bin!" " Gotte! Gotte! do you hear us ? "

Then Gotte rose up without a sound. She went out in the dark night and set light to a bundle of wood before the door of the little house in the woods. But at the same time she burnt a swallow's nest which hung under the eaves, and this brings ill luck, as every one knows.

And that was why Gotte could not sleep the following night because of a swallow which flew around her windows crying for its young ones.

They tried to kill it too, but no arrow could reach it.

"My fortune to any one who will kill the swallow," cried Gotte. But it was no use promising fortunes, no one could kill it. And thus Gotte lost her sleep and withered miserably at the side of a prince in a splendid castle.

SWISS

SOLOMON GESSNER

1730–1788

JEALOUSY[1]

THE most odious of all passions is jealousy; it is the most poisonous reptile that can inhabit our bosom. This Alexis found to his cost. He was in love with Daphne and she loved him. Both were handsome: he manly and brown, she white and innocent as the lily opening its petals to the first rosy kiss of the dawn. They had plighted their troth of eternal love, and Venus and the gods of love seemed to have filled their cup of happiness to the brim. Alexis' father had just recovered from a long and painful illness, and calling his son to his side said:

"Dear son, I have taken a vow to sacrifice six sheep to the goddess of health. Go and take them to her temple!"

It was two long days' journey to the temple of the goddess; but Alexis took leave of his sweetheart with tears in his eyes, as if he was going on a long sea-voyage, and sorrowfully he drove the sheep along before him. Thus going on his long way sighing, sighing like the breeze in the willow trees that line the brook, he passed the rich fields and meadows without seeing them. The finest views lay stretched before him and remained unnoticed. He only felt his love, he only saw his sweetheart; saw her in her cottage, saw her sitting by the spring in the shadow of the great rock, heard her call his name—and still he sighed. Thus he walked on behind his sheep, vexed because they were not as fleet as the deer, and finally arrived at the temple.

The sheep were slaughtered, the sacrifice made; on the wings of his love he hastened back towards his home. In a wooded glade, however, a thorn entered the sole of his foot, and his pain was so great

[1] The most noteworthy imaginative literature of Switzerland has been written in the German tongue, and indeed three of the following four stories are the work of authors usually classed among German writers, though they were of Swiss origin. In the German-speaking part of Switzerland a certain amount of vernacular literature has been produced in the German dialect known as "Swiss," but it is peculiarly local in its interest. Just as Gessner, Keller, and Meyer are usually classed with German authors, so is Edouard Rod included among the French, but it has seemed desirable to group them here in accordance with our territorial plan as the representatives of Switzerland in the art of the Short Story.—ED.

that he was hardly able to reach a hut that was lying close by. A kind old couple received him and soon treated his wound with healing herbs. "How unhappy I am," he kept on saying, sighing the while and counting every hour ; each minute seemed to him like a long winter's night, and to add to his misery some unkind goddess planted in his heart the seeds of jealousy. "Ye gods! What a thought!" he murmured to himself, looking around anxiously. "Daphne might be unfaithful! Ugly thought! But girls will be girls, and Daphne is beautiful. Who can look upon her without desiring her? And Daphis her neighbour has long desired her! And he is a fine fellow; who could hear him sing and remain unmoved? Who can play the flute as he plays it? His cottage stands close to Daphne's, and the space that divides them is but small. Oh leave me, leave me, wicked thoughts!"

But deeper and deeper this jealousy sank its root in his mind—torturing him by day and night. Often at night in his dreams and by day in his imagination he saw his sweetheart making her way to the spring in the shade of the trees to meet Daphis, who sang to her of his great love. He saw her gazing languishingly into his eyes and her bosom rising and falling in happy agitation. Or he saw his beloved resting in the soft shadows of the lofty trees asleep, saw Daphis stealthily approaching, gliding gently nearer and fixing his scorching gaze upon her every beauty. He bends over her, kisses her hand, and she doesn't wake. He kisses her cheeks, he kisses her lips—" And she doesn't wake!" he cries out at the top of his voice. "Oh miserable fellow that I am! What fearful pictures my brain creates! Why must I keep on thinking these dreadful thoughts, why torture myself with these fancies that are an offence against her innocence?"

Already he had lain there six days and his wound was still not quite healed. In vain the old couple begged him to delay. He could wait no longer, and embracing his benefactors and thanking them fervently he resumed his journey, travelling as fast as his wound would let him. Darkness began to fall when at last he came in sight of his loved one's cottage, and the full moon rose behind the wooded upland. "Ha, away with you, you ugly, torturing dreams! There my love awaits me, and to-night I shall weep with joy and hold her in my arms!" And saying this he hurried on. From under the rose-covered walk that led up to her gate he saw her slowly emerging. "Yes, it is she! Yes, it is Daphne, her slender lovely figure, her graceful walk, her snow-white dress! It is she, ye gods! But where is she going so late in the evening? It is dangerous for young girls to go out into the open fields so late at night. But perhaps she is coming out in the hope of meeting me?" he told himself. But there—a figure darts out from the covered walk behind her, runs to her side, and laughingly she takes his hands into hers. He hands her a basket of flowers, which with a graceful bow she hangs on her arm; and now they walk away from the cottage in the pale light of the full moon.

Terror-stricken, Alexis stands motionless, trembling from head to toe. "What do I see! It was only too true then, too true all that I feared; a compassionate goddess prepared me for this shock. Ah! poor wretch that I am, where, oh where is the goddess who warned me of this misfortune! Come to my aid now and avenge me; yes, avenge this infidelity, strike down these miserable beings and then let me die!"

Arm in arm the while that girlish figure and the youth went on their way in the moonlight towards the myrtle-grove where the little shrine of Venus stood, talking happily as they sauntered along.

"They are going into those myrtle-groves!" Alexis said to himself wrathfully, "into those shadows where she has so often pledged me her love! Now they are entering the wood. Ah! I have lost sight of them, and they, they will be sitting under yonder trees. But no, here they are again, I can see her white dress in the moonlight gleaming through the shrubs and the trunks. They have stopped; here is a fine open space and soft beautiful grass. Faithless ones! Yes, sit down there, opposite the watching moon, and there protest to one another your dishonourable and degrading passion. May all the devils persecute you! But what is this? The song of the nightingale and the cooing of the doves! How is it possible, when these low creatures sit there in their midst? They are moving on; yes, they are going to the temple of Venus; I shall go after them and listen, and spy on them."

With these words he made his way towards the grove, keeping carefully in the shadows. Nearer and nearer the couple in front of him drew to the temple whose white marble pillars, gleaming in the moonlight, reached high into the dark sky. "What, they dare to enter! Will the goddess of love bless this black outrage against her holiest vows?" Thus he spoke to himself as the girl, the basket of flowers still on her arm, ascended the steps and slowly made her way in between the stately pillars, while the youth, leaning against one of them, appeared to gaze after her lovingly. In the shadow of the temple Alexis approached closer and pulled himself up on to the pillared verandah. Mad with rage and despair he crept along in the shadow of one of the great pillars, and hugging it closely saw Daphne walking up to the statue of Venus, who, standing there in the rays of the moon in marble of milky whiteness, seems to shrink back in her holiness from the astonished gaze of the mortals who come to sacrifice at her shrine. Daphne sank on her knees before the goddess, deposited the wreaths and flowers at the foot of the pedestal, and sobbing loudly began in great misery to pray: " Listen to my prayers and accept the wreaths and flowers which I sacrifice at your shrine. The evening dew on them is mingled with my tears! Ah! Already six days have passed since Alexis left me! Oh, good and sweet goddess! Guide him back to my arms unhurt! Guard and watch over him on his way, and send him back to me as devoted and loving a sweetheart as he left me!"

In wonder Alexis listened to her prayers, then his eyes travelled to where the youth was standing, on whose face just then the rays of the full moon fell. Now he sees—it is Daphne's brother; he had accompanied her on her nightly pilgrimage to the temple, thinking it not wise to let so young a girl go there alone.

Alexis came out from behind the pillar. Daphne was overwhelmed with joy at seeing him, and he was full of gladness and shame. They embraced one another and then sank down in thankfulness before the goddess and prayed.

SWISS GOTTFRIED KELLER

1819–1890

A PRINCE IN DISGUISE

ON a dismal November day a poor devil of a tailor was walking along the country road to Goldach, a little wealthy town but a few miles from Seldwyla. The tailor carried nothing in his pocket but his thimble, which in lieu of coin he was incessantly twirling between his fingers; it was so cold that he was obliged to keep his hands in the pockets of his trousers, and his fingers began to ache smartly, what with this eternal twirling and twisting. He had lost his pay and his work at the same time, because some head tailor at Seldwyla had failed, and there was nothing for it but to take to the road. A couple of snowflakes that had blown into his mouth were the only breakfast he had had, and there was as little prospect of any dinner. Begging was made difficult, ay, seemed quite out of the question; because over his black Sunday suit, which was the only one he had, he wore an ample dark grey mantle faced with black velvet, which gave its wearer a noble and romantic exterior, the more so as his long black hair and little moustache were well cared for, and he was the happy possessor of pale, regular features.

Attire of the sort described had become a necessity to him, and he indulged in it with no evil or deceitful purpose; he was quite contented when he was not interfered with and left in peace to do his work, but he would sooner have starved than give up his mantle and Polish fur-cap, which he managed to wear with an inimitable grace.

For this reason he could work only in good-sized towns, where he did not become too conspicuous; when on the road and without savings he was in a sorry enough plight. Did he approach a house, he was looked at with surprise and curiosity, and there was nothing farther from the thoughts of the inhabitants than that he would beg; so the words died on his lips, the more so as he was not a possessor of many words, and he became in truth a martyr of his mantle, and suffered hunger as dark and dismal as the latter's velvet lining.

As he was wearily ascending a rise of ground he came upon a new and comfortable carriage, which a gentleman's coachman had fetched from Basle for his master, a foreign count who was awaiting it somewhere in Switzerland on an old estate he had bought or leased. The carriage was designed for travelling, and had all sorts of arrangements to hold luggage, so that it seemed to be heavily loaded, although it was empty. The coachman was walking by his horses on account of the steepness of the road. When he reached the top of the hill he got up on the box again, and asked the tailor if he would not have a ride; for it was beginning to rain, and he saw at a glance that the poor fellow was faintly and sorrowfully trudging along.

He gratefully and humbly accepted the offer, whereupon the carriage took him at a rapid pace over the rest of the road, so that in one short hour they passed, with a hollow, thundering sound, through the town gate of Goldach. Before the best hotel, called Zur Woge, the elegant turn-out stopped, and at once the groom pulled the bell violently, so that the wire nearly broke. Down came the host and his people and pulled open the carriage door; the children and neighbours came crowding about the splendid carriage, full of curiosity to see what kernel could be contained in this marvellous shell, and when the dumbfounded tailor came forth in his mantle, pale and handsome, gazing pensively upon the ground, he seemed to them to be a mysterious prince or count at the very least. The space between the carriage and the door of the hotel was narrow, and the rest of the pavement pretty well blocked by the curious crowd. It may have been due to a certain lack of presence of mind, or possibly of courage, that he did not break through the rabble and simply go on his way; he did not, but weakly allowed himself to be escorted into the house and upstairs, and did not become fully conscious of his new and remarkable position until he found himself in a comfortable dining-room, and his portentous mantle was being officiously removed.

"The gentleman wishes to dine?" said a voice. "Dinner will be served at once; it is nearly ready."

Without waiting for a reply the host rushed for the kitchen, and cried: "In the name of three devils! now we have nothing but beef and a mutton joint! I dare not cut the partridge-pie, because that was ordered for the gentlemen coming this evening. *Isn't* this a shame? The only day when we don't expect any such person, and when there is nothing in the house, so fine a gentleman must turn up! And the coachman has a coat-of-arms on his buttons, and the carriage is good enough for a duke! And the young man is so grand that he doesn't so much as open his mouth!" And the phlegmatic cook said:

"Well there is nothing to grumble about, sir. Of course he shall have the partridge-pie; he won't eat it up! We'll serve it on small plates for the gentlemen this evening. We can get out six platefuls!"

"Six platefuls? You must forget that the gentlemen are accustomed to eat their fill at *my* hotel!" answered the host; but the cook looked unmoved, and continued: "And so they shall! We must send for half-a-dozen of cutlets; we need them for the stranger as it is; and what he leaves I'll cut up into little squares and mix it in the pie. Just leave all that to me!"

But the honest host said, with a serious mien, "Cook, I have told you before that such things cannot be in this town and in this house! I wish to be respectable and honourable, and can afford to be so."

"Ye saints!" cried the cook, "one must do the best one can! Here are two snipes that I bought from the hunter this minute; I'll put them in the pie. A partridge-pie adulterated with snipe will be good enough for your gluttons! And then there are some trout; the biggest I threw into the water as that remarkable carriage came to the door; and there is some soup in that little pan. So then we have fish, beef, cutlets with vegetables, the joint, and the pie. Just give me the keys now, so that I can get out the sweetmeats and the dessert! And, by the way, you might do me the honour, sir, to entrust the key to me once for all, so that I wouldn't have to run after you for it and get into awful straits."

"Good woman, you must not bear me a grudge for that. I promised my wife on her deathbed never to give the key out of my hands, so it's a matter of principle, not of mistrust. Here are the cucumbers, and here are the cherries; here are the pears, and here the apricots; but this old, stale pastry cannot be used. Quick! send Lise to the pastry-cook's to get fresh cakes, three dishes full, and if he has a good tart he may send it also."

"Dear me, sir! you can't put all that on one gentleman's bill. It will cost you more than it is worth!"

"Never mind that. It's all for the honour! It won't kill me, and when a grand swell like that passes through our town he shall be able to say he dined well, though he was not expected, and it was in winter! I won't have it said of me as they say of the hosts of Seldwyla, that they eat everything good themselves and leave the bones for their customers. Go ahead, then, all of you, and do your best!"

. . . .

Without further delay he was asked to table, a chair was placed for him, and as the fragrant odour of the savoury soup, the like of which he had not smelled for many a day, robbed him completely of his will, he sat down in God's name and at once dipped his heavy spoon into the golden brown liquid. In deep silence did he refresh his wearied spirits, and he was waited upon in respectfully hushed awe.

When he had emptied his plate, and the host saw how he had relished it, he encouraged him politely to have another spoonful; it would do him good, the weather being so inclement. Now the trout was served adorned with greens, and the host helped him to a generous piece. But the tailor, tormented by anxiety, did not venture in his shyness boldly to use his knife, but coyly and shamefacedly dabbed at it with his fork. The cook, who was watching behind the door to see the grand gentleman, noticed it, and she said to her subordinates, "Praised be our Lord Jesus Christ! There is one who knows how to eat a fine fish, as he should; he does not saw the delicate thing with his knife as if he were butchering a calf. That is a person of quality. I'd swear to that if it were not wicked! And how handsome and sad he is! There isn't a doubt of it, he is in love with some grand lady whom they won't let him have. Ah yes, grand people have their troubles as well as others!" Meanwhile the host, seeing that his guest left his glass untouched, said deferentially, "My table wine is not to your honour's taste. Permit me to bring you a glass of good Bordeaux, which I can greatly recommend."

And then and there did the tailor commit his first spontaneous fault by obediently saying yes instead of no; and thereupon did the landlord of the Woge betake himself in person to his cellar to pick out a choice bottle; for he was greatly concerned to have it said that there was something first-class to be had in the place. When his guest, suffering under the torments of an evil conscience, ventured only to sip faint-heartedly of the contents of his glass, the host ran exulting into the kitchen, smacked his tongue, and cried: "The devil take me, there's one to the manner born; there's a judge of good wine for you. He takes it on his tongue as one would lay a ducat on the gold scales!" So dinner took its course, very slowly indeed, for the poor tailor ate and drank very coyly and undecidedly; and the host, to give him time, left everything on the table for longer than ordinary. For all that, what the guest had eaten up to this time was not worth speaking of; but now his hunger, which was constantly being tempted in so dangerous a manner, began to conquer his terror, and when the partridge-pie appeared the mood of the tailor suddenly changed, and one fixed thought began to master him. "Things are as they are," he said to himself, warmed and incited by a new glass of wine. "I were a fool now if I should bear the brunt of the coming shame and persecution without having eaten my fill for it! So look to it while it is time. This is likely to be the last dish; I will devote myself to this, come what may! What I once have in my stomach no king can rob me of!"

No sooner said than done. With the boldness of despair he attacked the savoury pie, with no thought of stopping, so that in less than five minutes it was half gone, and the cause of the gentlemen who had ordered it was sadly in want of support. Meat, mushrooms, balls, crust, and top he swallowed without distinction, only anxious to bag it all before a cruel destiny should overtake him. He drank his wine in a hearty draught, and put enormous bits of bread into his mouth; in short, it was a lively innings, as when before a storm the hay from the near meadow is cast into the barn with a pitch-fork. Again the host ran to the kitchen and cried: "Look, he is eating up the pie, while he scarcely touched the roast! And the Bordeaux he drinks by glassfuls!"

"Let him," said the cook. "He knows a partridge when he sees it! If he were a common fellow, he would have gorged on the roast!"

Meanwhile the coachman had had his horses fed, had eaten a substantial meal himself in the servants' room, and as he was in haste, he had ordered his horses to be harnessed again. The menials could not resist asking him, before it was too late, who his master was and what was his name. The coachman, a jolly and sly fellow, said, "Has he not told you himself?" "No," they said; and he replied, "It is no wonder. He doesn't have much to say from morning till night. Well, he is Count Strapinsky! He is going to stay here all day, perhaps longer, for he told me to take the carriage home."

He perpetrated this vicious joke to take revenge on the tailor, who had, as he thought, without giving him a word of thanks for his kindness, gone into the hotel to play the false *rôle* of a gentleman. Carrying his waggishness still further, he got up on his box without so much as asking what there was to pay for himself and his horses, cracked his whip, and drove out of town, no one interfering, for it was all put down on the bill of our friend the tailor.

KONRAD FERDINAND MEYER SWISS
1825–1898

PLAUTUS IN A NUNNERY

AT the end of a hot summer's day a group of cultured Florentines had gathered round Cosmos Medici, the "father of the fatherland," in front of a casino in the Medician Gardens to enjoy the cool evening air. Above them, in wondrously changing hues, was the clearest of evening skies.

Amongst the company, quietly drinking and chatting, the finely-chiselled features of a white-haired head stood out; on his eloquent lips seemed to hang the attention of all the company, yet the expression of the intelligent, mobile face was singularly mixed; over the gay forehead and the laughing mouth lay the shadow of a great sorrow.

"My dear Poggio," began Cosmos Medici, the intellect of the man showing in the well-set eyes in his ugly face, "the other day I looked again through your *Liber Facetiarum*, and though I know it all by heart, I enjoyed at least once more the admirable turning of your clever and happy phrases; it has since occurred to me that surely there must be still some story that your critical mind had excluded from this volume as being either too salacious or not salacious enough for its pages. Think, friend, and give us, who understand the slightest allusions and would forgive the coarsest joke, a 'Facetia inedita'; and then, talking and sipping your wine, you will forget your troubles!"

The new sorrow to which Cosmos referred, as something known to all, had fallen on the aged Poggio Bracciolini—now Secretary to the Florentine Republic, and formerly Secretary in turn to five Popes—at the hands of one of his clever and good-for-nothing sons. This unhappy youth had committed an offence akin to robbery and theft, and had brought not only misery, but also heavy monetary loss on his already deeply suffering old father.

"Those stories that would amuse you, Cosmos," replied Poggio, "I hardly now like to recall. Innocent of wrong as they were in my youth, they yet seem to me to testify to my then lack of balance and seriousness, and they may have some bearing on the results now showing so disastrously in my sons!"

"Don't moralise, Poggio!" interrupted one of the younger ones, "you who gave back to the world the Comedies of Plautus!"

"Thank you for your reminder, Romolo! Yes, thank you, for let the finding of Plautus be the Facetia with which I will amuse you to-night!"

"My Facetia," said Poggio, aping the style of the inevitable introduction to the Italian novel of the time, "concerns two crosses, a light one and a heavy one, and two barbarian nuns, a novice and an abbess."

"Great! Poggio," interrupted a neighbour, "the same style of Germanic vestals, I hope, as you mention in your *Letters of Travel*, the finest thing you ever wrote!"

"Oh, then I exaggerated, friends, knowing your tastes; however, here goes, and I venture you'll enjoy my barbarian females! Those days, dear Cosmos, when we struck the surplus heads off our holy Church, then distorted to a Lernæan Serpent, found me attending the Council of Constance. My spare time I divided between pondering the wretched composition of the Council—piety, cleverness, science, cunning, buffoonery—with all its attendant unchaste company mixed up together—and my search for old manuscripts in the surrounding convents. Various scents and clues led me to believe that in a neighbouring nunnery a Plautus lay hidden—think of it, friends—a Plautus, at a time when only a few scraps of that great Roman comic writer were known to the world! For nights I lay awake thinking of a way to secure this jewel. If only I had left everything and there and then had gone after this treasure instead of attending to the election of Pope Otto Colonna!

"Thus it happened that one of my followers—a blundering ass, and unfortunately one of our countrymen—to whom in my excitement I had given an inkling of the great find, had got there before me, and worse still, without getting the classic, *per fas et nefas*, had only succeeded in arousing the suspicion of the abbess. At last, in spite of the election of his Holiness, I got away, and hiring a sturdy mule and drover—one Anselino de Spiuga—I set out. Anselino, who, to my great surprise, had accepted my first small offer for his services, showed as we proceeded on our way a gradually increasing fit of depression, which in my happiness I laid myself out to dispel. I only partially succeeded, but I culled from him the following strange love-story.

"Coming to Constance some time back in the train of his Bishop he had later found work as a carpenter, and was employed in the building of an additional wing to a neighbouring convent. Here he got to know a maid named Gertrude who lived in the vicinity, and as the two spent much time in each other's company they mutually fell in love—'in all honour and chastity,' he added, 'for she is a good girl.' Suddenly she had given him up without apparent reason, and without telling him why, and to-morrow she was to take the veil—and now I knew why he had hired himself to me as drover for such a small sum; he was going to attend the ceremony, to see the girl for the last time, and to make sure with his own eyes how this maiden who had loved him, and who, strange to say, had expressed a deep abhorrence of the nunnery, a fear almost, was going to become a nun.

"He relapsed again into his brooding silence and asked to be left behind as soon as the convent came into view amongst the vineyards in the distance. On my inquiring about the abbess he told me that she was a nasty little woman, but a wonderful administrator, who had rehabilitated the convent, and whom the people called 'Brigittchen von Trogen.'

"I continued on my way, and arriving at the convent witnessed a queer performance. Some large unwieldy object, which I afterwards saw was a gruesome black cross of ancient make, was being raised now and again by one or the other of the large company assembled there. It was a motley crowd; not one man seemed able to lift the heavy cross, and every time it had been raised it would have come crashing down had not other helping hands supported it. Yells of vulgar laughter resounded when these attempts failed, and the crowd of peasants, townsfolk, pedlars, gipsies and wandering players who had been attracted here from Constance to witness the ceremony, grew bolder and rowdier as the huge wooden mugs filled with convent wine were handed round, passing from mouth to mouth. A queer figure the barbarian abbess made on the newly-cut grass; she skipped in and out of the throng full of glee—and as it seemed to me also full of her convent wine—shrieking and gesticulating wildly. 'Not one of you can lift this cross of our sainted Duchess Amalaswinta, yet to-morrow,' she said with a grin, 'Sister Gertrude will lift it up like a feather. Good people, this wonder has been performed for a thousand years and still it goes on!' I was sure now that this good abbess had imbibed her wine too freely on that bright summer's day.

"While I was lost in thought, trying to put two and two together, Anselino's story and the queer performance I was witnessing running through my brain, the barbarian abbess, with a roseate colour on her vulgar face, and with a bestial mouth, espied me.

"' Hi, there, Roman scribbler,' she called out. ' Come a little nearer and try to lift this cross of our sainted Amalaswinta ! '

" Every eye was on me, and then jeeringly and with rough Germanic pushes I was sent into the middle of the crowd. I excused myself, saying, ' Friends, look at my poor, short, weakly arms ! '

" ' Ho ! ho ! ' cried the abbess, ' the longer fingered are you, my fine fellow.' And really my fingers were rather long, having grown so through my occupation in continuous writing.

" Uproarious yells greeted this sally, and though I missed the exact point of it I mentally chalked it up against the abbess to be paid for presently. Annoyed I turned away and made my way to the chapel, the main entrance of which I found open, and entering there I sought peace and quietness in its fine and sombre interior. I stopped before a picture, which from its position in the nave I gathered to be something special, and on closer examination was not disappointed to find it so. The stone frame held a huge cross, an exact replica of the one I had seen upon the meadow, and beside it two figures ; one, a big powerful woman, a crown of thorns on her head, held up the cross on her broad shoulders, and yet was borne down by its weight, for her knees bent beneath her ; the other the small figure of a lovely child, with a halo around its head, also supported the cross, helping to lighten the tremendous burden. The figures were crude, but the painter had put into the faces all the life and soul that he was capable of, and he had succeeded in portraying in one profound despair and a deep compassion in the other.

" Stepping back to get a better view, I suddenly noticed, kneeling at the other side of the picture, the figure of a girl, apparently a native of the place—almost as well built as the Duchess of the picture—with the hood of her white cassock thrown back from a head crowned with a wealth of fair hair and a strong, well-shaped neck. She rose and, brushing away her tears, made as if to go. A novice, I thought, and, addressing her gently, begged her to explain to me the meaning of the painting.

" In simple language she told me that it represented a Duchess, the founder of this convent, who, having poisoned her husband, came here crowned with thorns and carrying that heavy cross to atone for her sins. Doubting her salvation she was supposed to have asked God for a sign of His forgiveness, and having had this cross made which no man could lift unaided, she would have broken down under it had not the Holy Virgin helped her to carry it in answer to her prayers.

"Seeing my doubting look, the girl brusquely insisted that the legend was perfectly true. I asked her name, and, as I had already guessed, it was Gertrude—the Gertrude of whom Anselino had spoken. Gaining her confidence, she confessed to me that she was taking the veil in fulfilment of a vow she had made after the death of her father when quite young; her mother had then fallen seriously ill, and she had, in her desperation at the thought of being left quite alone in the world, prayed to the Holy Virgin to spare her the mother until she should reach her twentieth year at least. A few weeks ago, near the end of the term set in all her prayers, her mother had died, and now the time had run out and she would gladly take the veil and give up her life to God. At the same time, she owned, that often, since she had learned to love Anselino, she had wavered in her resolution, but she would faithfully persist in it, provided the Holy Virgin also came to her aid, and helped her to carry that heavy cross on the morrow, as she had helped every novice since the time when the old Duchess entered the convent.

"I suggested that a clever girl might easily extricate herself by stumbling, but immediately her eyes flamed up and she said, 'Would you have me act a lie, sir? As surely as I want God, Father, Son, and Holy Ghost to help me in my last hour, so surely will I endeavour to carry that cross!' And with these words she raised her arms as if already holding it up. Her sleeves fell back and disclosed her well-moulded young arms, on which, as a true Florentine, I could not help but feast my eyes in artistic pleasure. She noticed this and, puckering her forehead, turned away offended.

"I sat down in one of the confessionals, rested my head in my hands, and pondering deeply, saw my way to gain that Plautus! I thought I saw at last through the incredible and through the fraud. This was my reasoning. The heavy cross being undoubtedly real, a barbarian woman a thousand years ago might have lifted it with the giant's strength of desperation and devotion; however, this deed could not have repeated itself, and for hundreds of years must have been accomplished by fraud. Who, and what, originated this fraud? Probably misplaced zeal to fill the convent, and calculated greed. Yet even Gertrude had assured me that she witnessed the feeble and ailing Lisbeth of Weinfelden carry that same cross just nine years ago.

"There must be two crosses, I told myself, a light one to be cleverly substituted for the heavy one at the right moment, and of the existence of that light fraudulent cross I was by then convinced. In this knowledge and in the fact that I had been one of the members of the Congress for the reformation and purification of the nunneries, I held two good weapons wherewith to fight my fine abbess. The net was closing upon her.

"Slowly I ascended the steps of the choir, and turning to the right, into a lofty and finely domed vestry, I found the place—adorned with many grand inscriptions—where the heavy black cross was usually stationed against the high wall. Two doors led off from here. One was locked, and opening the other I found myself in an ill-lit lumber-room, where, on rough shelves round the walls, the poor library of the convent reposed. I trembled with excitement at this discovery, and had I found here, covered in dust and cobwebs, those Comedies of Plautus, I would have kissed the dirt off the priceless pages. Alas, all I found were merely religious Rituals and Liturgies that left me cold. No Codex of Plautus! It was quite true, that stupid fellow had been before me, and the Plautus evidently had now been hidden by the crafty abbess. I found—and it was my only plunder—*The Confessions of St. Augustine*, and put it in my pocket to read at night before seeking rest. All at once, like lightning the abbess appeared, and rushing at me and feeling my gown, triumphantly produced the *St. Augustine*, which was nestling in my bosom.

"'Fellow, fellow!' she shrieked, 'I knew from your long nose that you were one of those southern book thieves who are the curse of our convents. But mark me, there is a difference between a befuddled monk of St. Gallus and a sturdy maid of Appenzell who keeps her brain clear. I know what you are after! We had another of your Lombardine robbers here the other day; and I found that, when he had finished admiring our holy relics, he tried to depart with a parchment of comic writings under his habit. We never knew we had this valuable pigskin of comic writings here, but I soon consulted the vicar at Dietenhofen, who likes a good mug of convent wine, and is a most learned man. "Goodness gracious!" he called out as soon as he had set his eyes on it, "Mother Abbess, this is worth something! This will build you another out-house and wine-press! Take it and hold it well, sleep on it and wait until you find an honest buyer!" And this I have done ever since, though I have found it pretty hard to rest on.'

"I had to hide a smile when I thought of the poor Plautus lying beneath the pillow of this virago's bed; but putting on my most solemn mien, I said:

"'Abbess, you mistake me. I am one of the fathers now assembled at Constance, one of the reverend persons charged with the reformation of the nunneries.' With these words I held before her a finely engrossed parchment which I had by me from my last sojourn in Rome. 'In the name,' I read out, 'and with the authority of the seventeenth solemn Council. The hands of none of our holy Vestals must be soiled by any unclean writings, whether in Latin or other language. The practice of trickery and imposture, whether traditional or otherwise, is prohibited, and must be punished without delay—even in the case of an abbess—with death at the stake.'

"She paled visibly, but immediately recovered herself, and with wonderful presence of mind said, 'God be thanked, that at last He is setting about the ordering of His holy Church!' and with these words produced from a cupboard in the corner a little volume, adding, 'This, a Lombardian cardinal left behind after his visit here, and the vicar of Dietenhofen pronounced it the profanest book he had ever seen, and the work of a cleric! So pray relieve us of this plague!' And she handed me—my *Facetiæ*.

"I knew this was pure accident, yet I was much chagrined, and began to hate this abbess thoroughly, especially so as I knew my writings to be desitute of any offensive remarks against holy Church.

"'It is well,' I said, 'and do you wish also to be proved innocent of the second, and more important, matter? I have witnessed your promise of a miracle on yonder meadow; beware, then, lest your miracle be examined.'

"Her knees began to give way and her eyes seemed to roll. 'Follow me,' I continued severely, 'and let us inquire into the working of that miracle!'

"We made our way to the vestry, where the heavy cross had been replaced, and I tried in vain to lift it. Resolutely I turned to the locked door at the side where I thought the second cross would be kept, and sternly commanded her to produce the key. With eyes protruding and terror-struck she cried, 'Lost, your holiness! Lost, these past ten years!'

"'Woman!' I cried in my hardest, most terrible tones, 'your life is in danger! If I find here a lighter cross which is a copy of yonder heavy one, you will burn at the stake, burn as sure as that heretic Huss and as guilty as he!'

"With chattering teeth and tottering knees she produced an old key and opened the door. And there stood against the wall the same black sinister cross, but light as cork. So perfectly was it fashioned after the other, that involuntarily I said aloud, 'A masterpiece! Perfect!' not in admiration of the fraud, but of the skill, the art that had fashioned this copy.

"'Jester, jester,' leered the brazen woman, who had been watching me closely, 'you have outwitted me, and I know your price, take your buffooning sheets of pigskin, which I will fetch you at once, keep your mouth shut and leave us in peace!' Quickly I decided what to do. I forced her to tell me how she had been initiated in this thousand-year-old fraud, how her predecessor on her death-bed had impressed her with the glory of keeping it up for the good of the convent and of holy Church, how she had been made to realise its deep significance and secret power, and finally she even insisted to me that in perpetrating the fraud she had done nothing unworthy.

"'I pardon you, so that holy Church may not be disgraced by any revelations,' I told her; but I also commanded her to burn the fraudulent cross immediately after the ceremony on the morrow had taken place—to prohibit the latter I thought unwise—and to produce the Plautus immediately.

"The abbess, grumbling and reluctant, obeyed, and I am sure my commands were quite in conformity with the wishes of the Council of Constance, though they were without the knowledge of the Council.

"I had taken the key from the lock of the all-important door and left it on the latch, while the abbess was fetching my Plautus, and had gone to my quarters at the inn across the way. Presently heavy knocks resounded on the oaken door of my room and the abbess furiously demanded the key. However, I told her calmly that it was not in my possession, which was quite true, for I had dropped it into a crevice between two pews in the chapel—where probably it still rests—and by and by the holy mother departed, moaning and lamenting pitifully. I was happy in the possession of my classic, and after beguiling my brain with the glorious treasure deep into the night I finally retired to rest.

"Startled out of my sleep I jumped up. It was morning. One half of the little window stood open and I heard from the chapel near by alternate wailing and groaning, and then again a stifled cry. Hastily I threw on some garments and hurried to the chapel. At the door of the vestry I halted, for there before the heavy cross I saw Gertrude on her knees beating the stone-flagged floor and wringing her hands, which were bleeding. She had been lying here all night in prayer and subjection; her voice was hoarse and her words came with difficulty from between her parched lips.

"'Mary, Mother of God, pity me! Let me be buried under the heavy cross for I cannot carry it! I hate the cell! I cannot live in it, I shall knock my head against the low ceiling, against the walls! But if you do help me to carry the cross, then lighten my heart also; for see, if you do not I shall dash out my brains on the flagstones!' Exhausted, she sank down.

"After a while I approached her gently, for I had made up my mind to save this girl, and though I had given the abbess my word—she had required this of me—not to speak to Gertrude, I saw my way to enlighten her.

"She saw me confusedly at first, but soon watched my actions more alertly, and later with perfect clearness. I walked up to the heavy cross and deliberately taking out my knife cut into it, near the cross-piece, a good sized notch. Then taking the requisite steps towards the unlocked door, where the other cross was hidden, I laughed loudly and called out, 'The truth on the wall, the lie in the hall!' Then clapping my hands and crying, 'He presto!' I called out, 'The lie on the wall, the truth in the hall!'

"Looking sideways at the novice I scrutinised her face and saw that her curiosity had been aroused, and knew that she would find out the rest for herself. I now quietly made my way back to my room, and throwing myself on my bed found a few hours more rest, until I was wakened again, this time by the ringing of bells and the singing of the crowds on their way to the convent.

"Just as I entered the vestry once more I saw Gertrude, pale as death, returning from a pilgrimage—a necessary part of the ceremonial to facilitate the changing of the crosses no doubt—to a neighbouring chapel. The preparation of the novice then began. In a circle of chanting nuns she first tied round her hips the thrice knotted cord, then slowly cast her shoes off her strong but well-formed feet, and having the crown of thorns handed to her pressed it viciously upon her hair, partly lacerating her forehead in doing so. The nuns drew back affrighted before her wild looks. Six of them—no doubt fully initiated into the sham—then placed the spurious cross upon her shoulders, imitating but poorly the carrying of a heavy load.

"But now events moved quickly. Gertrude, casting an eye rapidly on the part where I had heavily notched the real cross, found this one unmarked, and with a yell of rage slipping it off her shoulder, caught hold of it with both her hands and dashed it to pieces on the flagstones with a fearful cry. Then, with insane laughter, like one possessed, she ran to the vestry, and there in the unlocked closet found the real cross. With unearthly yells she hoisted it on her shoulders and staggered under it slowly and haltingly into full view of the congregation, in spite of the efforts of the abbess and her six co-conspirators to hold her back.

"'Now Mary, Mother of God, I pray you decide my fate honestly!' she screamed, and breathing heavily she tottered a few more steps, only to break down under the fearful load; again she raised herself with superhuman strength upon one knee and arm, only to collapse suddenly and completely and be crushed down under the heavy cross. This was the blood-stained truth and not the lying sham. A deep sigh escaped every breast in all that throng—which had witnessed this tragedy as if transfixed. The nuns were busily engaged trying to restore the bleeding girl to consciousness, and presently she opened her eyes, then stood up, passed her hand over her brow, and smiling slightly spoke in an almost clear voice full of happiness, 'You do not want me, Blessed Virgin, so I will give myself to another!' and ascending the steps of the choir she called, 'Anselino!' A deep manly voice answering her, she continued, 'Will you have me still?' 'Yes, with all my heart,' came the reply, and so descending again she went with swaying steps to the arms of her lover, her thorny crown still on her bleeding forehead.

"As I followed her down the choir steps my messenger from Constance touched my sleeve and brought me the news that at last the election of the Pope had been completed. When I looked up again Gertrude had disappeared. The crowd, however, was now seething with uproar and confusion, cries of 'Sham! Fraud! Shame!' against the abbess, mingled with shouts of 'Sinner! Traitress! Shameless hussy!' against Gertrude. The uproar was frightful. Whether either party knew the whole significance of the proceedings I know not, yet in any case the wonder-working cross was completely discredited, the power of the miracle gone for ever. To put an end to the raving of the people and the haranguing of the abbess, who in her fury yelled to me to get out of her sight, I ascended the chancel, and gaining some sort of silence for myself, proclaimed to the assembled Christians in sonorous tones, ' Habemus Pontificem Dominum Othonem de Colonna!' and started a rousing Te Deum; at first only the nuns joined in this, but soon all the multitude took part.

" *Plaudit amici!* I have finished. When, too, the Council at Constance, which lasted longer than this story, had finished, I returned with my Plautus and my superior, his Holiness, Martin V., over the mountains to Lombardy. But on our way we stayed at the inn at Spiuga, just north of the dangerous pass of the same name, where Anselino and Gertrude had made their home, and where she now carried the cross of matrimony.

" This, friend Cosmos, is my ' Facetia inedita.' "

With many acclamations Poggio was laughingly thanked by all his assembled friends, and the discussion went on to other things—parchments of the old world—the greatness of the present century.

SWISS

EDOUARD ROD
1857–1910

THE GOLDEN WEDDING

AT the end of the Rue Lafontaine, in Auteuil, leading to goodness knows where, a certain married couple had lived for the last five or six years. Their name was Walter, a cosmopolitan name which gives one no clue to their birth or station in life ; and their strange personalities caused as much talk in this quiet part of the world, where we fraternise somewhat, as if they were in the provinces.

Twice a day, at eleven o'clock and again at four, Monsieur Walter took a constitutional walk. He held himself very erect, and in spite of his seventy-five years his step was quite brisk. His complexion had that artificial look of freshness that is peculiar to well-preserved apples ; his frock-coat was very well-fitting, and he had the ribbon of some foreign order in his buttonhole. On wet days he curtailed his walks, went into a café, read the papers, and exchanged a few words with its frequenters. He spoke with affected brevity and with an accent which told as little as his name ; it was slightly guttural and therefore might be German, but the diphthongs were quite English, and the aspirates might have been those of a Russian. No sooner had he left a group of people than someone would ask, " Where the deuce does that fellow come from ? " At once conjectures would be offered. One man was sure that he was a German, trying to hide his nationality ; another thought he was an Englishman, with the saturnine temperament of that race ; a third would declare he was a Russian, whose delight was to make a mystery of himself.

As for Madame Walter, she never left home except on shopping expeditions, and spoke to no one but tradespeople. She was several years younger than her husband, but looked older : her hair was quite white, and her complexion mottled ; she stooped and was short-sighted ; and her whole mien was that of some poor soul who has seen much trouble. She did all her household duties with the aid of a charwoman, whose name was Marianne. This was the wife of a journeyman upholsterer ; she came in the early morning and left at mid-day, just when M. Walter came back to lunch after his daily walk.

Marianne's work was to clean out the rooms and do the heavier jobs, for Mme. Walter did all the cooking herself. Her cooking was perhaps plain, but was certainly excellent, and she was skilled in all kinds of foreign dishes, so that her cookery indicated her origin as little as her name.

Of the private life of the couple Marianne knew nothing at all. Once, when she had returned to the house to look for something she had accidentally left behind, she heard M. Walter's voice raised angrily in the dining-room. Two or three days later she made some excuse for repeating her action, and again she heard the man's irritable tones. But after this she was warned by Mme. Walter that if she were ever to come back to the flat except during " her proper hours " she would be instantly dismissed ; so Marianne restrained her curiosity. From the glimpse she had had of the household, however, Marianne gathered that M. Walter was a glutton and a tyrant, and that his wife shut herself up from the world so that no one should know of their quarrels. With this idea running in her mind, you can imagine her astonishment when Mme. Walter said to her one day : " Can you stay here the whole of to-morrow, Marianne ? I am having a dinner-party and I shall need you to help me."

Marianne knew that such a question was purely rhetorical and required no answer, but her curiosity got the better of her.

" Are you expecting visitors, madame ? " she asked.

Instead of withering her with a glance, the lady condescended to explain.

" No, I am not having visitors ; but to-morrow is the anniversary of our golden wedding, and we mean to have a rather special little dinner. I want to enjoy a meal without leaving the table after each course. You understand, I am sure."

Marianne understood perfectly, and with the subtle instinct of her class, which can grasp and unravel the complicated problems in the life of a neighbour, she knew at once that something mysterious was about to take place, and that the golden wedding would be something quite out of the ordinary.

. . . .

The golden wedding had, very naturally, not been forgotten by M. Walter. One day, after certain unpleasant remarks on a curry which was not hot enough for his taste, he had said : " By the way, do you know that the fourteenth of October will soon be here ? "

It was so long since any anniversary had made any difference in their lives, for even Easter, Christmas Day and New Year were passed over very quietly in this household, that Mme. Walter saw no significance in this date.

" Well ? " she asked.

" What ! is that all you have to say ? " her husband replied. " Does the date convey nothing to your mind ? But that's exactly like you : you have about as much heart as brains. . . Why, the fourteenth of October is the anniversary of our wedding—the fiftieth, my dear—our golden wedding day ! We ought to celebrate it somehow, don't you think ? . . . What do you say to a jolly little dinner, the kind you used to make when you were at your best, with a bottle of champagne to drink with the dessert ? That would revive our youth, wouldn't it ? "

A jolly little dinner with wine and dessert ! Yes, that was all M. Walter thought of when the date had suddenly occurred to him. Since he never on any occasion troubled himself about his wife, he did not perceive that she had suddenly grown very white and had refused to eat any more. In calm expectation he awaited the " great day."

As for Mme. Walter, she was completely overwhelmed. Fifty years ! was it really so long as all that ? For fifty years, then, she had dragged on in this slow sacrifice of her life ; for fifty years she had been growing old, and the whole time she had been waiting for the day when a ray of happiness or affection should come to her ; for fifty years she had felt those rebellious thoughts rising within her, and every time she had crushed them down.

Fifty years ago, when she was a young girl, fair-haired, pretty, intelligent, and warm-hearted, she had given her small hand trustingly into this man's keeping. But that happened far away, it doesn't matter where, in a southern land, on a warm, sunny day, amid the smiles of nature, amid songs, laughter, gaiety and dances. He was young and she had loved him. She believed in him utterly, and dreamed that a golden future awaited them under blue skies. Yet her disappointment began on the very day after the wedding, when she found that the heart of this man, whom she had endowed with every grace of soul, was ruled by a colossal egoism. The disillusionment had grown from day to day, from year to year, wrought by his absurd self-sufficiency, realised more fully as they journeyed together from one end of the world to the other, and perfected when he refused to share in griefs which should have been common to them but which he brushed aside from his vision as hurtful to his well-being. And yet, in spite of the tears she so often unwillingly shed, time had passed so quickly that now life held but little for her in the short years she had still to spend on earth, and there was little hope for her now save in the mysterious Beyond.

And yet even this last hope had been somewhat damaged by the withering egoism of her man. Had he not tarnished her pure faith with just such jests as he had thrown upon her girlish dreams of happiness ? And now, careless of the ruins in which he still contrived to stand upright, scorning the notion of treasuring any pleasant memory of bygone years, turning aside from those which still were possible, indifferent to past regrets as to the future menace, all he thought of now was a good dinner, with champagne at dessert ! Oh, wretched dinner ! If she could only make it into a means of revenge ! If the poor wretch could only have instilled into it all the bitterness, all the poisons she had absorbed drop by drop ! If it could only be the last dinner of their common life ! If she could only find courage to carry out, even at this latest hour, the plans she had so often played with, to break loose from her bondage and leave him to his own devices, while she would live out her remaining days far away from him !

. . . .

On the night of their golden wedding day M. Walter was in high good-humour, waiting for the " little dinner " such as his wife knew so well how to prepare and he to enjoy. To speak candidly, his good-humour was hardly less disagreeable than his bad temper : it showed itself in many little pleasantries in a bitter and malicious vein, and he underlined his thin jests with a grating laugh which was an outward expression of the creature's soul. Three or four times in the course of that day he spoke to his wife in this way, thinking himself a great wit. He had never loved her, he said brightly ; she was of no use except to prepare his meals ; and other clever little things he said which hurt as not the grossest insult could have done. To these his wife made no reply except by an occasional appealing look, but he never realised their grief-stricken significance. The hours went by.

At long last the gaudy clock which had followed them everywhere on their travels and divided their hours with its mellow chimes, struck six, and at the last stroke M. Walter, who returned from his constitutional with the most precise regularity, opened the dining-room door. The table was not even laid !

There is nothing in the world so heartrending as to find that some long-expected pleasure is to be deferred ; and the sight of that empty room, with its threat of delay in accomplishment of M. Walter's desires, put him in a state of actual fury. Hardly able to control himself, his face purple with rage, his lips brimming over with insults, he rushed into the kitchen. On the threshold he stood still in amazement, for there he found—Marianne ! And Marianne was there alone !

" Where is my wife ? " he asked.

" She has gone out," the woman replied.

" What, gone out ? Where ? What message did she leave ? "

" She said that you were not going to dine until seven o'clock to-day."

" Seven o'clock ! Another hour to wait ! And she has gone out ! Why did she go out ? "

That hour seemed a century of waiting. M. Walter had never before been so thwarted in his life. He paced up and down the room, trying to solve the puzzle which engrossed his whole attention. Why had his wife gone out, on this day of all days, and why had she altered the dinner-hour ? The riddle grew in his mind until it assumed gigantic proportions, and at last M. Walter, who was the least imaginative man on earth, came to entertain all kinds of mad notions ; it struck him that possibly his wife had suddenly lost her senses, and he could well imagine how annoying such a misfortune would be to him. When the clock had struck seven and the hands continued to creep round slowly, the dining-room became too small for him, and he began to pace about in all the other rooms of the flat, opening and shutting the doors, and counting his own steps for the sake of distraction ; and he ended up his walk with another visit to the kitchen. He felt sure that Marianne could enlighten him a little, but she held aloof. She watched him closely, a queer smile on her face, but luckily he was too much wrapped up in himself to be observant and he never noticed her looks. At last he broke the silence.

" Well," he queried, " she has not returned yet ? "

" Oh, I forgot to tell you, sir ; Mme. Walter told me to say that you were not to be anxious if she came back a little late."

" A little late ! " Why, it was a whole hour after the time fixed on for to-day! And the dinner, the festal dinner, the golden wedding dinner—she had handed it over to a charwoman who knew nothing in the world about cookery!

" What is there for dinner?" he asked Marianne roughly.

" Madame told me not to say anything about it to you, sir," the woman answered slyly, " because it was to be a surprise dinner."

A surprise dinner! This word cleared the air at once. Why, of course, his wife had gone out to purchase some rare and unheard-of delicacy; perhaps it had to come from a long way off and had not arrived until the afternoon train, and she could not bring it home any sooner! So she was a dutiful wife after all! His anger suddenly melted away into a feeling of vague and misty affection, and this helped to whet his appetite still more.

. . . . . .

There was the sound of a footstep on the stair, then the door opened, and Mme. Walter came in. She was looking rather pale, and was out of breath after her climb up four flights of stairs. Her hands were empty; she had brought no surprise parcels with her!

" Oh, so you are here at last! Why, it is nearly eight o'clock. What do you mean by such conduct?"

" I don't mean anything by it. I preferred to have dinner later to-day, that's all. Marianne, you may serve the dinner now."

M. Walter had assumed the attitude of a wrathful despot, and the calm reply had disconcerted him. The couple sat down silently at the table, and Marianne brought in a tureen of steaming soup.

" Pumpkin soup! Pumpkin soup! Why, you know I simply detest it!"

"Yes, but I am very fond of it," Mme. Walter replied calmly, in a tone that admitted of no reply; " and it is more than thirty years since I have tasted it."

M. Walter was dumbfounded. With his mouth wide open in astonishment, he looked at his wife, speechless. In the meantime Mme. Walter swallowed a few spoonfuls with difficulty, trying to look at her ease.

" Oh, here's the fish!"

" Look here, are you making fun of me? Why did you order a pike? And you have dressed it with sauce hollandaise, too! You know perfectly well that I only like sea fish!"

" Yes, but I like fresh-water fish and dislike the others."

In spite of this preference, Mme. Walter scarcely touched the portion on her plate. With dreaming eyes she gazed into the void, into the wasted past she had left behind her, in which her youth, beauty, high spirits, her love and her strength had been swallowed up; and she lived over again the fifty years of bondage that had been all her life. Her heart was black with hatred, and when her glance rested on her husband, sitting in bewilderment opposite her, feeling humiliated and vaguely nervous, she was full of triumph at the thought of the childish trick which had been her only sign of rebellion and revenge.

"This *is* a cheerful golden wedding and no mistake!" Marianne murmured to herself, as she brought in the jugged hare.

"Look here, is this a wager?" M. Walter broke out at last. "You have provided everything that I hate."

"But everything that I particularly like."

"Any one would say that you had done this on purpose."

"Oh, so you have seen through it at last, have you? Well, I may as well admit that I did arrange this dinner on purpose."

M. Walter rose, his face purple with rage, and he raised his fist.

"I arranged it on purpose," Mme. Walter repeated in her colourless voice.

Her calmness and rebellion seemed to him such enormities that M. Walter sat down again, silenced and somewhat alarmed.

"But look here," he said, "I don't understand all this. Explain yourself. Have you gone mad? Do you realise what you are saying? Isn't this my golden wedding?"

"Yes, but it is mine too, alas!" Mme. Walter answered. "And you need not think I have gone mad. And if you want me to explain what I have been thinking, I'll tell you. For fifty whole long years you have made me submit to your whims and give in to all your wishes without even once considering that I could have an idea of my own or a feeling that you would be capable of wounding. For fifty years I have been nothing but your slave. Well, I thought I should like you to be my slave for one hour, just one hour, to the very smallest details of our life. Afterwards you will resume your liberty, and I shall have to take up my yoke again. I should really have liked to shake you off altogether and then to have gone away and left you to yourself. But I simply can't do it: I am too old, and I'm afraid. Now, do you understand?"

The poor woman was trembling in every limb and her eyes were already dumbly pleading for pardon. While she was speaking M. Walter's face lit up. So that was all it was! It was a crisis that would soon be tided over; indeed, instinctively he felt that it had already passed and that he could now worry her, scold her and run her down, and that she would merely beg his pardon in return; and for the first time in his life, doubtless because his nerves had been on the rack and were now released, he was generous. His smile, then, was almost pleasant, and with a shrug of his shoulders he murmured: "After all, I suppose that women will be women until the end of time!"

Several tears had rolled down Mme. Walter's withered cheek into her empty plate. She dried her eyes, and then said very timidly: "We had better have the rest of the dinner brought in. I have cooked something for you that you like. It is a duck pie."

M. Walter's eyes brightened.

"From Amiens?" he asked.

She made a gesture of assent.

"Well, you have spoilt my appetite, but I think it will come back again later on. And the champagne—did you purposely omit that too?"

"No, it is there, in ice."

The old man's face grew bright at once.

"In ice!" he echoed in high glee. "Now you're yourself again! And you needn't leave me; I forgive you for everything!"